MARVEL-VERSE
SPIDER-MAN

MARVEL-VERSE
SPIDER-MAN

AMAZING SPIDER-MAN #32-33

SCRIPTER: **STAN LEE**
PLOTTER & ARTIST: **STEVE DITKO**
LETTERER: **ART SIMEK**
EDITOR: **STAN LEE**

MYTHOS: SPIDER-MAN

WRITER: **PAUL JENKINS**
ARTIST: **PAOLO RIVERA**
LETTERER: VC's **JOE CARAMAGNA**
ASSISTANT EDITOR: **AUBREY SITTERSON**
EDITOR: **STEPHEN WACKER**
EXECUTIVE EDITOR: **TOM BREVOORT**

MARVEL ADVENTURES SPIDER-MAN #2-3

WRITER: **ERICA DAVID**

PENCILER: **PATRICK SCHERBERGER**

INKER: **NORMAN LEE**

COLORISTS: **GURU-eFX's WES HARTMAN & ROBBY BEVARD**

LETTERER: **DAVE SHARPE**

COVER ART: **TONY S. DANIEL & SOTOCOLOR's J. RAUCH**

ASSISTANT EDITOR: **JOHN BARBER**

CONSULTING EDITOR: **MARK PANICCIA**

EDITOR: **MACKENZIE CADENHEAD**

SPIDER-MAN CREATED BY **STAN LEE & STEVE DITKO**

COLLECTION EDITOR: **JENNIFER GRÜNWALD** ASSISTANT EDITOR: **DANIEL KIRCHHOFFER**
ASSISTANT MANAGING EDITOR: **MAIA LOY** ASSISTANT MANAGING EDITOR: **LISA MONTALBANO**
ASSOCIATE MANAGER, DIGITAL ASSETS: **JOE HOCHSTEIN** MASTERWORKS EDITOR: **CORY SEDLMEIER**
VP PRODUCTION & SPECIAL PROJECTS: **JEFF YOUNGQUIST** RESEARCH: **JESS HARROLD**
BOOK DESIGNERS: **STACIE ZUCKER & ADAM DEL RE** WITH **JAY BOWEN**
SVP PRINT, SALES & MARKETING: **DAVID GABRIEL** EDITOR IN CHIEF: **C.B. CEBULSKI**

MARVEL-VERSE: SPIDER-MAN GN-TPB. Contains material originally published in magazine form as MYTHOS: SPIDER-MAN (2007) #1, AMAZING SPIDER-MAN (1963) #32-33 and MARVEL ADVENTURES SPIDER-MAN (2005) #2-3. First printing 2021. ISBN 978-1-302-93215-2. Published by MARVEL WORLDWIDE, INC., a subsidiary of MARVEL ENTERTAINMENT, LLC. OFFICE OF PUBLICATION: 1290 Avenue of the Americas, New York, NY 10104. © 2021 MARVEL. No similarity between any of the names, characters, persons, and/or institutions in this magazine with those of any living or dead person or institution is intended, and any such similarity which may exist is purely coincidental. **Printed in Canada.** KEVIN FEIGE, Chief Creative Officer; DAN BUCKLEY, President, Marvel Entertainment; JOE QUESADA, EVP & Creative Director; DAVID BOGART, Associate Publisher & SVP of Talent Affairs; TOM BREVOORT, VP, Executive Editor; NICK LOWE, Executive Editor, VP of Content, Digital Publishing; DAVID GABRIEL, VP of Print & Digital Publishing; JEFF YOUNGQUIST, VP of Production & Special Projects; ALEX MORALES, Director of Publishing Operations; DAN EDINGTON, Managing Editor; RICKEY PURDIN, Director of Talent Relations; JENNIFER GRÜNWALD, Senior Editor, Special Projects; SUSAN CRESPI, Production Manager; STAN LEE, Chairman Emeritus. For information regarding advertising in Marvel Comics or on Marvel.com, please contact Vit DeBellis, Custom Solutions & Integrated Advertising Manager, at vdebellis@marvel.com. For Marvel subscription inquiries, please call 888-511-5480. **Manufactured between 9/3/2021 and 10/5/2021 by SOLISCO PRINTERS, SCOTT, QC, CANADA.**

10 9 8 7 6 5 4 3 2 1

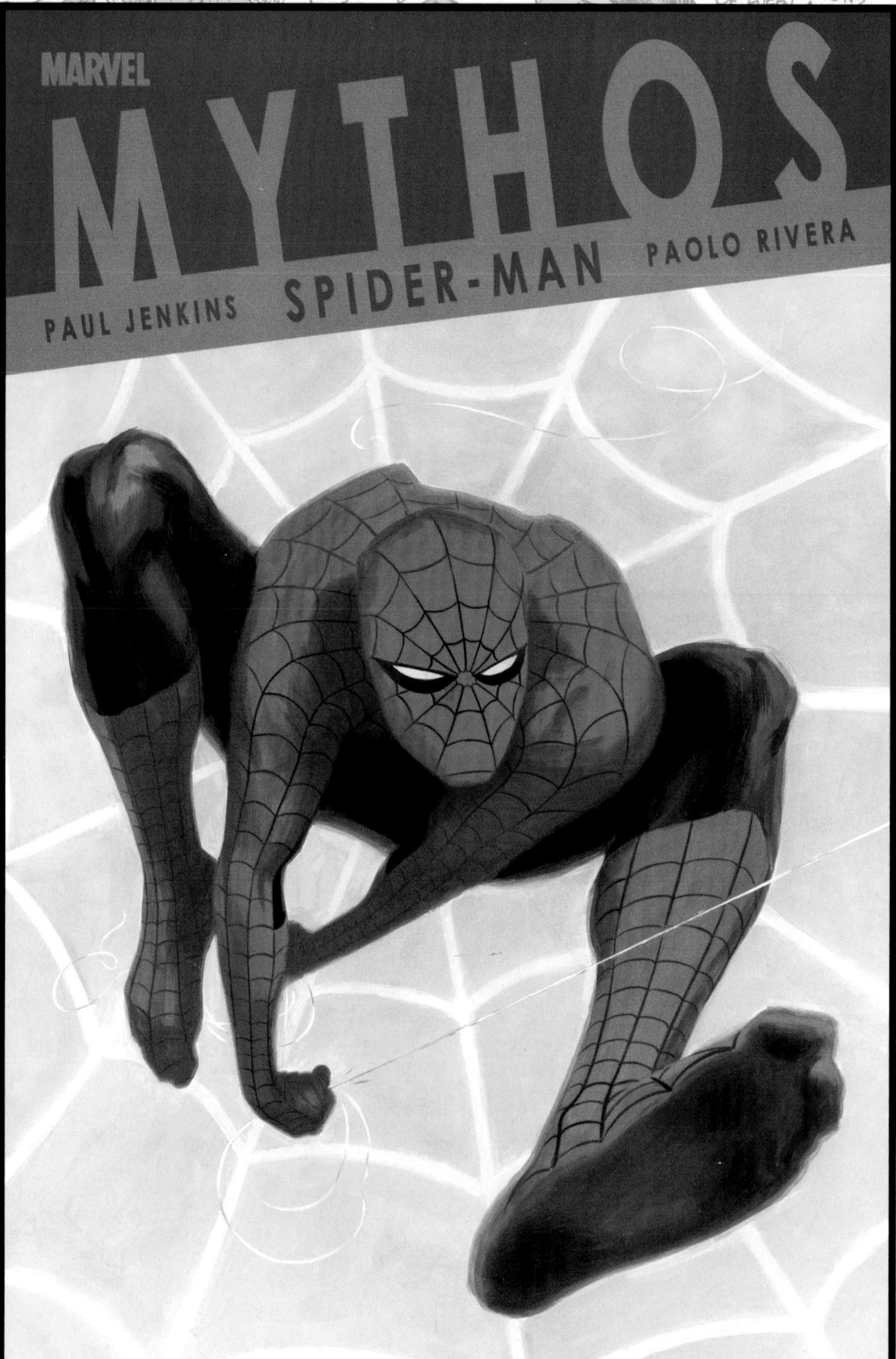
MARVEL
MYTHOS
SPIDER-MAN
PAUL JENKINS
PAOLO RIVERA

MYTHOS: SPIDER-MAN

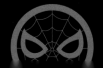

SWING INTO THIS MODERN RETELLING OF SPIDER-MAN'S
ORIGIN, AND LEARN HOW SPIDEY'S CAREER AS A SUPER

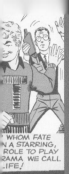

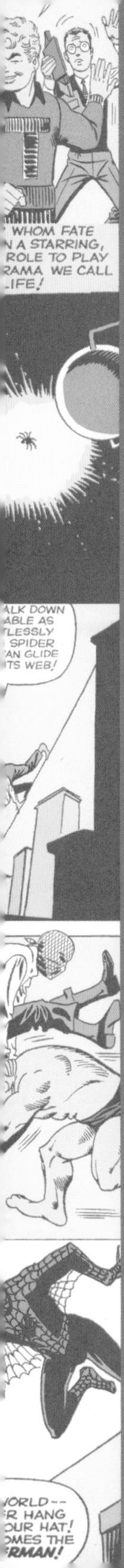

MYTHOS

While attending a demonstration in radiology, high-school student Peter Parker was bitten by a spider which had accidentally been exposed to RADIOACTIVE RAYS. Through a miracle of science, Peter soon found he had gained the proportionate speed, strength and agility of the arachnid and had, in effect, become a HUMAN SPIDER!

the AMAZING SPIDER-MAN®

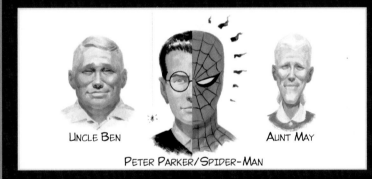

UNCLE BEN
AUNT MAY
PETER PARKER/SPIDER-MAN

Written by
PAUL JENKINS

Art by
PAOLO RIVERA

Letters by
VC'S JOE CARAMAGNA

Assistant Editor:
AUBREY SITTERSON

Editor:
STEPHEN WACKER

Executive Editor:
TOM BREVOORT

Editor In Chief:
JOE QUESADA

Publisher:
DAN BUCKLEY

Based on *Amazing Fantasy #15*, August 1962 by Stan Lee and Steve Ditko

Daily Chronicle
BAD NEWS, SON--YOUR UNCLE HAS BEEN SHOT--MURDERED!
NOT HALF SO SURPRISED AS YOU'RE GOING TO BE!
AND, A SHORT DISTANCE AWAY...
MY FAULT--ALL MY FAULT! IF ONLY I HAD STOPPED HIM WHEN I COULD HAVE! BUT I DIDN'T--AND NOW --UNCLE BEN-- IS DEAD...

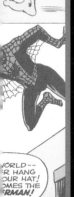

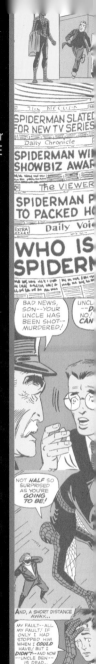

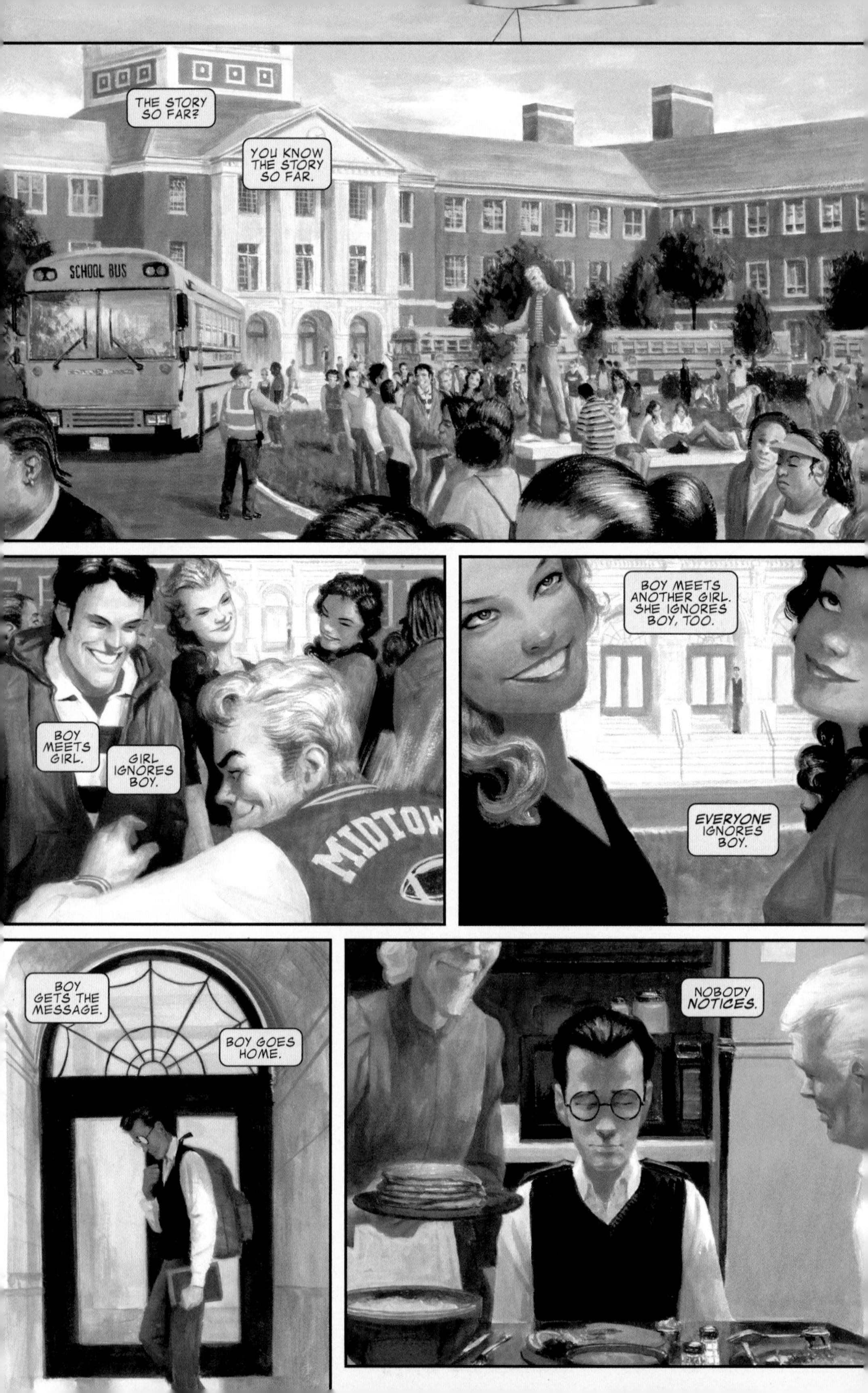

THE STORY SO FAR?
YOU KNOW THE STORY SO FAR.
SCHOOL BUS
BOY MEETS GIRL.
GIRL IGNORES BOY.
MIDTOW
BOY MEETS ANOTHER GIRL. SHE IGNORES BOY, TOO.
EVERYONE IGNORES BOY.
BOY GETS THE MESSAGE.
BOY GOES HOME.
NOBODY NOTICES.

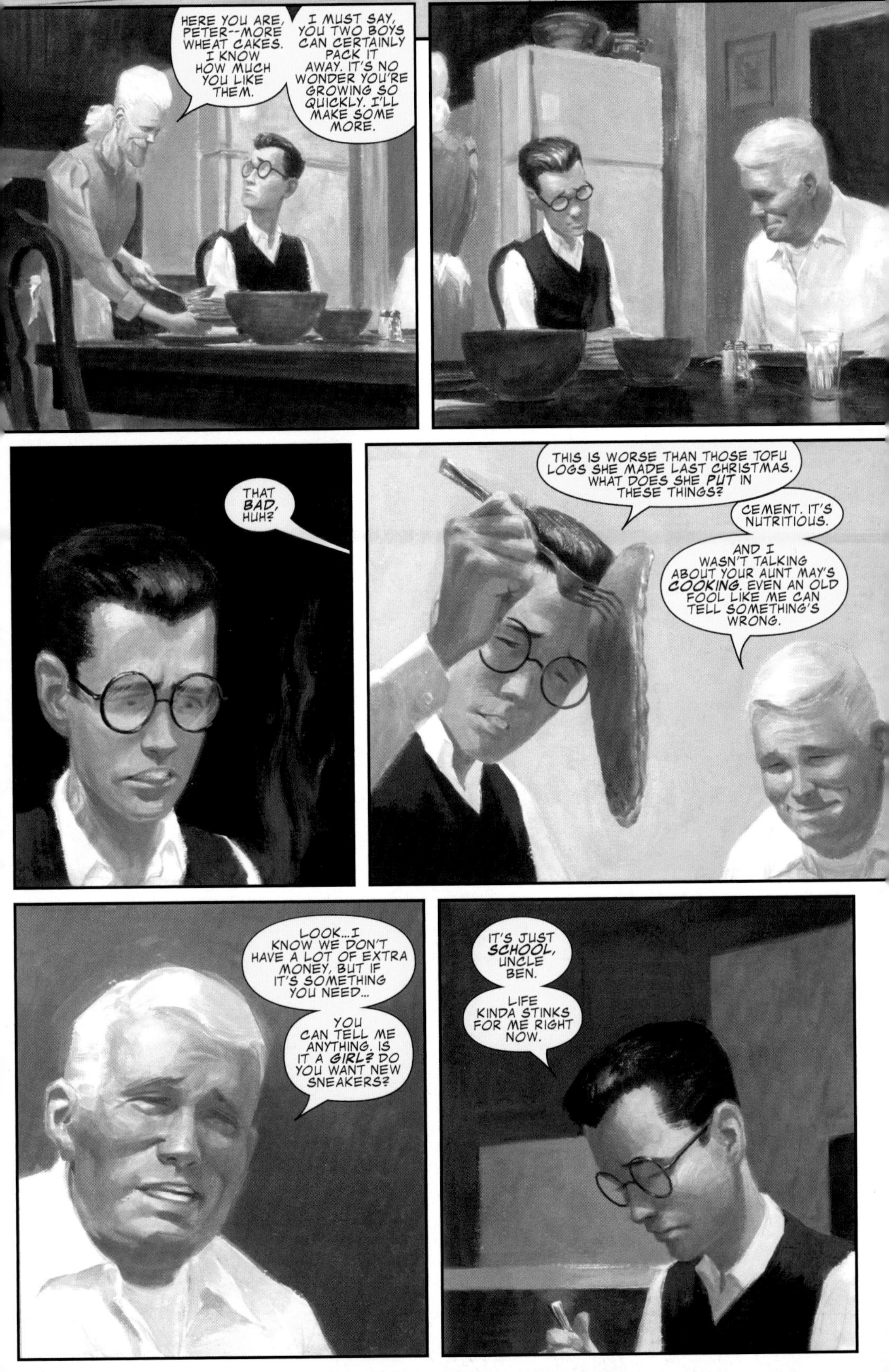

HERE YOU ARE, PETER--MORE WHEAT CAKES. I KNOW HOW MUCH YOU LIKE THEM.
I MUST SAY, YOU TWO BOYS CAN CERTAINLY PACK IT AWAY. IT'S NO WONDER YOU'RE GROWING SO QUICKLY. I'LL MAKE SOME MORE.
THAT BAD, HUH?
THIS IS WORSE THAN THOSE TOFU LOGS SHE MADE LAST CHRISTMAS. WHAT DOES SHE PUT IN THESE THINGS?
CEMENT. IT'S NUTRITIOUS.
AND I WASN'T TALKING ABOUT YOUR AUNT MAY'S COOKING. EVEN AN OLD FOOL LIKE ME CAN TELL SOMETHING'S WRONG.
LOOK...I KNOW WE DON'T HAVE A LOT OF EXTRA MONEY, BUT IF IT'S SOMETHING YOU NEED...
YOU CAN TELL ME ANYTHING. IS IT A GIRL? DO YOU WANT NEW SNEAKERS?
IT'S JUST SCHOOL, UNCLE BEN.
LIFE KINDA STINKS FOR ME RIGHT NOW.

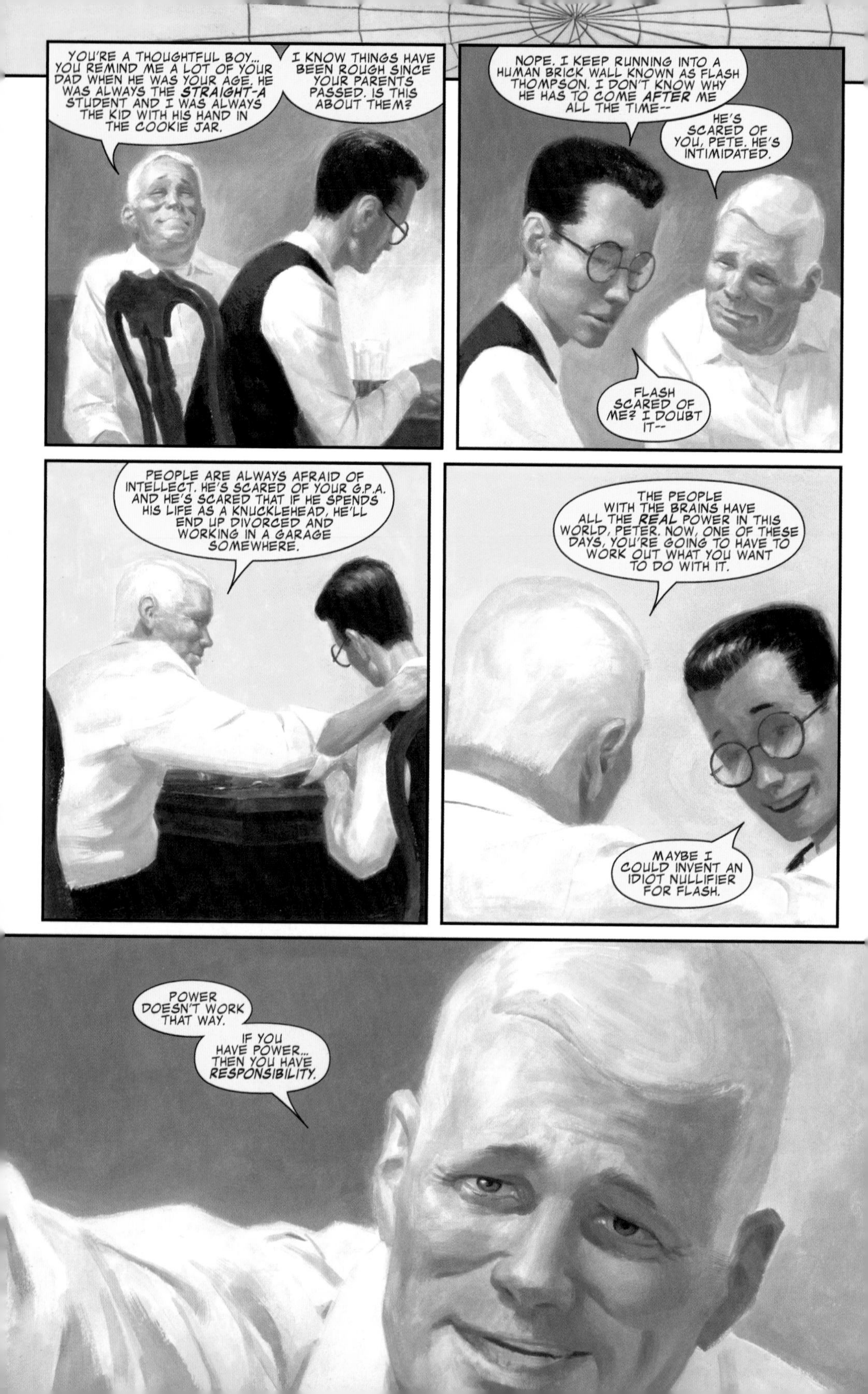

YOU'RE A THOUGHTFUL BOY... YOU REMIND ME A LOT OF YOUR DAD WHEN HE WAS YOUR AGE. HE WAS ALWAYS THE STRAIGHT-A STUDENT AND I WAS ALWAYS THE KID WITH HIS HAND IN THE COOKIE JAR.
I KNOW THINGS HAVE BEEN ROUGH SINCE YOUR PARENTS PASSED. IS THIS ABOUT THEM?
NOPE. I KEEP RUNNING INTO A HUMAN BRICK WALL KNOWN AS FLASH THOMPSON. I DON'T KNOW WHY HE HAS TO COME AFTER ME ALL THE TIME--
HE'S SCARED OF YOU, PETE. HE'S INTIMIDATED.
FLASH SCARED OF ME? I DOUBT IT--
PEOPLE ARE ALWAYS AFRAID OF INTELLECT. HE'S SCARED OF YOUR G.P.A. AND HE'S SCARED THAT IF HE SPENDS HIS LIFE AS A KNUCKLEHEAD, HE'LL END UP DIVORCED AND WORKING IN A GARAGE SOMEWHERE.
THE PEOPLE WITH THE BRAINS HAVE ALL THE REAL POWER IN THIS WORLD, PETER. NOW, ONE OF THESE DAYS, YOU'RE GOING TO HAVE TO WORK OUT WHAT YOU WANT TO DO WITH IT.
MAYBE I COULD INVENT AN IDIOT NULLIFIER FOR FLASH.
POWER DOESN'T WORK THAT WAY.
IF YOU HAVE POWER... THEN YOU HAVE RESPONSIBILITY.

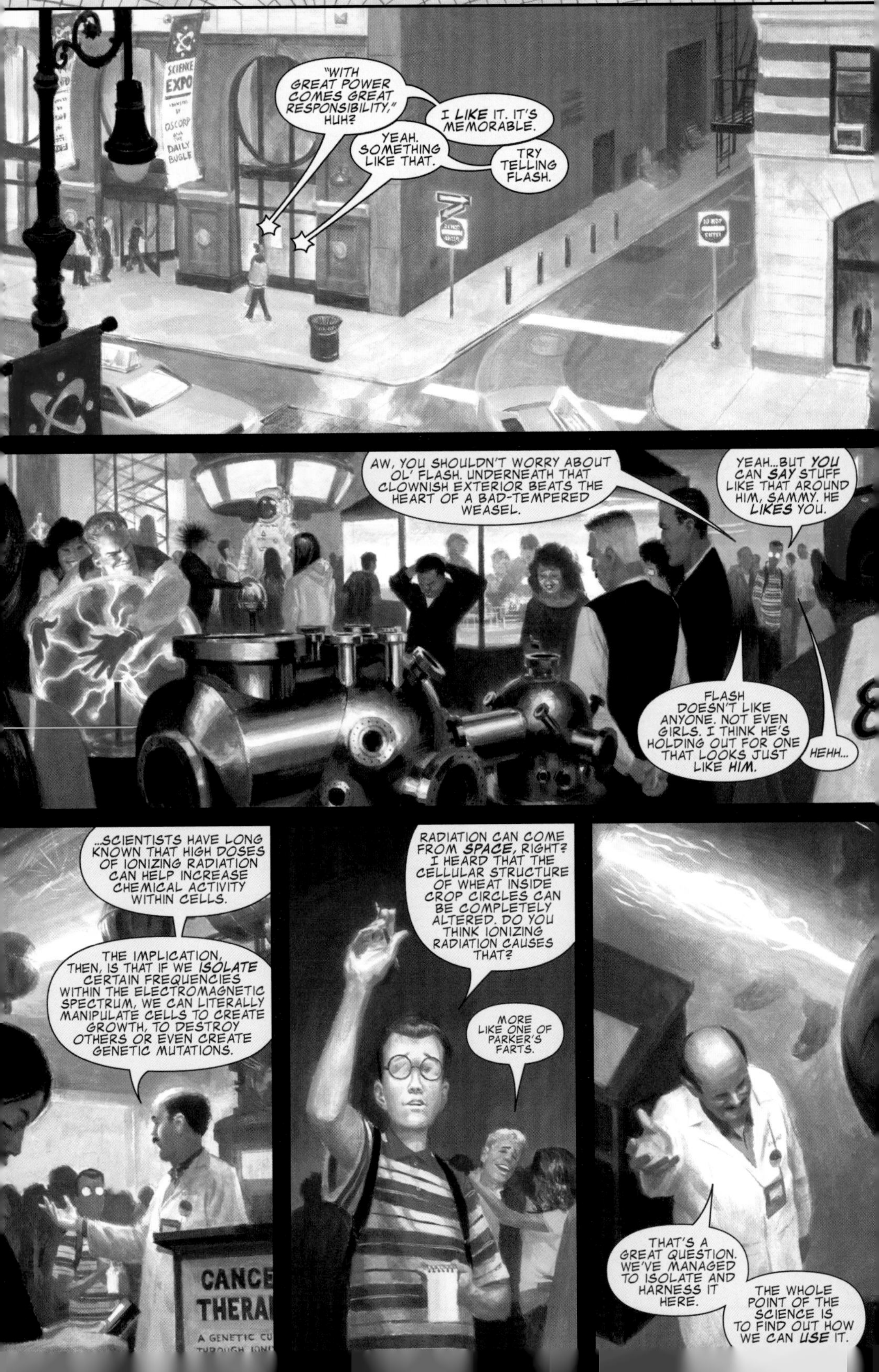
SCIENCE EXPO
OSCORP
DAILY BUGLE
"WITH GREAT POWER COMES GREAT RESPONSIBILITY," HUH?
I LIKE IT. IT'S MEMORABLE.
YEAH. SOMETHING LIKE THAT.
TRY TELLING FLASH.
AW, YOU SHOULDN'T WORRY ABOUT OL' FLASH. UNDERNEATH THAT CLOWNISH EXTERIOR BEATS THE HEART OF A BAD-TEMPERED WEASEL.
YEAH...BUT YOU CAN SAY STUFF LIKE THAT AROUND HIM, SAMMY. HE LIKES YOU.
FLASH DOESN'T LIKE ANYONE. NOT EVEN GIRLS. I THINK HE'S HOLDING OUT FOR ONE THAT LOOKS JUST LIKE HIM.
HEHH...
...SCIENTISTS HAVE LONG KNOWN THAT HIGH DOSES OF IONIZING RADIATION CAN HELP INCREASE CHEMICAL ACTIVITY WITHIN CELLS.
THE IMPLICATION, THEN, IS THAT IF WE ISOLATE CERTAIN FREQUENCIES WITHIN THE ELECTROMAGNETIC SPECTRUM, WE CAN LITERALLY MANIPULATE CELLS TO CREATE GROWTH, TO DESTROY OTHERS OR EVEN CREATE GENETIC MUTATIONS.
CANCE THERA
RADIATION CAN COME FROM SPACE, RIGHT? I HEARD THAT THE CELLULAR STRUCTURE OF WHEAT INSIDE CROP CIRCLES CAN BE COMPLETELY ALTERED. DO YOU THINK IONIZING RADIATION CAUSES THAT?
MORE LIKE ONE OF PARKER'S FARTS.
THAT'S A GREAT QUESTION. WE'VE MANAGED TO ISOLATE AND HARNESS IT HERE.
THE WHOLE POINT OF THE SCIENCE IS TO FIND OUT HOW WE CAN USE IT.

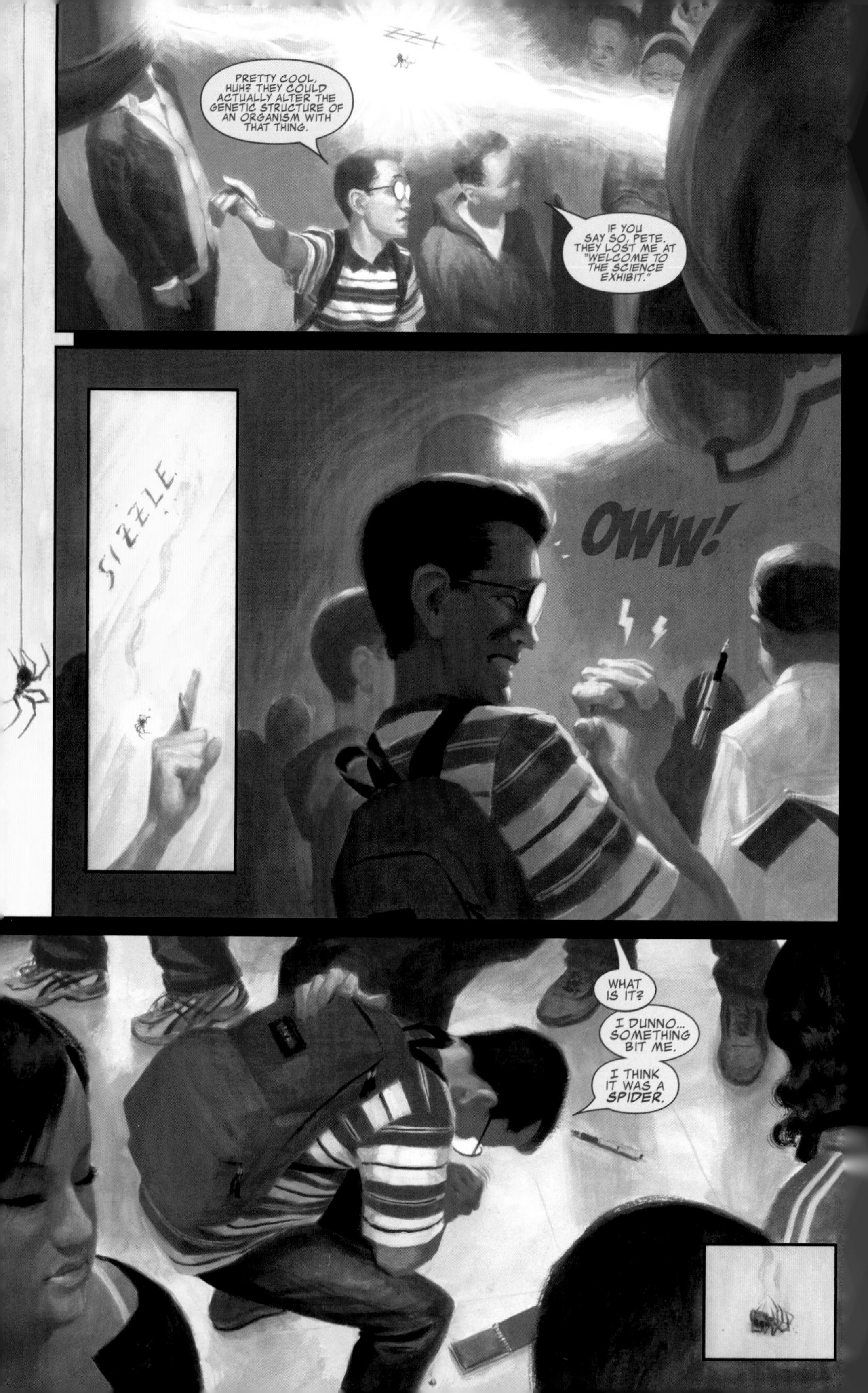
ZZZT
PRETTY COOL, HUH? THEY COULD ACTUALLY ALTER THE GENETIC STRUCTURE OF AN ORGANISM WITH THAT THING.
IF YOU SAY SO, PETE. THEY LOST ME AT "WELCOME TO THE SCIENCE EXHIBIT."
SIZZLE
OWW!
WHAT IS IT?
I DUNNO... SOMETHING BIT ME.
I THINK IT WAS A SPIDER.

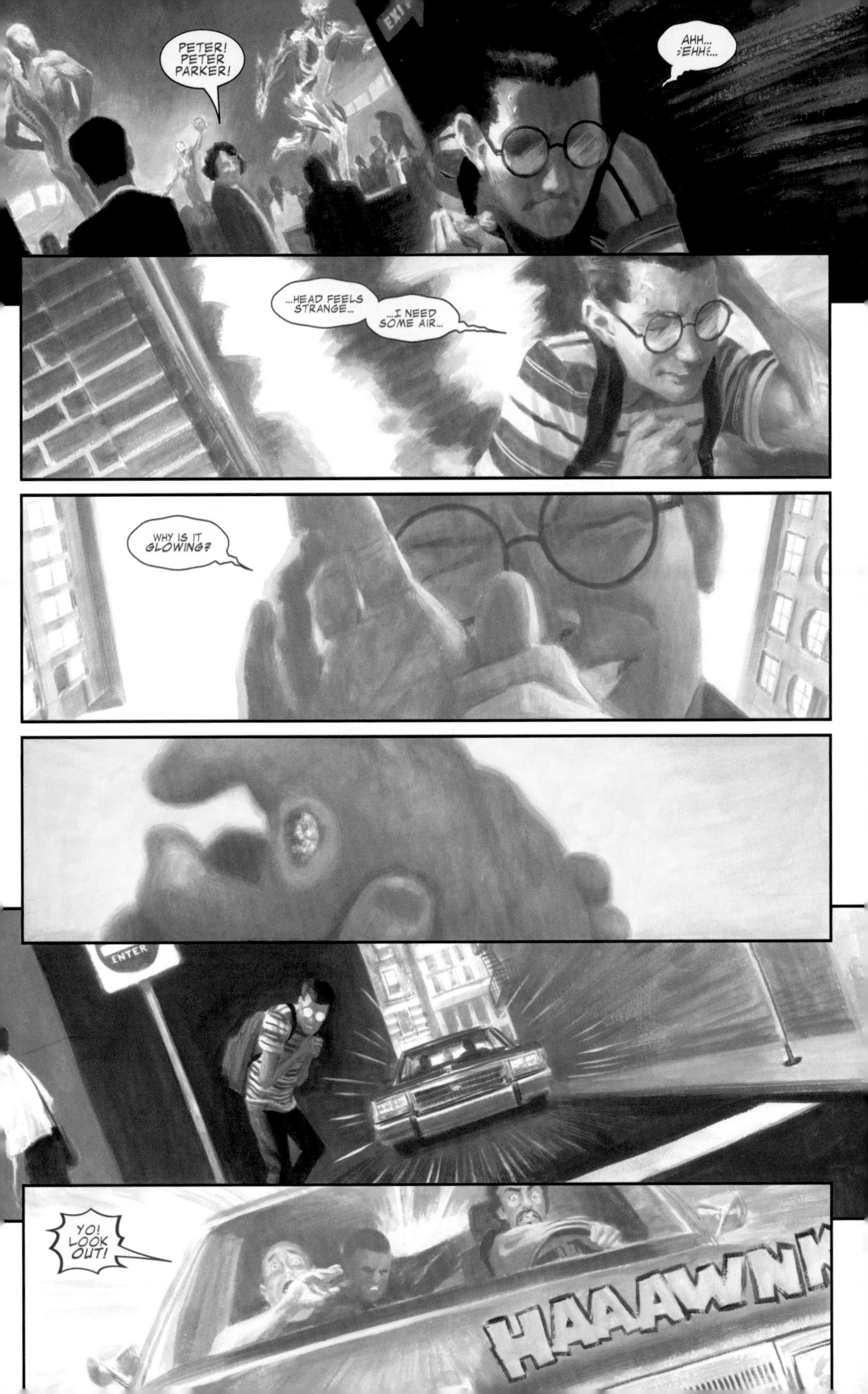
PETER! PETER PARKER!
AHH... EHH...
...HEAD FEELS STRANGE...
...I NEED SOME AIR...
WHY IS IT GLOWING?
ENTER
YO! LOOK OUT!
HAAAWNK

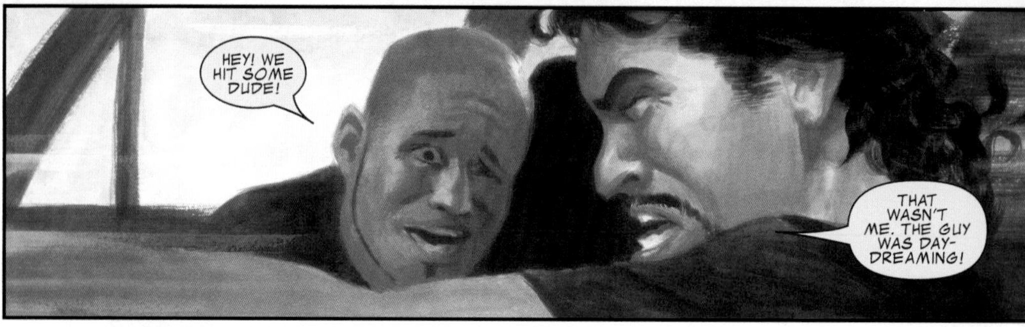
HEY! WE HIT SOME DUDE!
THAT WASN'T ME. THE GUY WAS DAY-DREAMING!

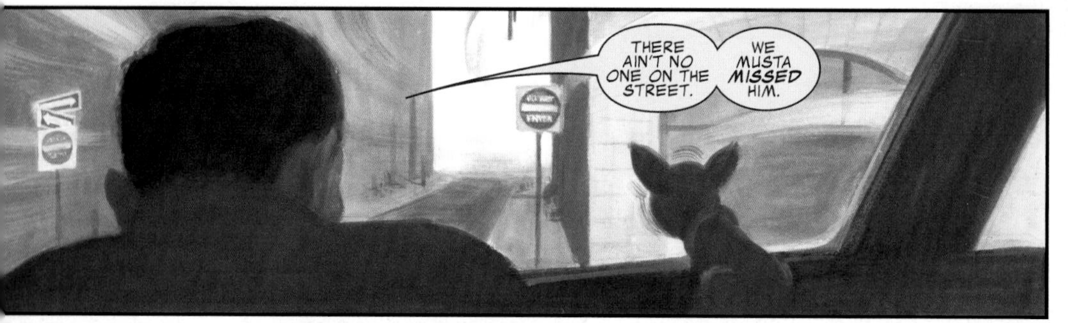
THERE AIN'T NO ONE ON THE STREET.
WE MUSTA *MISSED* HIM.

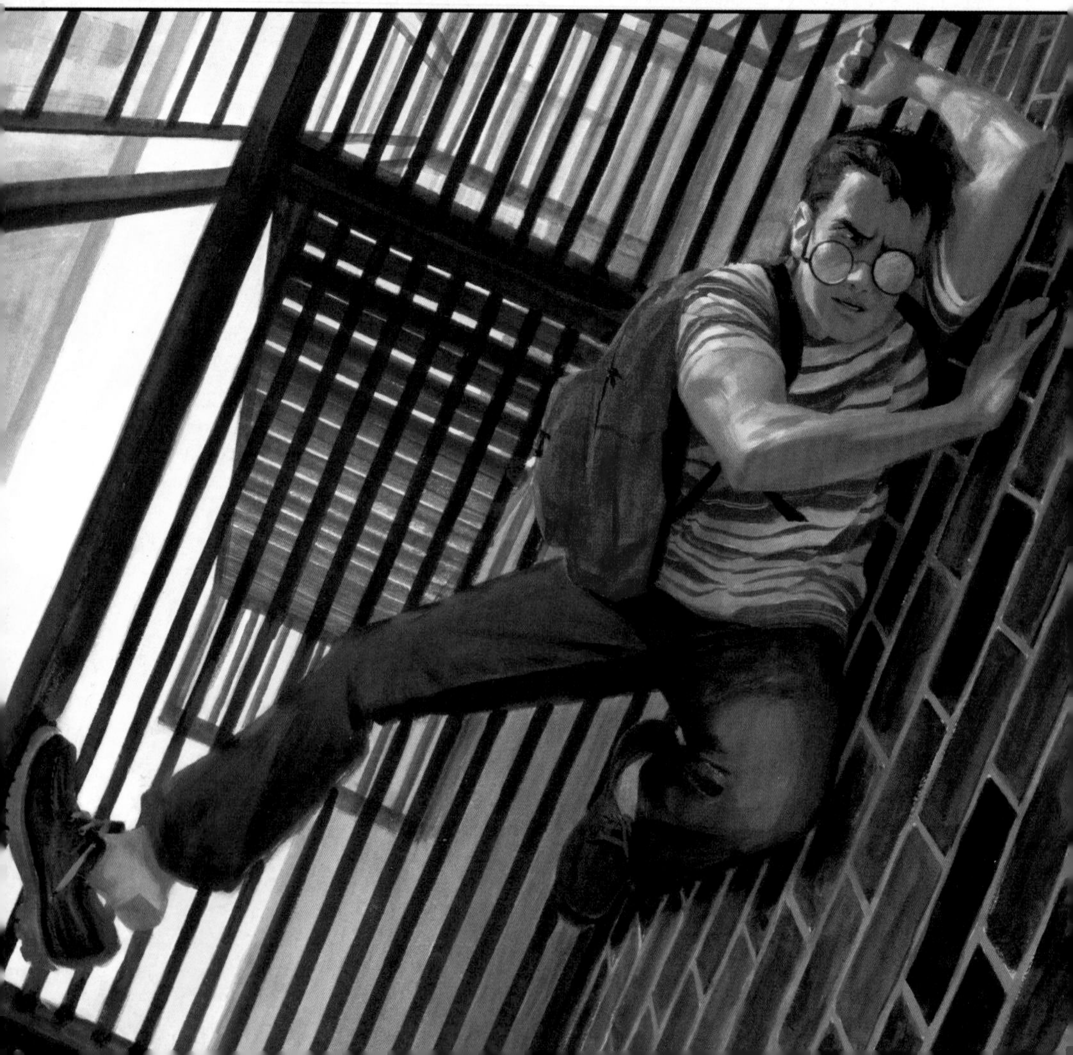

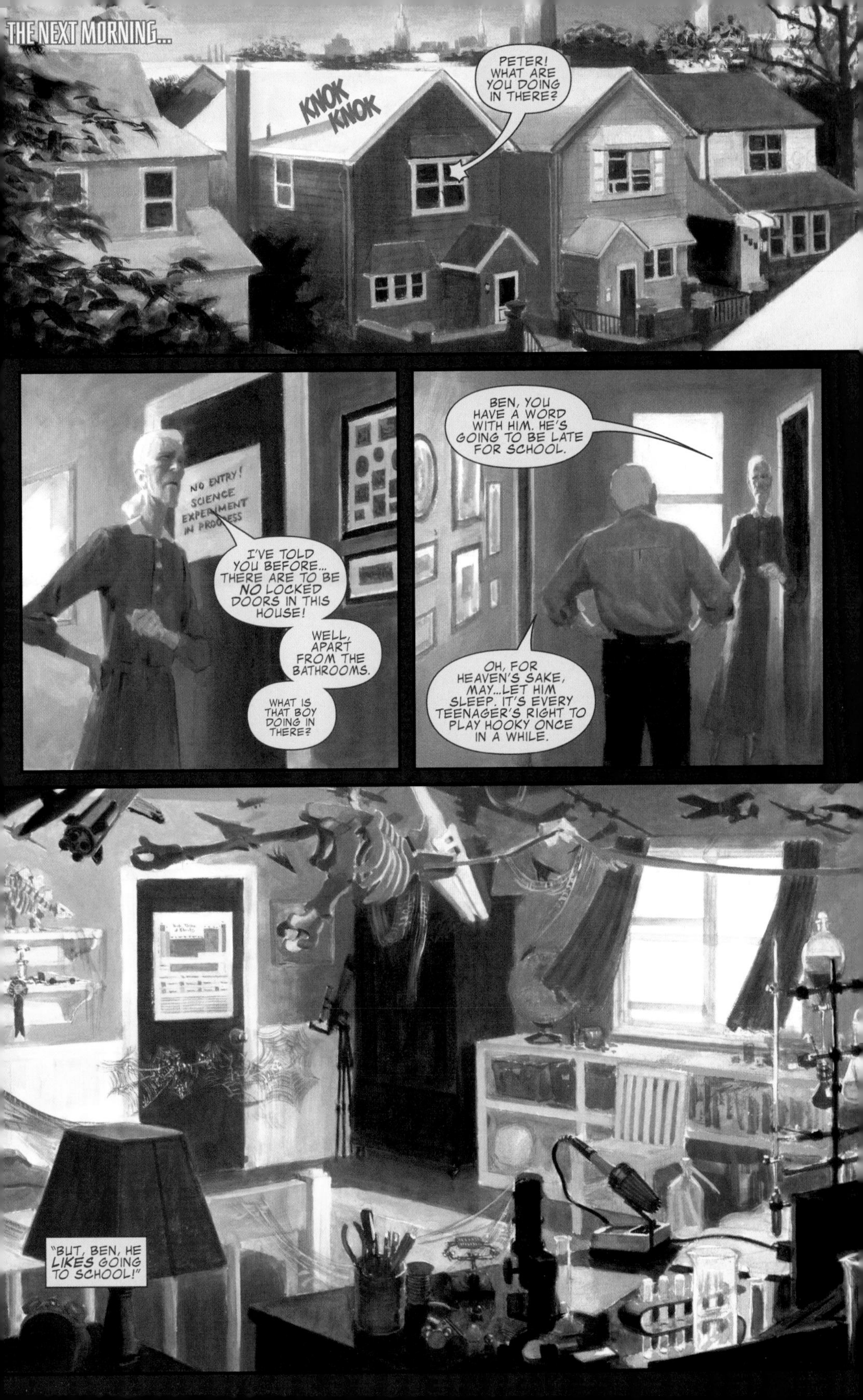
THE NEXT MORNING...
KNOK KNOK
PETER! WHAT ARE YOU DOING IN THERE?
NO ENTRY! SCIENCE EXPERIMENT IN PROGRESS
I'VE TOLD YOU BEFORE... THERE ARE TO BE NO LOCKED DOORS IN THIS HOUSE!
WELL, APART FROM THE BATHROOMS.
WHAT IS THAT BOY DOING IN THERE?
BEN, YOU HAVE A WORD WITH HIM. HE'S GOING TO BE LATE FOR SCHOOL.
OH, FOR HEAVEN'S SAKE, MAY...LET HIM SLEEP. IT'S EVERY TEENAGER'S RIGHT TO PLAY HOOKY ONCE IN A WHILE.
"BUT, BEN, HE LIKES GOING TO SCHOOL!"

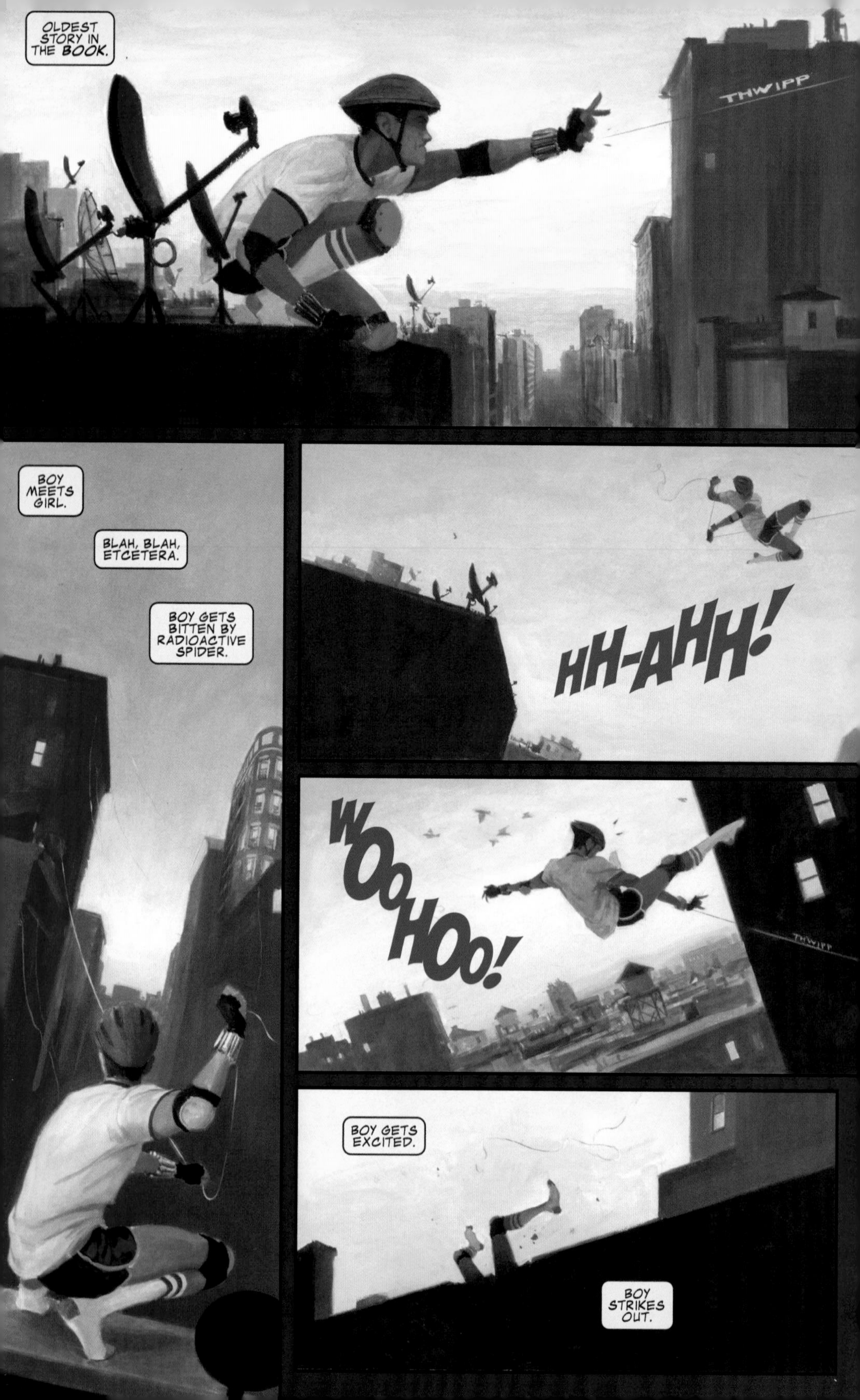
OLDEST STORY IN THE BOOK.
THWIPP
BOY MEETS GIRL.
BLAH, BLAH, ETCETERA.
BOY GETS BITTEN BY RADIOACTIVE SPIDER.
HH-AHH!
WOOHOO!
THWIPP
BOY GETS EXCITED.
BOY STRIKES OUT.

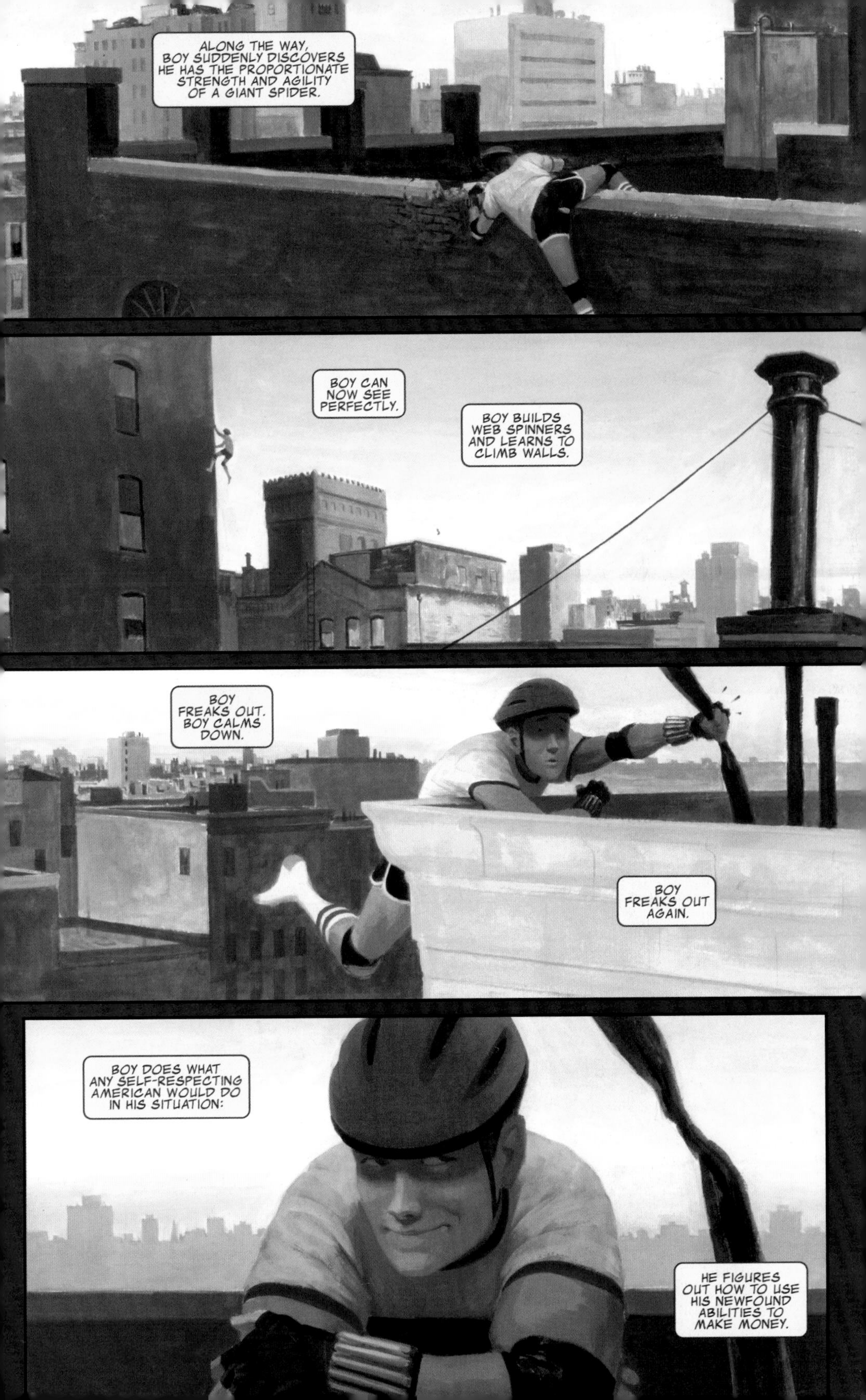
ALONG THE WAY, BOY SUDDENLY DISCOVERS HE HAS THE PROPORTIONATE STRENGTH AND AGILITY OF A GIANT SPIDER.
BOY CAN NOW SEE PERFECTLY.
BOY BUILDS WEB SPINNERS AND LEARNS TO CLIMB WALLS.
BOY FREAKS OUT. BOY CALMS DOWN.
BOY FREAKS OUT AGAIN.
BOY DOES WHAT ANY SELF-RESPECTING AMERICAN WOULD DO IN HIS SITUATION:
HE FIGURES OUT HOW TO USE HIS NEWFOUND ABILITIES TO MAKE MONEY.

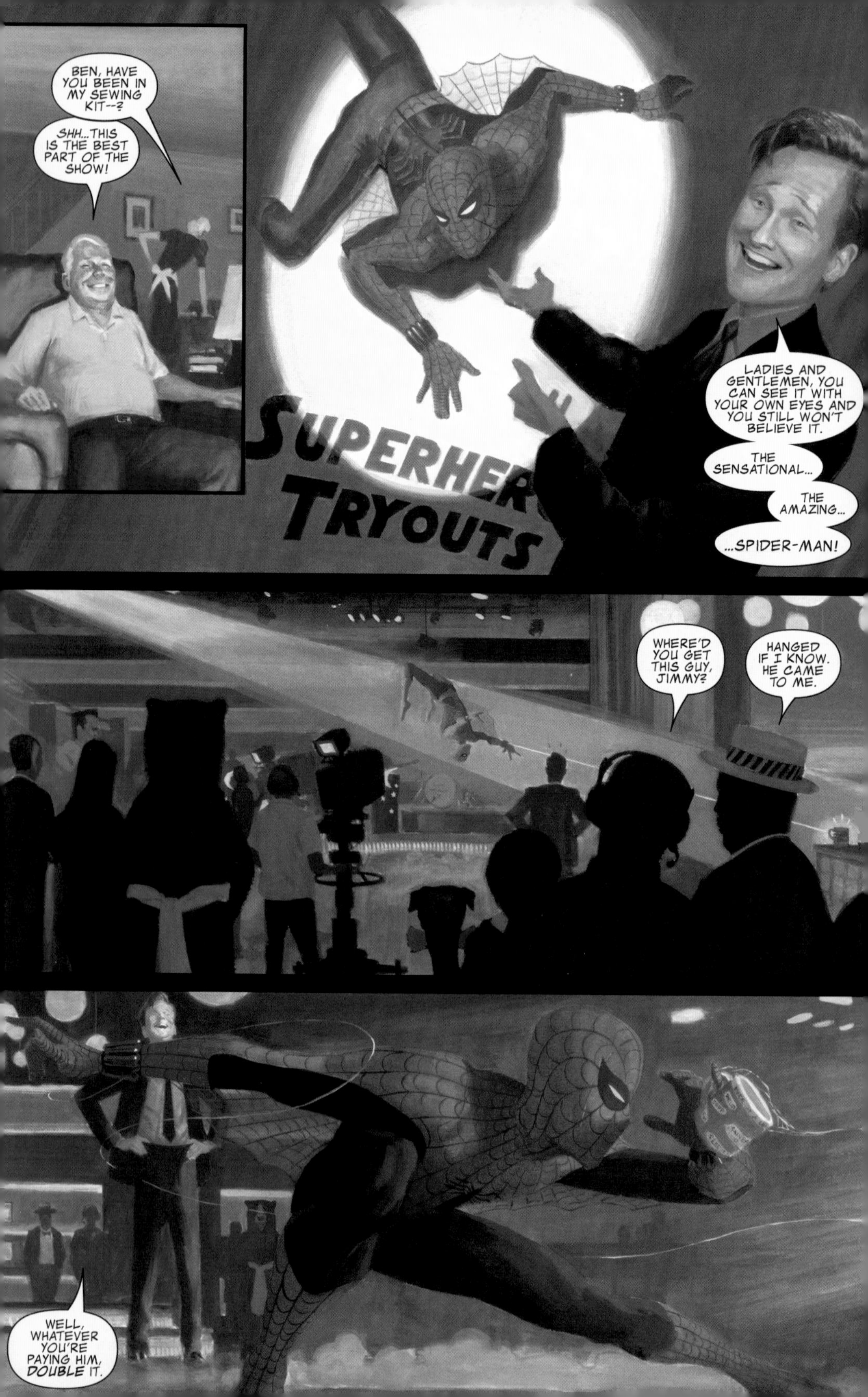
BEN, HAVE YOU BEEN IN MY SEWING KIT--?
SHH...THIS IS THE BEST PART OF THE SHOW!
SUPERHERO TRYOUTS
LADIES AND GENTLEMEN, YOU CAN SEE IT WITH YOUR OWN EYES AND YOU STILL WON'T BELIEVE IT.
THE SENSATIONAL...
THE AMAZING...
...SPIDER-MAN!
WHERE'D YOU GET THIS GUY, JIMMY?
HANGED IF I KNOW. HE CAME TO ME.
WELL, WHATEVER YOU'RE PAYING HIM, *DOUBLE* IT.

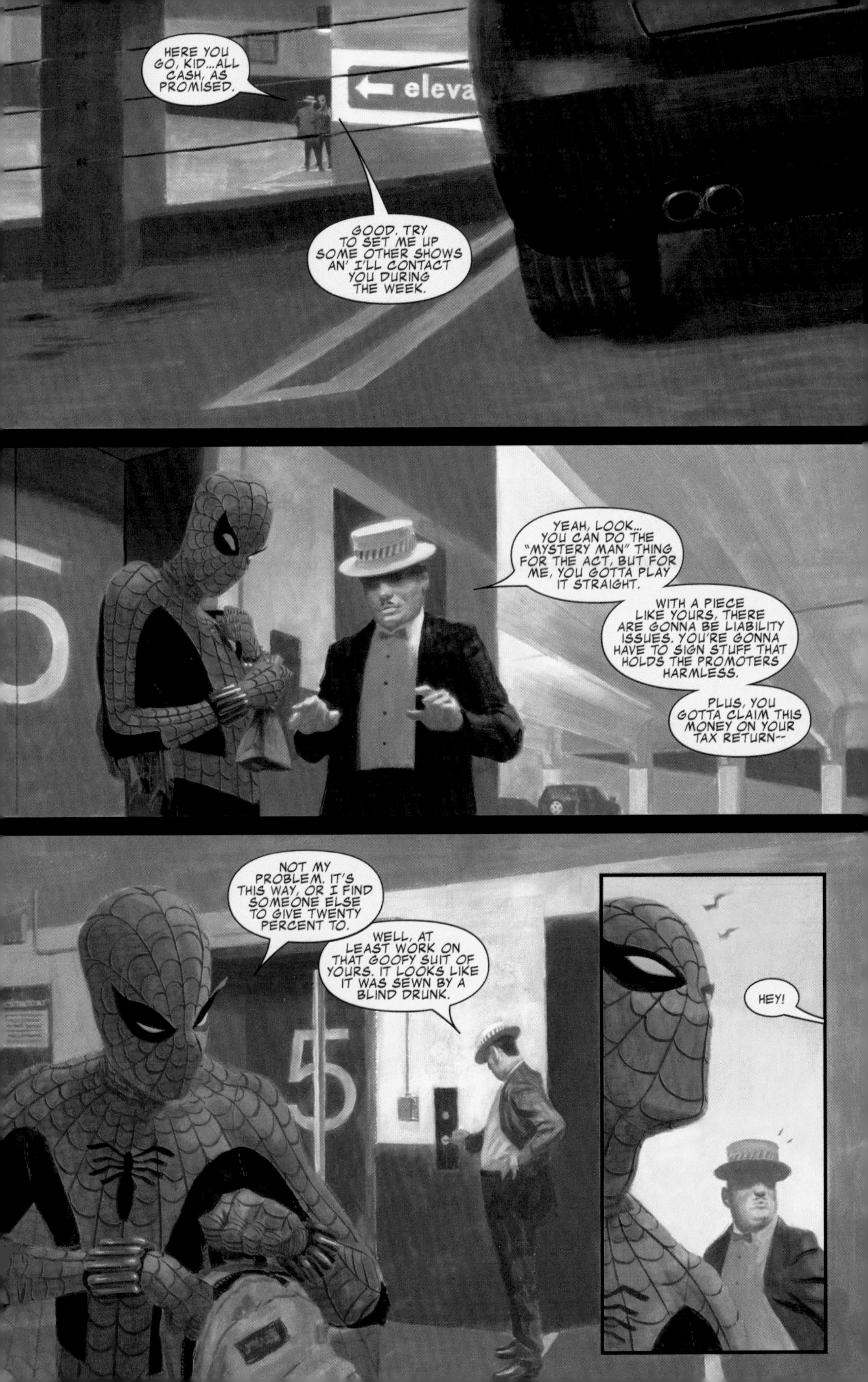
HERE YOU GO, KID...ALL CASH, AS PROMISED.
GOOD. TRY TO SET ME UP SOME OTHER SHOWS AN' I'LL CONTACT YOU DURING THE WEEK.
eleva
YEAH, LOOK... YOU CAN DO THE "MYSTERY MAN" THING FOR THE ACT, BUT FOR ME, YOU GOTTA PLAY IT STRAIGHT.
WITH A PIECE LIKE YOURS, THERE ARE GONNA BE LIABILITY ISSUES. YOU'RE GONNA HAVE TO SIGN STUFF THAT HOLDS THE PROMOTERS HARMLESS.
PLUS, YOU GOTTA CLAIM THIS MONEY ON YOUR TAX RETURN--
NOT MY PROBLEM. IT'S THIS WAY, OR I FIND SOMEONE ELSE TO GIVE TWENTY PERCENT TO.
WELL, AT LEAST WORK ON THAT GOOFY SUIT OF YOURS. IT LOOKS LIKE IT WAS SEWN BY A BLIND DRUNK.
HEY!

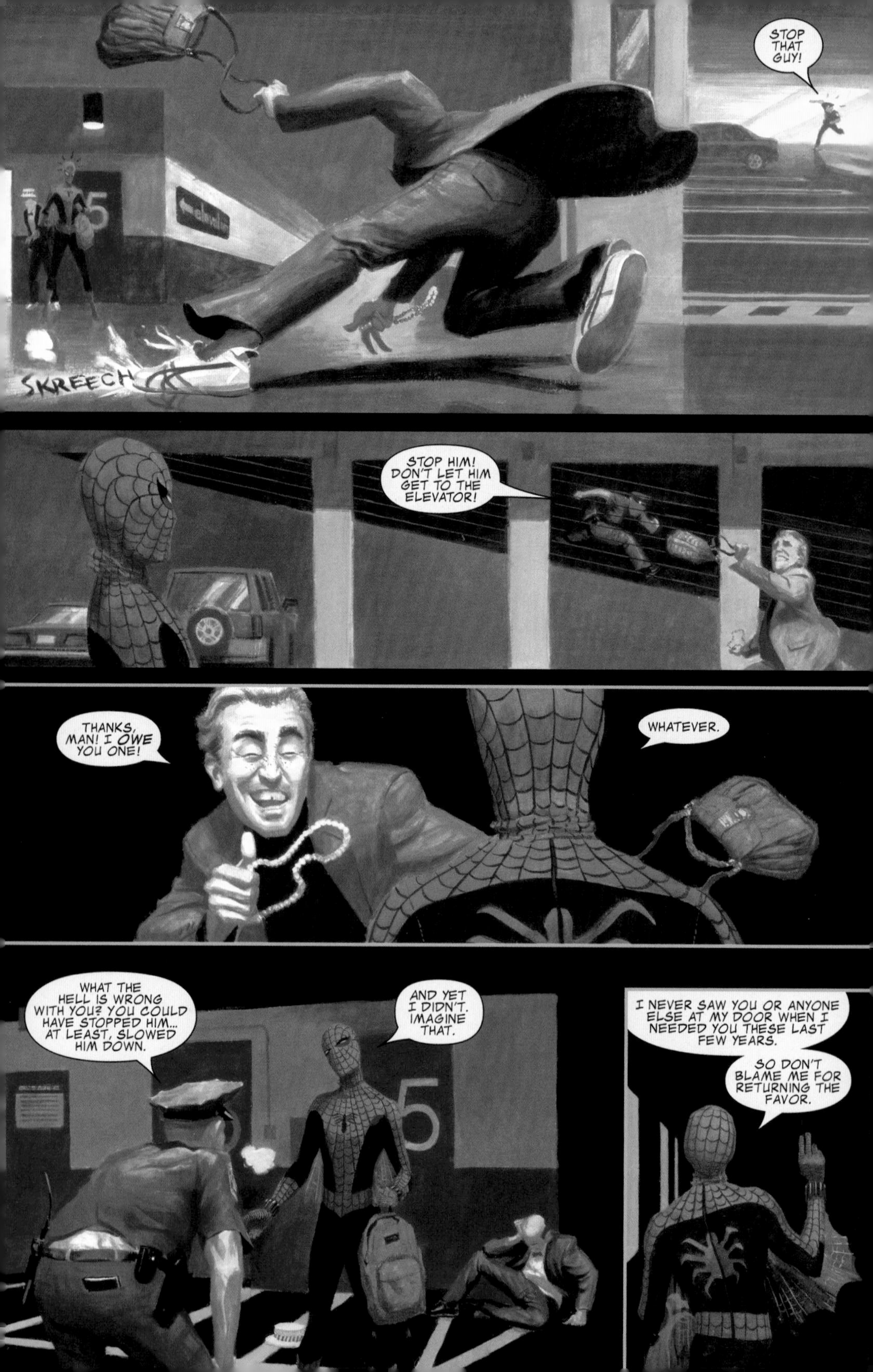
STOP THAT GUY!
SKREECH
STOP HIM! DON'T LET HIM GET TO THE ELEVATOR!
THANKS, MAN! I OWE YOU ONE!
WHATEVER.
WHAT THE HELL IS WRONG WITH YOU? YOU COULD HAVE STOPPED HIM... AT LEAST, SLOWED HIM DOWN.
AND YET I DIDN'T. IMAGINE THAT.
I NEVER SAW YOU OR ANYONE ELSE AT MY DOOR WHEN I NEEDED YOU THESE LAST FEW YEARS.
SO DON'T BLAME ME FOR RETURNING THE FAVOR.

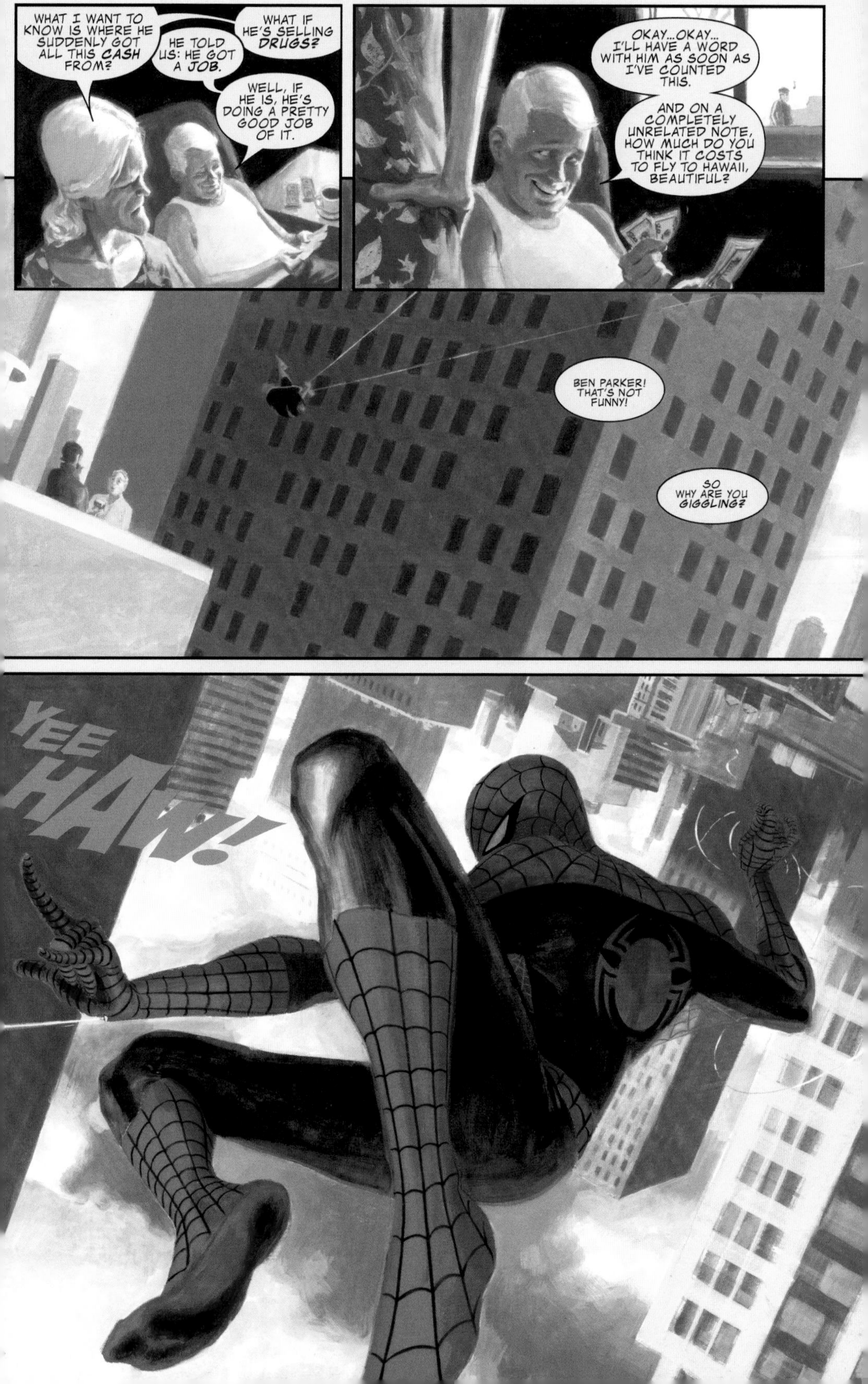
WHAT I WANT TO KNOW IS WHERE HE SUDDENLY GOT ALL THIS CASH FROM?
WHAT IF HE'S SELLING DRUGS?
HE TOLD US: HE GOT A JOB.
WELL, IF HE IS, HE'S DOING A PRETTY GOOD JOB OF IT.
OKAY...OKAY... I'LL HAVE A WORD WITH HIM AS SOON AS I'VE COUNTED THIS.
AND ON A COMPLETELY UNRELATED NOTE, HOW MUCH DO YOU THINK IT COSTS TO FLY TO HAWAII, BEAUTIFUL?
BEN PARKER! THAT'S NOT FUNNY!
SO WHY ARE YOU GIGGLING?
YEE HAW!

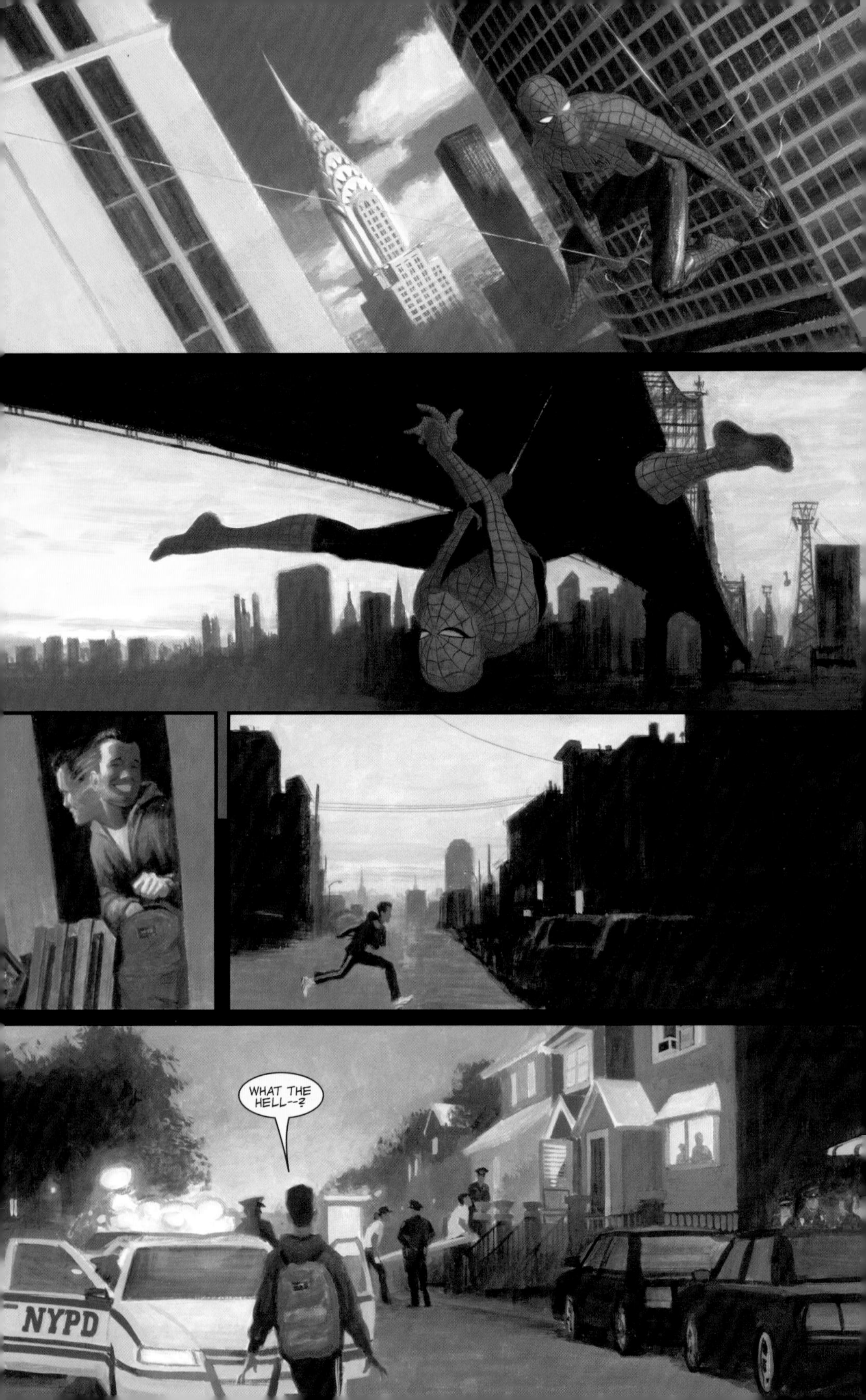
WHAT THE HELL--?
NYPD

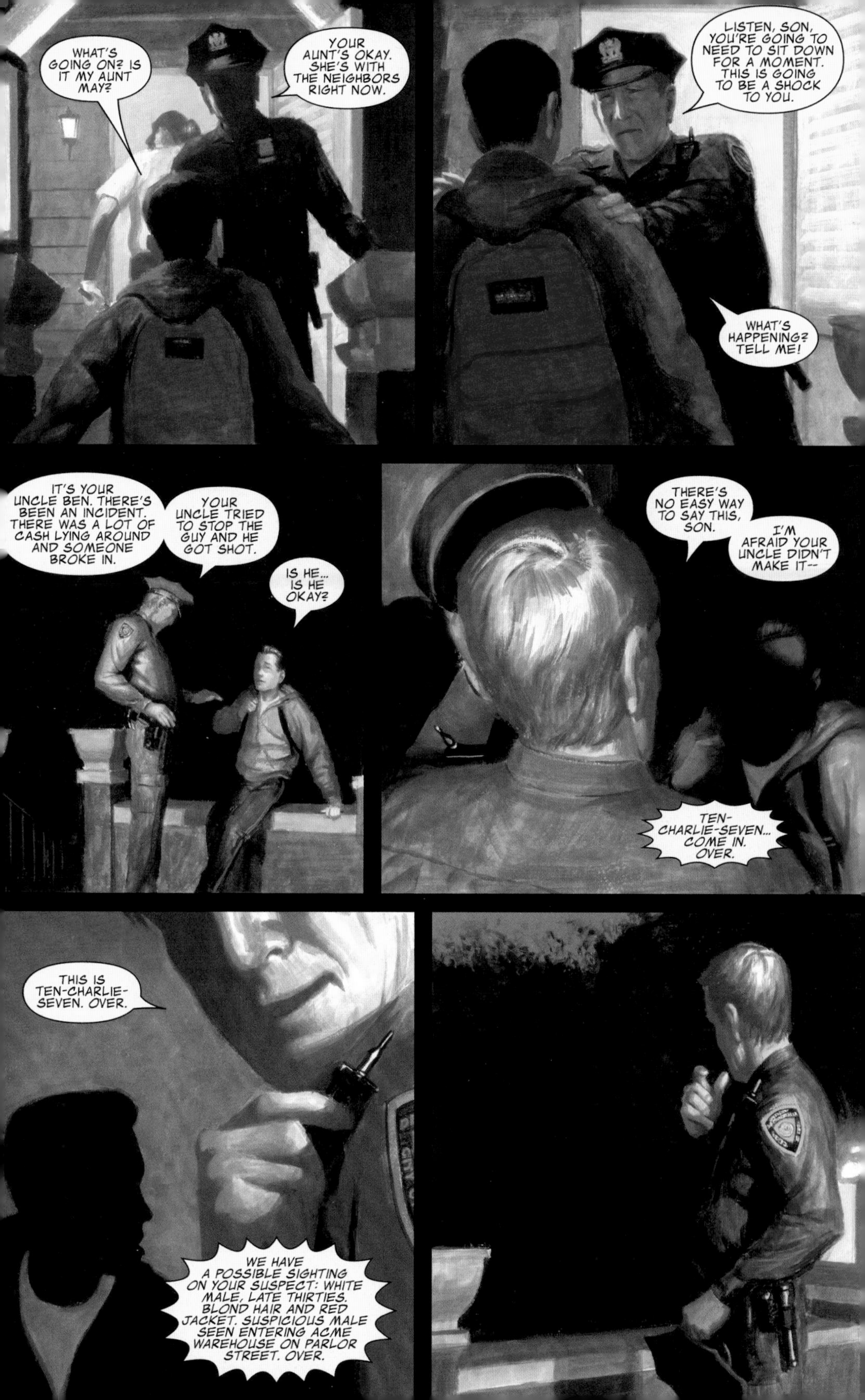
WHAT'S GOING ON? IS IT MY AUNT MAY?
YOUR AUNT'S OKAY. SHE'S WITH THE NEIGHBORS RIGHT NOW.
LISTEN, SON, YOU'RE GOING TO NEED TO SIT DOWN FOR A MOMENT. THIS IS GOING TO BE A SHOCK TO YOU.
WHAT'S HAPPENING? TELL ME!
IT'S YOUR UNCLE BEN. THERE'S BEEN AN INCIDENT. THERE WAS A LOT OF CASH LYING AROUND AND SOMEONE BROKE IN.
YOUR UNCLE TRIED TO STOP THE GUY AND HE GOT SHOT.
IS HE... IS HE OKAY?
THERE'S NO EASY WAY TO SAY THIS, SON.
I'M AFRAID YOUR UNCLE DIDN'T MAKE IT--
TEN-CHARLIE-SEVEN... COME IN. OVER.
THIS IS TEN-CHARLIE-SEVEN. OVER.
WE HAVE A POSSIBLE SIGHTING ON YOUR SUSPECT: WHITE MALE, LATE THIRTIES. BLOND HAIR AND RED JACKET. SUSPICIOUS MALE SEEN ENTERING ACME WAREHOUSE ON PARLOR STREET. OVER.

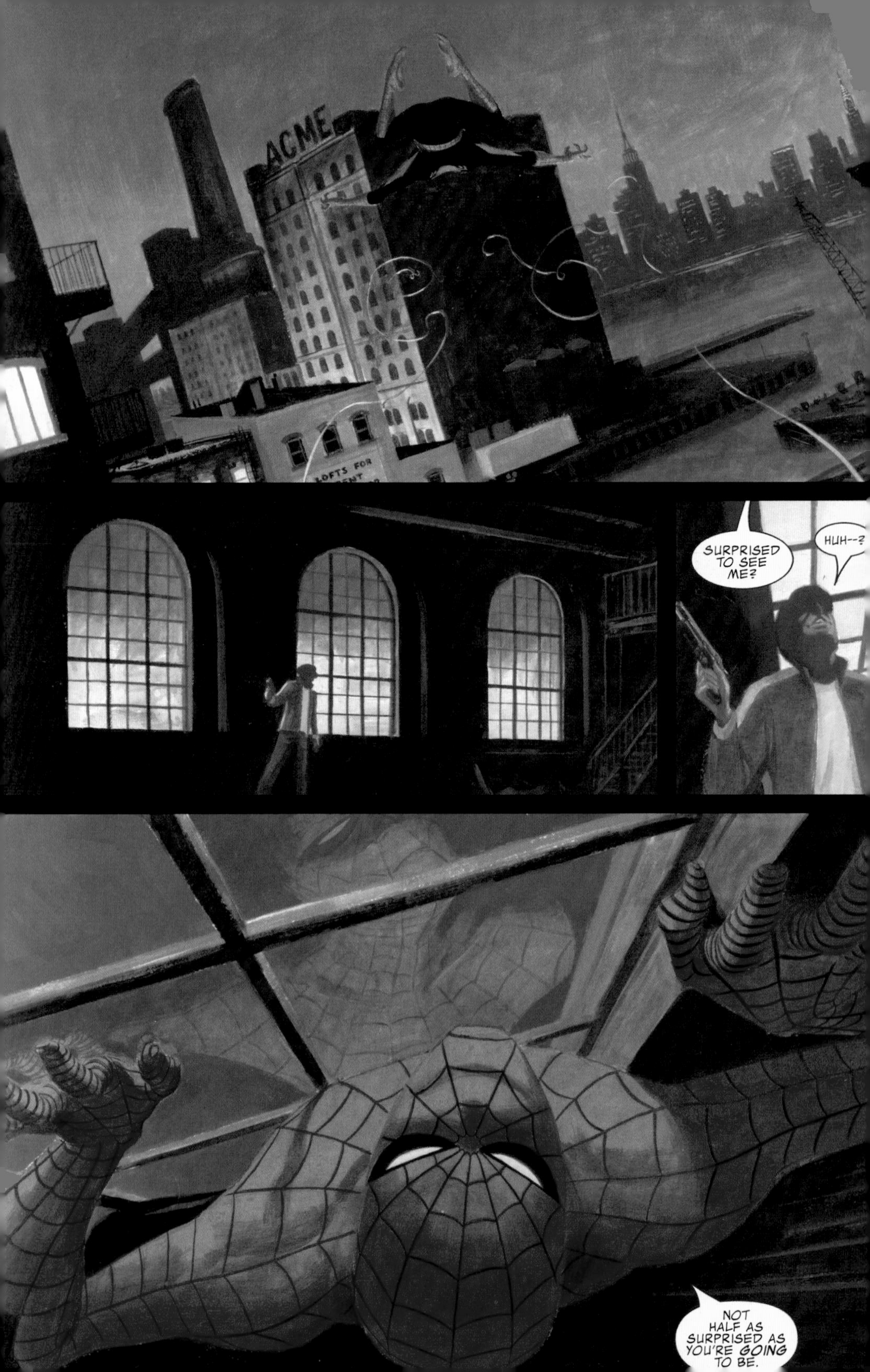
ACME
LOFTS FOR
SURPRISED TO SEE ME?
HUH--?
NOT HALF AS SURPRISED AS YOU'RE *GOING* TO BE.

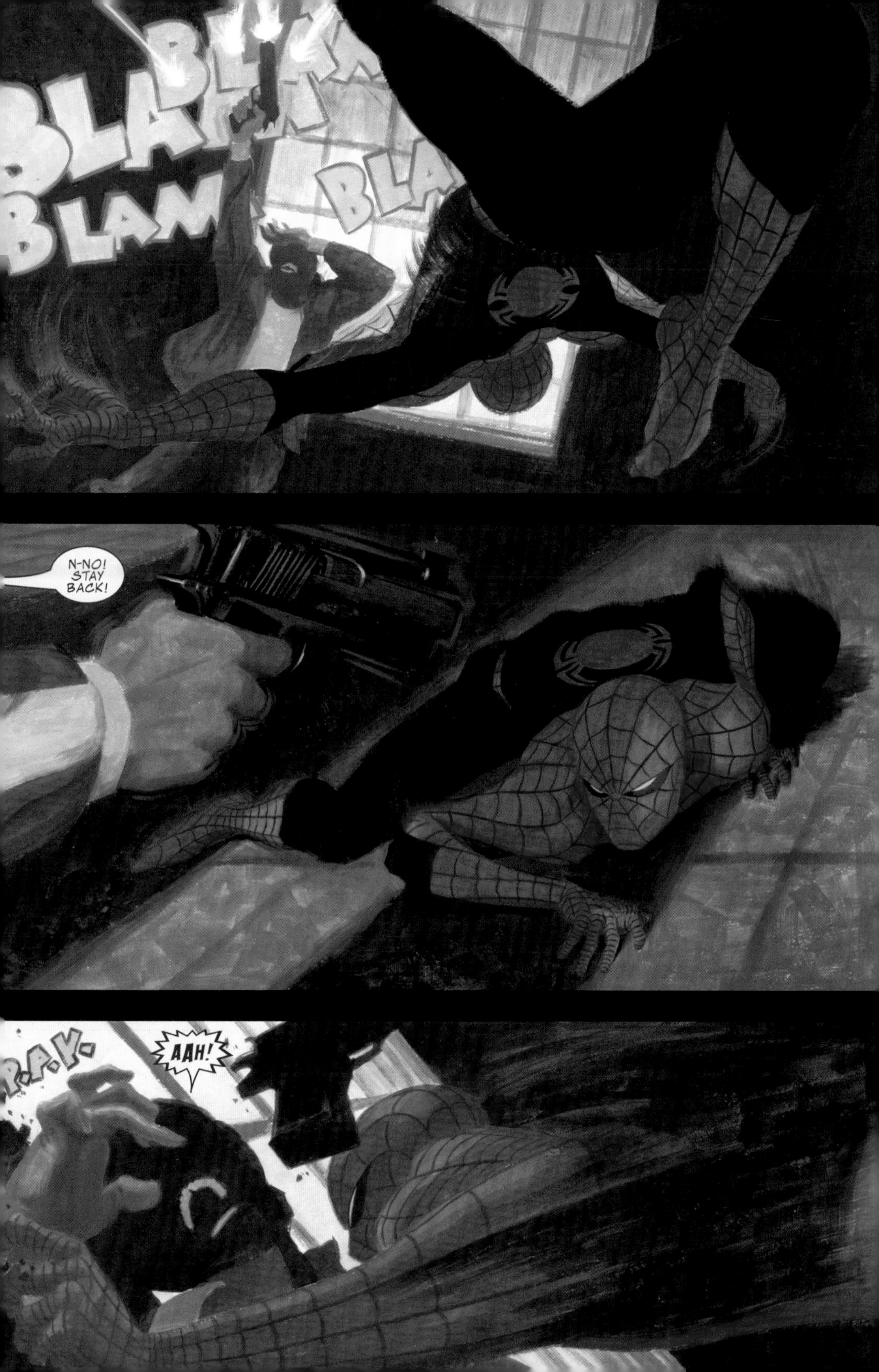
BLAM
BLAM
BLAM
N-NO! STAY BACK!
P.A.K.
AAH!

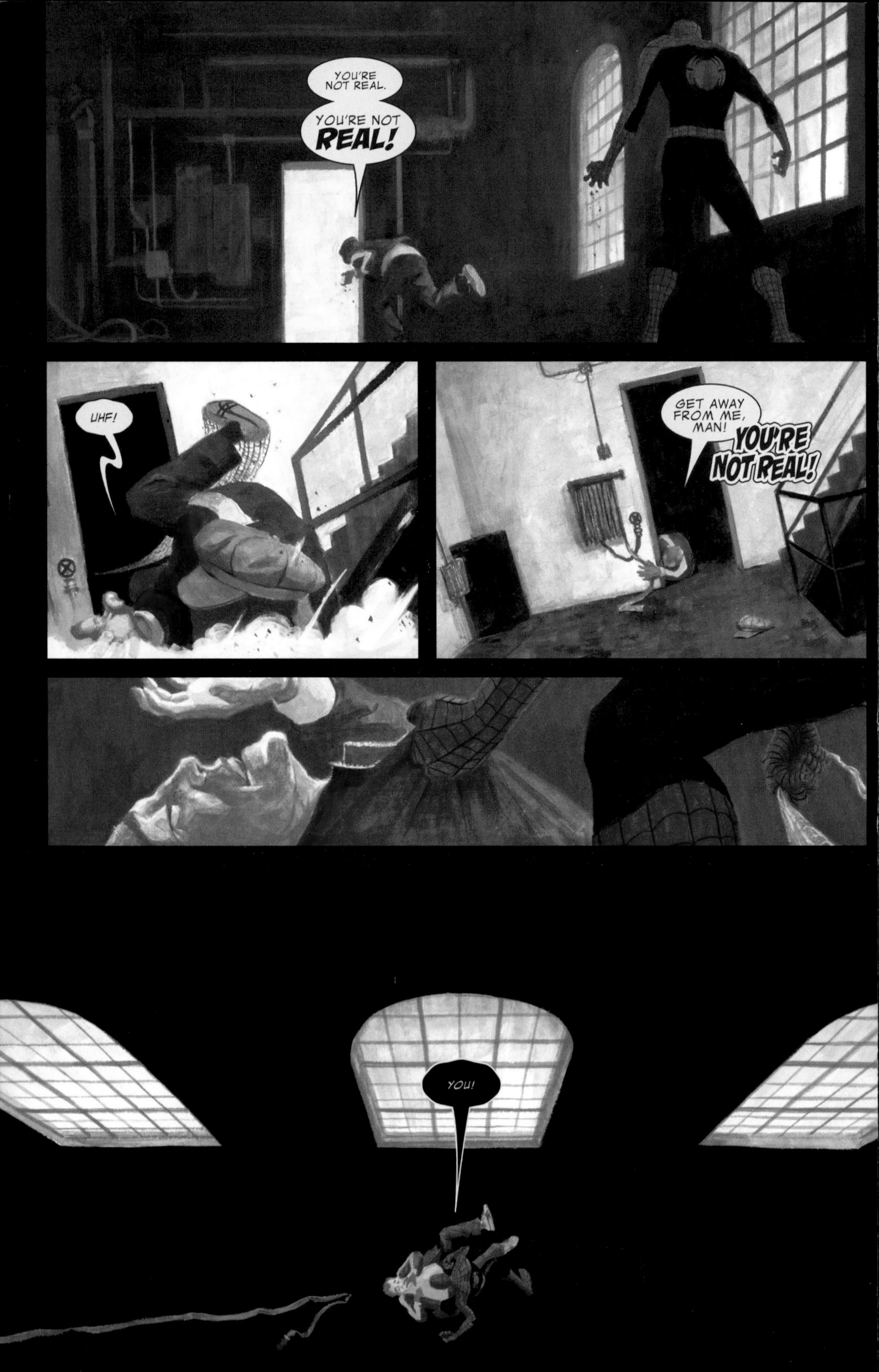
YOU'RE NOT REAL.
YOU'RE NOT REAL!
UHF!
GET AWAY FROM ME, MAN!
YOU'RE NOT REAL!
YOU!

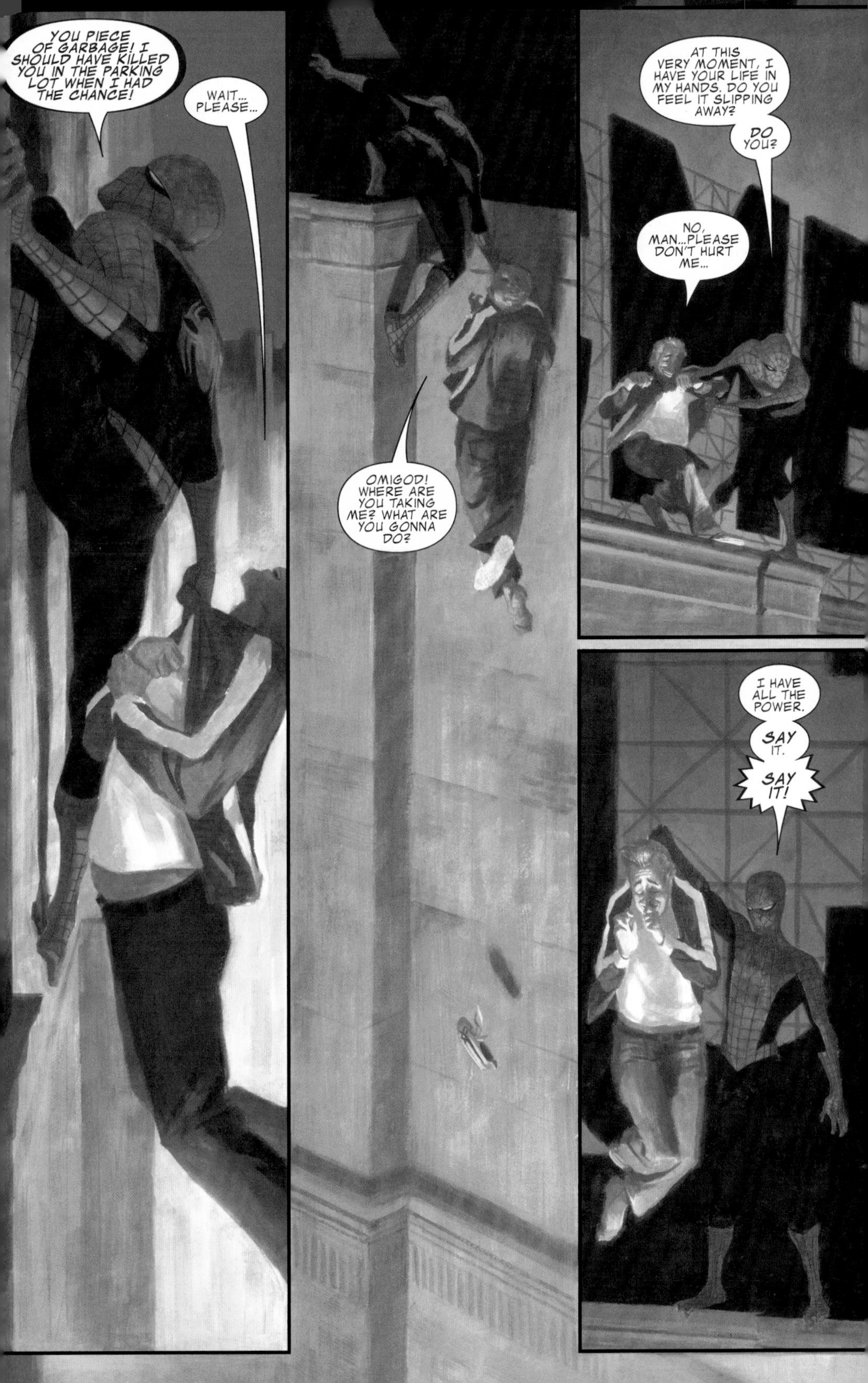

YOU PIECE OF GARBAGE! I SHOULD HAVE KILLED YOU IN THE PARKING LOT WHEN I HAD THE CHANCE!
WAIT... PLEASE...
OMIGOD! WHERE ARE YOU TAKING ME? WHAT ARE YOU GONNA DO?
AT THIS VERY MOMENT, I HAVE YOUR LIFE IN MY HANDS. DO YOU FEEL IT SLIPPING AWAY?
DO YOU?
NO, MAN...PLEASE DON'T HURT ME...
I HAVE ALL THE POWER.
SAY IT.
SAY IT!

C'MON, DUDE...

SAY IT. TELL ME I HAVE ALL THE POWER.

YOU HAVE ALL THE POWER! YOU HAVE ALL THE POWER!

AND DON'T YOU EVER *FORGET* IT.

OH...GOD... ;AH-HEHH;... I DON'T NEED TO BE DEAD RIGHT NOW...

YOU KILLED A GOOD MAN TONIGHT. WHAT DO YOU *THINK* I SHOULD DO?

I DIDN'T *MEAN* TO--

I OUGHT TO KILL YOU RIGHT NOW!

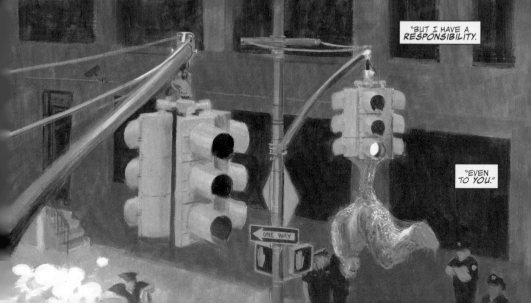

"BUT I HAVE A *RESPONSIBILITY.*

"EVEN TO *YOU.*"

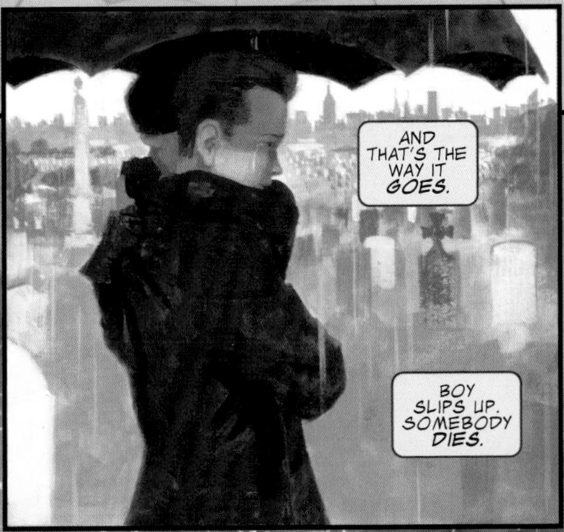
AND THAT'S THE WAY IT GOES.
BOY SLIPS UP. SOMEBODY DIES.
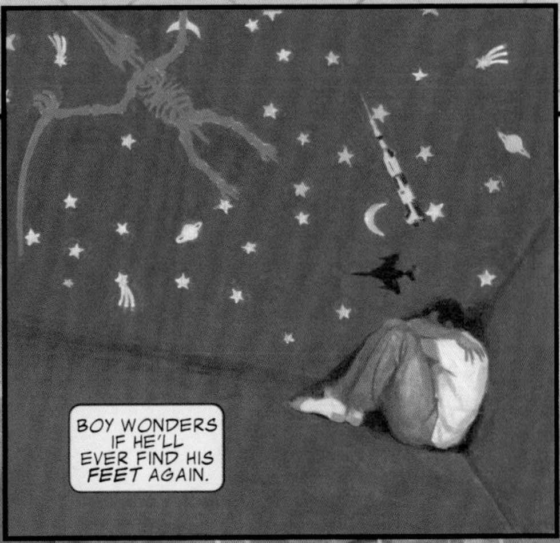
BOY WONDERS IF HE'LL EVER FIND HIS FEET AGAIN.
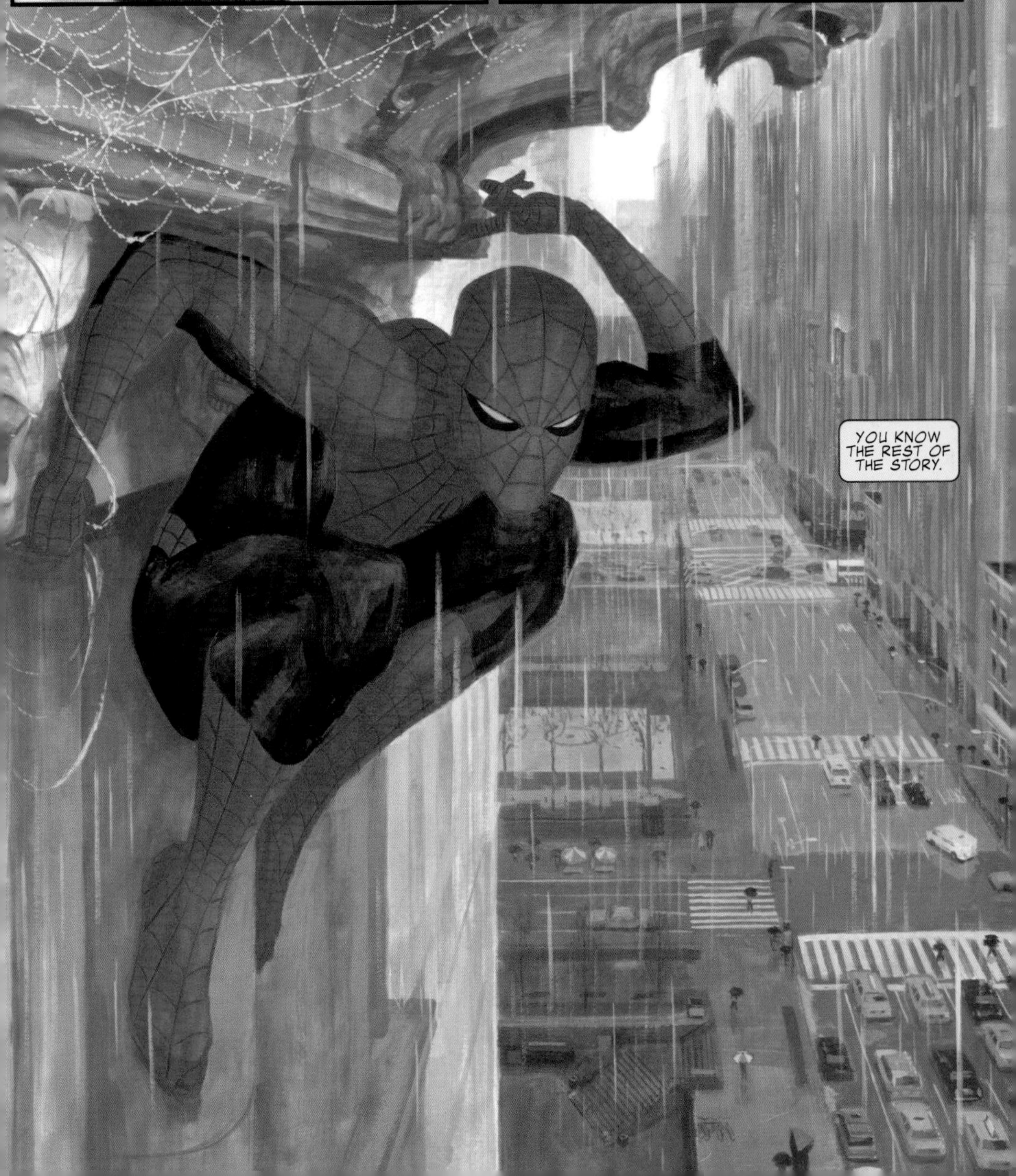
YOU KNOW THE REST OF THE STORY.

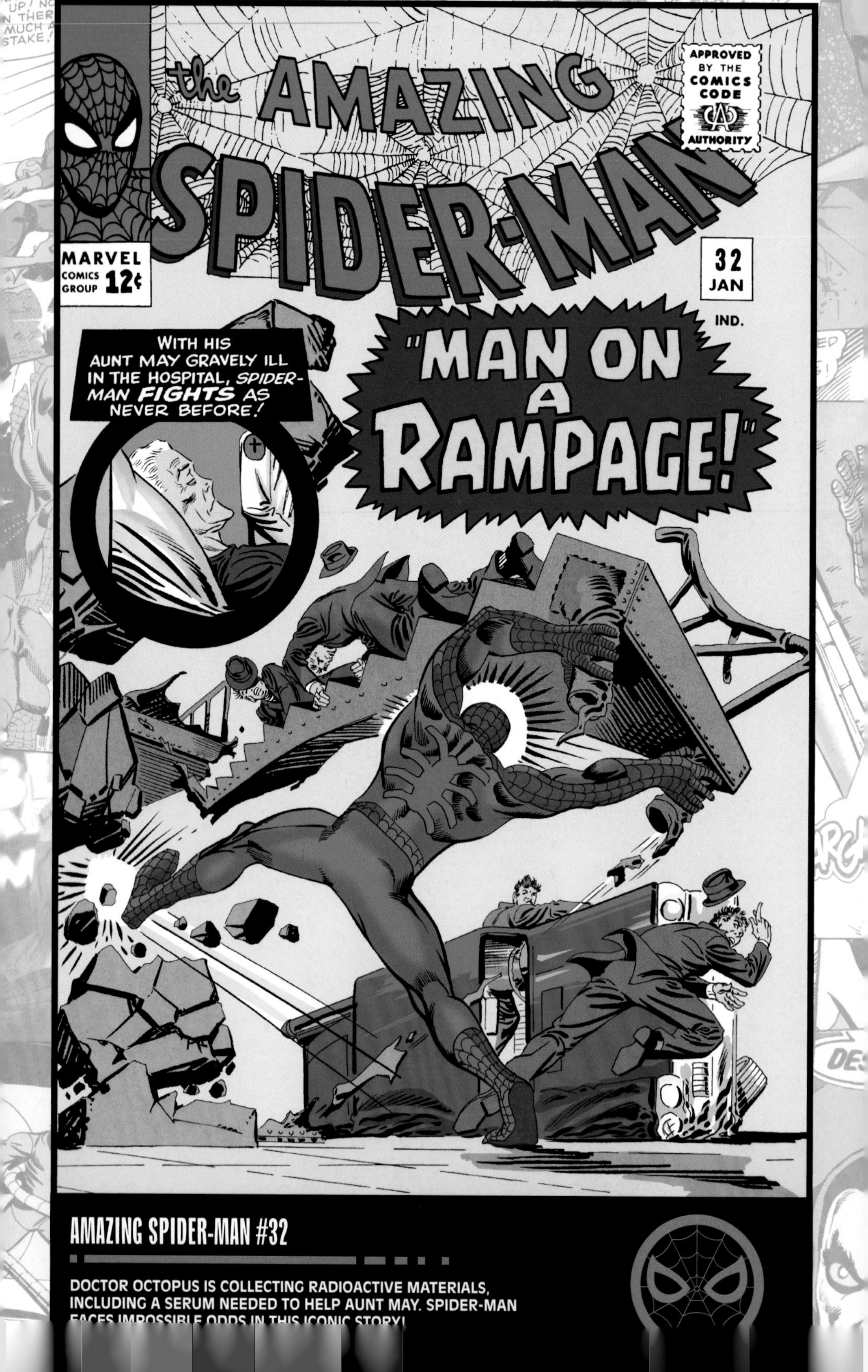

the AMAZING SPIDER-MAN
APPROVED BY THE COMICS CODE AUTHORITY
MARVEL COMICS GROUP 12¢
32 JAN
IND.
"MAN ON A RAMPAGE!"
WITH HIS AUNT MAY GRAVELY ILL IN THE HOSPITAL, SPIDER-MAN FIGHTS AS NEVER BEFORE!

AMAZING SPIDER-MAN #32

DOCTOR OCTOPUS IS COLLECTING RADIOACTIVE MATERIALS, INCLUDING A SERUM NEEDED TO HELP AUNT MAY. SPIDER-MAN FACES IMPOSSIBLE ODDS IN THIS ICONIC STORY!

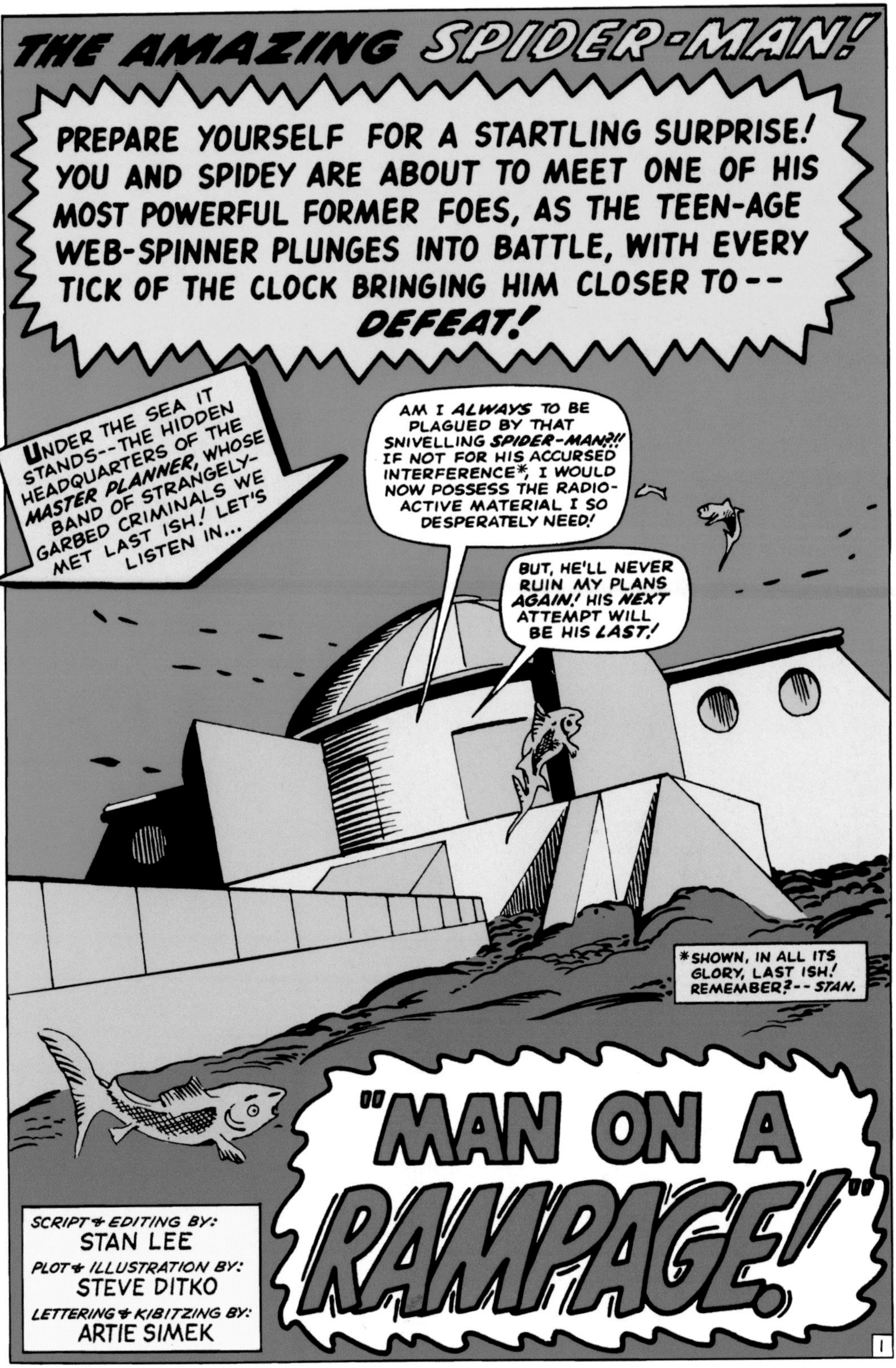
THE AMAZING SPIDER-MAN!
PREPARE YOURSELF FOR A STARTLING SURPRISE! YOU AND SPIDEY ARE ABOUT TO MEET ONE OF HIS MOST POWERFUL FORMER FOES, AS THE TEEN-AGE WEB-SPINNER PLUNGES INTO BATTLE, WITH EVERY TICK OF THE CLOCK BRINGING HIM CLOSER TO -- DEFEAT!
UNDER THE SEA IT STANDS--THE HIDDEN HEADQUARTERS OF THE MASTER PLANNER, WHOSE BAND OF STRANGELY-GARBED CRIMINALS WE MET LAST ISH! LET'S LISTEN IN...
AM I ALWAYS TO BE PLAGUED BY THAT SNIVELLING SPIDER-MAN?!! IF NOT FOR HIS ACCURSED INTERFERENCE*, I WOULD NOW POSSESS THE RADIO-ACTIVE MATERIAL I SO DESPERATELY NEED!
BUT, HE'LL NEVER RUIN MY PLANS AGAIN! HIS NEXT ATTEMPT WILL BE HIS LAST!
*SHOWN, IN ALL ITS GLORY, LAST ISH! REMEMBER?-- STAN.
"MAN ON A RAMPAGE!"
SCRIPT & EDITING BY: STAN LEE
PLOT & ILLUSTRATION BY: STEVE DITKO
LETTERING & KIBITZING BY: ARTIE SIMEK
1

MY EXPERIMENTS ARE ALMOST *COMPLETE!* I AM CLOSE TO THE *MASTERY* OF LINGERING RADIATION!

AND *STILL* MY SECRET IS *SAFE!* NO ONE KNOWS WHO THE *MASTER PLANNER* REALLY IS!

IT WAS RADIATION THAT CHANGED MY ENTIRE LIFE-- THAT CAUSED ME TO BECOME WHAT I AM TODAY!

AND, THANKS TO RADIATION, THE WORLD WILL SOON AGAIN BE MENACED BY--

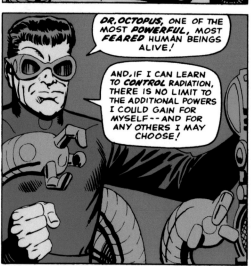

DR. OCTOPUS, ONE OF THE MOST *POWERFUL,* MOST *FEARED* HUMAN BEINGS ALIVE!

AND, IF I CAN LEARN TO *CONTROL* RADIATION, THERE IS NO LIMIT TO THE ADDITIONAL POWERS I COULD GAIN FOR MYSELF--AND FOR ANY OTHERS I MAY CHOOSE!

ATTENTION, DEPUTY SQUAD LEADER! THIS IS THE *MASTER PLANNER!* HAVE YOUR MEN CONTINUE TO SEARCH FOR ANY AND ALL ATOMIC EQUIPMENT FOR ME!

YES SIR! WE WILL CONTINUE UNTIL YOU ISSUE NEW ORDERS! OVER AND OUT!

WHILE, ON THE SURFACE, AS *PETER PARKER* WALKS THRU THE PRESS ROOM OF THE *DAILY BUGLE...*

I WAS *HOPING* PETER WOULD SHOW UP! I SIMPLY *HAVE* TO SPEAK TO HIM!

PETER! WAIT A MOMENT! I WANT TO *TALK* TO YOU!

HE'S TRYING TO PRETEND HE DIDN'T *HEAR* ME! BUT I WON'T *LET* HIM--!

PETER PARKER! YOU *CAN'T* KEEP AVOIDING ME THAT WAY-- AS THOUGH WE'RE NO MORE THAN STRANGERS!

I *HOPED* SHE'D BE OUT TO LUNCH! I DIDN'T WANT TO FACE HER!

YOU *MUST* TELL ME WHAT'S WRONG! WHAT HAVE I SAID-- OR DONE--?

HOW CAN I TELL HER THE TRUTH? SHE THINKS SHE *LOVES* ME --BUT IF SHE EVER FOUND OUT I'M *SPIDER-MAN,* SHE'D DROP ME LIKE A HOT POTATO!

2

Panel 1:

AND THEN, *NED LEEDS*, THE YOUNG REPORTER WHO HAS ASKED BETTY BRANT TO *MARRY* HIM, ENTERS THE SCENE...

PETER, YOU'RE NOT BEING *FAIR* TO BETTY! SHE *DESERVES* AN ANSWER FROM YOU!

NED, PLEASE DON'T INTERFERE!

NOW'S MY CHANCE TO MAKE HER *ANGRY* AT ME!

Panel 2:

BUTT OUT, CREEP! I DON'T OWE BETTY *ANYTHING!* WE HAD A FEW LAUGHS TOGETHER, THAT'S ALL! MAYBE I'VE *OUTGROWN* HER!

PETER--!

WHAT'S GOTTEN *INTO* YOU, FELLA? YOU SOUND-- *DIFFERENT!*

Panel 3:

IT'S EASY FOR *HIM* TO BE CALM! *HE* DOESN'T LOVE A GIRL WHO'D *HATE* HIM IF SHE LEARNED ABOUT HIS SECRET IDENTITY!

I'VE *GOT* TO MAKE HER HATE ME! A CLEAN BREAK IS THE BEST THING FOR *ALL* OF US!

LOOK, PARKER, WHY DON'T WE TALK THIS OVER *CALMLY?*

HANDS OFF, LEEDS! I'VE *MORE* IMPORTANT THINGS TO DO!

Panel 4:

BUT YOU KNOW HOW *I* FEEL ABOUT BETTY! IF *YOU'RE* NOT INTERESTED, WHY DON'T YOU JUST *SAY SO, AND-- ;UHNNN!*

PETER! STOP IT!

I'M *SICK* OF PEOPLE TRYING TO TELL ME WHAT TO DO! NOW *GET LOST!*

THM P!

Panel 5:

AND, ON THE OTHER SIDE OF THE DOOR, WE FIND...

WHAT IN BLAZES IS GOING *ON* OUT THERE??!

Panel 6:

SORRY, MR. JAMESON! I GUESS I JUST GOT CARRIED AWAY!

PARKER! I NEVER THOUGHT OF *YOU* AS THE VIOLENT TYPE! WHAT ARE YOU *DOING* HERE, ANYWAY?

I -EH- BROUGHT YOU SOME NEWS PHOTOS!

Panel 7:

THAT'S THAT! BETTY MUST *DESPISE* ME NOW! NEVER KNOWING HOW MUCH I REALLY *LOVE* HER-- OR HOW MUCH TOUGHER THIS IS FOR *ME!*

AFTER ALL, SHE'LL PROBABLY END UP MARRYING NED AND FORGET ABOUT ME!

BUT, *I'LL* CARRY A TORCH-- FOREVER!

ALL RIGHT-- LET'S *SEE* THE PHOTOS!

Panel 8:

YOU CALL *THESE* NEWS PHOTOS?? JUST A FEW SHOTS OF SOME STRIKERS PICKETING A DEPARTMENT STORE! YOU'RE *SLIPPING*, PARKER!

I KNOW IT! WITH AUNT MAY IN THE HOSPITAL, I HAVEN'T BEEN ABLE TO DO *ANYTHING* RIGHT!

Panel 9:

CAN'T *USE* 'EM! DON'T WASTE MY TIME UNLESS YOU HAVE SOMETHING *GOOD!*

YOU OLD SKINFLINT! YOU'VE *FORGOTTEN* ALL THE GREAT *EXCLUSIVES* I GAVE YOU IN THE PAST!

DON'T JUST *STAND* THERE! THIS ISN'T VISITORS' DAY! GOODBYE!

3

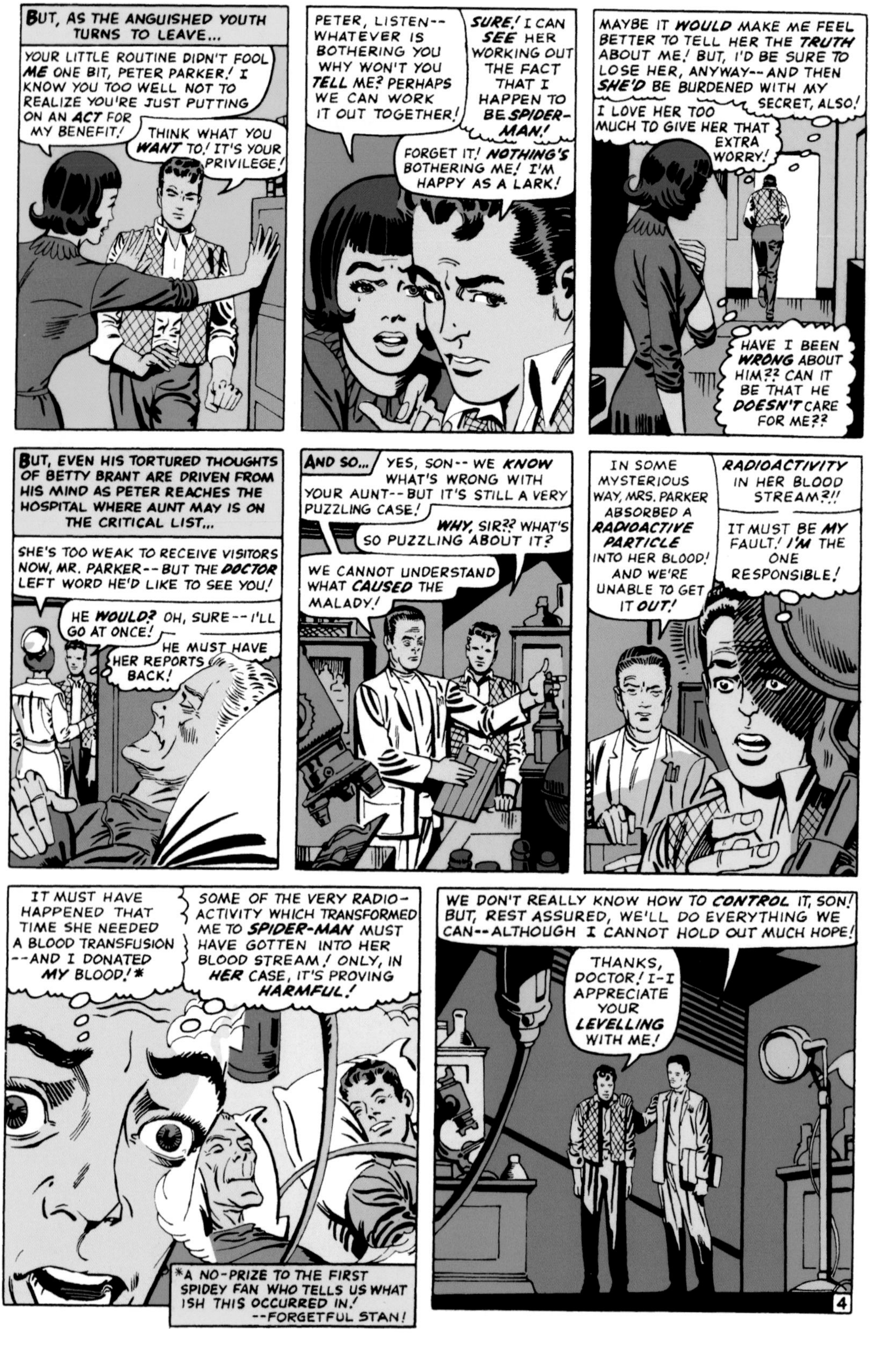
BUT, AS THE ANGUISHED YOUTH TURNS TO LEAVE...
YOUR LITTLE ROUTINE DIDN'T FOOL ME ONE BIT, PETER PARKER! I KNOW YOU TOO WELL NOT TO REALIZE YOU'RE JUST PUTTING ON AN ACT FOR MY BENEFIT!
THINK WHAT YOU WANT TO! IT'S YOUR PRIVILEGE!
PETER, LISTEN-- WHATEVER IS BOTHERING YOU WHY WON'T YOU TELL ME? PERHAPS WE CAN WORK IT OUT TOGETHER!
SURE! I CAN SEE HER WORKING OUT THE FACT THAT I HAPPEN TO BE SPIDER-MAN!
FORGET IT! NOTHING'S BOTHERING ME! I'M HAPPY AS A LARK!
MAYBE IT WOULD MAKE ME FEEL BETTER TO TELL HER THE TRUTH ABOUT ME! BUT, I'D BE SURE TO LOSE HER, ANYWAY-- AND THEN SHE'D BE BURDENED WITH MY SECRET, ALSO!
I LOVE HER TOO MUCH TO GIVE HER THAT EXTRA WORRY!
HAVE I BEEN WRONG ABOUT HIM?? CAN IT BE THAT HE DOESN'T CARE FOR ME??
BUT, EVEN HIS TORTURED THOUGHTS OF BETTY BRANT ARE DRIVEN FROM HIS MIND AS PETER REACHES THE HOSPITAL WHERE AUNT MAY IS ON THE CRITICAL LIST...
SHE'S TOO WEAK TO RECEIVE VISITORS NOW, MR. PARKER-- BUT THE DOCTOR LEFT WORD HE'D LIKE TO SEE YOU!
HE WOULD? OH, SURE-- I'LL GO AT ONCE!
HE MUST HAVE HER REPORTS BACK!
AND SO...
YES, SON-- WE KNOW WHAT'S WRONG WITH YOUR AUNT-- BUT IT'S STILL A VERY PUZZLING CASE!
WHY, SIR?? WHAT'S SO PUZZLING ABOUT IT?
WE CANNOT UNDERSTAND WHAT CAUSED THE MALADY!
IN SOME MYSTERIOUS WAY, MRS. PARKER ABSORBED A RADIOACTIVE PARTICLE INTO HER BLOOD! AND WE'RE UNABLE TO GET IT OUT!
RADIOACTIVITY IN HER BLOOD STREAM?!!
IT MUST BE MY FAULT! I'M THE ONE RESPONSIBLE!
IT MUST HAVE HAPPENED THAT TIME SHE NEEDED A BLOOD TRANSFUSION --AND I DONATED MY BLOOD!*
SOME OF THE VERY RADIO-ACTIVITY WHICH TRANSFORMED ME TO SPIDER-MAN MUST HAVE GOTTEN INTO HER BLOOD STREAM! ONLY, IN HER CASE, IT'S PROVING HARMFUL!
*A NO-PRIZE TO THE FIRST SPIDEY FAN WHO TELLS US WHAT ISH THIS OCCURRED IN! --FORGETFUL STAN!
WE DON'T REALLY KNOW HOW TO CONTROL IT, SON! BUT, REST ASSURED, WE'LL DO EVERYTHING WE CAN--ALTHOUGH I CANNOT HOLD OUT MUCH HOPE!
THANKS, DOCTOR! I-I APPRECIATE YOUR LEVELLING WITH ME!
4

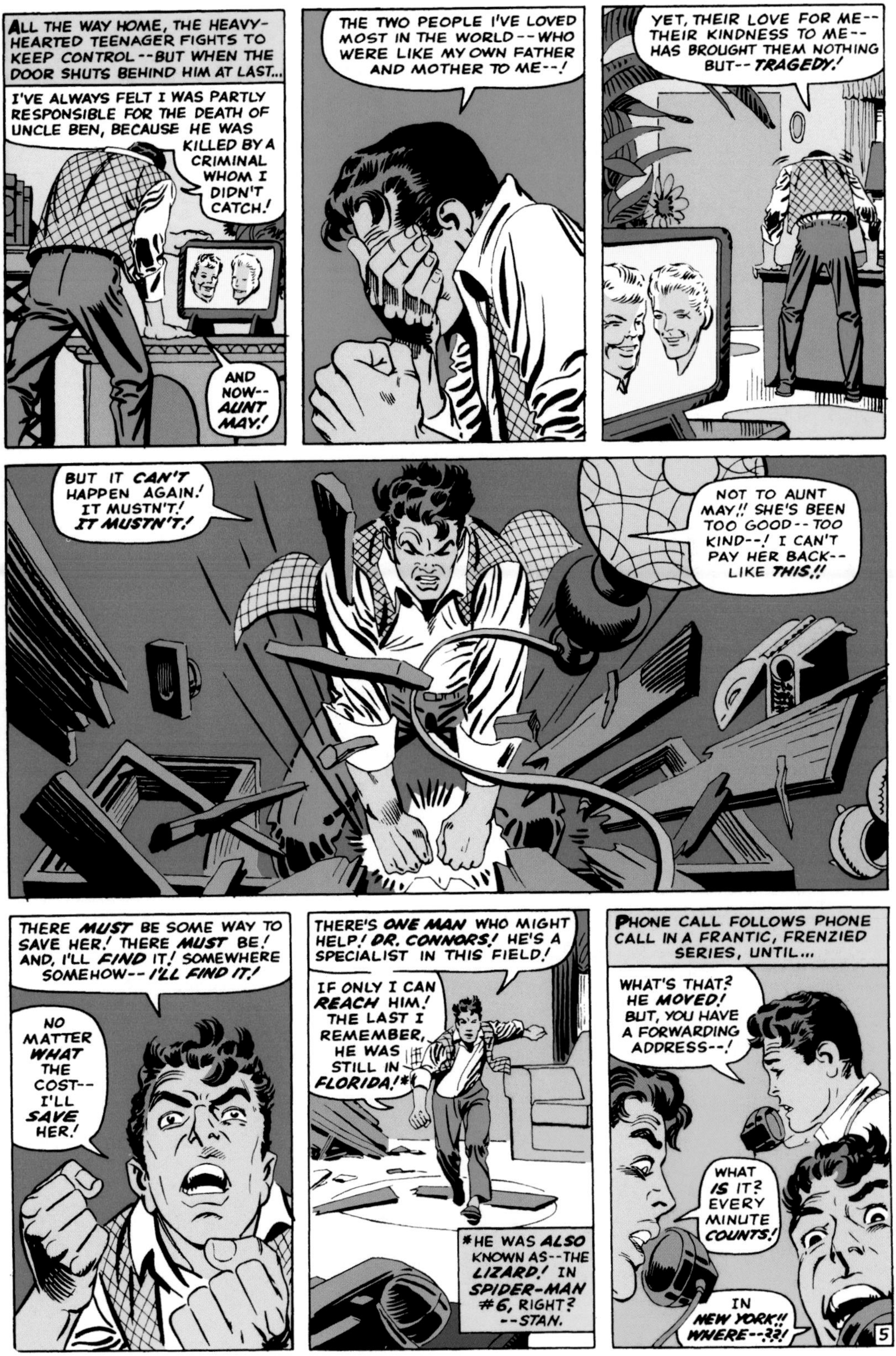
ALL THE WAY HOME, THE HEAVY-HEARTED TEENAGER FIGHTS TO KEEP CONTROL--BUT WHEN THE DOOR SHUTS BEHIND HIM AT LAST...
I'VE ALWAYS FELT I WAS PARTLY RESPONSIBLE FOR THE DEATH OF UNCLE BEN, BECAUSE HE WAS KILLED BY A CRIMINAL WHOM I DIDN'T CATCH!
AND NOW--AUNT MAY!
THE TWO PEOPLE I'VE LOVED MOST IN THE WORLD--WHO WERE LIKE MY OWN FATHER AND MOTHER TO ME--!
YET, THEIR LOVE FOR ME--THEIR KINDNESS TO ME--HAS BROUGHT THEM NOTHING BUT--TRAGEDY!
BUT IT CAN'T HAPPEN AGAIN! IT MUSTN'T! IT MUSTN'T!
NOT TO AUNT MAY!! SHE'S BEEN TOO GOOD--TOO KIND--! I CAN'T PAY HER BACK--LIKE THIS!!
THERE MUST BE SOME WAY TO SAVE HER! THERE MUST BE! AND, I'LL FIND IT! SOMEWHERE SOMEHOW--I'LL FIND IT!
NO MATTER WHAT THE COST--I'LL SAVE HER!
THERE'S ONE MAN WHO MIGHT HELP! DR. CONNORS! HE'S A SPECIALIST IN THIS FIELD!
IF ONLY I CAN REACH HIM! THE LAST I REMEMBER, HE WAS STILL IN FLORIDA!*
*HE WAS ALSO KNOWN AS--THE LIZARD! IN SPIDER-MAN #6, RIGHT? --STAN.
PHONE CALL FOLLOWS PHONE CALL IN A FRANTIC, FRENZIED SERIES, UNTIL...
WHAT'S THAT? HE MOVED! BUT, YOU HAVE A FORWARDING ADDRESS--!
WHAT IS IT? EVERY MINUTE COUNTS!
IN NEW YORK!! WHERE--??!
5

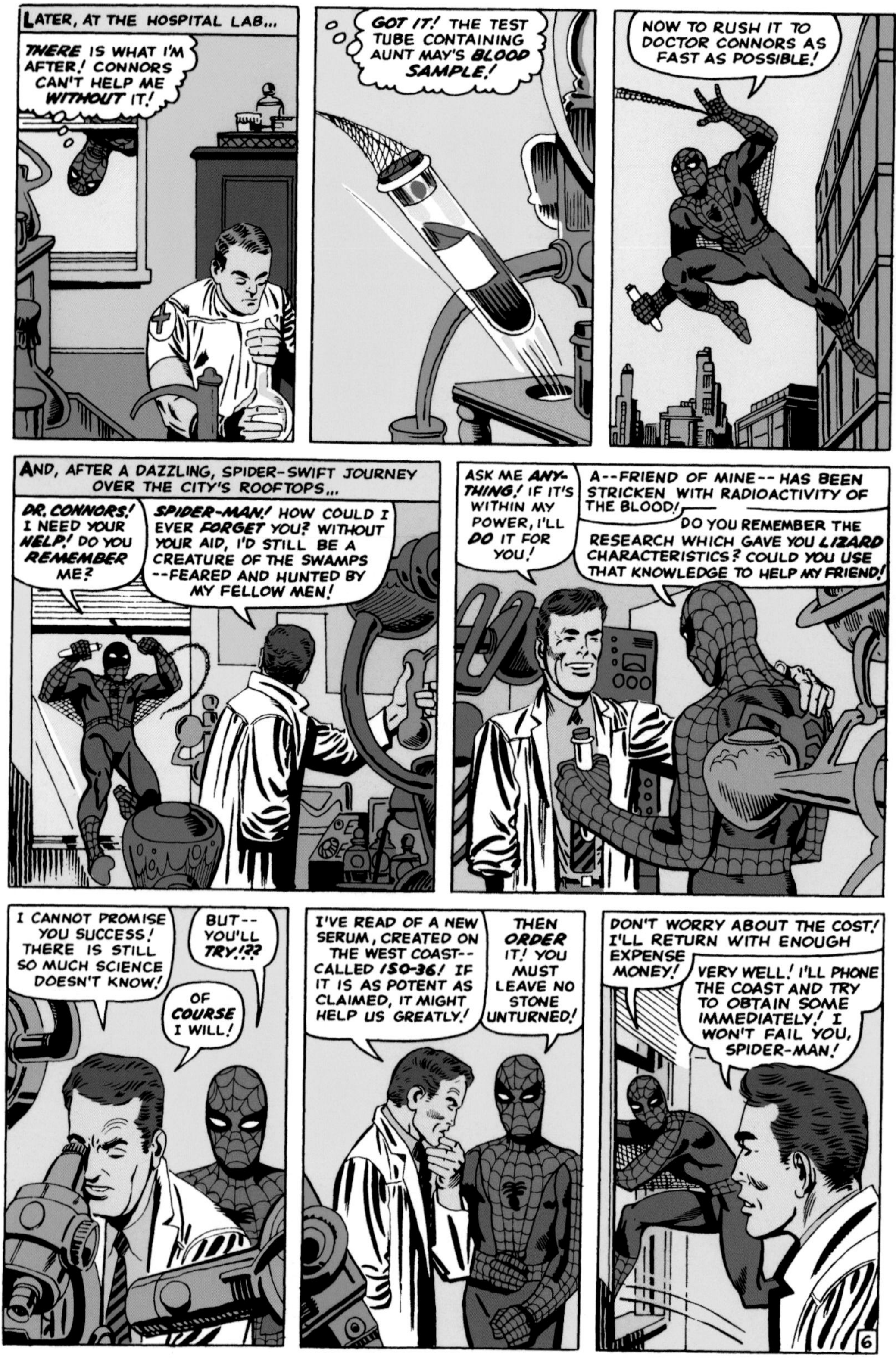
LATER, AT THE HOSPITAL LAB...
THERE IS WHAT I'M AFTER! CONNORS CAN'T HELP ME WITHOUT IT!
GOT IT! THE TEST TUBE CONTAINING AUNT MAY'S BLOOD SAMPLE!
NOW TO RUSH IT TO DOCTOR CONNORS AS FAST AS POSSIBLE!
AND, AFTER A DAZZLING, SPIDER-SWIFT JOURNEY OVER THE CITY'S ROOFTOPS...
DR. CONNORS! I NEED YOUR HELP! DO YOU REMEMBER ME?
SPIDER-MAN! HOW COULD I EVER FORGET YOU? WITHOUT YOUR AID, I'D STILL BE A CREATURE OF THE SWAMPS --FEARED AND HUNTED BY MY FELLOW MEN!
ASK ME ANYTHING! IF IT'S WITHIN MY POWER, I'LL DO IT FOR YOU!
A--FRIEND OF MINE-- HAS BEEN STRICKEN WITH RADIOACTIVITY OF THE BLOOD!
DO YOU REMEMBER THE RESEARCH WHICH GAVE YOU LIZARD CHARACTERISTICS? COULD YOU USE THAT KNOWLEDGE TO HELP MY FRIEND?
I CANNOT PROMISE YOU SUCCESS! THERE IS STILL SO MUCH SCIENCE DOESN'T KNOW!
BUT-- YOU'LL TRY!??
OF COURSE I WILL!
I'VE READ OF A NEW SERUM, CREATED ON THE WEST COAST-- CALLED ISO-36! IF IT IS AS POTENT AS CLAIMED, IT MIGHT HELP US GREATLY!
THEN ORDER IT! YOU MUST LEAVE NO STONE UNTURNED!
DON'T WORRY ABOUT THE COST! I'LL RETURN WITH ENOUGH EXPENSE MONEY!
VERY WELL! I'LL PHONE THE COAST AND TRY TO OBTAIN SOME IMMEDIATELY! I WON'T FAIL YOU, SPIDER-MAN!
6

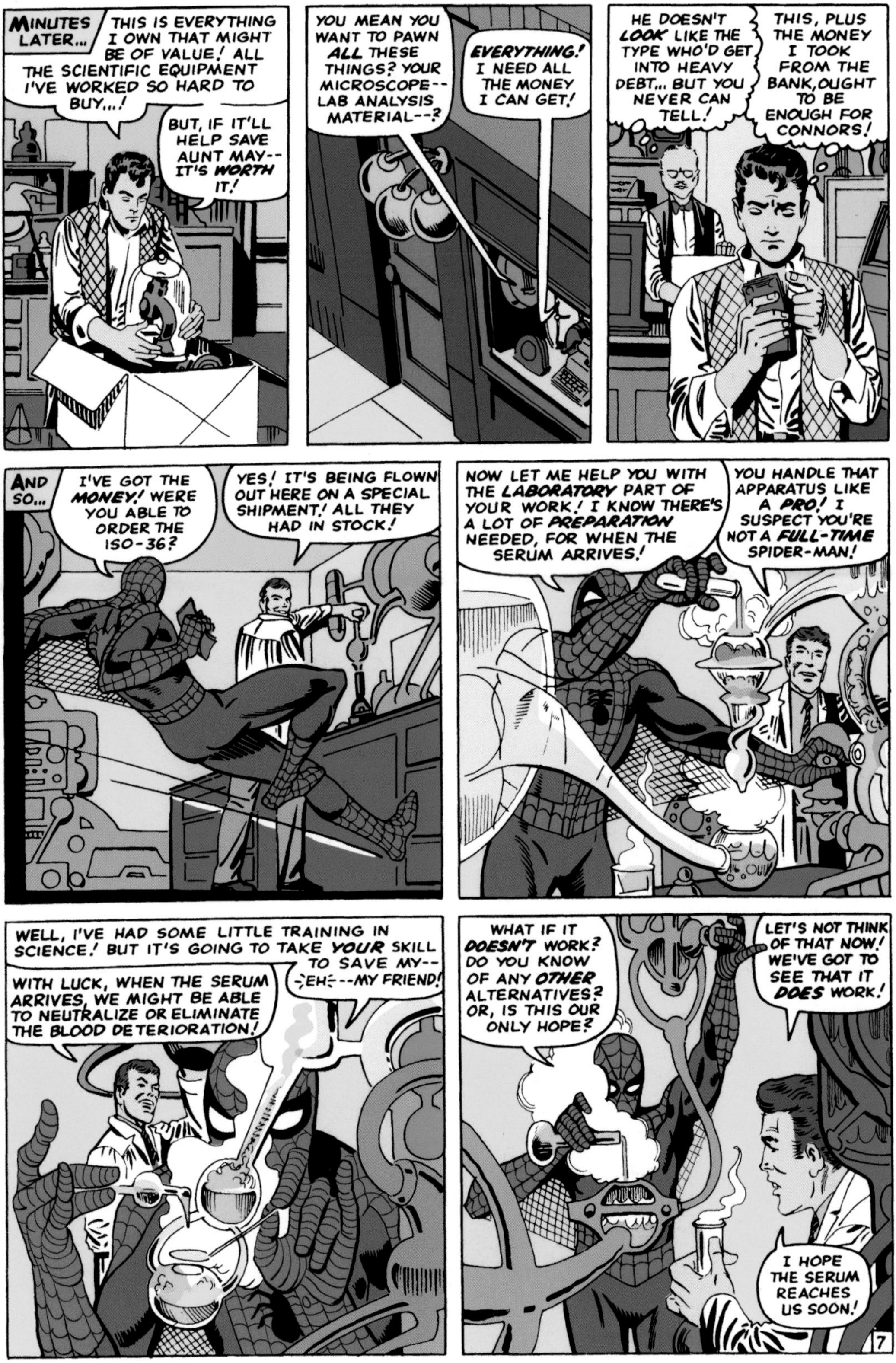
MINUTES LATER...
THIS IS EVERYTHING I OWN THAT MIGHT BE OF VALUE! ALL THE SCIENTIFIC EQUIPMENT I'VE WORKED SO HARD TO BUY...!
BUT, IF IT'LL HELP SAVE AUNT MAY-- IT'S WORTH IT!
YOU MEAN YOU WANT TO PAWN ALL THESE THINGS? YOUR MICROSCOPE-- LAB ANALYSIS MATERIAL--?
EVERYTHING! I NEED ALL THE MONEY I CAN GET!
HE DOESN'T LOOK LIKE THE TYPE WHO'D GET INTO HEAVY DEBT... BUT YOU NEVER CAN TELL!
THIS, PLUS THE MONEY I TOOK FROM THE BANK, OUGHT TO BE ENOUGH FOR CONNORS!
AND SO...
I'VE GOT THE MONEY! WERE YOU ABLE TO ORDER THE ISO-36?
YES! IT'S BEING FLOWN OUT HERE ON A SPECIAL SHIPMENT! ALL THEY HAD IN STOCK!
NOW LET ME HELP YOU WITH THE LABORATORY PART OF YOUR WORK! I KNOW THERE'S A LOT OF PREPARATION NEEDED, FOR WHEN THE SERUM ARRIVES!
YOU HANDLE THAT APPARATUS LIKE A PRO! I SUSPECT YOU'RE NOT A FULL-TIME SPIDER-MAN!
WELL, I'VE HAD SOME LITTLE TRAINING IN SCIENCE! BUT IT'S GOING TO TAKE YOUR SKILL TO SAVE MY--
-EH- --MY FRIEND!
WITH LUCK, WHEN THE SERUM ARRIVES, WE MIGHT BE ABLE TO NEUTRALIZE OR ELIMINATE THE BLOOD DETERIORATION!
WHAT IF IT DOESN'T WORK? DO YOU KNOW OF ANY OTHER ALTERNATIVES? OR, IS THIS OUR ONLY HOPE?
LET'S NOT THINK OF THAT NOW! WE'VE GOT TO SEE THAT IT DOES WORK!
I HOPE THE SERUM REACHES US SOON!
7

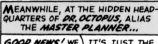

MEANWHILE, AT THE HIDDEN HEAD-QUARTERS OF *DR. OCTOPUS*, ALIAS THE *MASTER PLANNER*...

GOOD NEWS! WE JUST LEARNED OF A SHIPMENT OF *ISO-36* ARRIVING FROM THE WEST COAST!

IT'S JUST THE THING I NEED TO CARRY OUT MY RESEARCH! WHAT A STROKE OF *LUCK!*

USE EVERY AVAILABLE MAN! DON'T LET *ANY-THING* STOP YOU! I *MUST* HAVE THAT SERUM!

EVERYTHING IS ARRANGED! WE WILL NOT FAIL!

I HEARD OF *ISO-36* SOME MONTHS AGO, WHEN IT WAS MERELY IN THE DEVELOPMENT STAGE! IT COULD BE THE ONE VITAL KEY TO MY EXPERIMENTS!

AND *FATE* IS PLACING IT WITHIN MY GRASP!

LATER THAT DAY, AFTER THE LANDING OF A CROSS-COUNTRY JET...

DR. CONNORS MUST WANT THIS SERUM PRETTY BAD TO PAY SUCH A HIGH PREMIUM PRICE FOR ITS DELIVERY!

THOK!

WE'LL TAKE THAT!

GOOD WORK! I *GOT* IT!

NOW, LET'S GET *OUT* OF HERE-- WHILE WE *CAN!*

NO! *NO!* COME *BACK!* YOU MUSTN'T--!

SECONDS LATER, AT THE LABORATORY OF DOCTOR CONNORS...

WHAT'S THAT?!! THE SERUM-- STOLEN AT THE AIRPORT!!

YOU SAY THE DESCRIP-TION FITS THE *MASTER PLANNER'S* GANG...!

HE GOT THE *SERUM??!*

DON'T STOP YOUR PRELIMINARY EXPERIMENTING! I'LL BE *BACK*-- WITH THE SERUM!

THIS TIME THE MASTER PLANNER HAS GONE *TOO FAR!* WHEREVER HE IS-- WHOEVER HE IS-- I'LL *GET* HIM!

MY MONEY'S ON YOU, MISTER! GOOD LUCK!

8

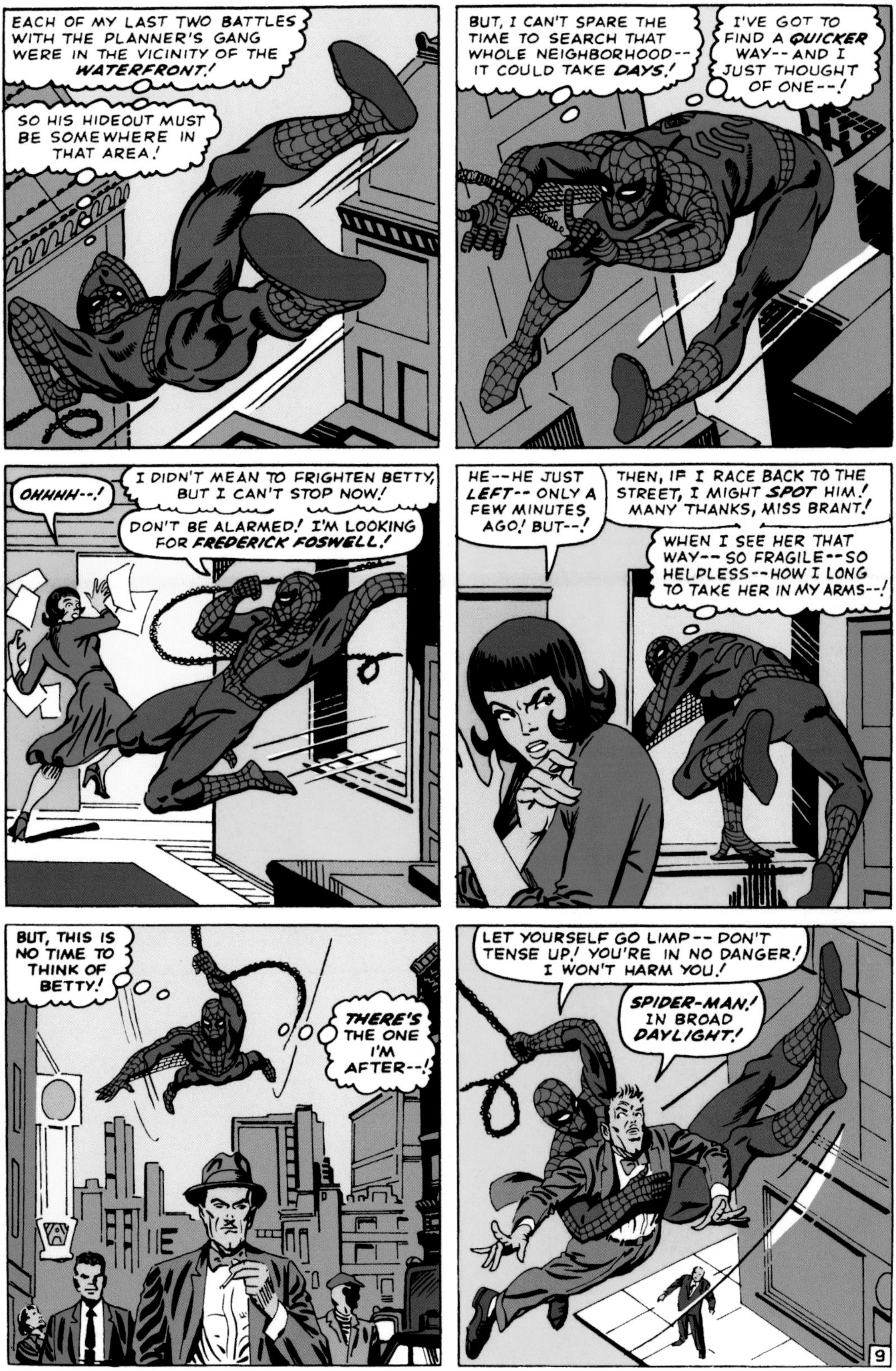
EACH OF MY LAST TWO BATTLES WITH THE PLANNER'S GANG WERE IN THE VICINITY OF THE WATERFRONT!
SO HIS HIDEOUT MUST BE SOMEWHERE IN THAT AREA!
BUT, I CAN'T SPARE THE TIME TO SEARCH THAT WHOLE NEIGHBORHOOD-- IT COULD TAKE DAYS!
I'VE GOT TO FIND A QUICKER WAY-- AND I JUST THOUGHT OF ONE--!
OHHHH--!
I DIDN'T MEAN TO FRIGHTEN BETTY, BUT I CAN'T STOP NOW!
DON'T BE ALARMED! I'M LOOKING FOR FREDERICK FOSWELL!
HE--HE JUST LEFT-- ONLY A FEW MINUTES AGO! BUT--!
THEN, IF I RACE BACK TO THE STREET, I MIGHT SPOT HIM! MANY THANKS, MISS BRANT!
WHEN I SEE HER THAT WAY-- SO FRAGILE--SO HELPLESS--HOW I LONG TO TAKE HER IN MY ARMS--!
BUT, THIS IS NO TIME TO THINK OF BETTY!
THERE'S THE ONE I'M AFTER--!
LET YOURSELF GO LIMP-- DON'T TENSE UP! YOU'RE IN NO DANGER! I WON'T HARM YOU!
SPIDER-MAN! IN BROAD DAYLIGHT!
9

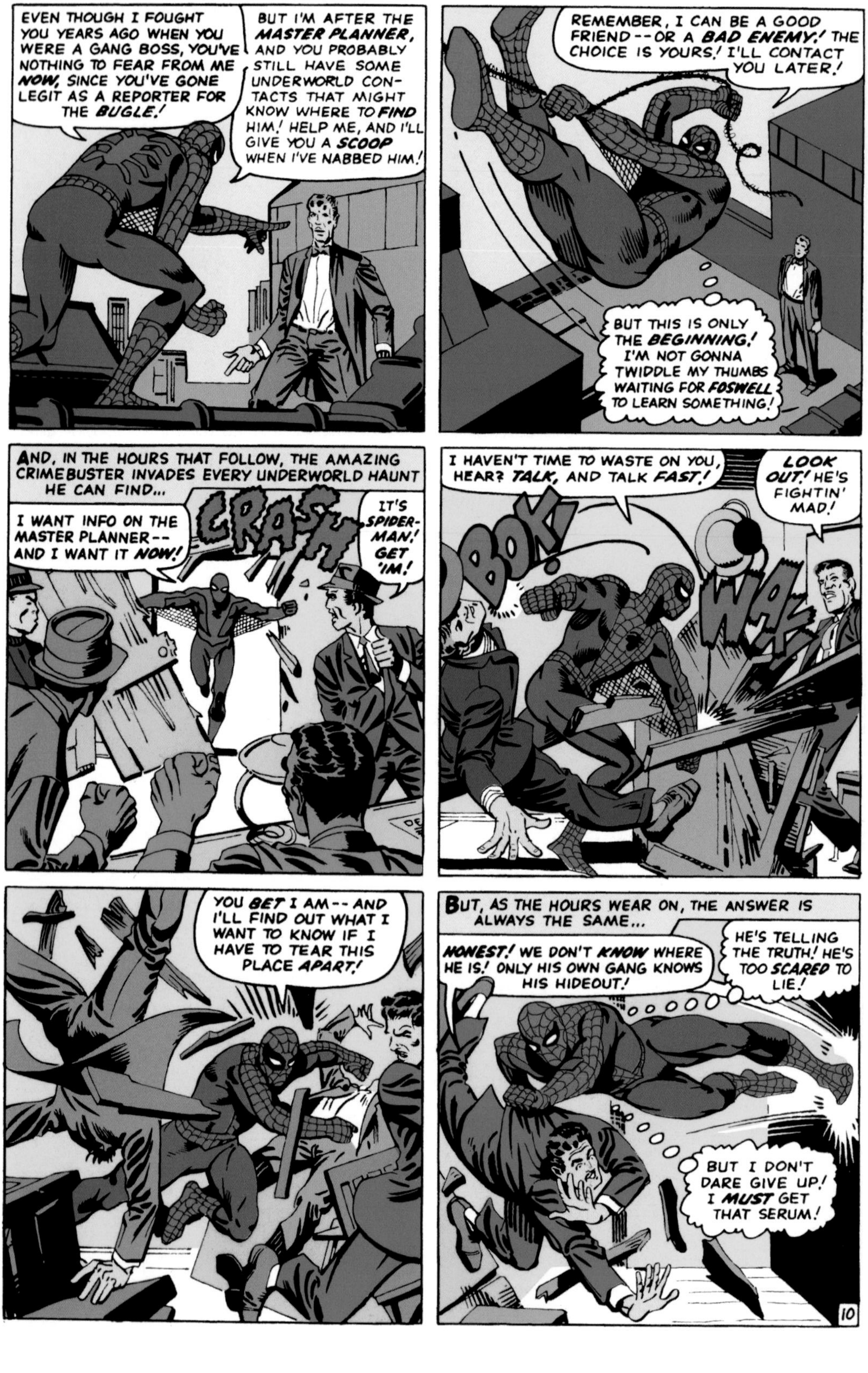
EVEN THOUGH I FOUGHT YOU YEARS AGO WHEN YOU WERE A GANG BOSS, YOU'VE NOTHING TO FEAR FROM ME NOW, SINCE YOU'VE GONE LEGIT AS A REPORTER FOR THE BUGLE!
BUT I'M AFTER THE MASTER PLANNER, AND YOU PROBABLY STILL HAVE SOME UNDERWORLD CONTACTS THAT MIGHT KNOW WHERE TO FIND HIM! HELP ME, AND I'LL GIVE YOU A SCOOP WHEN I'VE NABBED HIM!
REMEMBER, I CAN BE A GOOD FRIEND--OR A BAD ENEMY! THE CHOICE IS YOURS! I'LL CONTACT YOU LATER!
BUT THIS IS ONLY THE BEGINNING! I'M NOT GONNA TWIDDLE MY THUMBS WAITING FOR FOSWELL TO LEARN SOMETHING!
AND, IN THE HOURS THAT FOLLOW, THE AMAZING CRIMEBUSTER INVADES EVERY UNDERWORLD HAUNT HE CAN FIND...
I WANT INFO ON THE MASTER PLANNER-- AND I WANT IT NOW!
CRASH
IT'S SPIDER-MAN! GET 'IM!
I HAVEN'T TIME TO WASTE ON YOU, HEAR? TALK, AND TALK FAST!
LOOK OUT! HE'S FIGHTIN' MAD!
BOK!
WAK
YOU BET I AM--AND I'LL FIND OUT WHAT I WANT TO KNOW IF I HAVE TO TEAR THIS PLACE APART!
BUT, AS THE HOURS WEAR ON, THE ANSWER IS ALWAYS THE SAME...
HONEST! WE DON'T KNOW WHERE HE IS! ONLY HIS OWN GANG KNOWS HIS HIDEOUT!
HE'S TELLING THE TRUTH! HE'S TOO SCARED TO LIE!
BUT I DON'T DARE GIVE UP! I MUST GET THAT SERUM!
10

MEANWHILE, AT THE HOSPITAL...

I WAS AFRAID OF THIS! SHE'S GETTING WEAKER-- SLIPPING INTO A COMA...

AND THERE IS NOTHING MORE THAT WE CAN DO FOR HER!

SHE IS PUTTING UP A VALIANT FIGHT-- SHE HAS A TREMENDOUS WILL TO LIVE!

BUT NOW, HER FATE IS IN THE HANDS OF A POWER FAR GREATER THAN OURS!

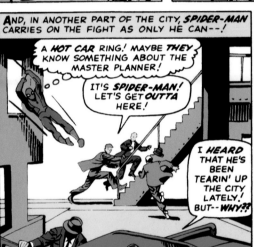

AND, IN ANOTHER PART OF THE CITY, *SPIDER-MAN* CARRIES ON THE FIGHT AS ONLY HE CAN--!

A *HOT CAR* RING! MAYBE *THEY* KNOW SOMETHING ABOUT THE MASTER PLANNER!

IT'S *SPIDER-MAN!* LET'S GET *OUTTA* HERE!

I *HEARD* THAT HE'S BEEN TEARIN' UP THE CITY LATELY! BUT-- *WHY??*

HOLD IT! NOBODY LEAVES UNTIL I *SAY* SO!! THAT MEANS *NOBODY!*

CRASH!

H-HE RIPPED OUT THE WHOLE BLAMED *STAIRCASE!!*

GET BACK *DOWN* THERE! I'VE GOT SOME QUESTIONS --AND YOU BETTER HAVE THE *ANSWERS!*

SK-R-A-K-K

AND *DROP THOSE GUNS* BEFORE I *REALLY* GET MAD!! I'M THRU TREATING YOU PUNKS WITH KID GLOVES!

M-MAYBE WE BETTER DO LIKE HE SAYS.?!!

I HEAR YA TALKIN', CHARLIE!

11

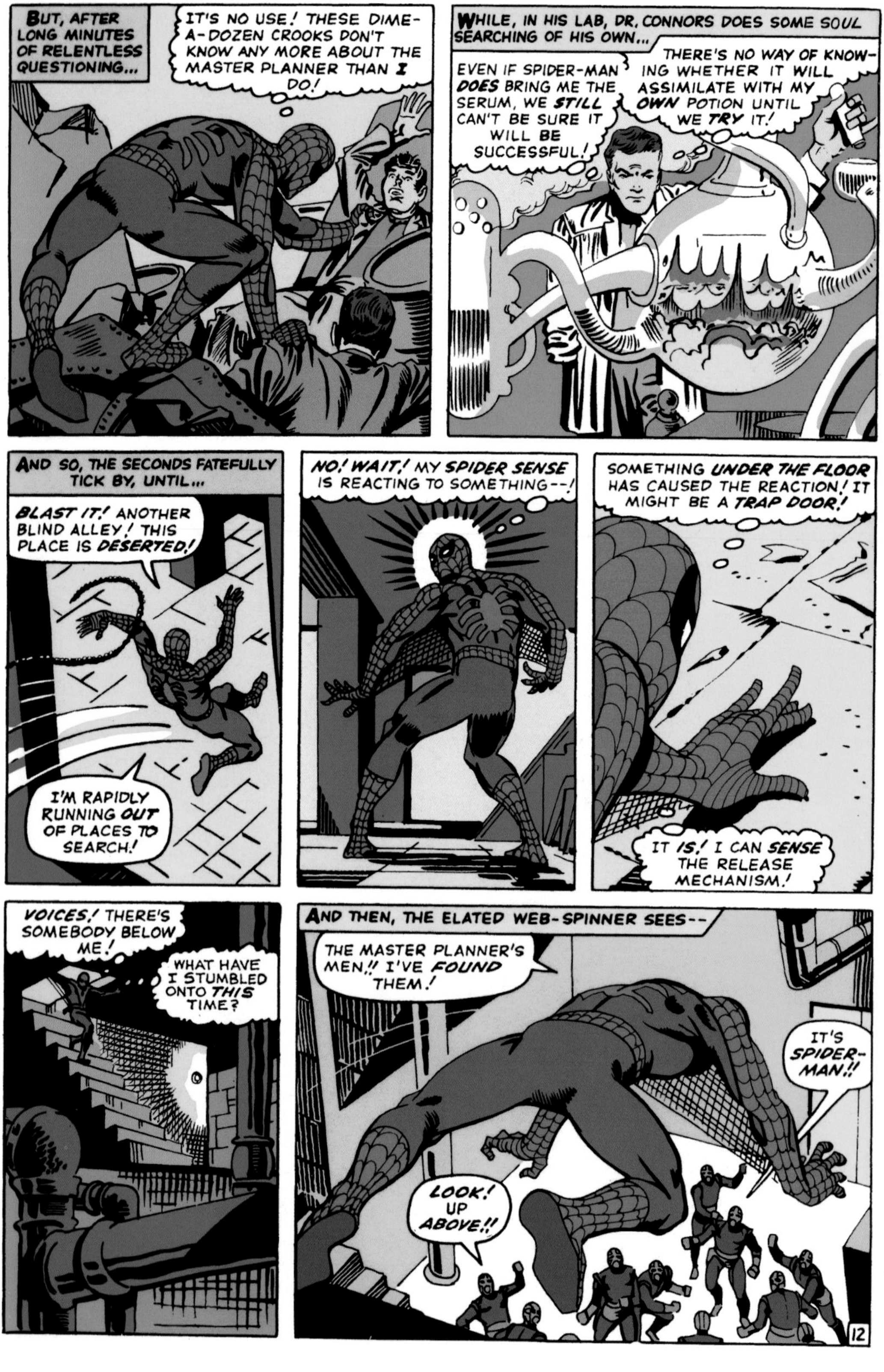
BUT, AFTER LONG MINUTES OF RELENTLESS QUESTIONING...
IT'S NO USE! THESE DIME-A-DOZEN CROOKS DON'T KNOW ANY MORE ABOUT THE MASTER PLANNER THAN I DO!
WHILE, IN HIS LAB, DR. CONNORS DOES SOME SOUL SEARCHING OF HIS OWN...
EVEN IF SPIDER-MAN DOES BRING ME THE SERUM, WE STILL CAN'T BE SURE IT WILL BE SUCCESSFUL!
THERE'S NO WAY OF KNOWING WHETHER IT WILL ASSIMILATE WITH MY OWN POTION UNTIL WE TRY IT!
AND SO, THE SECONDS FATEFULLY TICK BY, UNTIL...
BLAST IT! ANOTHER BLIND ALLEY! THIS PLACE IS DESERTED!
I'M RAPIDLY RUNNING OUT OF PLACES TO SEARCH!
NO! WAIT! MY SPIDER SENSE IS REACTING TO SOMETHING--!
SOMETHING UNDER THE FLOOR HAS CAUSED THE REACTION! IT MIGHT BE A TRAP DOOR!
IT IS! I CAN SENSE THE RELEASE MECHANISM!
VOICES! THERE'S SOMEBODY BELOW ME!
WHAT HAVE I STUMBLED ONTO THIS TIME?
AND THEN, THE ELATED WEB-SPINNER SEES--
THE MASTER PLANNER'S MEN!! I'VE FOUND THEM!
IT'S SPIDER-MAN!!
LOOK! UP ABOVE!!
12

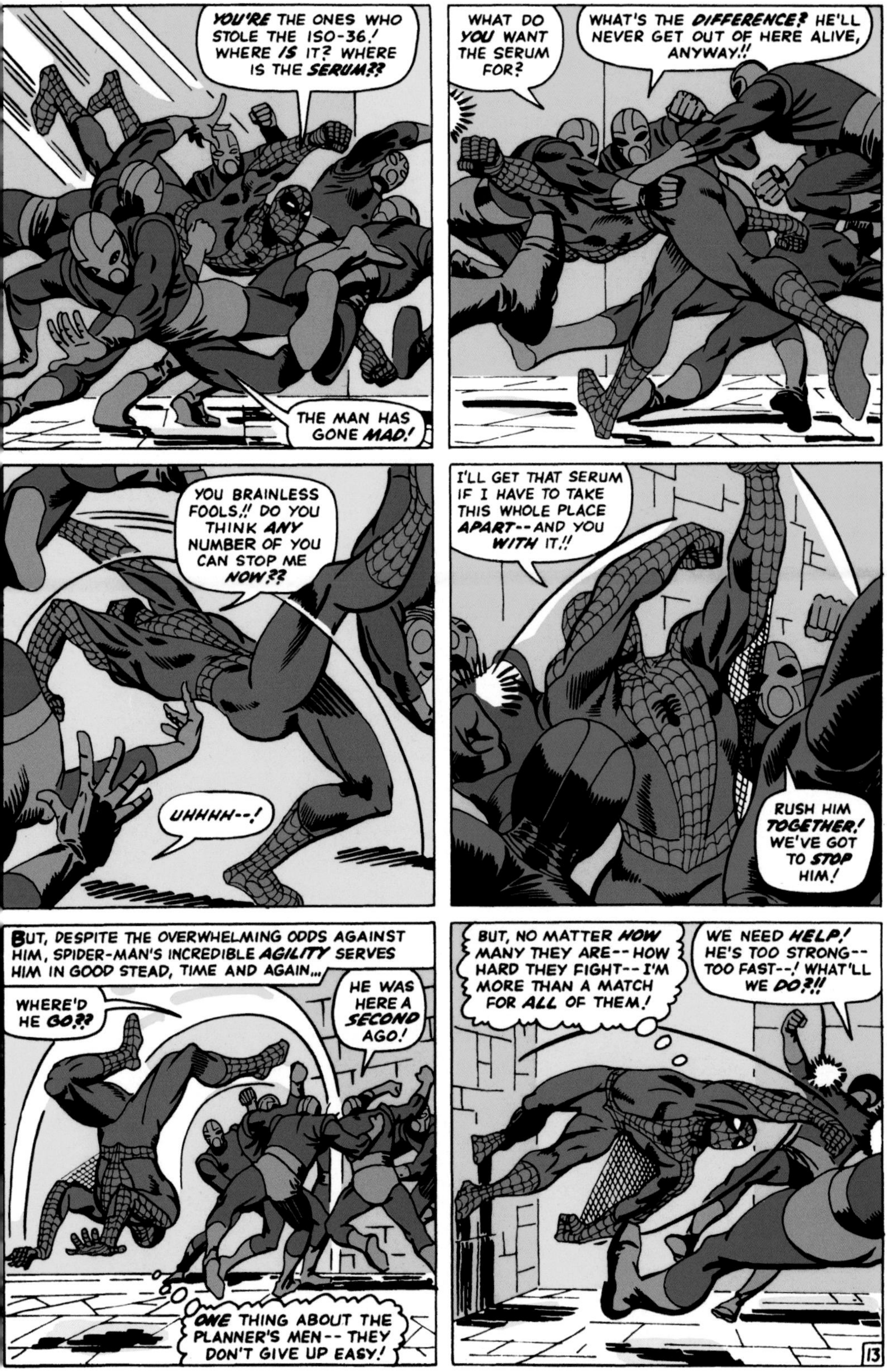
YOU'RE THE ONES WHO STOLE THE ISO-36! WHERE IS IT? WHERE IS THE SERUM??
THE MAN HAS GONE MAD!
WHAT DO YOU WANT THE SERUM FOR?
WHAT'S THE DIFFERENCE? HE'LL NEVER GET OUT OF HERE ALIVE, ANYWAY!!
YOU BRAINLESS FOOLS!! DO YOU THINK ANY NUMBER OF YOU CAN STOP ME NOW??
UHHHH--!
I'LL GET THAT SERUM IF I HAVE TO TAKE THIS WHOLE PLACE APART--AND YOU WITH IT!!
RUSH HIM TOGETHER! WE'VE GOT TO STOP HIM!
BUT, DESPITE THE OVERWHELMING ODDS AGAINST HIM, SPIDER-MAN'S INCREDIBLE AGILITY SERVES HIM IN GOOD STEAD, TIME AND AGAIN...
WHERE'D HE GO??
HE WAS HERE A SECOND AGO!
ONE THING ABOUT THE PLANNER'S MEN-- THEY DON'T GIVE UP EASY!
BUT, NO MATTER HOW MANY THEY ARE-- HOW HARD THEY FIGHT-- I'M MORE THAN A MATCH FOR ALL OF THEM!
WE NEED HELP! HE'S TOO STRONG-- TOO FAST--! WHAT'LL WE DO?!!
13

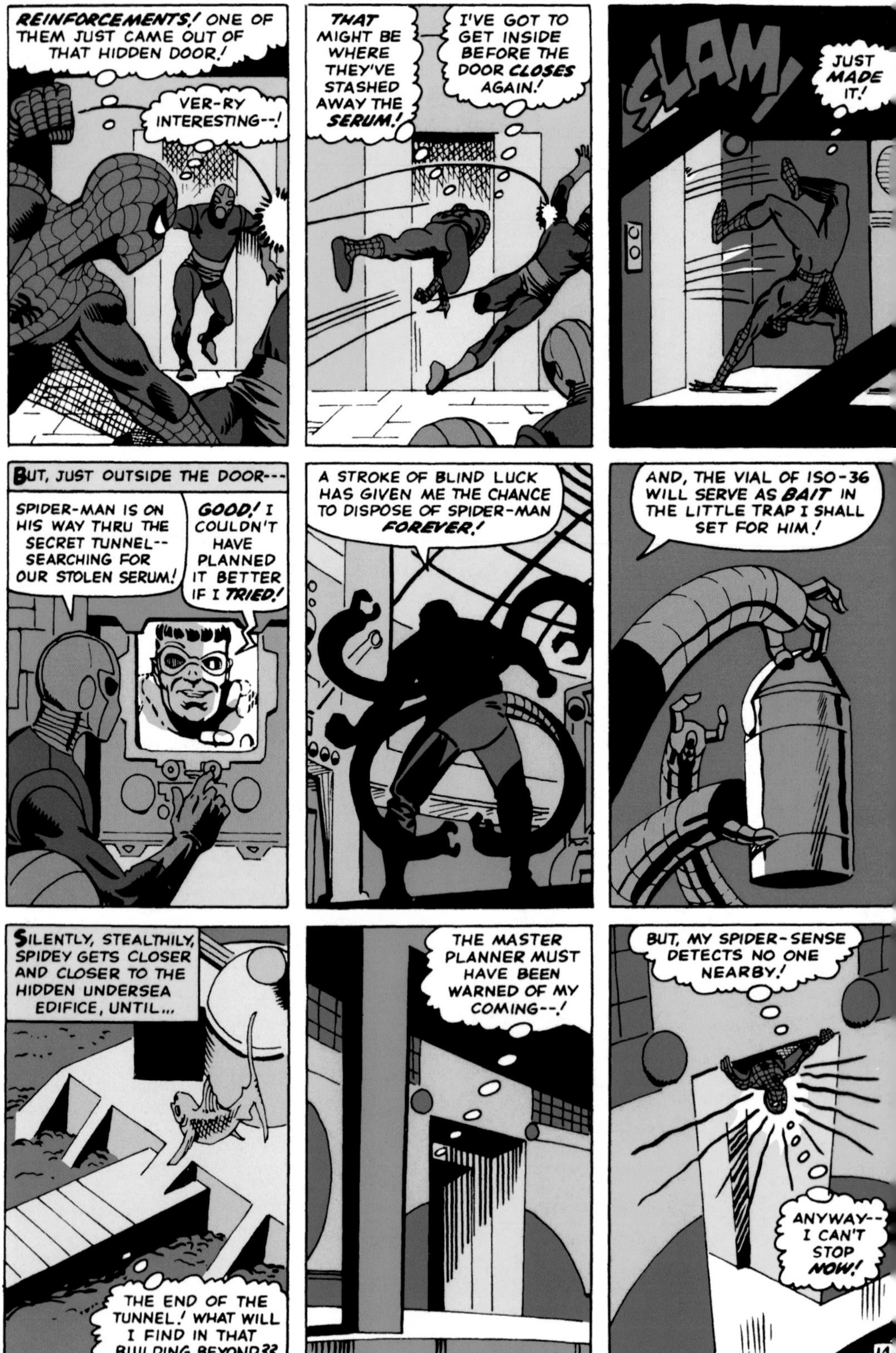
REINFORCEMENTS! ONE OF THEM JUST CAME OUT OF THAT HIDDEN DOOR!
VER-RY INTERESTING--!
THAT MIGHT BE WHERE THEY'VE STASHED AWAY THE SERUM!
I'VE GOT TO GET INSIDE BEFORE THE DOOR CLOSES AGAIN!
SLAM!
JUST MADE IT!
BUT, JUST OUTSIDE THE DOOR---
SPIDER-MAN IS ON HIS WAY THRU THE SECRET TUNNEL--SEARCHING FOR OUR STOLEN SERUM!
GOOD! I COULDN'T HAVE PLANNED IT BETTER IF I TRIED!
A STROKE OF BLIND LUCK HAS GIVEN ME THE CHANCE TO DISPOSE OF SPIDER-MAN FOREVER!
AND, THE VIAL OF ISO-36 WILL SERVE AS BAIT IN THE LITTLE TRAP I SHALL SET FOR HIM!
SILENTLY, STEALTHILY, SPIDEY GETS CLOSER AND CLOSER TO THE HIDDEN UNDERSEA EDIFICE, UNTIL...
THE END OF THE TUNNEL! WHAT WILL I FIND IN THAT BUILDING BEYOND??
THE MASTER PLANNER MUST HAVE BEEN WARNED OF MY COMING--!
BUT, MY SPIDER-SENSE DETECTS NO ONE NEARBY!
ANYWAY--I CAN'T STOP NOW!
14

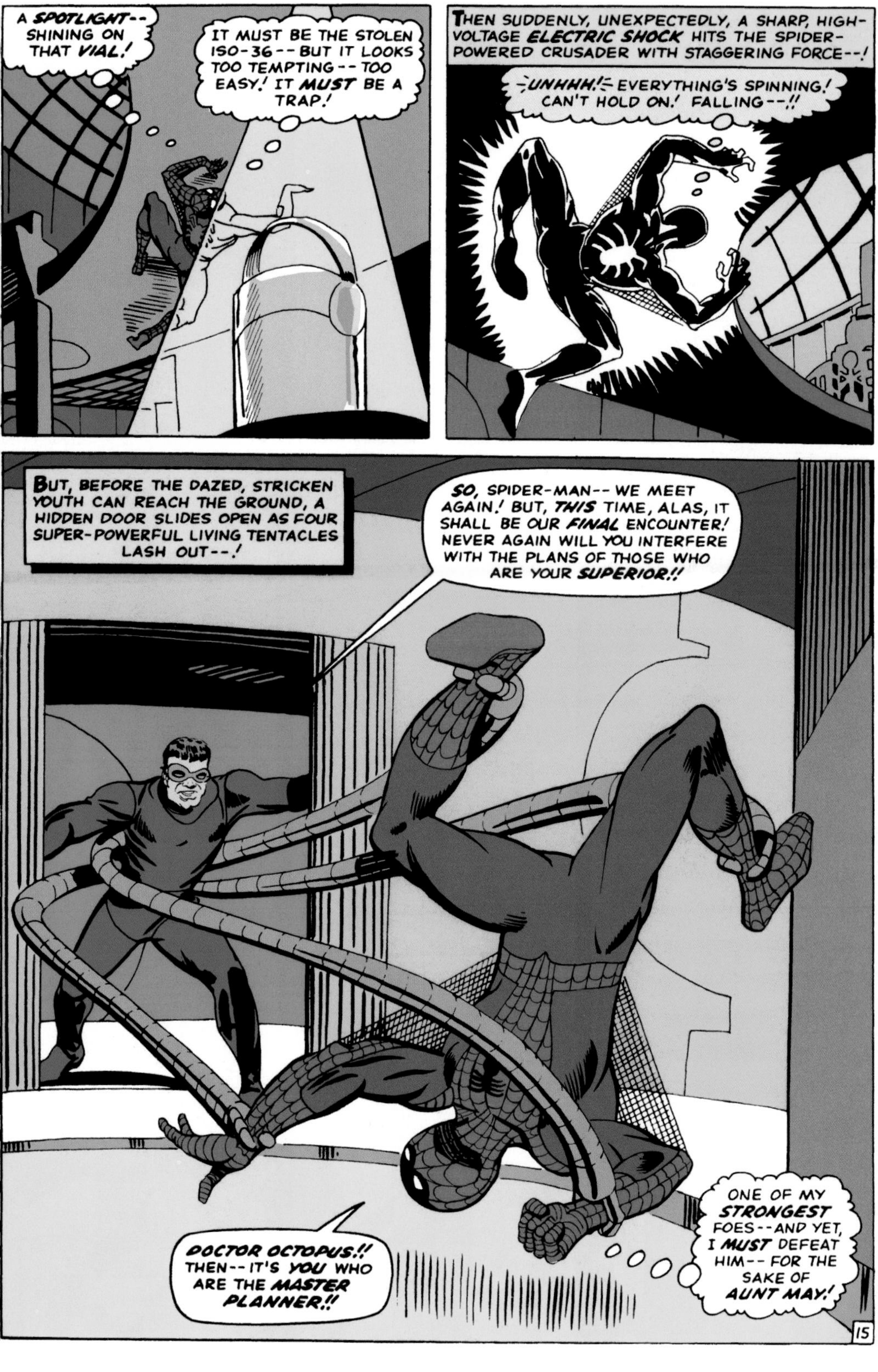
A SPOTLIGHT-- SHINING ON THAT VIAL!
IT MUST BE THE STOLEN ISO-36-- BUT IT LOOKS TOO TEMPTING-- TOO EASY! IT MUST BE A TRAP!
THEN SUDDENLY, UNEXPECTEDLY, A SHARP, HIGH-VOLTAGE ELECTRIC SHOCK HITS THE SPIDER-POWERED CRUSADER WITH STAGGERING FORCE--!
-UNHHH!- EVERYTHING'S SPINNING! CAN'T HOLD ON! FALLING--!!
BUT, BEFORE THE DAZED, STRICKEN YOUTH CAN REACH THE GROUND, A HIDDEN DOOR SLIDES OPEN AS FOUR SUPER-POWERFUL LIVING TENTACLES LASH OUT--!
SO, SPIDER-MAN-- WE MEET AGAIN! BUT, THIS TIME, ALAS, IT SHALL BE OUR FINAL ENCOUNTER! NEVER AGAIN WILL YOU INTERFERE WITH THE PLANS OF THOSE WHO ARE YOUR SUPERIOR!!
DOCTOR OCTOPUS!! THEN-- IT'S YOU WHO ARE THE MASTER PLANNER!!
ONE OF MY STRONGEST FOES-- AND YET, I MUST DEFEAT HIM-- FOR THE SAKE OF AUNT MAY!

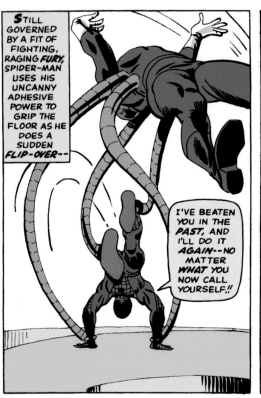

STILL GOVERNED BY A FIT OF FIGHTING, RAGING *FURY*, SPIDER-MAN USES HIS UNCANNY ADHESIVE POWER TO GRIP THE FLOOR AS HE DOES A SUDDEN *FLIP-OVER*--

I'VE BEATEN YOU IN THE *PAST*, AND I'LL DO IT *AGAIN*--NO MATTER *WHAT* YOU NOW CALL YOURSELF.!!

YOU ARROGANT FOOL.! YOU'RE FIGHTING ON *MY* TERMS NOW.! YOU HAVEN'T A *CHANCE* HERE, AGAINST *ME*!

WE'LL *SEE* ABOUT THAT.!

I *KNEW* HE'D HAVE TO RELEASE HIS GRIP ON ME IN ORDER TO USE HIS ARMS TO *SAVE* HIMSELF.!

I SHOULD HAVE *SUSPECTED* THAT HE'D BE THE MASTER PLANNER-- SINCE ALL HIS CRIMES DEALT WITH THE THEFT OF ATOMIC AND RADIOACTIVE MATERIAL.!

SO YOU'RE LASHING OUT AT ME WITH YOUR *ARMS* AGAIN.! *GOOD.!* IT'S JUST WHAT I EXPECTED YOU TO DO!

YOU'RE *BLUFFING.!* THERE'S NO WAY YOU CAN COPE WITH MY FLEXIBLE, CLUTCHING ARMS-- *UNHHHH.!*

KEEP TALKING, BIG MAN-- AND I'LL JUST PRACTICE A LITTLE *KNOT-TYING* WHILE YOU DO!

HE'S *TOO STRONG.!* HE'LL FREE HIMSELF IN SECONDS! BUT, AT LEAST I GAINED SOME BREATHING TIME!

AND I'VE MADE HIM LOSE THE ADVANTAGE OF *SURPRISE.!*

16

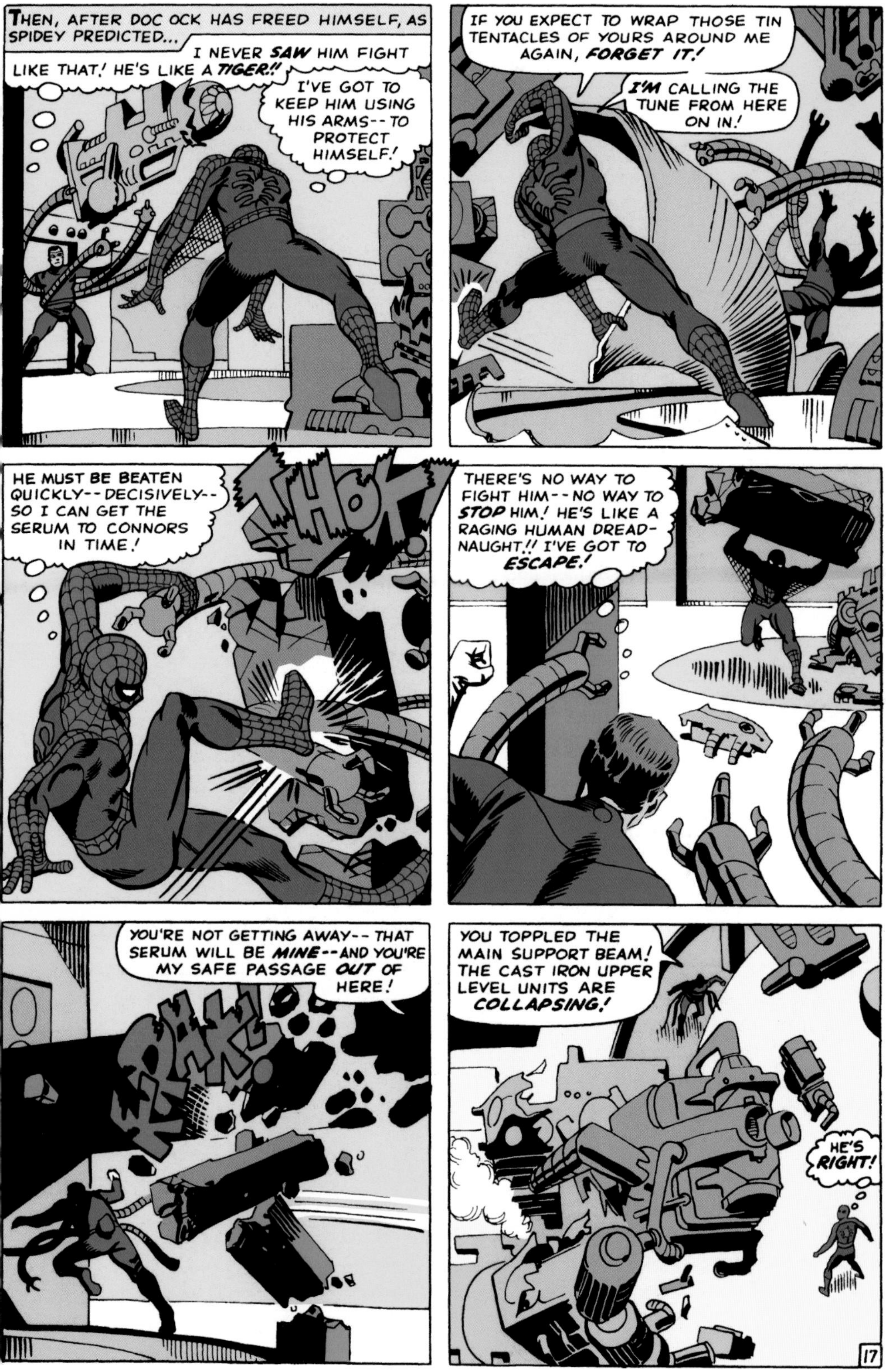

THEN, AFTER DOC OCK HAS FREED HIMSELF, AS SPIDEY PREDICTED...
I NEVER SAW HIM FIGHT LIKE THAT! HE'S LIKE A TIGER!!
I'VE GOT TO KEEP HIM USING HIS ARMS--TO PROTECT HIMSELF!
IF YOU EXPECT TO WRAP THOSE TIN TENTACLES OF YOURS AROUND ME AGAIN, FORGET IT!
I'M CALLING THE TUNE FROM HERE ON IN!
HE MUST BE BEATEN QUICKLY--DECISIVELY--SO I CAN GET THE SERUM TO CONNORS IN TIME!
THOK!
THERE'S NO WAY TO FIGHT HIM--NO WAY TO STOP HIM! HE'S LIKE A RAGING HUMAN DREAD-NAUGHT!! I'VE GOT TO ESCAPE!
YOU'RE NOT GETTING AWAY--THAT SERUM WILL BE MINE--AND YOU'RE MY SAFE PASSAGE OUT OF HERE!
KRAK!
YOU TOPPLED THE MAIN SUPPORT BEAM! THE CAST IRON UPPER LEVEL UNITS ARE COLLAPSING!
HE'S RIGHT!

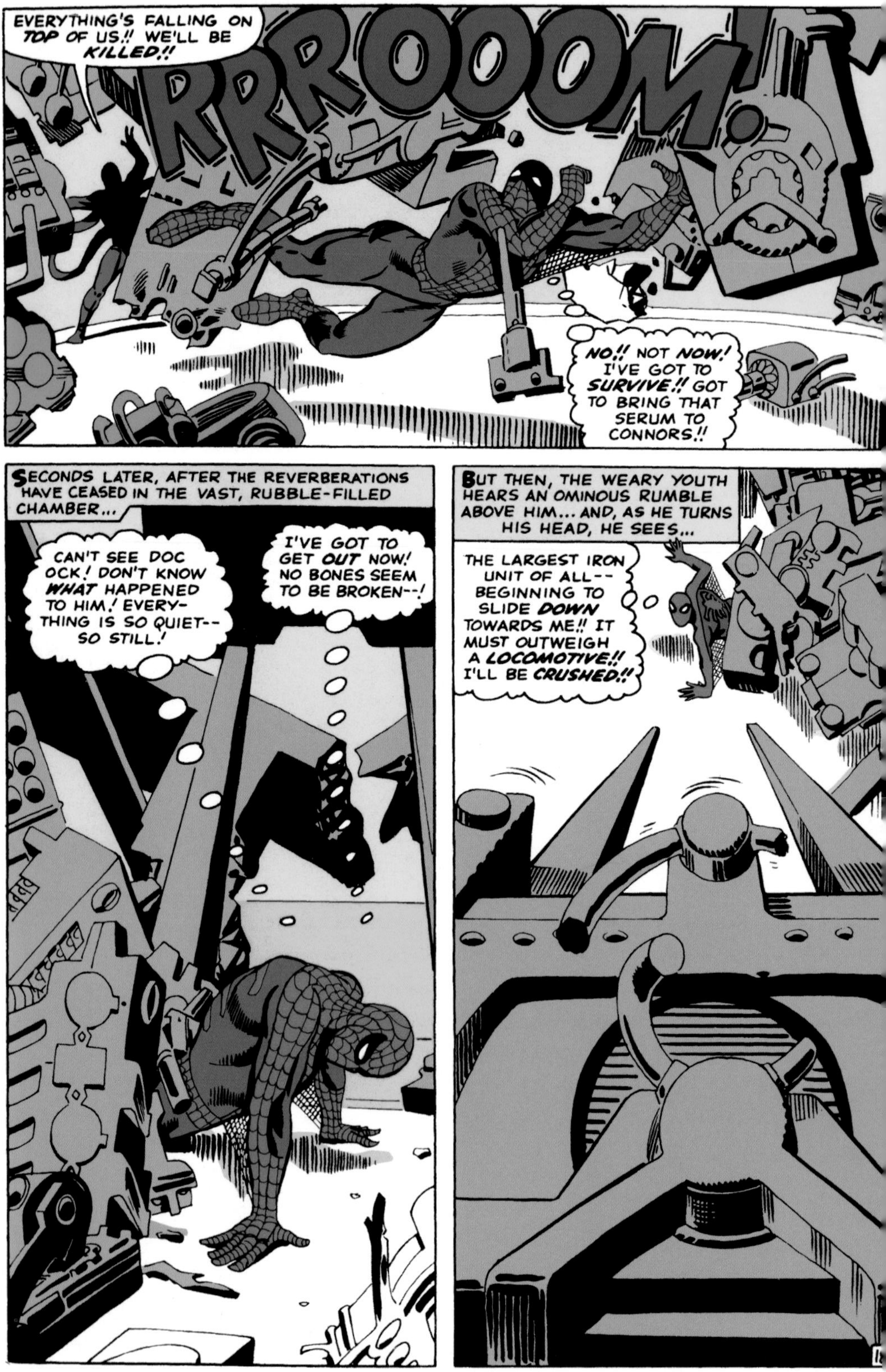

EVERYTHING'S FALLING ON TOP OF US!! WE'LL BE KILLED!!
RRROOOM!
NO!! NOT NOW! I'VE GOT TO SURVIVE!! GOT TO BRING THAT SERUM TO CONNORS!!
SECONDS LATER, AFTER THE REVERBERATIONS HAVE CEASED IN THE VAST, RUBBLE-FILLED CHAMBER...
CAN'T SEE DOC OCK! DON'T KNOW WHAT HAPPENED TO HIM! EVERYTHING IS SO QUIET-- SO STILL!
I'VE GOT TO GET OUT NOW! NO BONES SEEM TO BE BROKEN--!
BUT THEN, THE WEARY YOUTH HEARS AN OMINOUS RUMBLE ABOVE HIM... AND, AS HE TURNS HIS HEAD, HE SEES...
THE LARGEST IRON UNIT OF ALL-- BEGINNING TO SLIDE DOWN TOWARDS ME!! IT MUST OUTWEIGH A LOCOMOTIVE!! I'LL BE CRUSHED!!

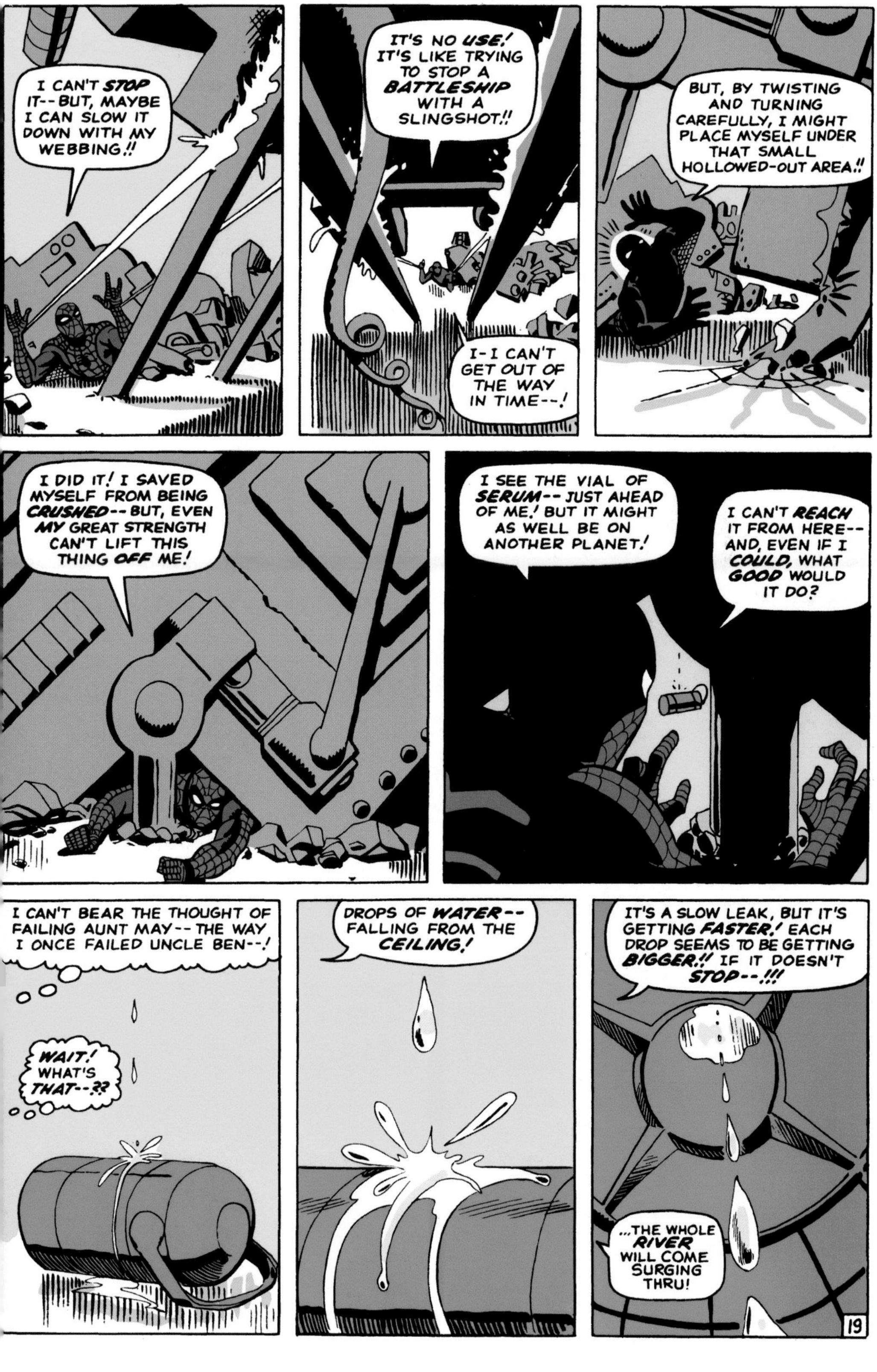
I CAN'T STOP IT--BUT, MAYBE I CAN SLOW IT DOWN WITH MY WEBBING!!
IT'S NO USE! IT'S LIKE TRYING TO STOP A BATTLESHIP WITH A SLINGSHOT!!
I-I CAN'T GET OUT OF THE WAY IN TIME--!
BUT, BY TWISTING AND TURNING CAREFULLY, I MIGHT PLACE MYSELF UNDER THAT SMALL HOLLOWED-OUT AREA!!
I DID IT! I SAVED MYSELF FROM BEING CRUSHED--BUT, EVEN MY GREAT STRENGTH CAN'T LIFT THIS THING OFF ME!
I SEE THE VIAL OF SERUM--JUST AHEAD OF ME! BUT IT MIGHT AS WELL BE ON ANOTHER PLANET!
I CAN'T REACH IT FROM HERE--AND, EVEN IF I COULD, WHAT GOOD WOULD IT DO?
I CAN'T BEAR THE THOUGHT OF FAILING AUNT MAY--THE WAY I ONCE FAILED UNCLE BEN--!
WAIT! WHAT'S THAT--??
DROPS OF WATER--FALLING FROM THE CEILING!
IT'S A SLOW LEAK, BUT IT'S GETTING FASTER! EACH DROP SEEMS TO BE GETTING BIGGER!! IF IT DOESN'T STOP--!!!
...THE WHOLE RIVER WILL COME SURGING THRU!
19

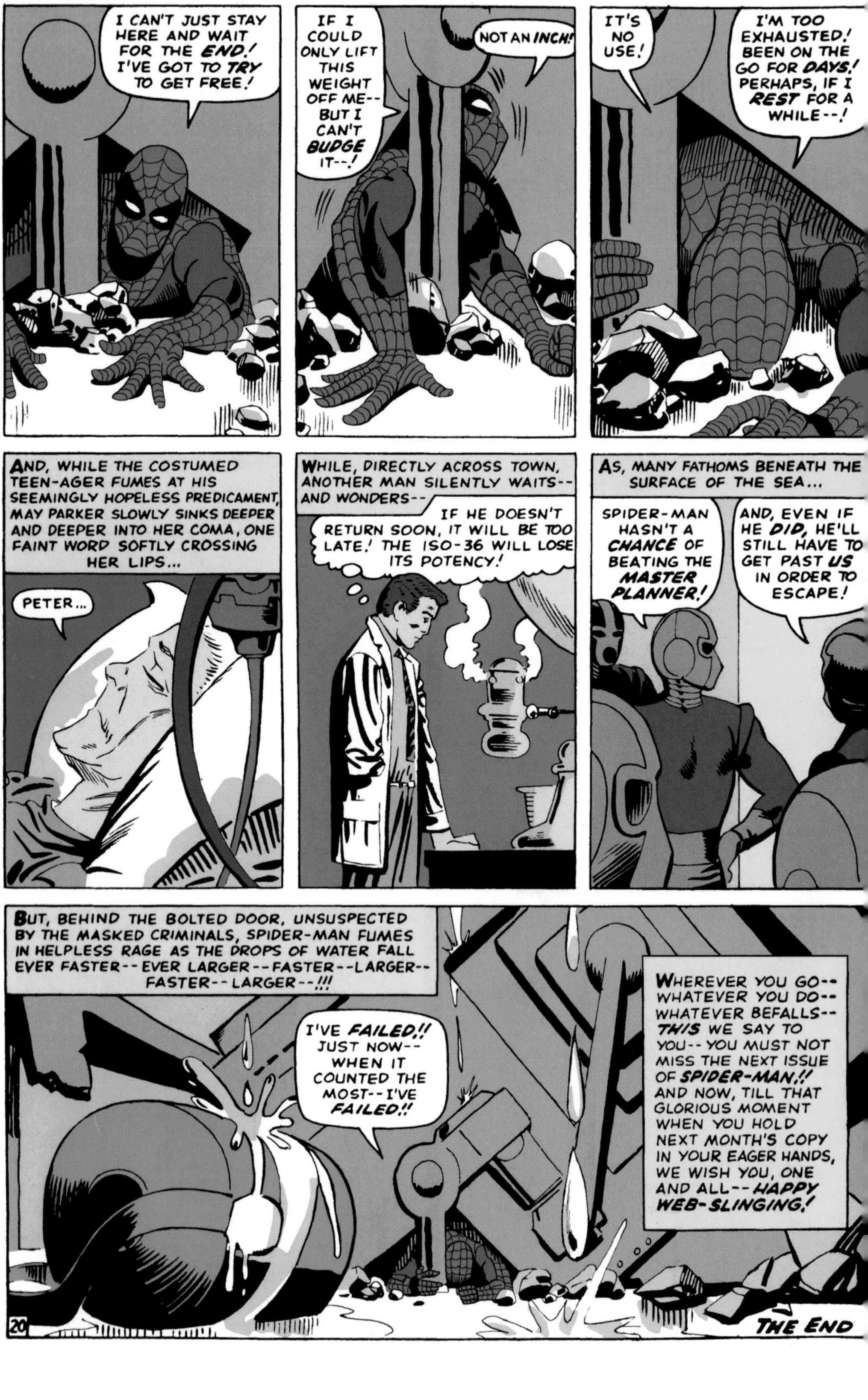
I CAN'T JUST STAY HERE AND WAIT FOR THE END! I'VE GOT TO TRY TO GET FREE!
IF I COULD ONLY LIFT THIS WEIGHT OFF ME-- BUT I CAN'T BUDGE IT--!
NOT AN INCH!
IT'S NO USE!
I'M TOO EXHAUSTED! BEEN ON THE GO FOR DAYS! PERHAPS, IF I REST FOR A WHILE--!
AND, WHILE THE COSTUMED TEEN-AGER FUMES AT HIS SEEMINGLY HOPELESS PREDICAMENT, MAY PARKER SLOWLY SINKS DEEPER AND DEEPER INTO HER COMA, ONE FAINT WORD SOFTLY CROSSING HER LIPS...
PETER...
WHILE, DIRECTLY ACROSS TOWN, ANOTHER MAN SILENTLY WAITS-- AND WONDERS--
IF HE DOESN'T RETURN SOON, IT WILL BE TOO LATE! THE ISO-36 WILL LOSE ITS POTENCY!
AS, MANY FATHOMS BENEATH THE SURFACE OF THE SEA...
SPIDER-MAN HASN'T A CHANCE OF BEATING THE MASTER PLANNER!
AND, EVEN IF HE DID, HE'LL STILL HAVE TO GET PAST US IN ORDER TO ESCAPE!
BUT, BEHIND THE BOLTED DOOR, UNSUSPECTED BY THE MASKED CRIMINALS, SPIDER-MAN FUMES IN HELPLESS RAGE AS THE DROPS OF WATER FALL EVER FASTER-- EVER LARGER--FASTER--LARGER-- FASTER--LARGER--!!!
I'VE FAILED!! JUST NOW-- WHEN IT COUNTED THE MOST--I'VE FAILED!!
WHEREVER YOU GO-- WHATEVER YOU DO-- WHATEVER BEFALLS-- THIS WE SAY TO YOU-- YOU MUST NOT MISS THE NEXT ISSUE OF SPIDER-MAN!! AND NOW, TILL THAT GLORIOUS MOMENT WHEN YOU HOLD NEXT MONTH'S COPY IN YOUR EAGER HANDS, WE WISH YOU, ONE AND ALL--HAPPY WEB-SLINGING!
20
THE END

APPROVED BY THE COMICS CODE AUTHORITY
the AMAZING SPIDER-MAN
MARVEL COMICS GROUP 12¢
33 FEB
IND.
"The FINAL CHAPTER!"

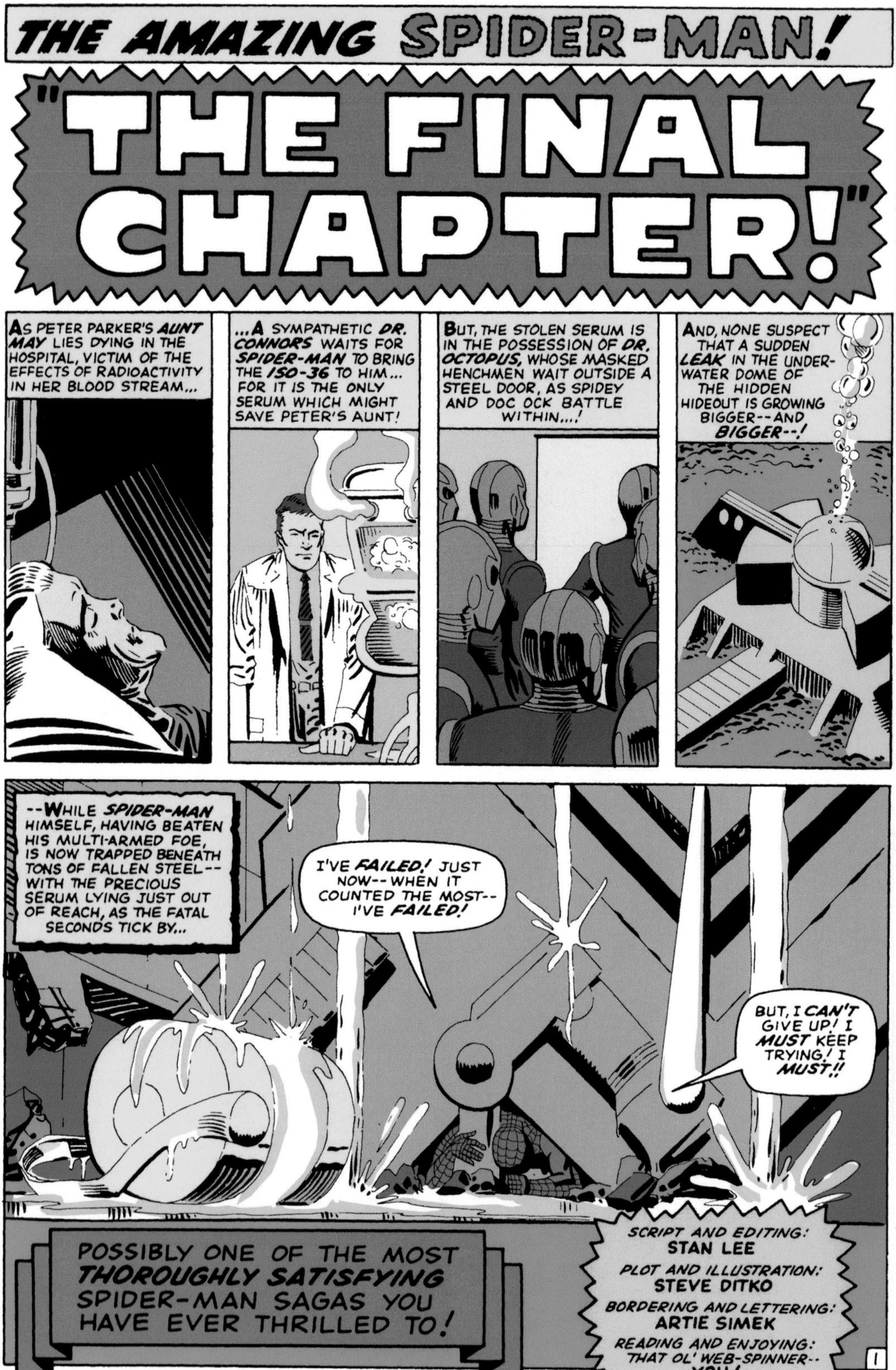
THE AMAZING SPIDER-MAN!
"THE FINAL CHAPTER!"
AS PETER PARKER'S AUNT MAY LIES DYING IN THE HOSPITAL, VICTIM OF THE EFFECTS OF RADIOACTIVITY IN HER BLOOD STREAM...
...A SYMPATHETIC DR. CONNORS WAITS FOR SPIDER-MAN TO BRING THE ISO-36 TO HIM... FOR IT IS THE ONLY SERUM WHICH MIGHT SAVE PETER'S AUNT!
BUT, THE STOLEN SERUM IS IN THE POSSESSION OF DR. OCTOPUS, WHOSE MASKED HENCHMEN WAIT OUTSIDE A STEEL DOOR, AS SPIDEY AND DOC OCK BATTLE WITHIN...!
AND, NONE SUSPECT THAT A SUDDEN LEAK IN THE UNDER-WATER DOME OF THE HIDDEN HIDEOUT IS GROWING BIGGER--AND BIGGER--!
--WHILE SPIDER-MAN HIMSELF, HAVING BEATEN HIS MULTI-ARMED FOE, IS NOW TRAPPED BENEATH TONS OF FALLEN STEEL--WITH THE PRECIOUS SERUM LYING JUST OUT OF REACH, AS THE FATAL SECONDS TICK BY...
I'VE FAILED! JUST NOW--WHEN IT COUNTED THE MOST--I'VE FAILED!
BUT, I CAN'T GIVE UP! I MUST KEEP TRYING! I MUST!!
POSSIBLY ONE OF THE MOST THOROUGHLY SATISFYING SPIDER-MAN SAGAS YOU HAVE EVER THRILLED TO!
SCRIPT AND EDITING: STAN LEE
PLOT AND ILLUSTRATION: STEVE DITKO
BORDERING AND LETTERING: ARTIE SIMEK
READING AND ENJOYING: THAT OL' WEB-SPINNER--YOU!
1

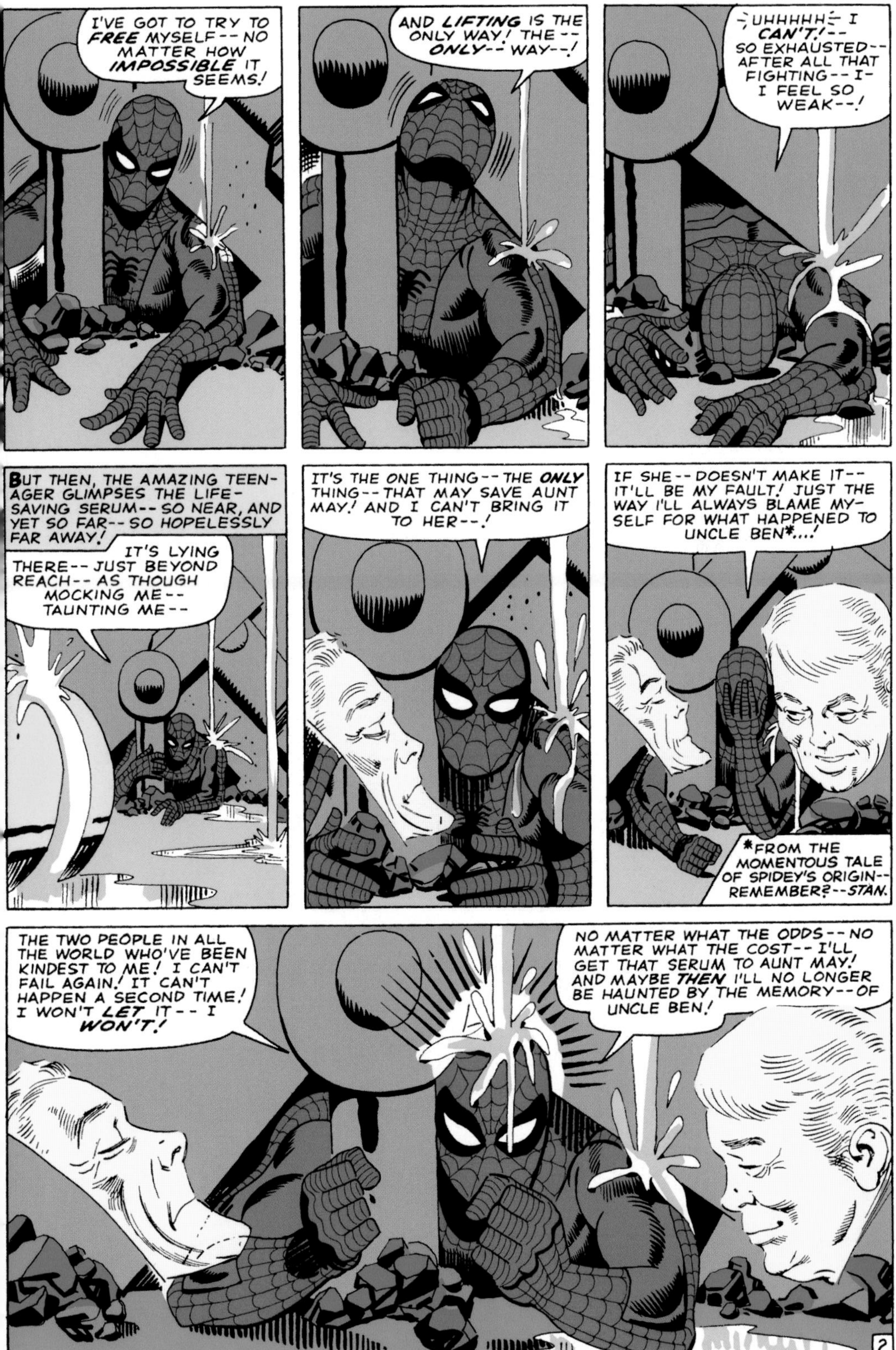

I'VE GOT TO TRY TO FREE MYSELF-- NO MATTER HOW IMPOSSIBLE IT SEEMS!
AND LIFTING IS THE ONLY WAY! THE-- ONLY-- WAY--!
UHHHHH-- I CAN'T!-- SO EXHAUSTED-- AFTER ALL THAT FIGHTING-- I-- I FEEL SO WEAK--!
BUT THEN, THE AMAZING TEEN-AGER GLIMPSES THE LIFE-SAVING SERUM-- SO NEAR, AND YET SO FAR-- SO HOPELESSLY FAR AWAY!
IT'S LYING THERE-- JUST BEYOND REACH-- AS THOUGH MOCKING ME-- TAUNTING ME--
IT'S THE ONE THING-- THE ONLY THING-- THAT MAY SAVE AUNT MAY! AND I CAN'T BRING IT TO HER--!
IF SHE-- DOESN'T MAKE IT-- IT'LL BE MY FAULT! JUST THE WAY I'LL ALWAYS BLAME MY-SELF FOR WHAT HAPPENED TO UNCLE BEN*...!
*FROM THE MOMENTOUS TALE OF SPIDEY'S ORIGIN-- REMEMBER?-- STAN.
THE TWO PEOPLE IN ALL THE WORLD WHO'VE BEEN KINDEST TO ME! I CAN'T FAIL AGAIN! IT CAN'T HAPPEN A SECOND TIME! I WON'T LET IT-- I WON'T!
NO MATTER WHAT THE ODDS-- NO MATTER WHAT THE COST-- I'LL GET THAT SERUM TO AUNT MAY! AND MAYBE THEN I'LL NO LONGER BE HAUNTED BY THE MEMORY-- OF UNCLE BEN!
2

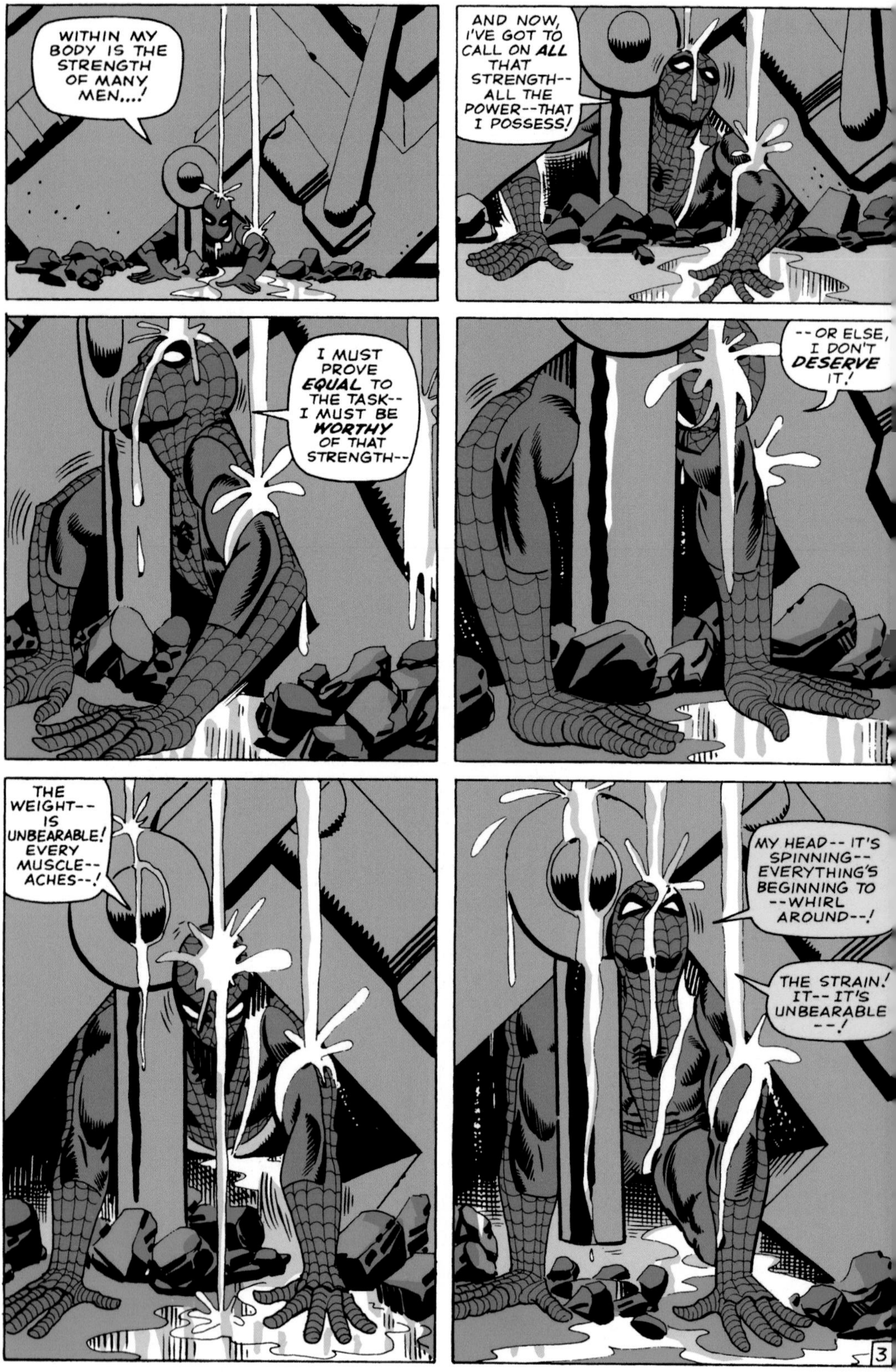
WITHIN MY BODY IS THE STRENGTH OF MANY MEN...!
AND NOW, I'VE GOT TO CALL ON ALL THAT STRENGTH-- ALL THE POWER--THAT I POSSESS!
I MUST PROVE EQUAL TO THE TASK-- I MUST BE WORTHY OF THAT STRENGTH--
--OR ELSE, I DON'T DESERVE IT!
THE WEIGHT-- IS UNBEARABLE! EVERY MUSCLE-- ACHES--!
MY HEAD-- IT'S SPINNING-- EVERYTHING'S BEGINNING TO --WHIRL AROUND--!
THE STRAIN! IT-- IT'S UNBEARABLE --!
3

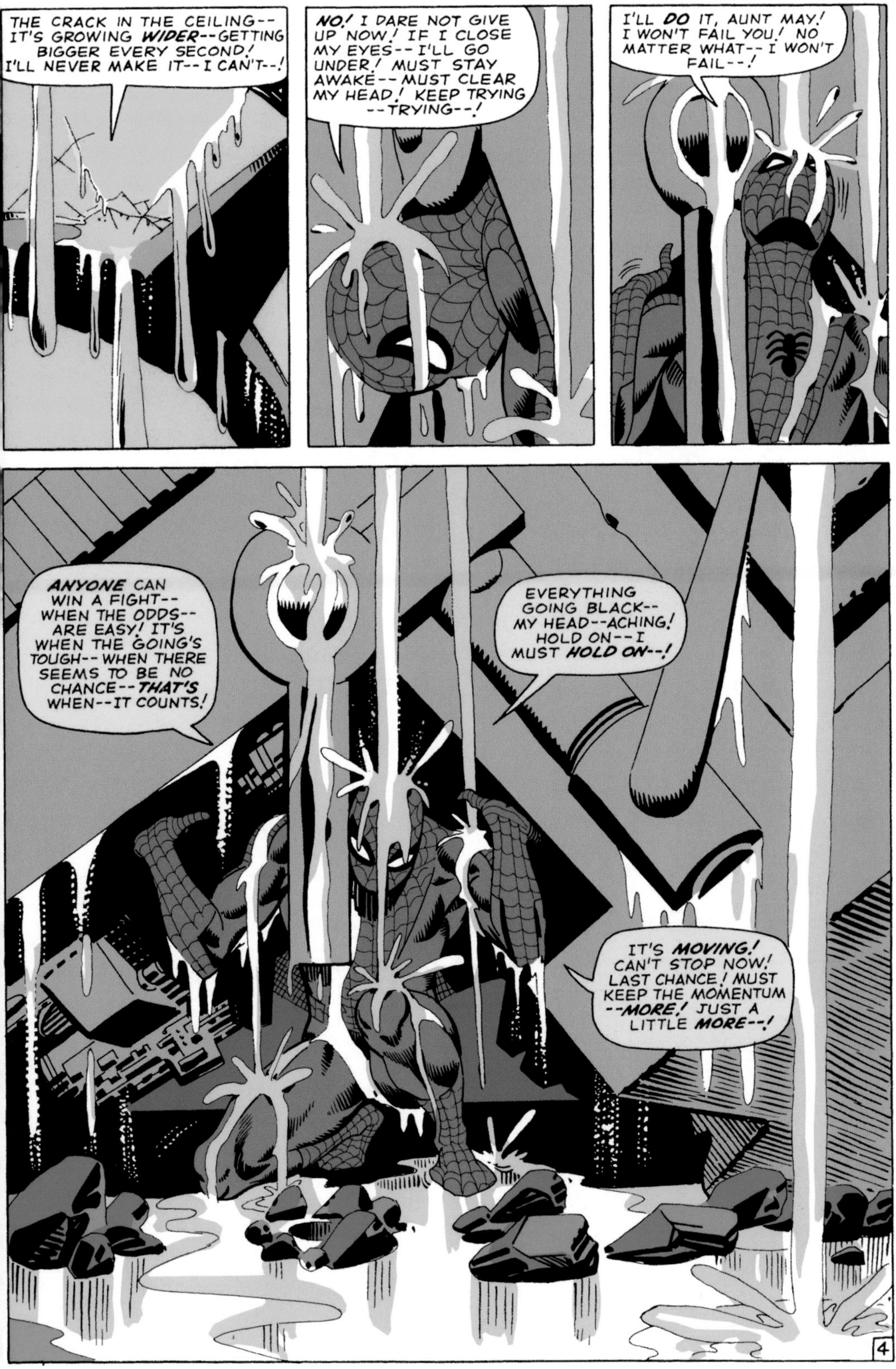
THE CRACK IN THE CEILING-- IT'S GROWING WIDER--GETTING BIGGER EVERY SECOND! I'LL NEVER MAKE IT--I CAN'T--!
NO! I DARE NOT GIVE UP NOW! IF I CLOSE MY EYES--I'LL GO UNDER! MUST STAY AWAKE--MUST CLEAR MY HEAD! KEEP TRYING --TRYING--!
I'LL DO IT, AUNT MAY! I WON'T FAIL YOU! NO MATTER WHAT--I WON'T FAIL--!
ANYONE CAN WIN A FIGHT-- WHEN THE ODDS-- ARE EASY! IT'S WHEN THE GOING'S TOUGH--WHEN THERE SEEMS TO BE NO CHANCE--THAT'S WHEN--IT COUNTS!
EVERYTHING GOING BLACK-- MY HEAD--ACHING! HOLD ON--I MUST HOLD ON--!
IT'S MOVING! CAN'T STOP NOW! LAST CHANCE! MUST KEEP THE MOMENTUM --MORE! JUST A LITTLE MORE--!

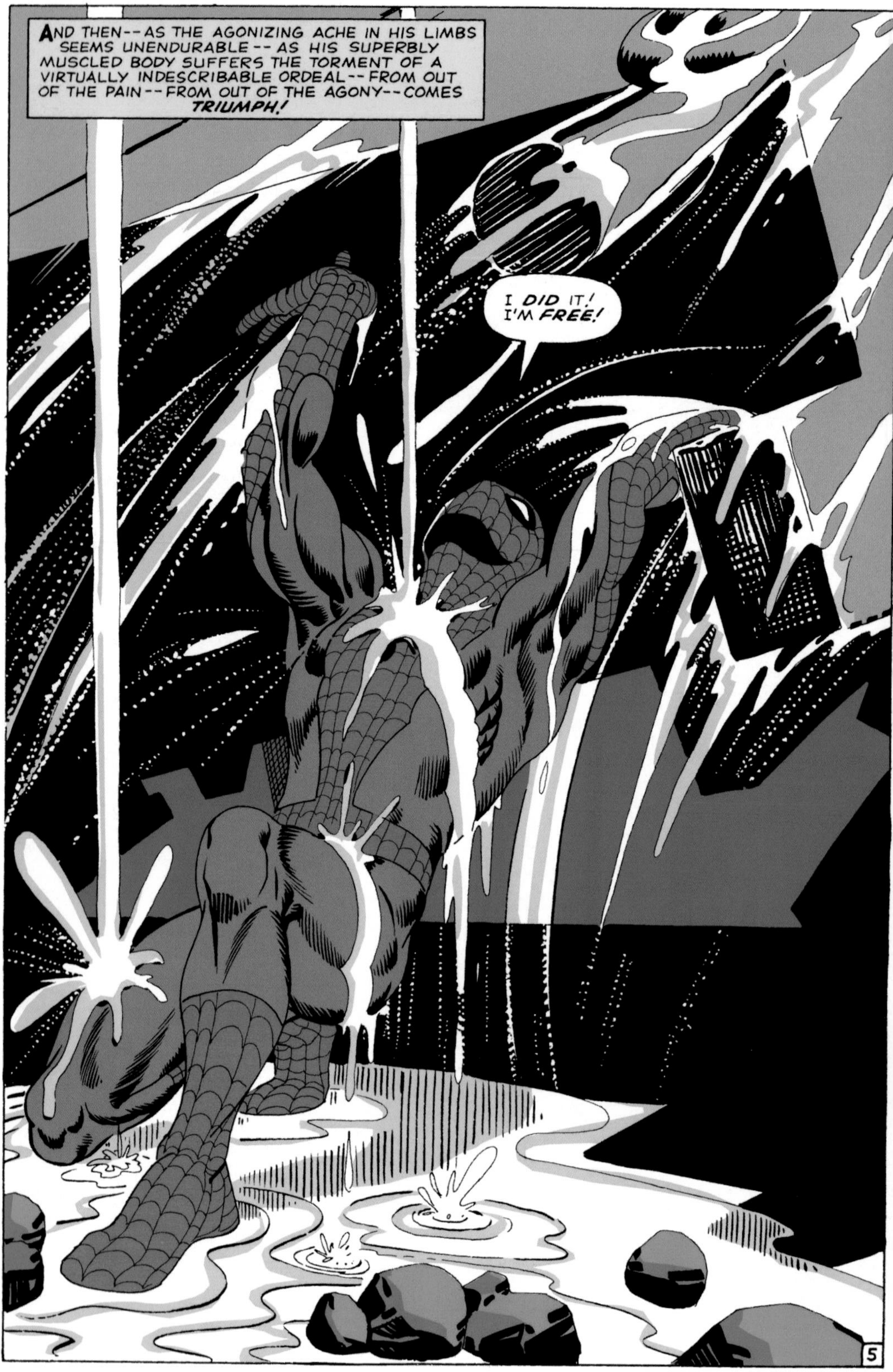
AND THEN--AS THE AGONIZING ACHE IN HIS LIMBS SEEMS UNENDURABLE--AS HIS SUPERBLY MUSCLED BODY SUFFERS THE TORMENT OF A VIRTUALLY INDESCRIBABLE ORDEAL--FROM OUT OF THE PAIN--FROM OUT OF THE AGONY--COMES *TRIUMPH!*
I *DID* IT! I'M *FREE!*
5

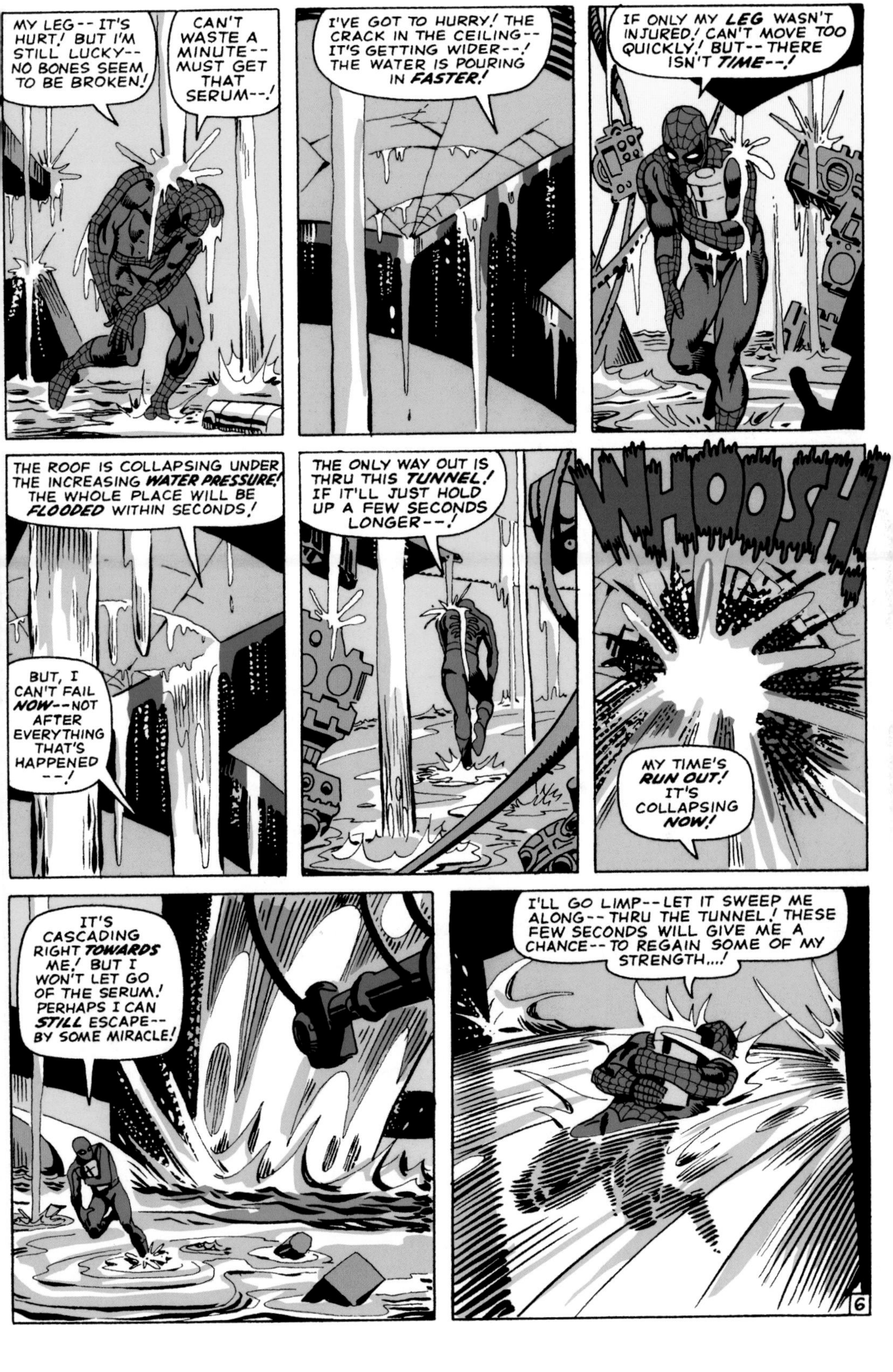
MY LEG-- IT'S HURT! BUT I'M STILL LUCKY-- NO BONES SEEM TO BE BROKEN!
CAN'T WASTE A MINUTE-- MUST GET THAT SERUM--!
I'VE GOT TO HURRY! THE CRACK IN THE CEILING-- IT'S GETTING WIDER--! THE WATER IS POURING IN FASTER!
IF ONLY MY LEG WASN'T INJURED! CAN'T MOVE TOO QUICKLY! BUT-- THERE ISN'T TIME--!
THE ROOF IS COLLAPSING UNDER THE INCREASING WATER PRESSURE! THE WHOLE PLACE WILL BE FLOODED WITHIN SECONDS!
BUT, I CAN'T FAIL NOW--NOT AFTER EVERYTHING THAT'S HAPPENED--!
THE ONLY WAY OUT IS THRU THIS TUNNEL! IF IT'LL JUST HOLD UP A FEW SECONDS LONGER--!
WHOOSH
MY TIME'S RUN OUT! IT'S COLLAPSING NOW!
IT'S CASCADING RIGHT TOWARDS ME! BUT I WON'T LET GO OF THE SERUM! PERHAPS I CAN STILL ESCAPE-- BY SOME MIRACLE!
I'LL GO LIMP--LET IT SWEEP ME ALONG--THRU THE TUNNEL! THESE FEW SECONDS WILL GIVE ME A CHANCE--TO REGAIN SOME OF MY STRENGTH...!
6

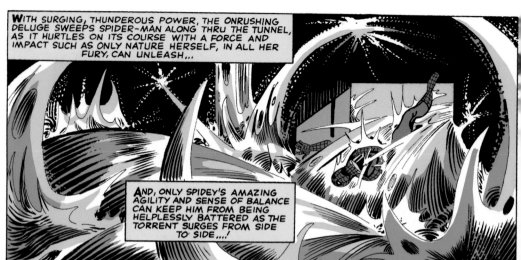

WITH SURGING, THUNDEROUS POWER, THE ONRUSHING DELUGE SWEEPS SPIDER-MAN ALONG THRU THE TUNNEL, AS IT HURTLES ON ITS COURSE WITH A FORCE AND IMPACT SUCH AS ONLY NATURE HERSELF, IN ALL HER FURY, CAN UNLEASH,...

AND, ONLY SPIDEY'S AMAZING AGILITY AND SENSE OF BALANCE CAN KEEP HIM FROM BEING HELPLESSLY BATTERED AS THE TORRENT SURGES FROM SIDE TO SIDE,....!

THE TUNNEL IS ALMOST COMPLETELY *INUNDATED!* I CAN HOLD MY BREATH FAR LONGER THAN A NORMAL MAN-- BUT NOT *FOREVER!*

I'VE GOT TO FIND A WAY OUT--BEFORE I *DROWN!*

THAT *DOOR--* AT THE END OF THE TUNNEL! IT'S MY ONLY CHANCE!

THE RELENTLESS HAMMERING OF TONS OF WATER SHOULD BREAK IT DOWN BY THE TIME I REACH IT!

MUSTN'T GET *CARELESS* NOW! HAVE TO KEEP SWERVING--DODGING-- AVOIDING THE WRECKAGE WHICH COULD TANGLE ME UP!

AND THEN, SECONDS LATER...

I'M *THRU!* THERE'S *AIR* TO BREATHE! *AIR!*

7

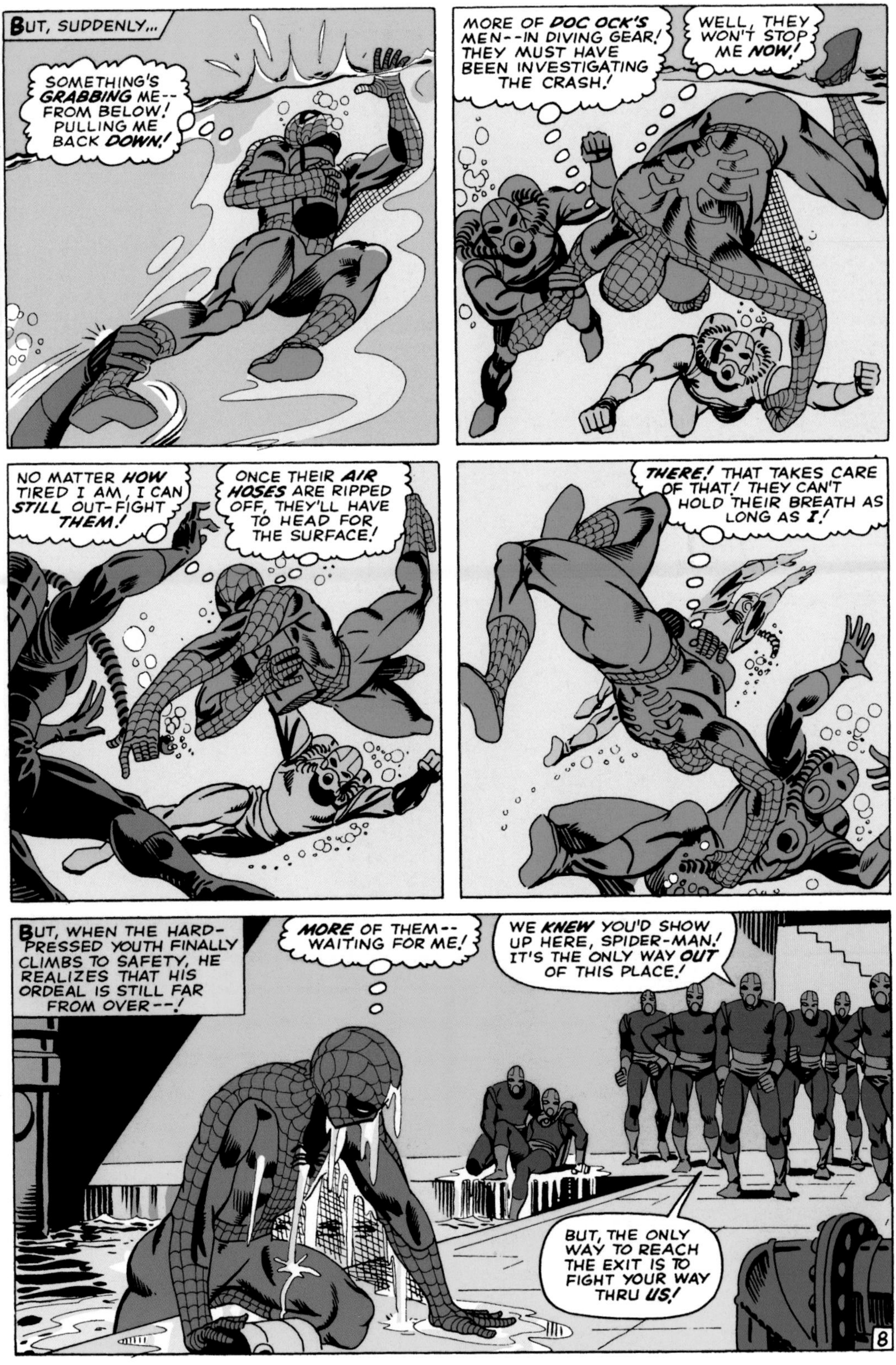

BUT, SUDDENLY...
SOMETHING'S GRABBING ME-- FROM BELOW! PULLING ME BACK DOWN!
MORE OF DOC OCK'S MEN--IN DIVING GEAR! THEY MUST HAVE BEEN INVESTIGATING THE CRASH!
WELL, THEY WON'T STOP ME NOW!
NO MATTER HOW TIRED I AM, I CAN STILL OUT-FIGHT THEM!
ONCE THEIR AIR HOSES ARE RIPPED OFF, THEY'LL HAVE TO HEAD FOR THE SURFACE!
THERE! THAT TAKES CARE OF THAT! THEY CAN'T HOLD THEIR BREATH AS LONG AS I!
BUT, WHEN THE HARD-PRESSED YOUTH FINALLY CLIMBS TO SAFETY, HE REALIZES THAT HIS ORDEAL IS STILL FAR FROM OVER--!
MORE OF THEM-- WAITING FOR ME!
WE KNEW YOU'D SHOW UP HERE, SPIDER-MAN! IT'S THE ONLY WAY OUT OF THIS PLACE!
BUT, THE ONLY WAY TO REACH THE EXIT IS TO FIGHT YOUR WAY THRU US!
8

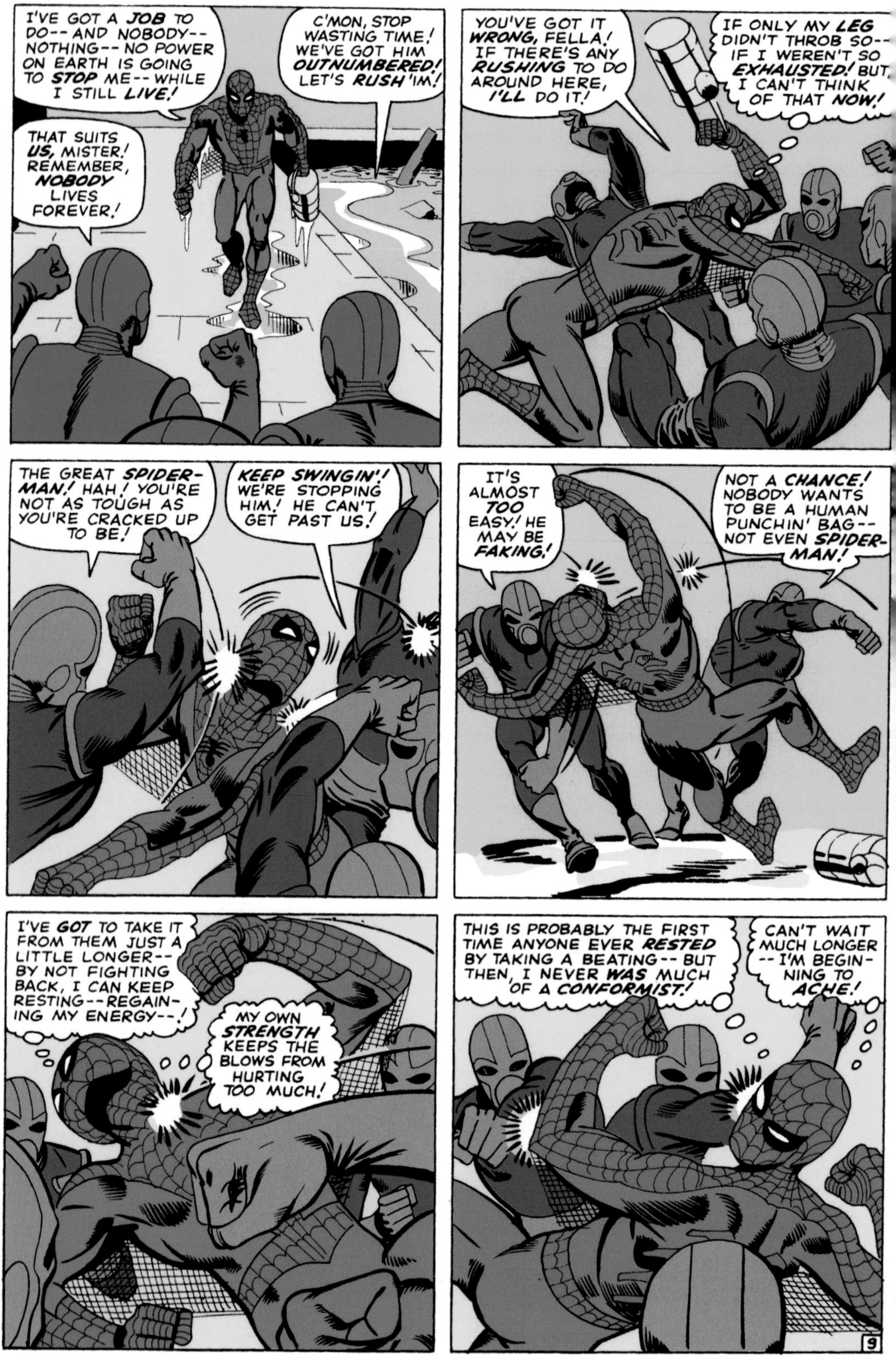

I'VE GOT A JOB TO DO-- AND NOBODY-- NOTHING-- NO POWER ON EARTH IS GOING TO STOP ME-- WHILE I STILL LIVE!
C'MON, STOP WASTING TIME! WE'VE GOT HIM OUTNUMBERED! LET'S RUSH 'IM!
THAT SUITS US, MISTER! REMEMBER, NOBODY LIVES FOREVER!
YOU'VE GOT IT WRONG, FELLA! IF THERE'S ANY RUSHING TO DO AROUND HERE, I'LL DO IT!
IF ONLY MY LEG DIDN'T THROB SO-- IF I WEREN'T SO EXHAUSTED! BUT I CAN'T THINK OF THAT NOW!
THE GREAT SPIDER-MAN! HAH! YOU'RE NOT AS TOUGH AS YOU'RE CRACKED UP TO BE!
KEEP SWINGIN'! WE'RE STOPPING HIM! HE CAN'T GET PAST US!
IT'S ALMOST TOO EASY! HE MAY BE FAKING!
NOT A CHANCE! NOBODY WANTS TO BE A HUMAN PUNCHIN' BAG-- NOT EVEN SPIDER-MAN!
I'VE GOT TO TAKE IT FROM THEM JUST A LITTLE LONGER-- BY NOT FIGHTING BACK, I CAN KEEP RESTING-- REGAINING MY ENERGY--!
MY OWN STRENGTH KEEPS THE BLOWS FROM HURTING TOO MUCH!
THIS IS PROBABLY THE FIRST TIME ANYONE EVER RESTED BY TAKING A BEATING-- BUT THEN, I NEVER WAS MUCH OF A CONFORMIST!
CAN'T WAIT MUCH LONGER -- I'M BEGINNING TO ACHE!
9

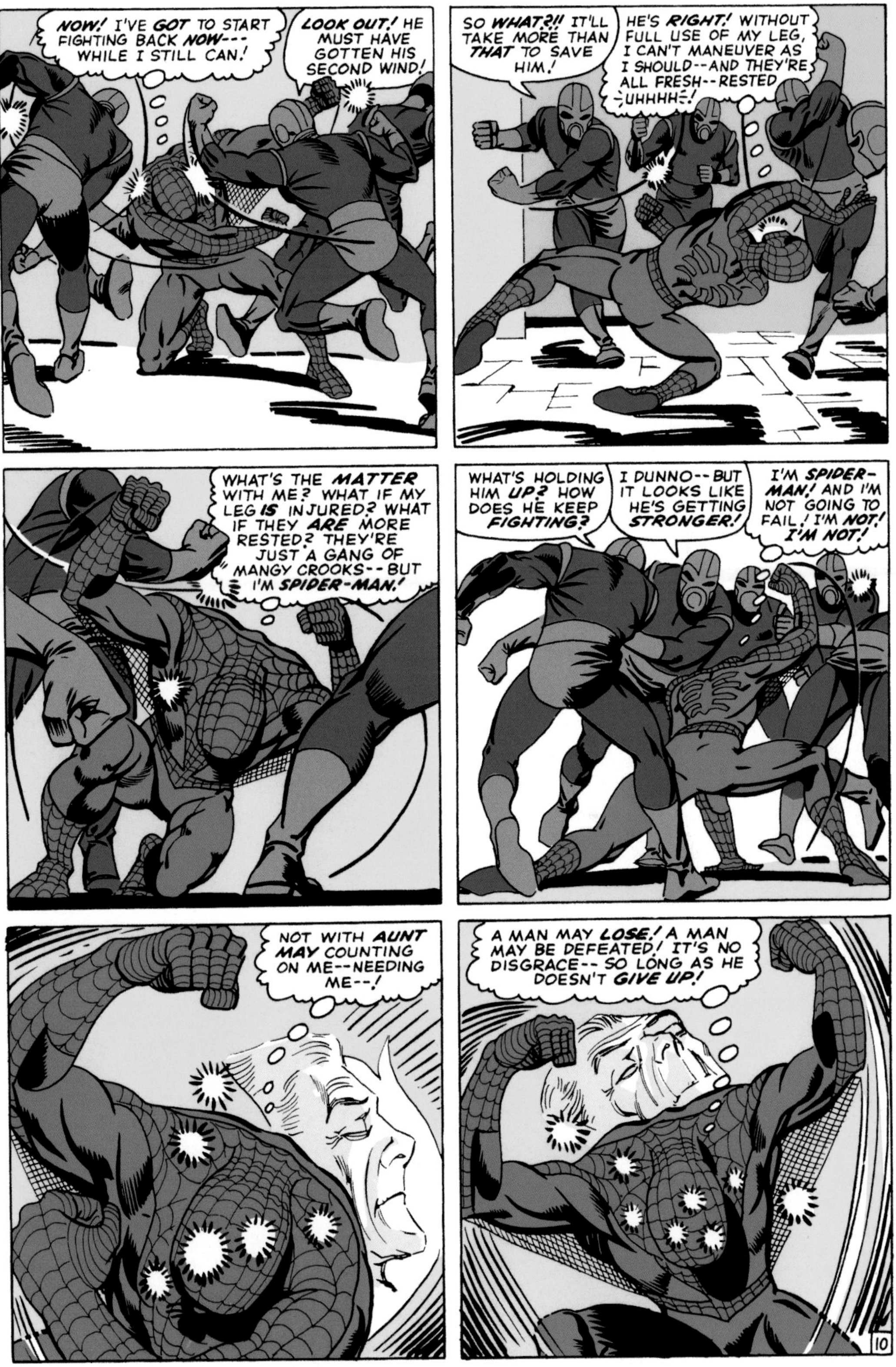
NOW! I'VE GOT TO START FIGHTING BACK NOW--- WHILE I STILL CAN!
LOOK OUT! HE MUST HAVE GOTTEN HIS SECOND WIND!
SO WHAT?!! IT'LL TAKE MORE THAN THAT TO SAVE HIM!
HE'S RIGHT! WITHOUT FULL USE OF MY LEG, I CAN'T MANEUVER AS I SHOULD--AND THEY'RE ALL FRESH--RESTED --UHHHH--!
WHAT'S THE MATTER WITH ME? WHAT IF MY LEG IS INJURED? WHAT IF THEY ARE MORE RESTED? THEY'RE JUST A GANG OF MANGY CROOKS--BUT I'M SPIDER-MAN!
WHAT'S HOLDING HIM UP? HOW DOES HE KEEP FIGHTING?
I DUNNO--BUT IT LOOKS LIKE HE'S GETTING STRONGER!
I'M SPIDER-MAN! AND I'M NOT GOING TO FAIL! I'M NOT! I'M NOT!
NOT WITH AUNT MAY COUNTING ON ME--NEEDING ME--!
A MAN MAY LOSE! A MAN MAY BE DEFEATED! IT'S NO DISGRACE-- SO LONG AS HE DOESN'T GIVE UP!
10

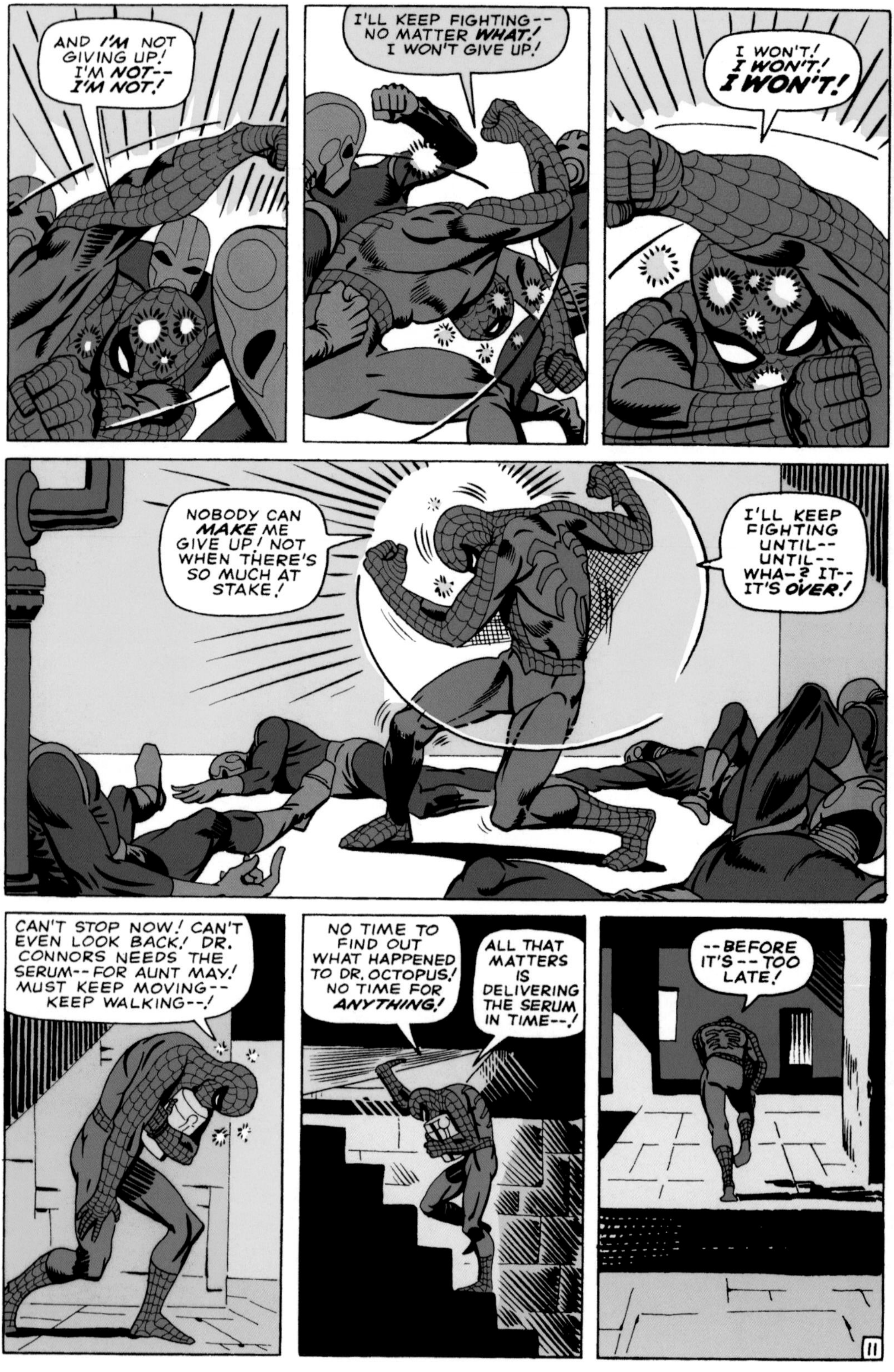
AND I'M NOT GIVING UP! I'M NOT-- I'M NOT!
I'LL KEEP FIGHTING-- NO MATTER WHAT! I WON'T GIVE UP!
I WON'T! I WON'T! I WON'T!
NOBODY CAN MAKE ME GIVE UP! NOT WHEN THERE'S SO MUCH AT STAKE!
I'LL KEEP FIGHTING UNTIL-- UNTIL-- WHA-? IT-- IT'S OVER!
CAN'T STOP NOW! CAN'T EVEN LOOK BACK! DR. CONNORS NEEDS THE SERUM--FOR AUNT MAY! MUST KEEP MOVING-- KEEP WALKING--!
NO TIME TO FIND OUT WHAT HAPPENED TO DR. OCTOPUS! NO TIME FOR ANYTHING!
ALL THAT MATTERS IS DELIVERING THE SERUM IN TIME--!
--BEFORE IT'S--TOO LATE!
11

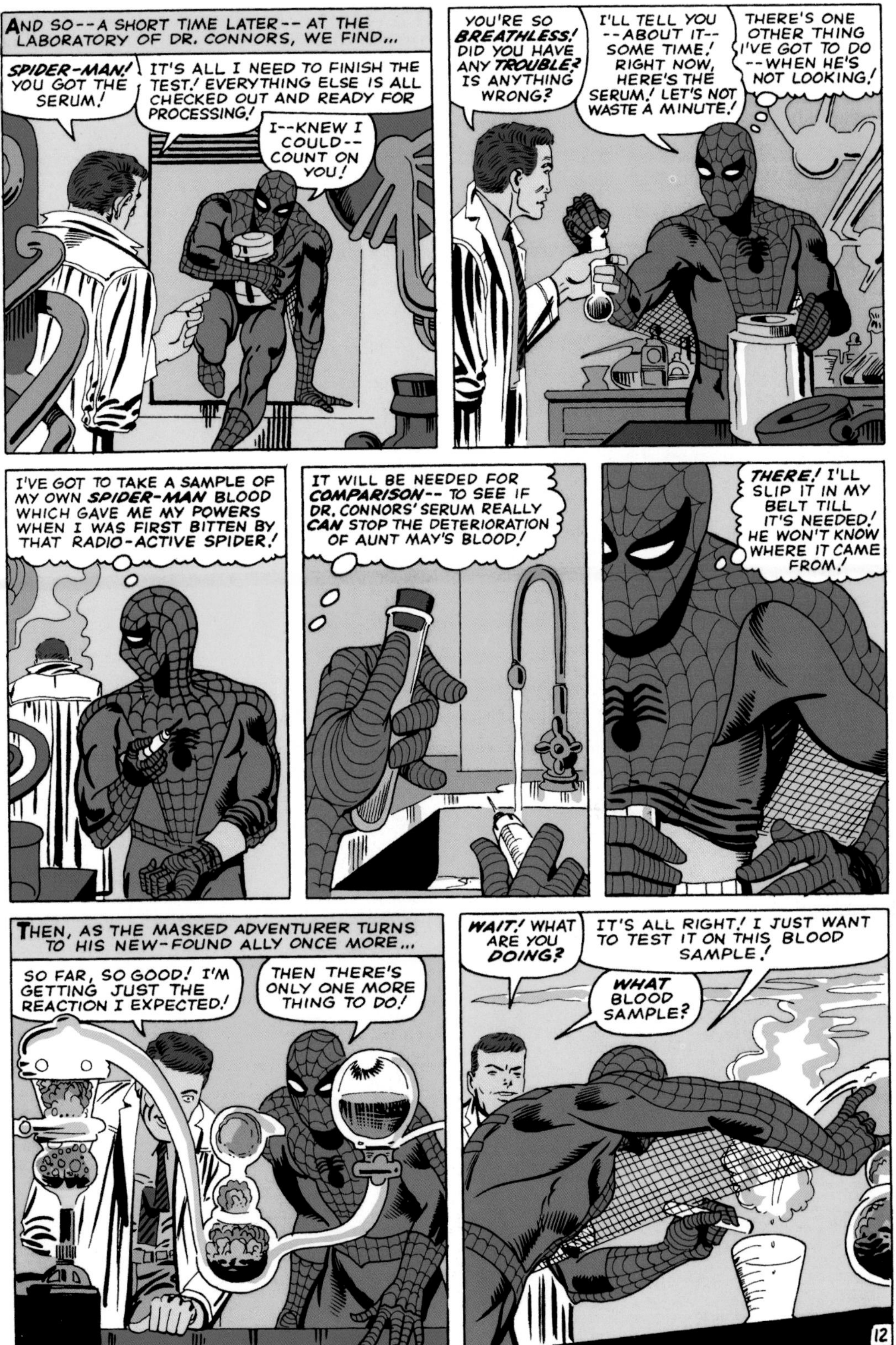
AND SO--A SHORT TIME LATER--AT THE LABORATORY OF DR. CONNORS, WE FIND...
SPIDER-MAN! YOU GOT THE SERUM!
IT'S ALL I NEED TO FINISH THE TEST! EVERYTHING ELSE IS ALL CHECKED OUT AND READY FOR PROCESSING!
I--KNEW I COULD--COUNT ON YOU!
YOU'RE SO BREATHLESS! DID YOU HAVE ANY TROUBLE? IS ANYTHING WRONG?
I'LL TELL YOU --ABOUT IT-- SOME TIME! RIGHT NOW, HERE'S THE SERUM! LET'S NOT WASTE A MINUTE!
THERE'S ONE OTHER THING I'VE GOT TO DO --WHEN HE'S NOT LOOKING!
I'VE GOT TO TAKE A SAMPLE OF MY OWN SPIDER-MAN BLOOD WHICH GAVE ME MY POWERS WHEN I WAS FIRST BITTEN BY THAT RADIO-ACTIVE SPIDER!
IT WILL BE NEEDED FOR COMPARISON-- TO SEE IF DR. CONNORS' SERUM REALLY CAN STOP THE DETERIORATION OF AUNT MAY'S BLOOD!
THERE! I'LL SLIP IT IN MY BELT TILL IT'S NEEDED! HE WON'T KNOW WHERE IT CAME FROM!
THEN, AS THE MASKED ADVENTURER TURNS TO HIS NEW-FOUND ALLY ONCE MORE...
SO FAR, SO GOOD! I'M GETTING JUST THE REACTION I EXPECTED!
THEN THERE'S ONLY ONE MORE THING TO DO!
WAIT! WHAT ARE YOU DOING?
IT'S ALL RIGHT! I JUST WANT TO TEST IT ON THIS BLOOD SAMPLE!
WHAT BLOOD SAMPLE?
12

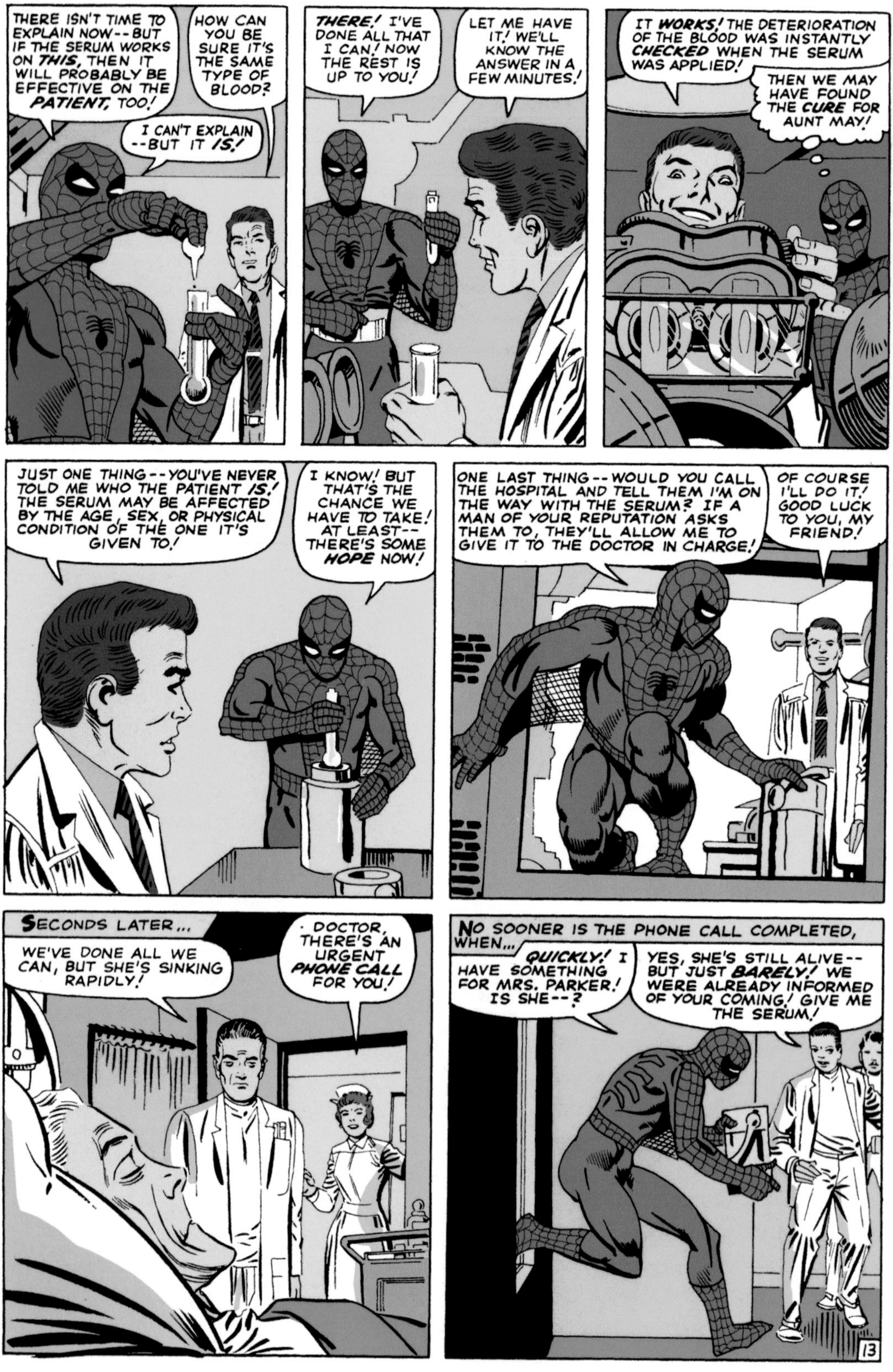
THERE ISN'T TIME TO EXPLAIN NOW--BUT IF THE SERUM WORKS ON THIS, THEN IT WILL PROBABLY BE EFFECTIVE ON THE PATIENT, TOO!
HOW CAN YOU BE SURE IT'S THE SAME TYPE OF BLOOD?
I CAN'T EXPLAIN --BUT IT IS!
THERE! I'VE DONE ALL THAT I CAN! NOW THE REST IS UP TO YOU!
LET ME HAVE IT! WE'LL KNOW THE ANSWER IN A FEW MINUTES!
IT WORKS! THE DETERIORATION OF THE BLOOD WAS INSTANTLY CHECKED WHEN THE SERUM WAS APPLIED!
THEN WE MAY HAVE FOUND THE CURE FOR AUNT MAY!
JUST ONE THING--YOU'VE NEVER TOLD ME WHO THE PATIENT IS! THE SERUM MAY BE AFFECTED BY THE AGE, SEX, OR PHYSICAL CONDITION OF THE ONE IT'S GIVEN TO!
I KNOW! BUT THAT'S THE CHANCE WE HAVE TO TAKE! AT LEAST--THERE'S SOME HOPE NOW!
ONE LAST THING--WOULD YOU CALL THE HOSPITAL AND TELL THEM I'M ON THE WAY WITH THE SERUM? IF A MAN OF YOUR REPUTATION ASKS THEM TO, THEY'LL ALLOW ME TO GIVE IT TO THE DOCTOR IN CHARGE!
OF COURSE I'LL DO IT! GOOD LUCK TO YOU, MY FRIEND!
SECONDS LATER...
WE'VE DONE ALL WE CAN, BUT SHE'S SINKING RAPIDLY!
DOCTOR, THERE'S AN URGENT PHONE CALL FOR YOU!
NO SOONER IS THE PHONE CALL COMPLETED, WHEN...
QUICKLY! I HAVE SOMETHING FOR MRS. PARKER! IS SHE--?
YES, SHE'S STILL ALIVE--BUT JUST BARELY! WE WERE ALREADY INFORMED OF YOUR COMING! GIVE ME THE SERUM!
13

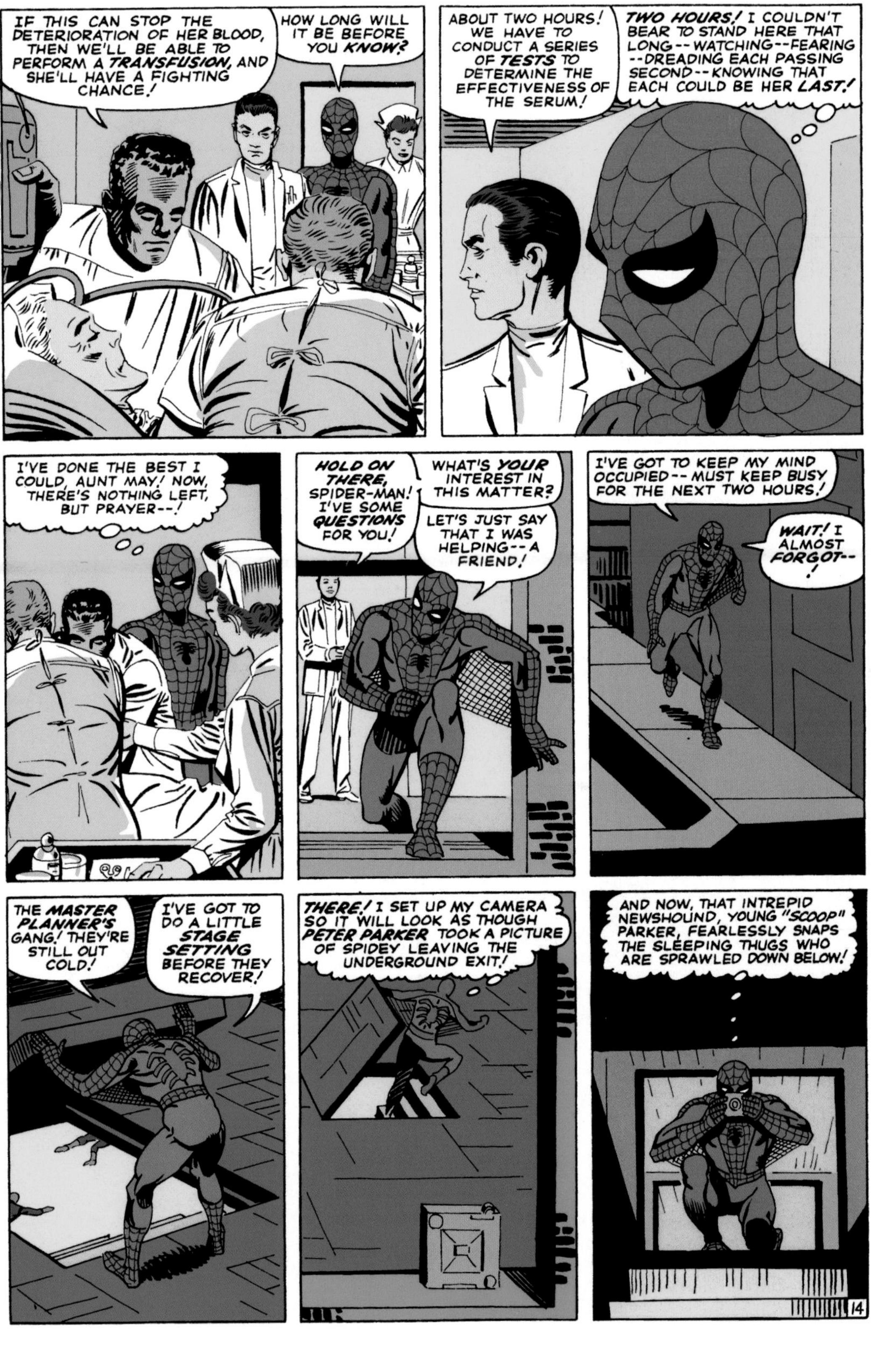
IF THIS CAN STOP THE DETERIORATION OF HER BLOOD, THEN WE'LL BE ABLE TO PERFORM A TRANSFUSION, AND SHE'LL HAVE A FIGHTING CHANCE!
HOW LONG WILL IT BE BEFORE YOU KNOW?
ABOUT TWO HOURS! WE HAVE TO CONDUCT A SERIES OF TESTS TO DETERMINE THE EFFECTIVENESS OF THE SERUM!
TWO HOURS! I COULDN'T BEAR TO STAND HERE THAT LONG--WATCHING--FEARING--DREADING EACH PASSING SECOND--KNOWING THAT EACH COULD BE HER LAST!
I'VE DONE THE BEST I COULD, AUNT MAY! NOW, THERE'S NOTHING LEFT, BUT PRAYER--!
HOLD ON THERE, SPIDER-MAN! I'VE SOME QUESTIONS FOR YOU!
WHAT'S YOUR INTEREST IN THIS MATTER?
LET'S JUST SAY THAT I WAS HELPING--A FRIEND!
I'VE GOT TO KEEP MY MIND OCCUPIED--MUST KEEP BUSY FOR THE NEXT TWO HOURS!
WAIT! I ALMOST FORGOT--!
THE MASTER PLANNER'S GANG! THEY'RE STILL OUT COLD!
I'VE GOT TO DO A LITTLE STAGE SETTING BEFORE THEY RECOVER!
THERE! I SET UP MY CAMERA SO IT WILL LOOK AS THOUGH PETER PARKER TOOK A PICTURE OF SPIDEY LEAVING THE UNDERGROUND EXIT!
AND NOW, THAT INTREPID NEWSHOUND, YOUNG "SCOOP" PARKER, FEARLESSLY SNAPS THE SLEEPING THUGS WHO ARE SPRAWLED DOWN BELOW!
14

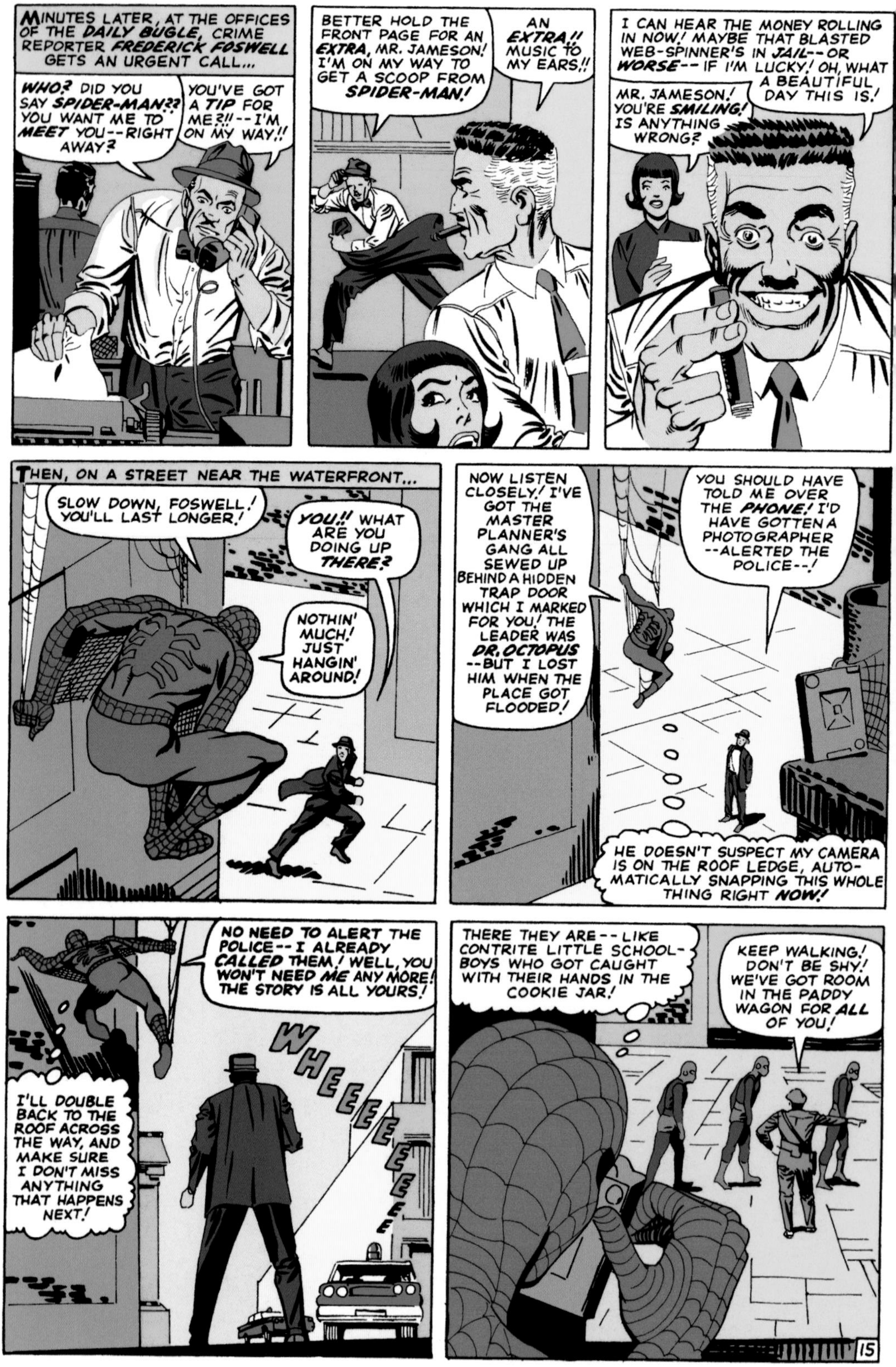
MINUTES LATER, AT THE OFFICES OF THE DAILY BUGLE, CRIME REPORTER FREDERICK FOSWELL GETS AN URGENT CALL...
WHO? DID YOU SAY SPIDER-MAN?? YOU WANT ME TO MEET YOU--RIGHT AWAY?
YOU'VE GOT A TIP FOR ME?!!--I'M ON MY WAY!!
BETTER HOLD THE FRONT PAGE FOR AN EXTRA, MR. JAMESON! I'M ON MY WAY TO GET A SCOOP FROM SPIDER-MAN!
AN EXTRA!! MUSIC TO MY EARS!!
I CAN HEAR THE MONEY ROLLING IN NOW! MAYBE THAT BLASTED WEB-SPINNER'S IN JAIL--OR WORSE--IF I'M LUCKY! OH, WHAT A BEAUTIFUL DAY THIS IS!
MR. JAMESON! YOU'RE SMILING! IS ANYTHING WRONG?
THEN, ON A STREET NEAR THE WATERFRONT...
SLOW DOWN, FOSWELL! YOU'LL LAST LONGER!
YOU!! WHAT ARE YOU DOING UP THERE?
NOTHIN' MUCH! JUST HANGIN' AROUND!
NOW LISTEN CLOSELY! I'VE GOT THE MASTER PLANNER'S GANG ALL SEWED UP BEHIND A HIDDEN TRAP DOOR WHICH I MARKED FOR YOU! THE LEADER WAS DR. OCTOPUS--BUT I LOST HIM WHEN THE PLACE GOT FLOODED!
YOU SHOULD HAVE TOLD ME OVER THE PHONE! I'D HAVE GOTTEN A PHOTOGRAPHER--ALERTED THE POLICE--!
HE DOESN'T SUSPECT MY CAMERA IS ON THE ROOF LEDGE, AUTOMATICALLY SNAPPING THIS WHOLE THING RIGHT NOW!
NO NEED TO ALERT THE POLICE--I ALREADY CALLED THEM! WELL, YOU WON'T NEED ME ANY MORE! THE STORY IS ALL YOURS!
I'LL DOUBLE BACK TO THE ROOF ACROSS THE WAY, AND MAKE SURE I DON'T MISS ANYTHING THAT HAPPENS NEXT!
WHEEEEEEEEE
THERE THEY ARE--LIKE CONTRITE LITTLE SCHOOLBOYS WHO GOT CAUGHT WITH THEIR HANDS IN THE COOKIE JAR!
KEEP WALKING! DON'T BE SHY! WE'VE GOT ROOM IN THE PADDY WAGON FOR ALL OF YOU!

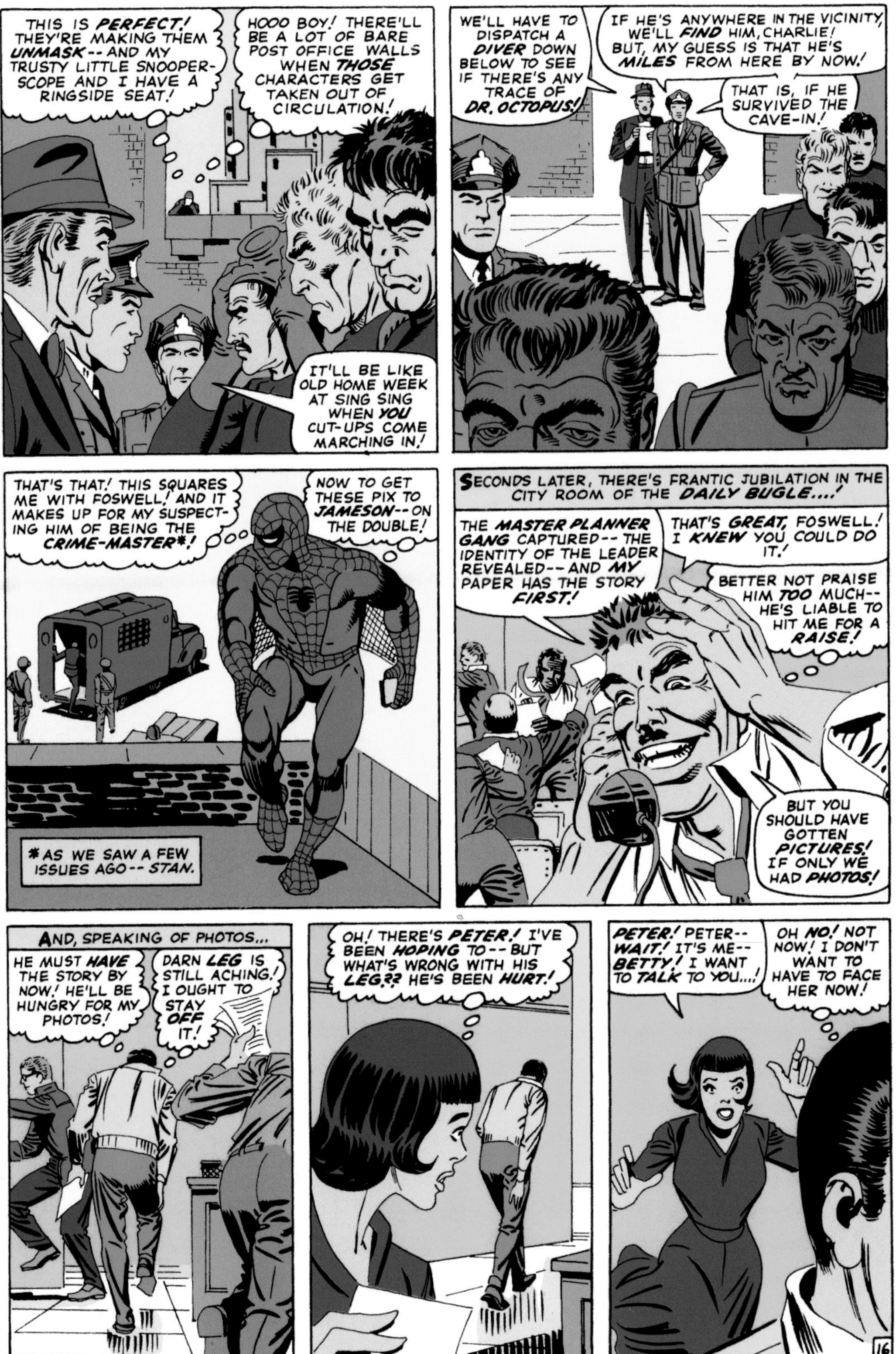
THIS IS PERFECT! THEY'RE MAKING THEM UNMASK-- AND MY TRUSTY LITTLE SNOOPER-SCOPE AND I HAVE A RINGSIDE SEAT!
HOOO BOY! THERE'LL BE A LOT OF BARE POST OFFICE WALLS WHEN THOSE CHARACTERS GET TAKEN OUT OF CIRCULATION!
IT'LL BE LIKE OLD HOME WEEK AT SING SING WHEN YOU CUT-UPS COME MARCHING IN!
WE'LL HAVE TO DISPATCH A DIVER DOWN BELOW TO SEE IF THERE'S ANY TRACE OF DR. OCTOPUS!
IF HE'S ANYWHERE IN THE VICINITY, WE'LL FIND HIM, CHARLIE! BUT, MY GUESS IS THAT HE'S MILES FROM HERE BY NOW!
THAT IS, IF HE SURVIVED THE CAVE-IN!
THAT'S THAT! THIS SQUARES ME WITH FOSWELL! AND IT MAKES UP FOR MY SUSPECTING HIM OF BEING THE CRIME-MASTER*!
NOW TO GET THESE PIX TO JAMESON-- ON THE DOUBLE!
*AS WE SAW A FEW ISSUES AGO-- STAN.
SECONDS LATER, THERE'S FRANTIC JUBILATION IN THE CITY ROOM OF THE DAILY BUGLE....!
THE MASTER PLANNER GANG CAPTURED-- THE IDENTITY OF THE LEADER REVEALED-- AND MY PAPER HAS THE STORY FIRST!
THAT'S GREAT, FOSWELL! I KNEW YOU COULD DO IT!
BETTER NOT PRAISE HIM TOO MUCH-- HE'S LIABLE TO HIT ME FOR A RAISE!
BUT YOU SHOULD HAVE GOTTEN PICTURES! IF ONLY WE HAD PHOTOS!
AND, SPEAKING OF PHOTOS...
HE MUST HAVE THE STORY BY NOW! HE'LL BE HUNGRY FOR MY PHOTOS!
DARN LEG IS STILL ACHING! I OUGHT TO STAY OFF IT!
OH! THERE'S PETER! I'VE BEEN HOPING TO-- BUT WHAT'S WRONG WITH HIS LEG?? HE'S BEEN HURT!
PETER! PETER-- WAIT! IT'S ME-- BETTY! I WANT TO TALK TO YOU....!
OH NO! NOT NOW! I DON'T WANT TO HAVE TO FACE HER NOW!

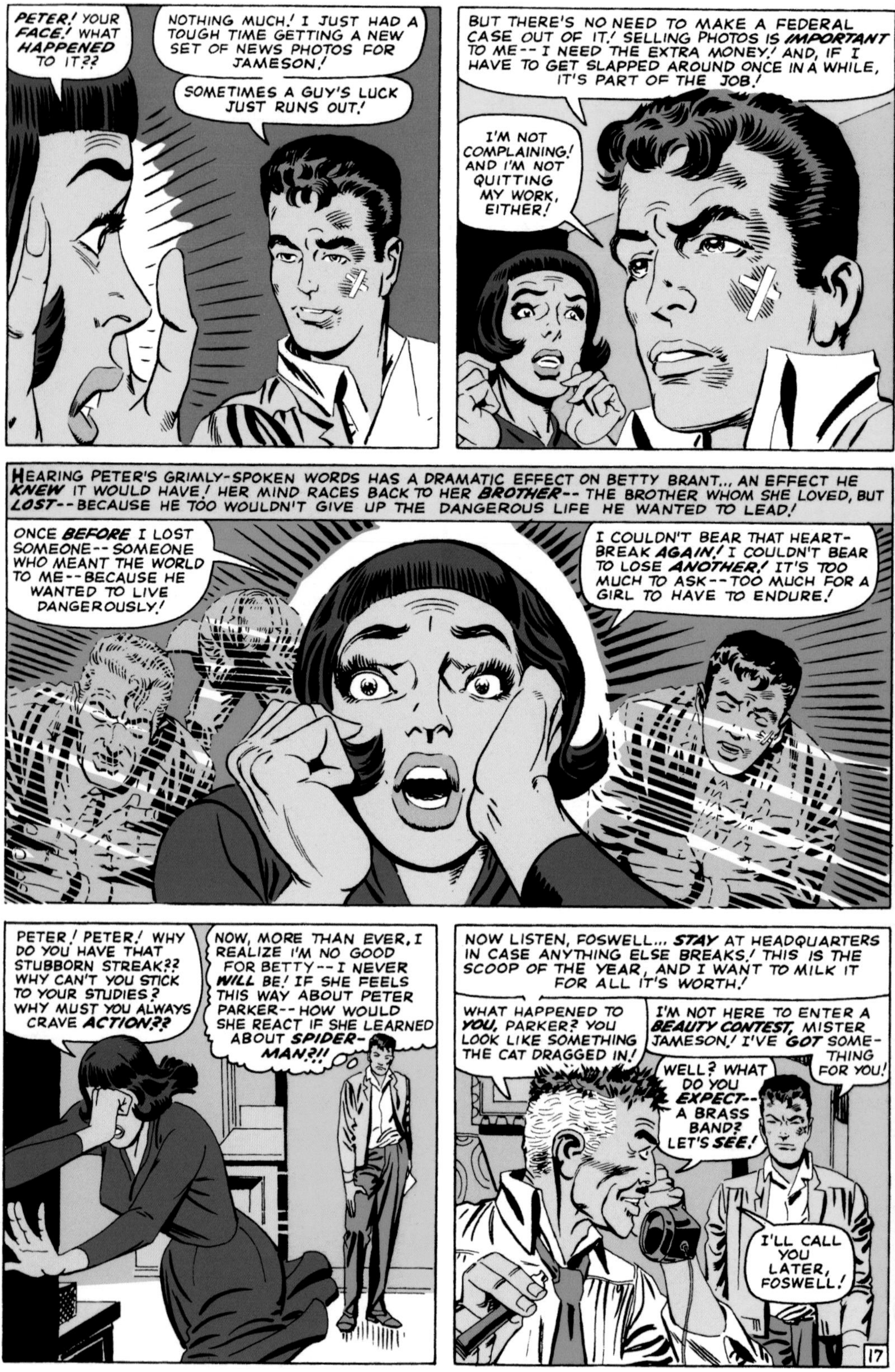
PETER! YOUR FACE! WHAT HAPPENED TO IT??
NOTHING MUCH! I JUST HAD A TOUGH TIME GETTING A NEW SET OF NEWS PHOTOS FOR JAMESON!
SOMETIMES A GUY'S LUCK JUST RUNS OUT!
BUT THERE'S NO NEED TO MAKE A FEDERAL CASE OUT OF IT! SELLING PHOTOS IS IMPORTANT TO ME-- I NEED THE EXTRA MONEY! AND, IF I HAVE TO GET SLAPPED AROUND ONCE IN A WHILE, IT'S PART OF THE JOB!
I'M NOT COMPLAINING! AND I'M NOT QUITTING MY WORK, EITHER!
HEARING PETER'S GRIMLY-SPOKEN WORDS HAS A DRAMATIC EFFECT ON BETTY BRANT... AN EFFECT HE KNEW IT WOULD HAVE! HER MIND RACES BACK TO HER BROTHER-- THE BROTHER WHOM SHE LOVED, BUT LOST--BECAUSE HE TOO WOULDN'T GIVE UP THE DANGEROUS LIFE HE WANTED TO LEAD!
ONCE BEFORE I LOST SOMEONE--SOMEONE WHO MEANT THE WORLD TO ME--BECAUSE HE WANTED TO LIVE DANGEROUSLY!
I COULDN'T BEAR THAT HEART-BREAK AGAIN! I COULDN'T BEAR TO LOSE ANOTHER! IT'S TOO MUCH TO ASK--TOO MUCH FOR A GIRL TO HAVE TO ENDURE!
PETER! PETER! WHY DO YOU HAVE THAT STUBBORN STREAK?? WHY CAN'T YOU STICK TO YOUR STUDIES? WHY MUST YOU ALWAYS CRAVE ACTION??
NOW, MORE THAN EVER, I REALIZE I'M NO GOOD FOR BETTY--I NEVER WILL BE! IF SHE FEELS THIS WAY ABOUT PETER PARKER--HOW WOULD SHE REACT IF SHE LEARNED ABOUT SPIDER-MAN?!!
NOW LISTEN, FOSWELL... STAY AT HEADQUARTERS IN CASE ANYTHING ELSE BREAKS! THIS IS THE SCOOP OF THE YEAR, AND I WANT TO MILK IT FOR ALL IT'S WORTH!
WHAT HAPPENED TO YOU, PARKER? YOU LOOK LIKE SOMETHING THE CAT DRAGGED IN!
I'M NOT HERE TO ENTER A BEAUTY CONTEST, MISTER JAMESON! I'VE GOT SOME-THING FOR YOU!
WELL? WHAT DO YOU EXPECT-- A BRASS BAND? LET'S SEE!
I'LL CALL YOU LATER, FOSWELL!
17

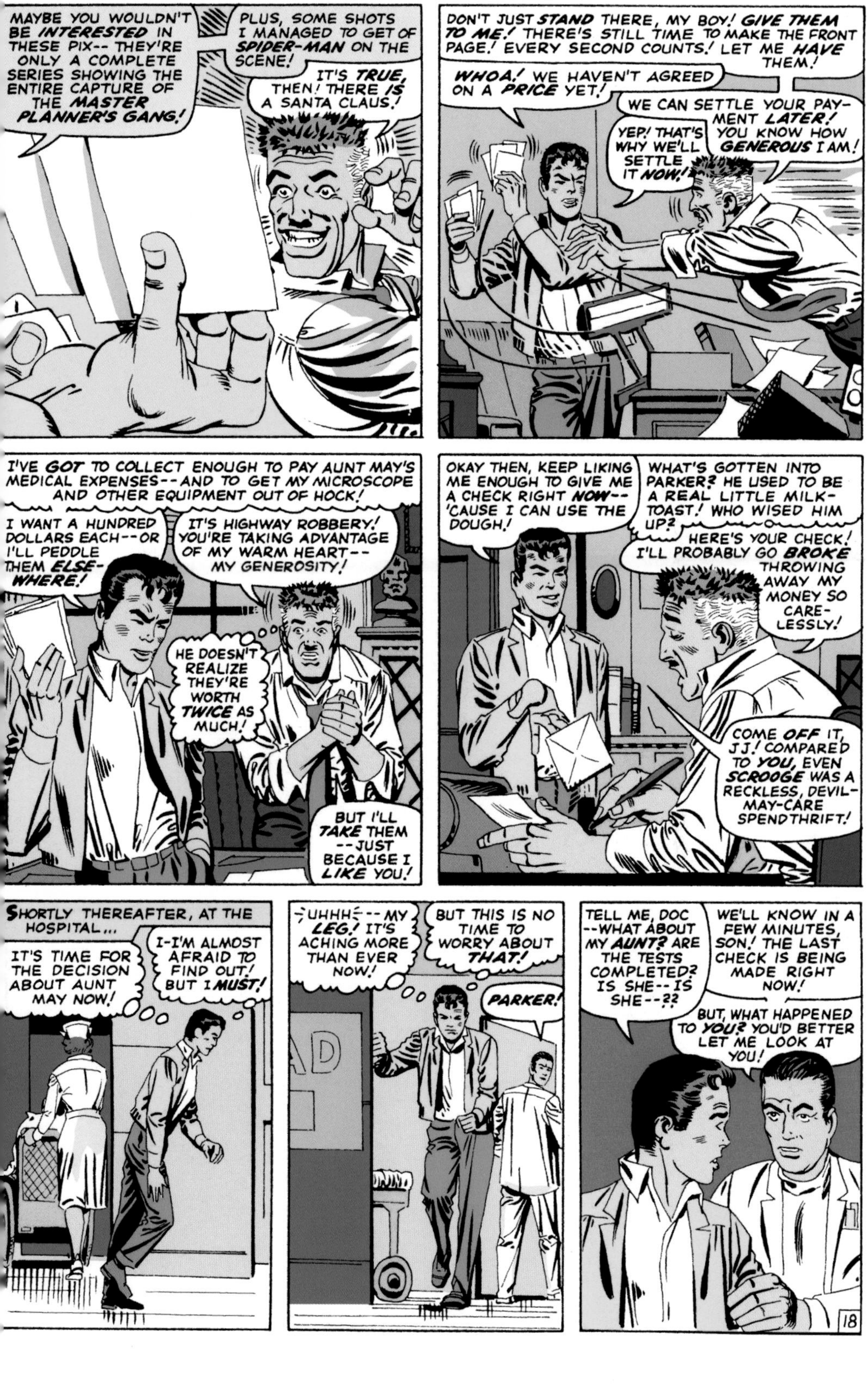

MAYBE YOU WOULDN'T BE INTERESTED IN THESE PIX-- THEY'RE ONLY A COMPLETE SERIES SHOWING THE ENTIRE CAPTURE OF THE MASTER PLANNER'S GANG!
PLUS, SOME SHOTS I MANAGED TO GET OF SPIDER-MAN ON THE SCENE!
IT'S TRUE, THEN! THERE IS A SANTA CLAUS!
DON'T JUST STAND THERE, MY BOY! GIVE THEM TO ME! THERE'S STILL TIME TO MAKE THE FRONT PAGE! EVERY SECOND COUNTS! LET ME HAVE THEM!
WHOA! WE HAVEN'T AGREED ON A PRICE YET!
WE CAN SETTLE YOUR PAYMENT LATER! YOU KNOW HOW GENEROUS I AM!
YEP! THAT'S WHY WE'LL SETTLE IT NOW!
I'VE GOT TO COLLECT ENOUGH TO PAY AUNT MAY'S MEDICAL EXPENSES--AND TO GET MY MICROSCOPE AND OTHER EQUIPMENT OUT OF HOCK!
I WANT A HUNDRED DOLLARS EACH--OR I'LL PEDDLE THEM ELSEWHERE!
IT'S HIGHWAY ROBBERY! YOU'RE TAKING ADVANTAGE OF MY WARM HEART--MY GENEROSITY!
HE DOESN'T REALIZE THEY'RE WORTH TWICE AS MUCH!
BUT I'LL TAKE THEM --JUST BECAUSE I LIKE YOU!
OKAY THEN, KEEP LIKING ME ENOUGH TO GIVE ME A CHECK RIGHT NOW-- 'CAUSE I CAN USE THE DOUGH!
WHAT'S GOTTEN INTO PARKER? HE USED TO BE A REAL LITTLE MILK-TOAST! WHO WISED HIM UP?
HERE'S YOUR CHECK! I'LL PROBABLY GO BROKE THROWING AWAY MY MONEY SO CARELESSLY!
COME OFF IT, J.J.! COMPARED TO YOU, EVEN SCROOGE WAS A RECKLESS, DEVIL-MAY-CARE SPENDTHRIFT!
SHORTLY THEREAFTER, AT THE HOSPITAL...
IT'S TIME FOR THE DECISION ABOUT AUNT MAY NOW!
I-I'M ALMOST AFRAID TO FIND OUT! BUT I MUST!
UHHH--MY LEG! IT'S ACHING MORE THAN EVER NOW!
BUT THIS IS NO TIME TO WORRY ABOUT THAT!
PARKER!
TELL ME, DOC --WHAT ABOUT MY AUNT? ARE THE TESTS COMPLETED? IS SHE--IS SHE--??
WE'LL KNOW IN A FEW MINUTES, SON! THE LAST CHECK IS BEING MADE RIGHT NOW!
BUT, WHAT HAPPENED TO YOU? YOU'D BETTER LET ME LOOK AT YOU!

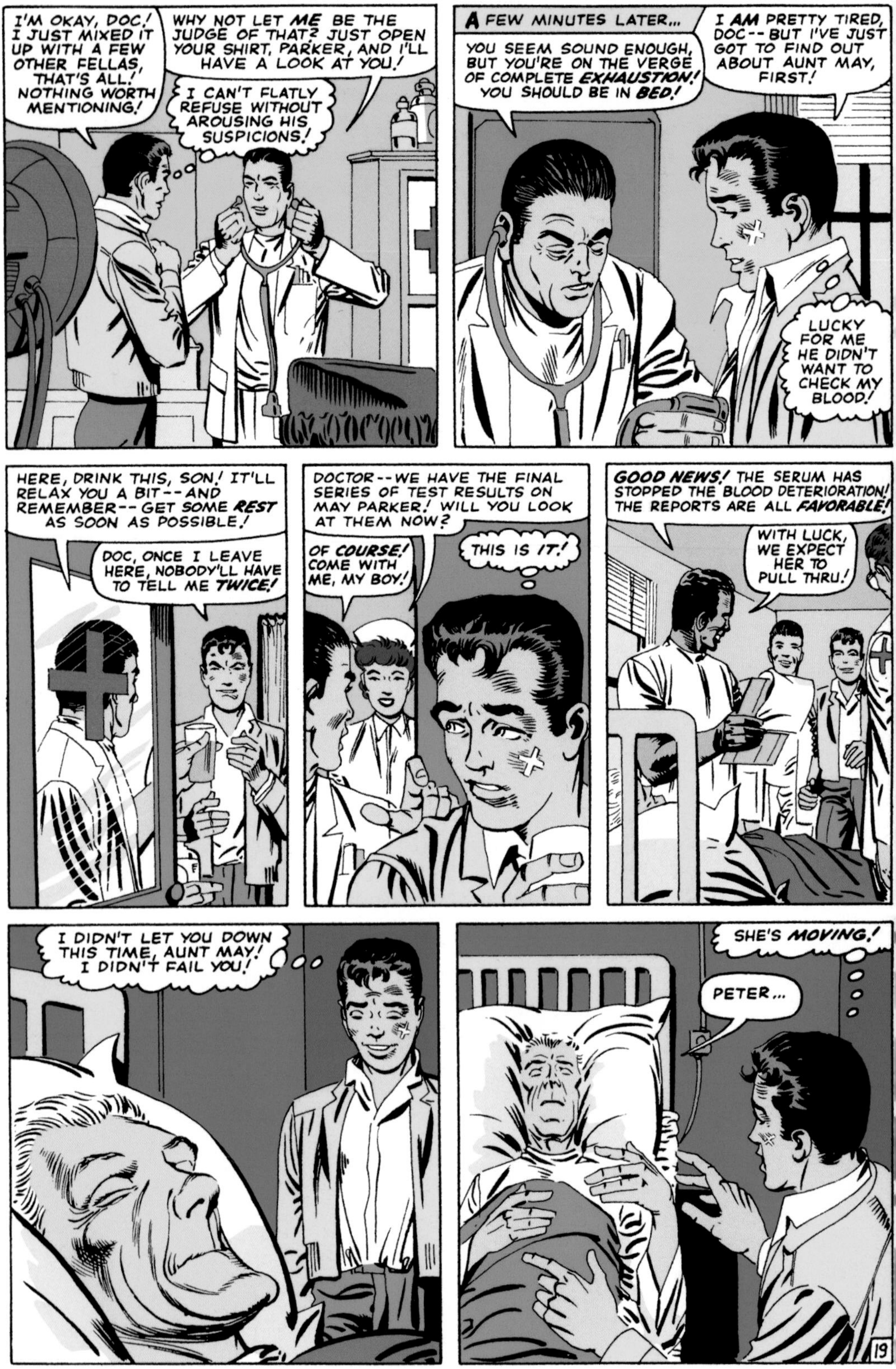
I'M OKAY, DOC! I JUST MIXED IT UP WITH A FEW OTHER FELLAS, THAT'S ALL! NOTHING WORTH MENTIONING!
WHY NOT LET ME BE THE JUDGE OF THAT? JUST OPEN YOUR SHIRT, PARKER, AND I'LL HAVE A LOOK AT YOU!
I CAN'T FLATLY REFUSE WITHOUT AROUSING HIS SUSPICIONS!
A FEW MINUTES LATER...
YOU SEEM SOUND ENOUGH, BUT YOU'RE ON THE VERGE OF COMPLETE EXHAUSTION! YOU SHOULD BE IN BED!
I AM PRETTY TIRED, DOC--BUT I'VE JUST GOT TO FIND OUT ABOUT AUNT MAY, FIRST!
LUCKY FOR ME HE DIDN'T WANT TO CHECK MY BLOOD!
HERE, DRINK THIS, SON! IT'LL RELAX YOU A BIT--AND REMEMBER--GET SOME REST AS SOON AS POSSIBLE!
DOC, ONCE I LEAVE HERE, NOBODY'LL HAVE TO TELL ME TWICE!
DOCTOR--WE HAVE THE FINAL SERIES OF TEST RESULTS ON MAY PARKER! WILL YOU LOOK AT THEM NOW?
OF COURSE! COME WITH ME, MY BOY!
THIS IS IT!
GOOD NEWS! THE SERUM HAS STOPPED THE BLOOD DETERIORATION! THE REPORTS ARE ALL FAVORABLE!
WITH LUCK, WE EXPECT HER TO PULL THRU!
I DIDN'T LET YOU DOWN THIS TIME, AUNT MAY! I DIDN'T FAIL YOU!
SHE'S MOVING!
PETER...

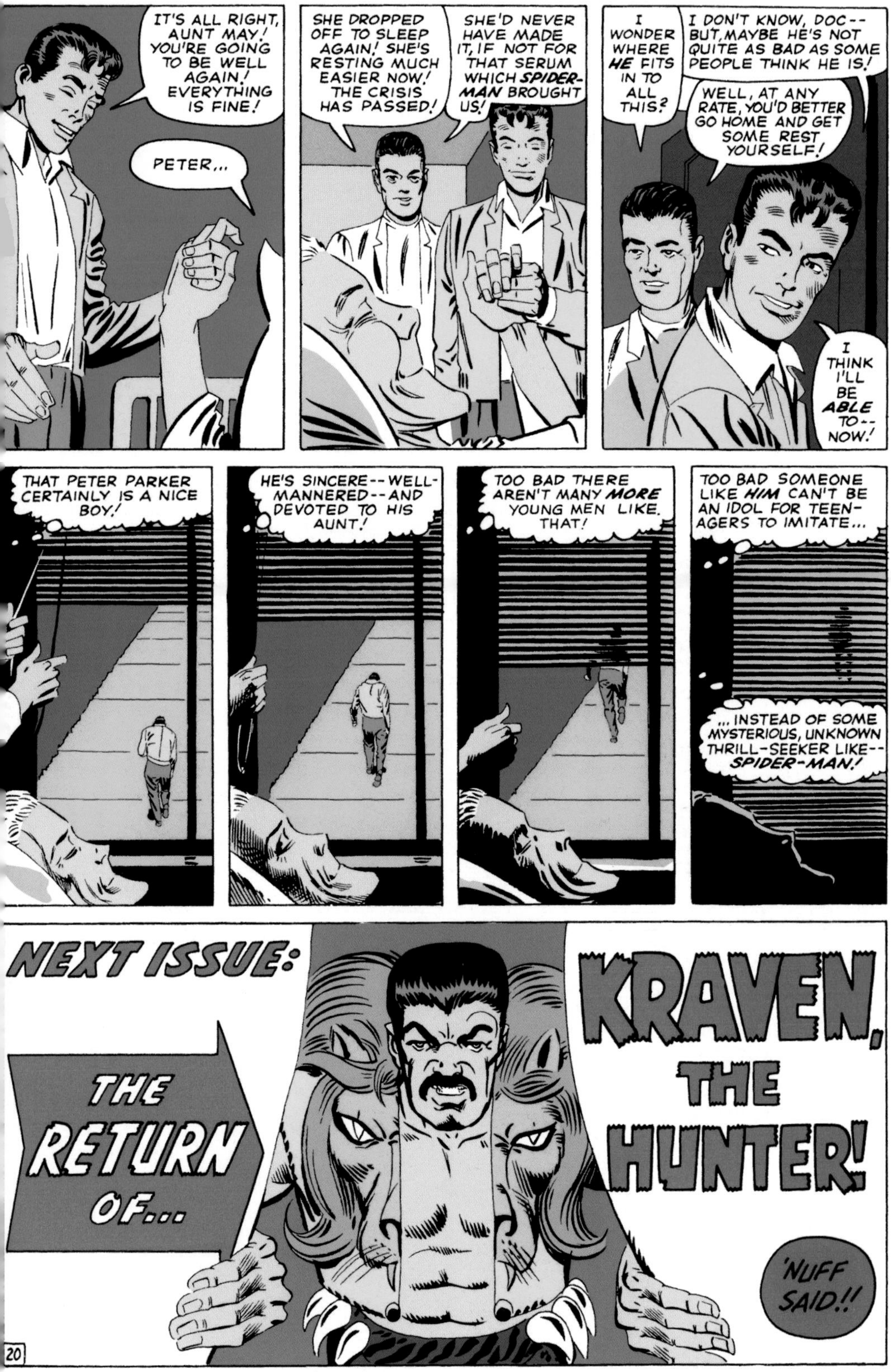
IT'S ALL RIGHT, AUNT MAY! YOU'RE GOING TO BE WELL AGAIN! EVERYTHING IS FINE!
PETER...
SHE DROPPED OFF TO SLEEP AGAIN! SHE'S RESTING MUCH EASIER NOW! THE CRISIS HAS PASSED!
SHE'D NEVER HAVE MADE IT, IF NOT FOR THAT SERUM WHICH SPIDER-MAN BROUGHT US!
I WONDER WHERE HE FITS IN TO ALL THIS?
I DON'T KNOW, DOC-- BUT, MAYBE HE'S NOT QUITE AS BAD AS SOME PEOPLE THINK HE IS!
WELL, AT ANY RATE, YOU'D BETTER GO HOME AND GET SOME REST YOURSELF!
I THINK I'LL BE ABLE TO-- NOW!
THAT PETER PARKER CERTAINLY IS A NICE BOY!
HE'S SINCERE-- WELL-MANNERED-- AND DEVOTED TO HIS AUNT!
TOO BAD THERE AREN'T MANY MORE YOUNG MEN LIKE THAT!
TOO BAD SOMEONE LIKE HIM CAN'T BE AN IDOL FOR TEEN-AGERS TO IMITATE...
... INSTEAD OF SOME MYSTERIOUS, UNKNOWN THRILL-SEEKER LIKE-- SPIDER-MAN!
NEXT ISSUE:
THE RETURN OF...
KRAVEN, THE HUNTER!
'NUFF SAID!!
20

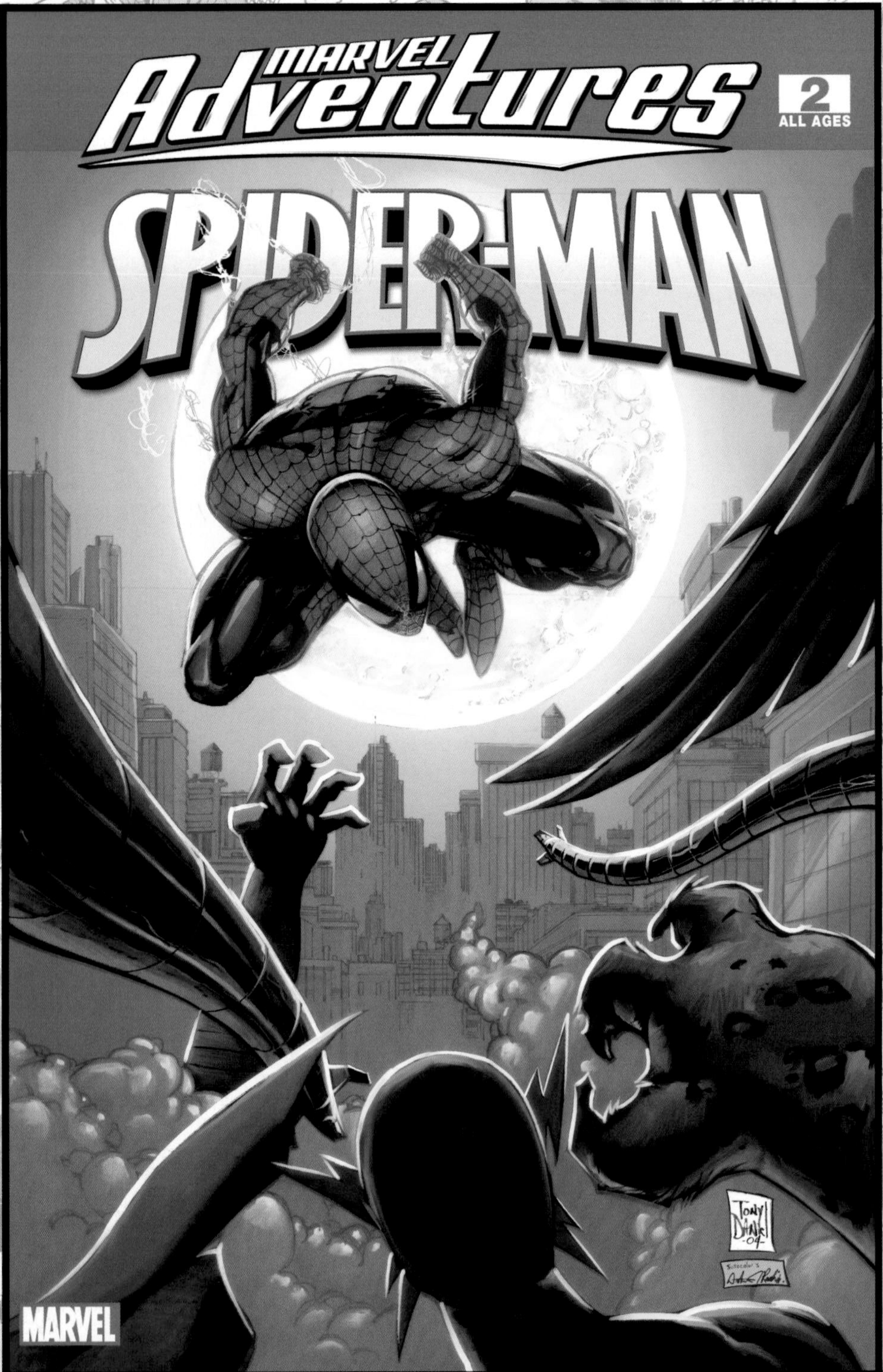
MARVEL
Adventures
2
ALL AGES
SPIDER-MAN
MARVEL

MARVEL ADVENTURES SPIDER-MAN #2

WITH SPIDEY'S POWERS ON THE FRITZ, NOW IS THE WORST TIME FOR SIX OF HIS MOST SINISTER VILLAINS TO BAND TOGETHER TO BRING DOWN THE WALL-CRAWLER!

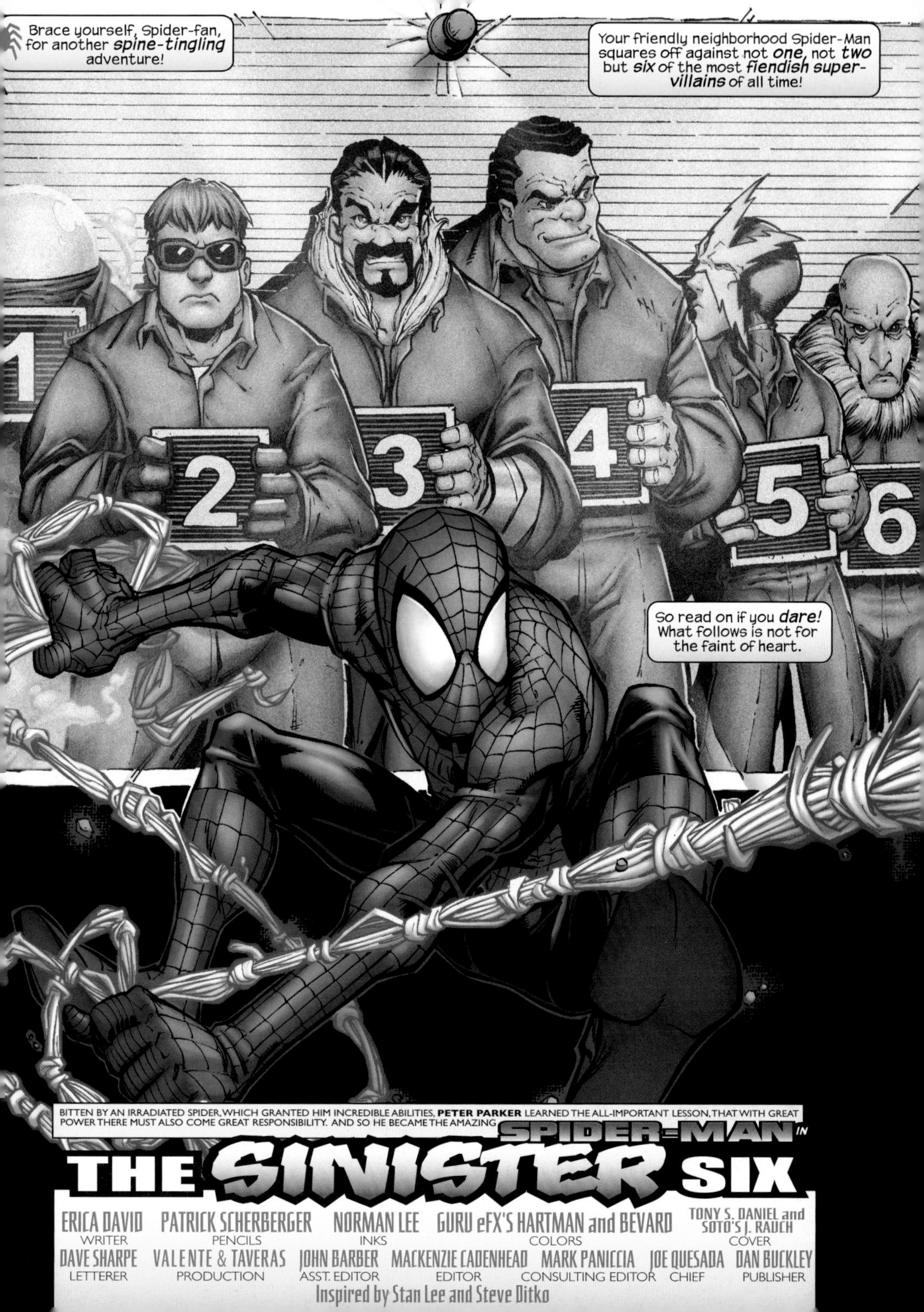

Brace yourself, Spider-fan, for another spine-tingling adventure!
Your friendly neighborhood Spider-Man squares off against not one, not two but six of the most fiendish super-villains of all time!
1
2
3
4
5
6
So read on if you dare! What follows is not for the faint of heart.
BITTEN BY AN IRRADIATED SPIDER, WHICH GRANTED HIM INCREDIBLE ABILITIES, PETER PARKER LEARNED THE ALL-IMPORTANT LESSON, THAT WITH GREAT POWER THERE MUST ALSO COME GREAT RESPONSIBILITY. AND SO HE BECAME THE AMAZING
SPIDER-MAN IN
THE SINISTER SIX
ERICA DAVID WRITER
PATRICK SCHERBERGER PENCILS
NORMAN LEE INKS
GURU eFX'S HARTMAN and BEVARD COLORS
TONY S. DANIEL and SOTO'S J. RAUCH COVER
DAVE SHARPE LETTERER
VALENTE & TAVERAS PRODUCTION
JOHN BARBER ASST. EDITOR
MACKENZIE CADENHEAD EDITOR
MARK PANICCIA CONSULTING EDITOR
JOE QUESADA CHIEF
DAN BUCKLEY PUBLISHER
Inspired by Stan Lee and Steve Ditko

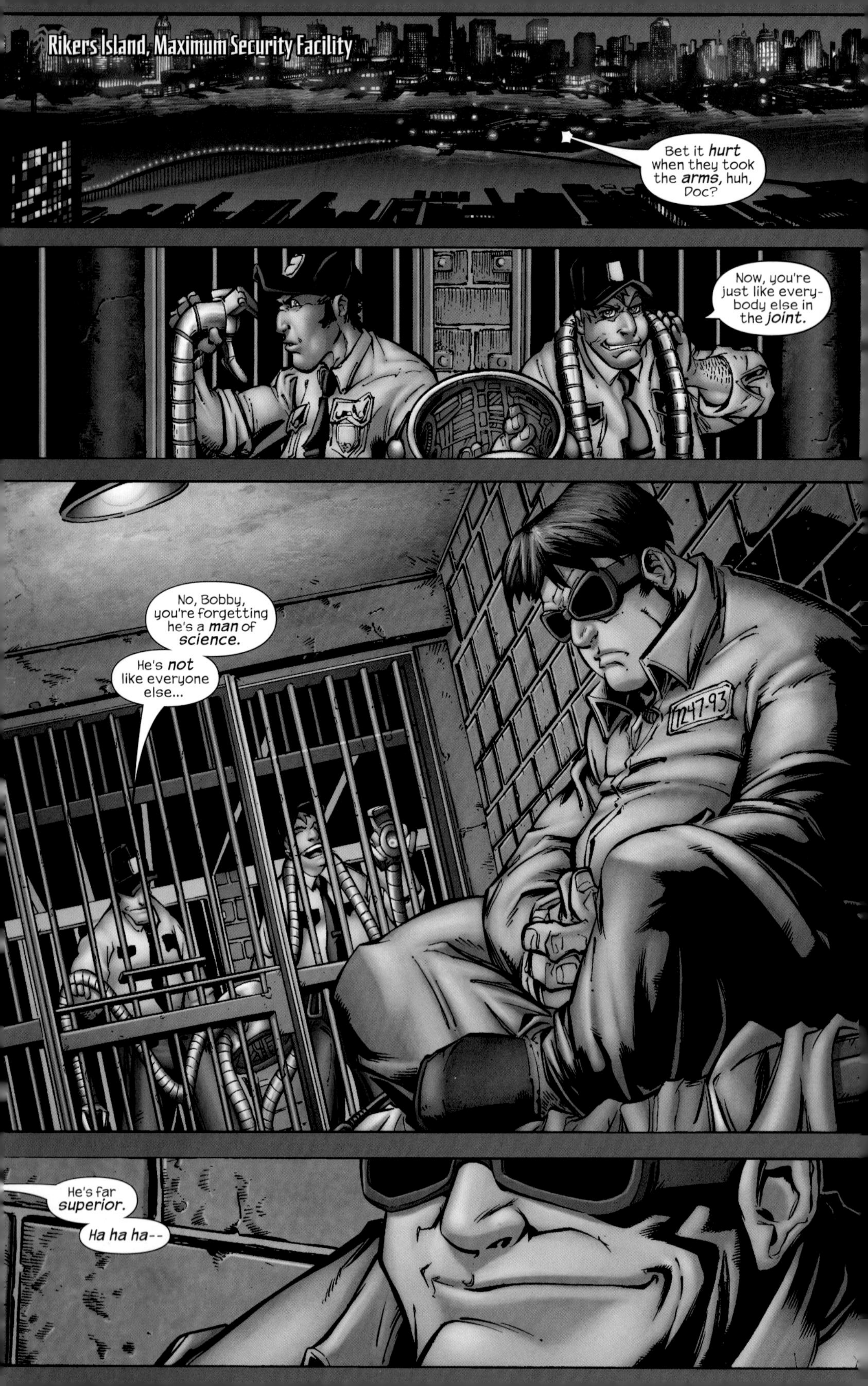
Rikers Island, Maximum Security Facility
Bet it hurt when they took the arms, huh, Doc?
Now, you're just like every-body else in the joint.
No, Bobby, you're forgetting he's a man of science.
He's not like everyone else...
1247-93
He's far superior.
Ha ha ha--

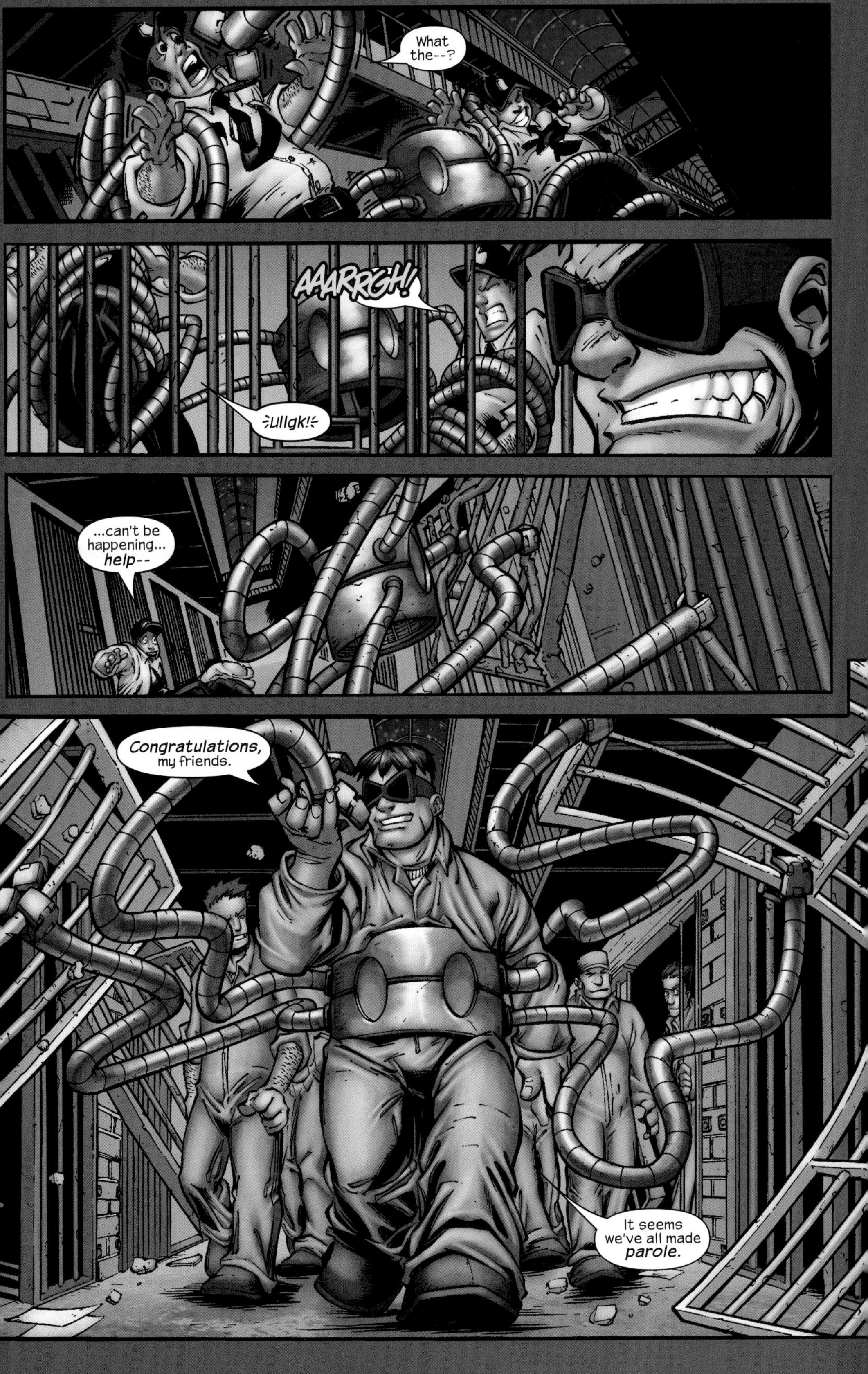
What the--?
AAARRGH!
Ullgk!
...can't be happening... help--
Congratulations, my friends.
It seems we've all made parole.

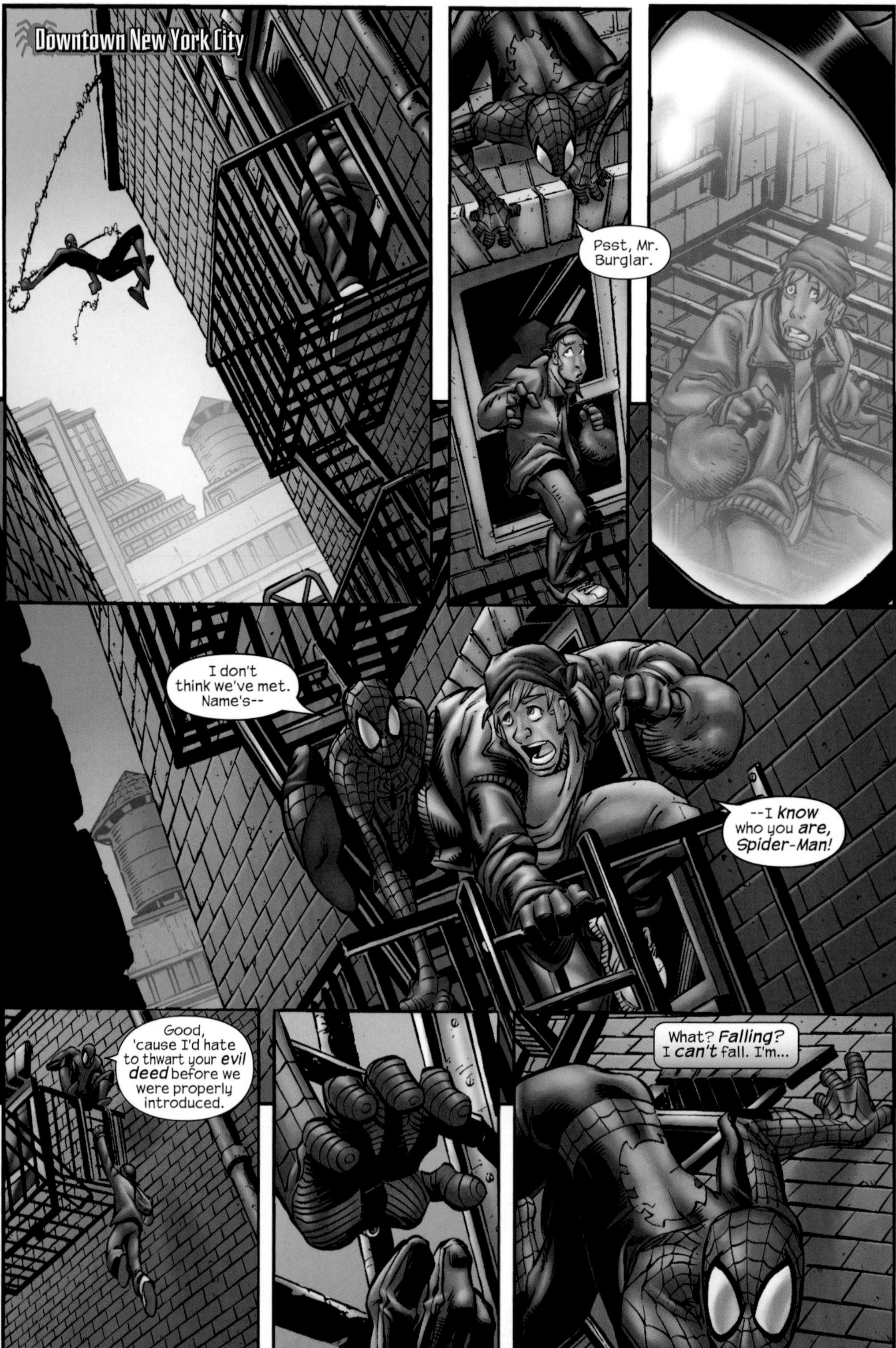
Downtown New York City
Psst, Mr. Burglar.
I don't think we've met. Name's--
--I *know* who you *are*, Spider-Man!
Good, 'cause I'd hate to thwart your *evil deed* before we were properly introduced.
What? *Falling?* I *can't* fall. I'm...

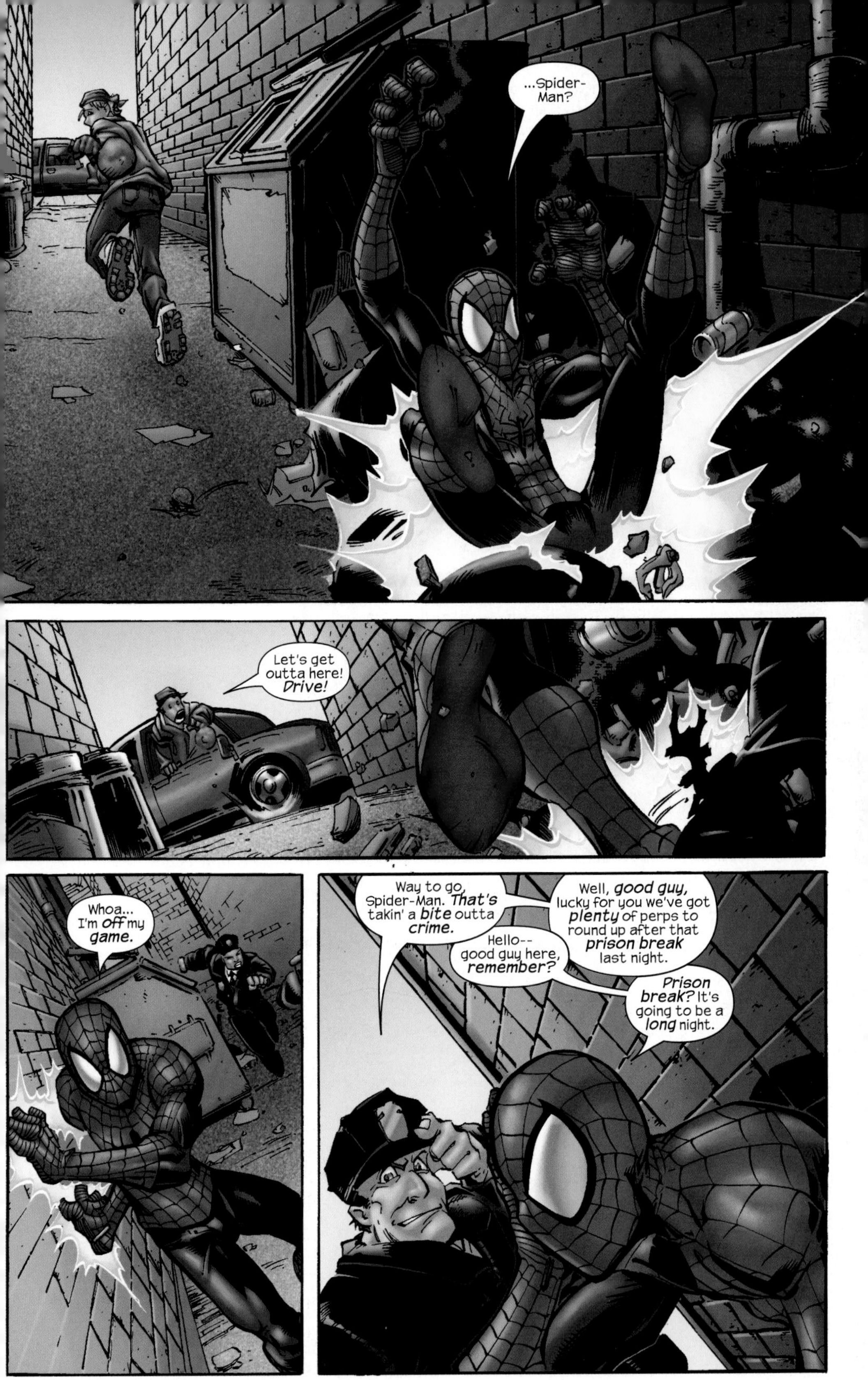
...Spider-Man?
Let's get outta here! Drive!
Whoa... I'm off my game.
Way to go, Spider-Man. That's takin' a bite outta crime.
Hello-- good guy here, remember?
Well, good guy, lucky for you we've got plenty of perps to round up after that prison break last night.
Prison break? It's going to be a long night.

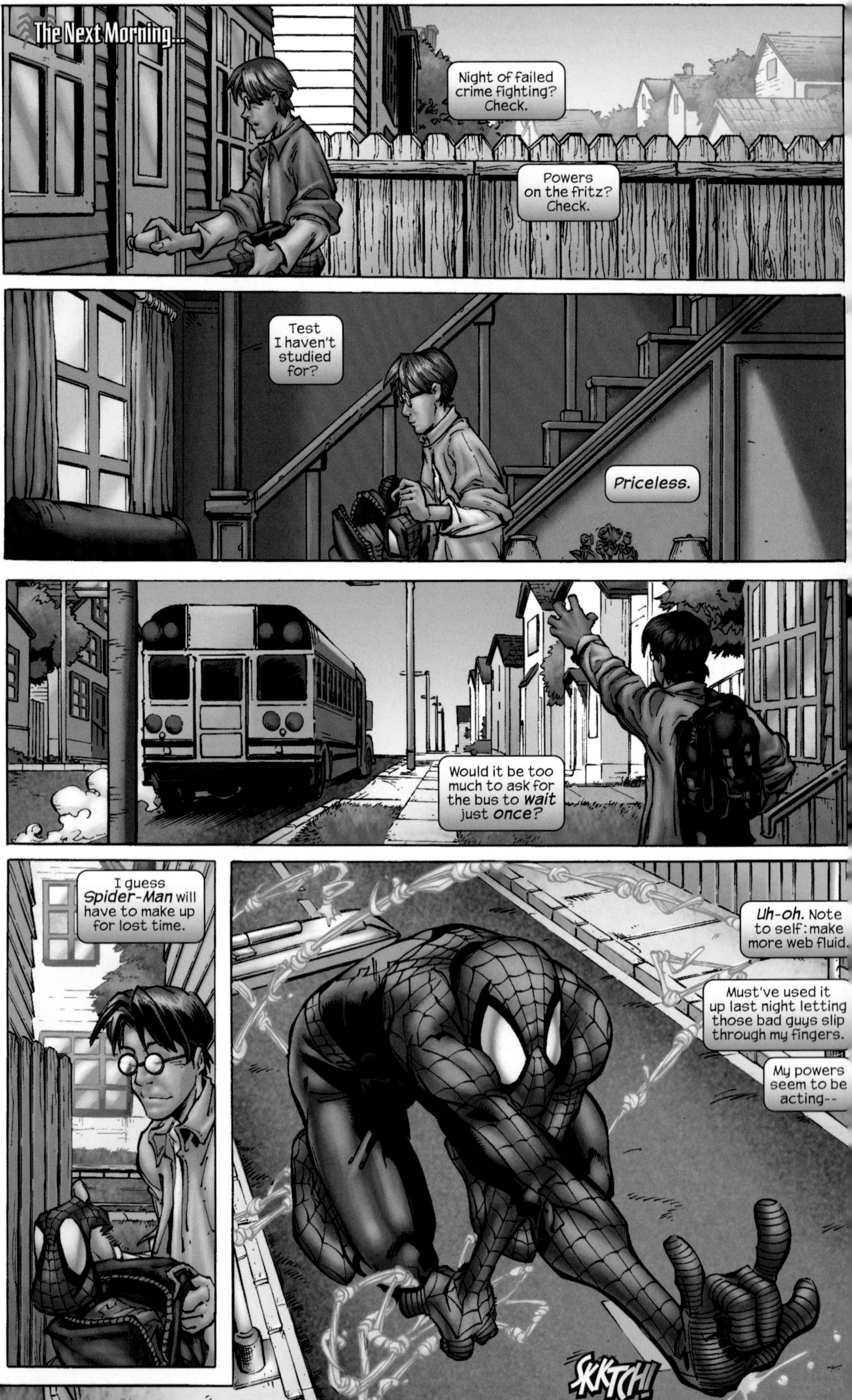
The Next Morning...
Night of failed crime fighting? Check.
Powers on the fritz? Check.
Test I haven't studied for?
Priceless.
Would it be too much to ask for the bus to *wait* just *once?*
I guess *Spider-Man* will have to make up for lost time.
Uh-oh. Note to self: make more web fluid.
Must've used it up last night letting those bad guys slip through my fingers.
My powers seem to be acting--
SKKTCH!

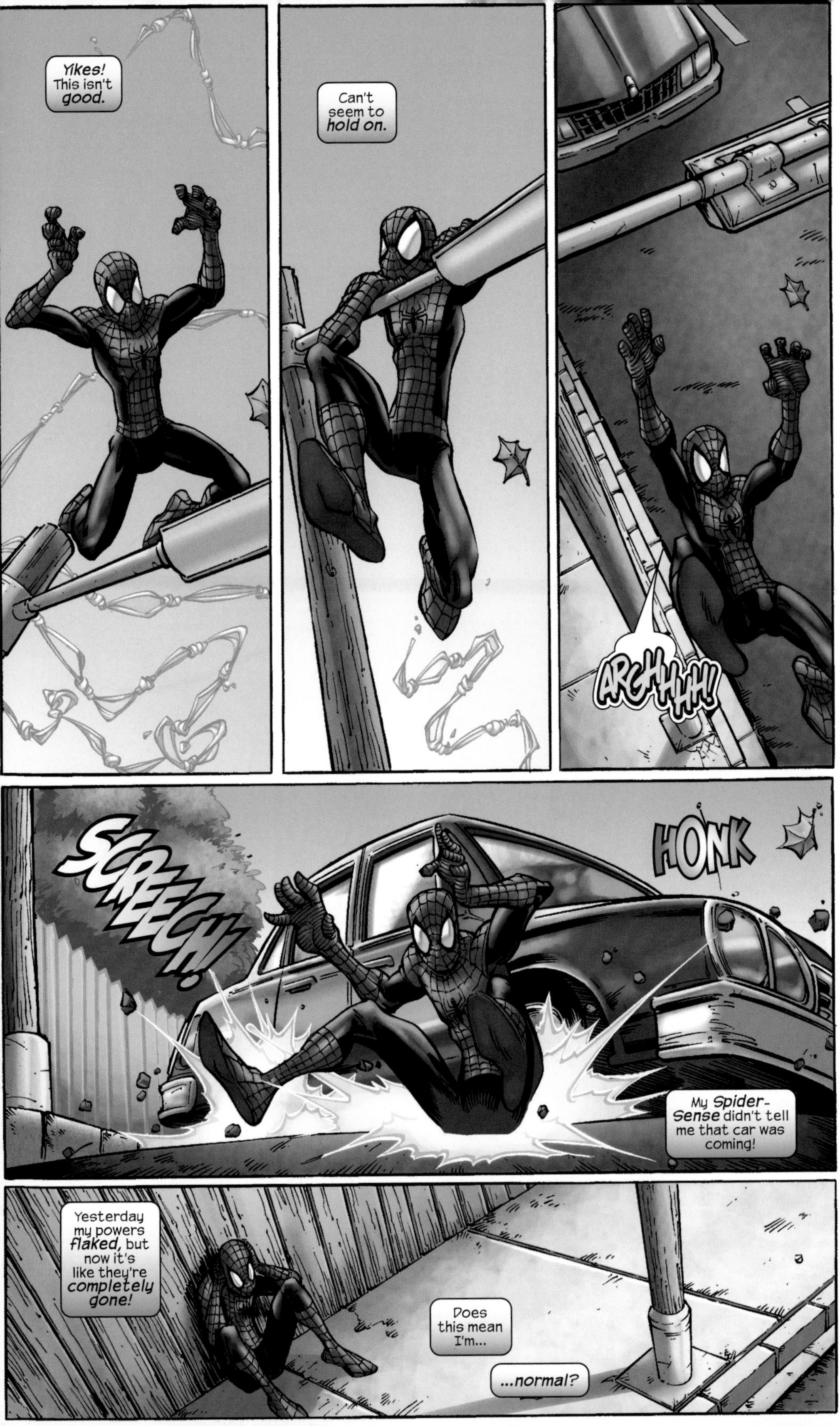
Yikes! This isn't good.
Can't seem to hold on.
ARGHHHH!
SCREECH!
HONK
My Spider-Sense didn't tell me that car was coming!
Yesterday my powers flaked, but now it's like they're completely gone!
Does this mean I'm...
...normal?

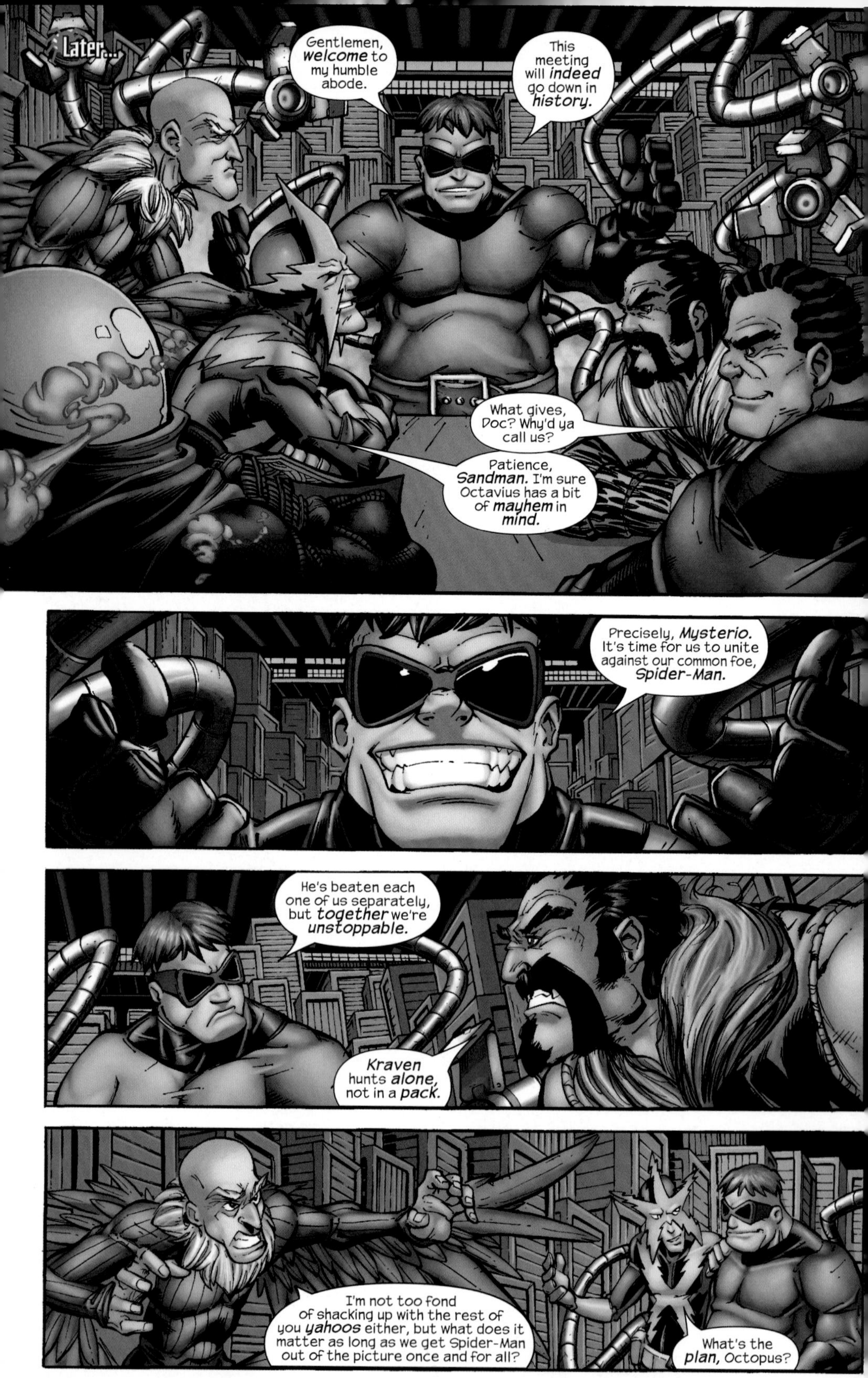
Later...
Gentlemen, welcome to my humble abode.
This meeting will indeed go down in history.
What gives, Doc? Why'd ya call us?
Patience, Sandman. I'm sure Octavius has a bit of mayhem in mind.
Precisely, Mysterio. It's time for us to unite against our common foe, Spider-Man.
He's beaten each one of us separately, but together we're unstoppable.
Kraven hunts alone, not in a pack.
I'm not too fond of shacking up with the rest of you yahoos either, but what does it matter as long as we get Spider-Man out of the picture once and for all?
What's the plan, Octopus?

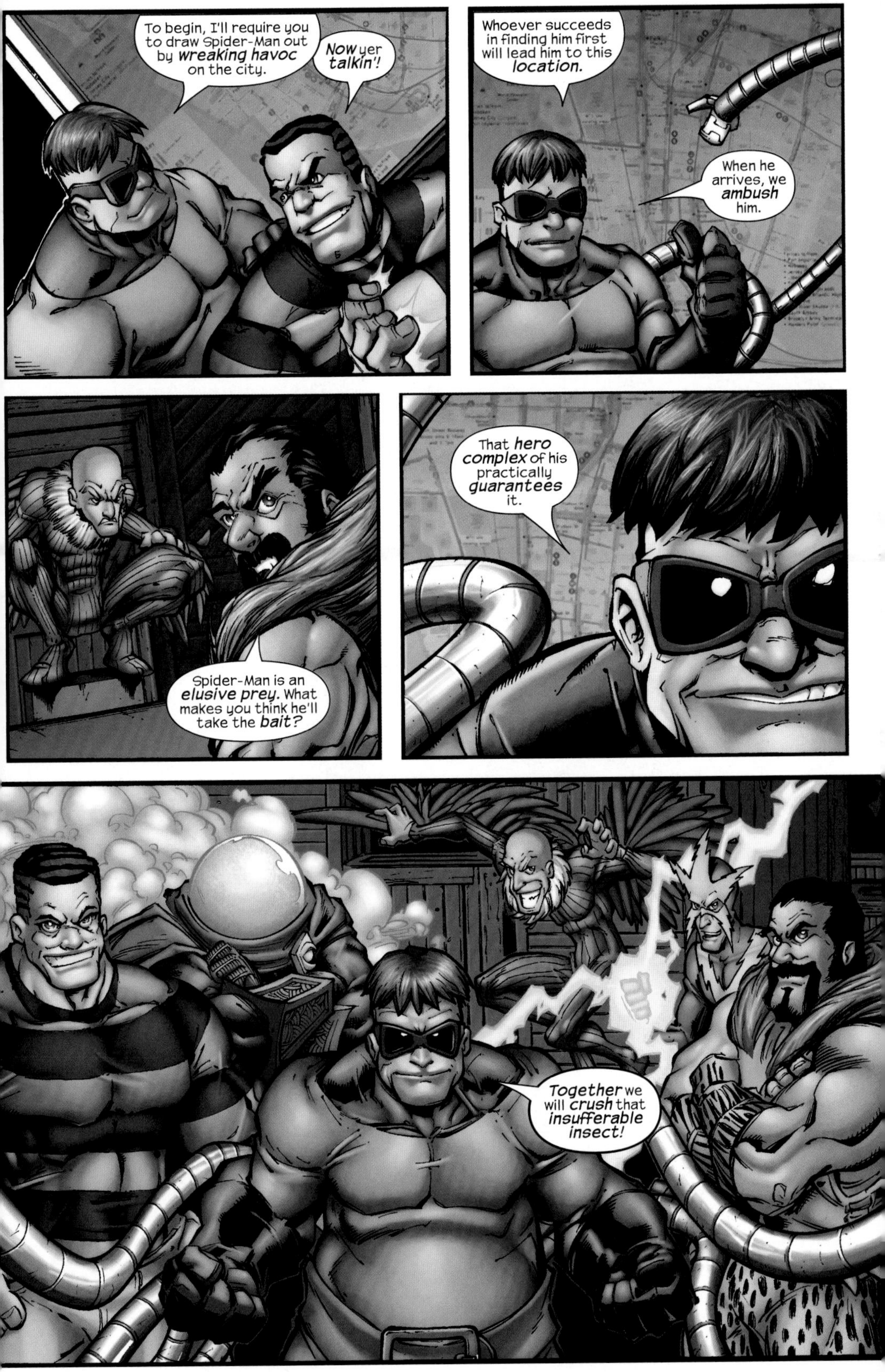
To begin, I'll require you to draw Spider-Man out by *wreaking havoc* on the city.
Now yer *talkin'!*
Whoever succeeds in finding him first will lead him to this *location.*
When he arrives, we *ambush* him.
Spider-Man is an *elusive prey.* What makes you think he'll take the *bait?*
That *hero complex* of his practically *guarantees* it.
Together we will *crush* that *insufferable insect!*

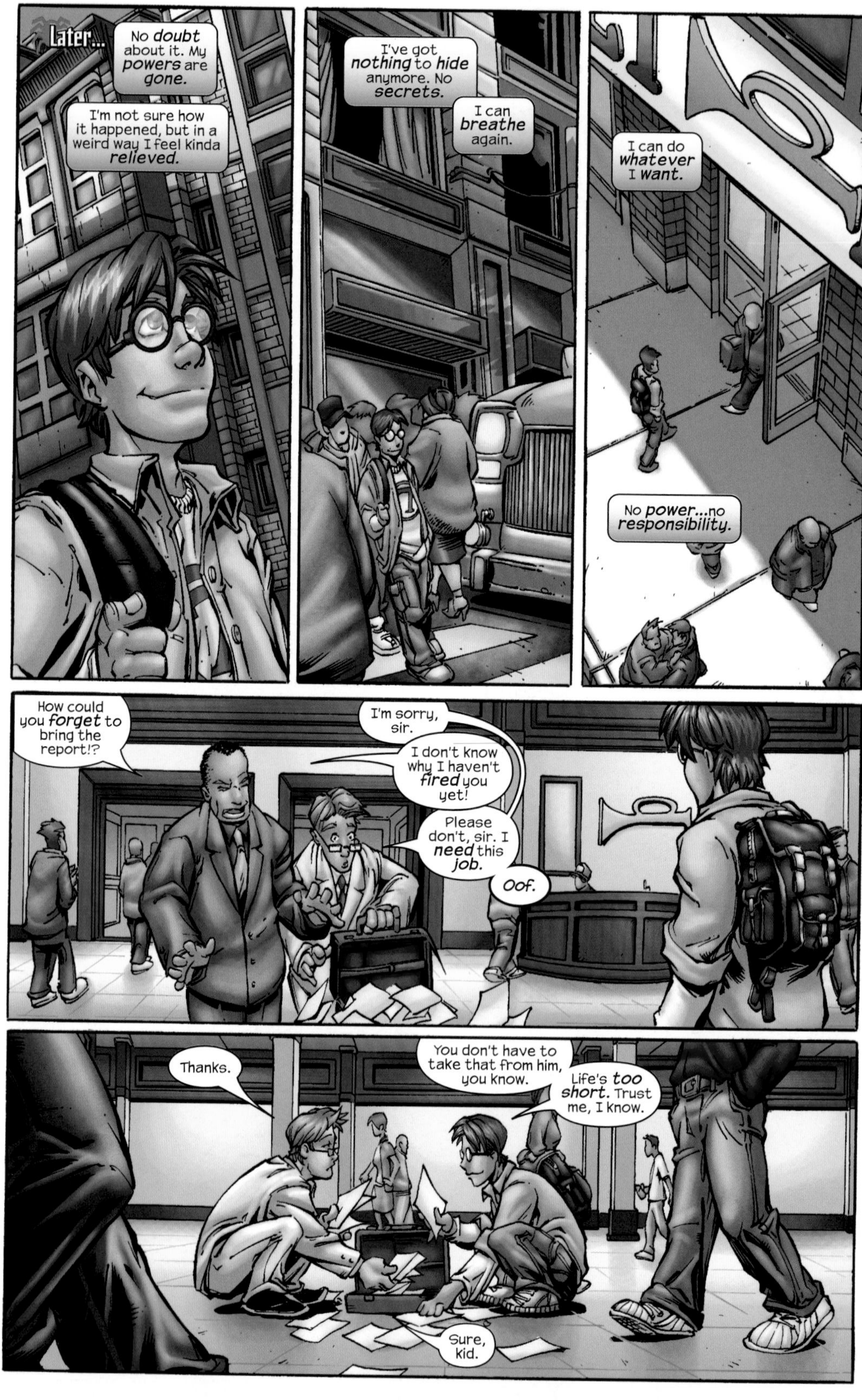
Later...
No doubt about it. My powers are gone.
I'm not sure how it happened, but in a weird way I feel kinda relieved.
I've got nothing to hide anymore. No secrets.
I can breathe again.
I can do whatever I want.
No power...no responsibility.
How could you forget to bring the report!?
I'm sorry, sir.
I don't know why I haven't fired you yet!
Please don't, sir. I need this job.
Oof.
Thanks.
You don't have to take that from him, you know.
Life's too short. Trust me, I know.
Sure, kid.

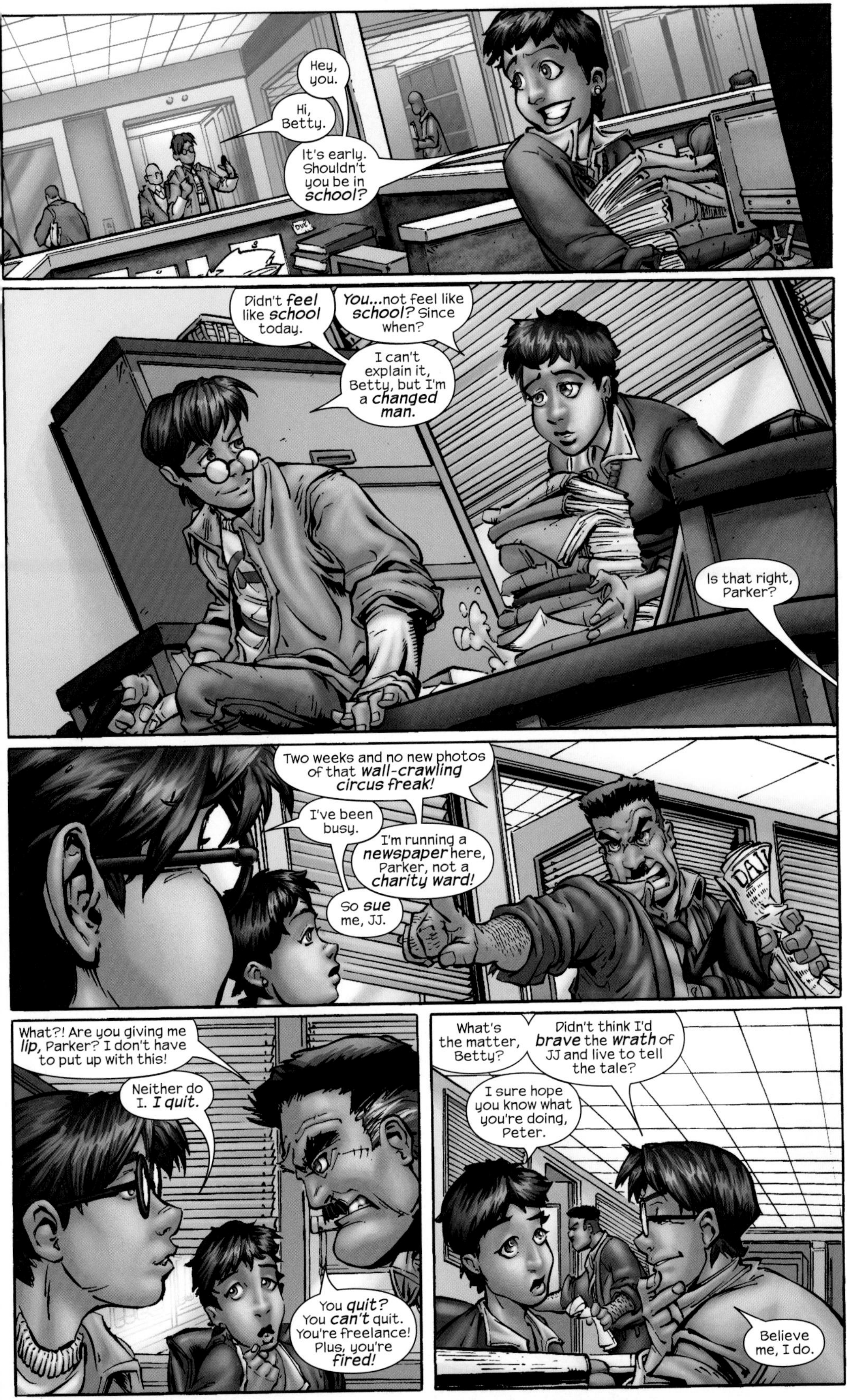
Hey, you.
Hi, Betty.
It's early. Shouldn't you be in *school?*
Didn't *feel* like *school* today.
*You...*not feel like *school?* Since when?
I can't explain it, Betty, but I'm a *changed man.*
Is that right, Parker?
Two weeks and no new photos of that *wall-crawling circus freak!*
I've been busy.
I'm running a *newspaper* here, Parker, not a *charity ward!*
So *sue* me, JJ.
What?! Are you giving me *lip,* Parker? I don't have to put up with this!
Neither do I. *I quit.*
You *quit?* You *can't* quit. You're freelance! Plus, you're *fired!*
What's the matter, Betty?
Didn't think I'd *brave* the *wrath* of JJ and live to tell the tale?
I sure hope you know what you're doing, Peter.
Believe me, I do.

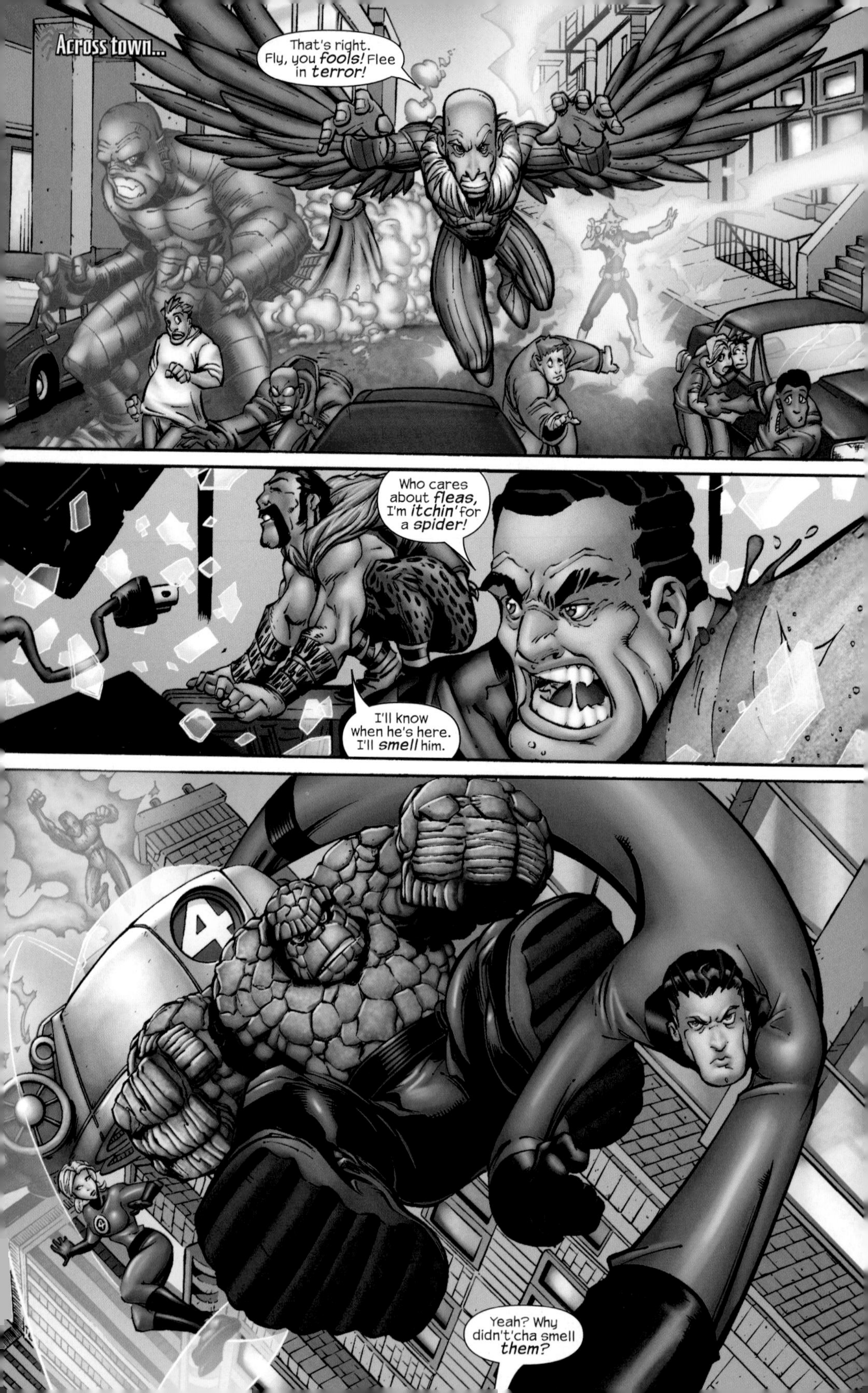
Across town...
That's right. Fly, you fools! Flee in terror!
Who cares about fleas, I'm itchin' for a spider!
I'll know when he's here. I'll smell him.
Yeah? Why didn't'cha smell them?

The Fantastic *Four!* I don't believe we invited *you* to our party.

Guess we'll have to *crash* it, then.

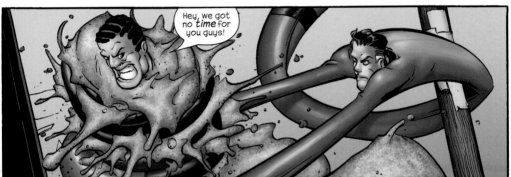

Hey, we got no *time* for you guys!

Well, *I* got time for *you!*

Clobberin' *time,* that is!

What Thing *means* to say is that you can't go around *terrorizing* people!

Not on *our* watch.

Save your *energy,* boys. They're not *worth* it.

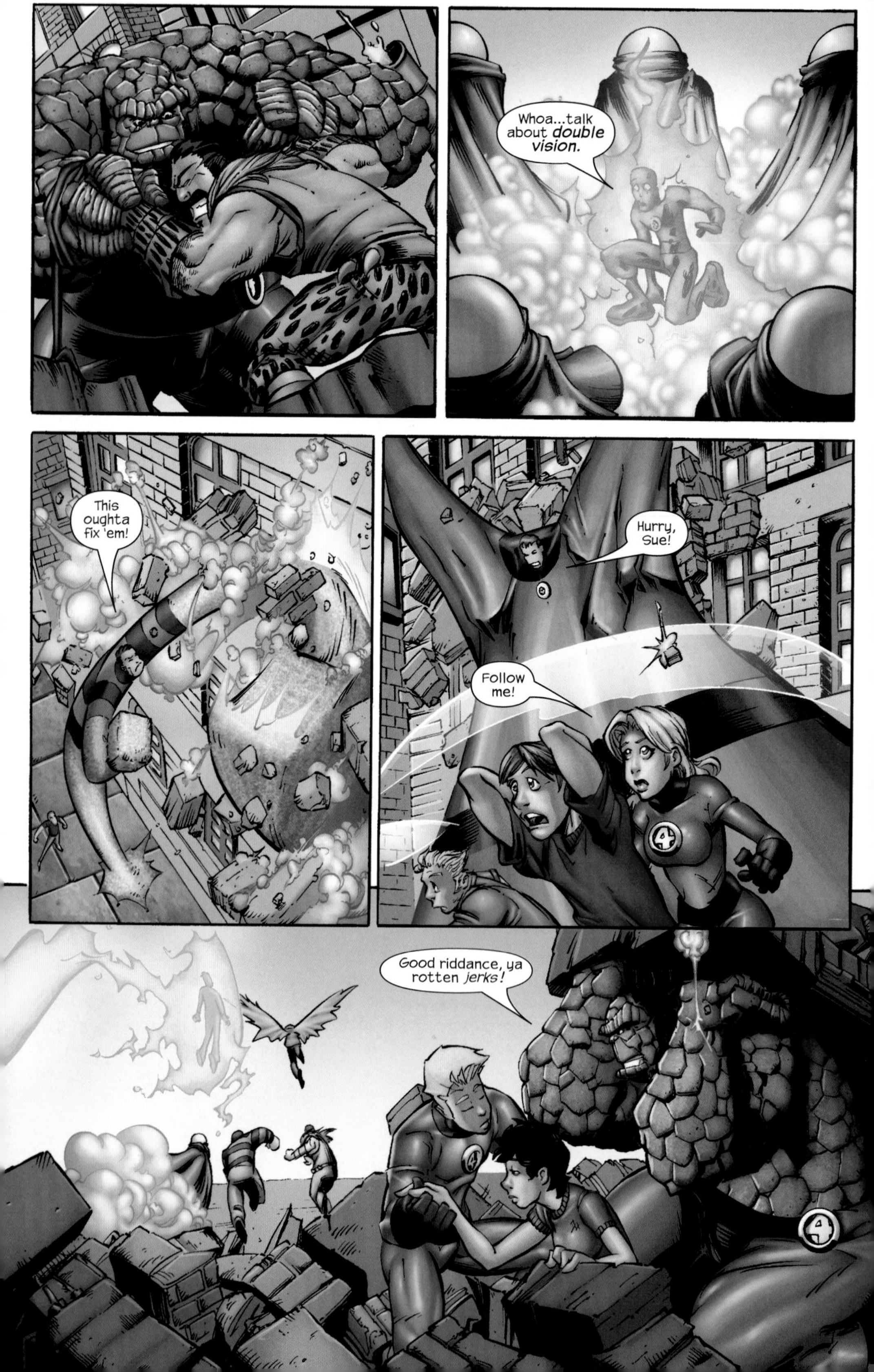
Whoa...talk about *double vision.*
This oughta fix 'em!
Hurry, Sue!
Follow me!
Good riddance, ya rotten *jerks!*

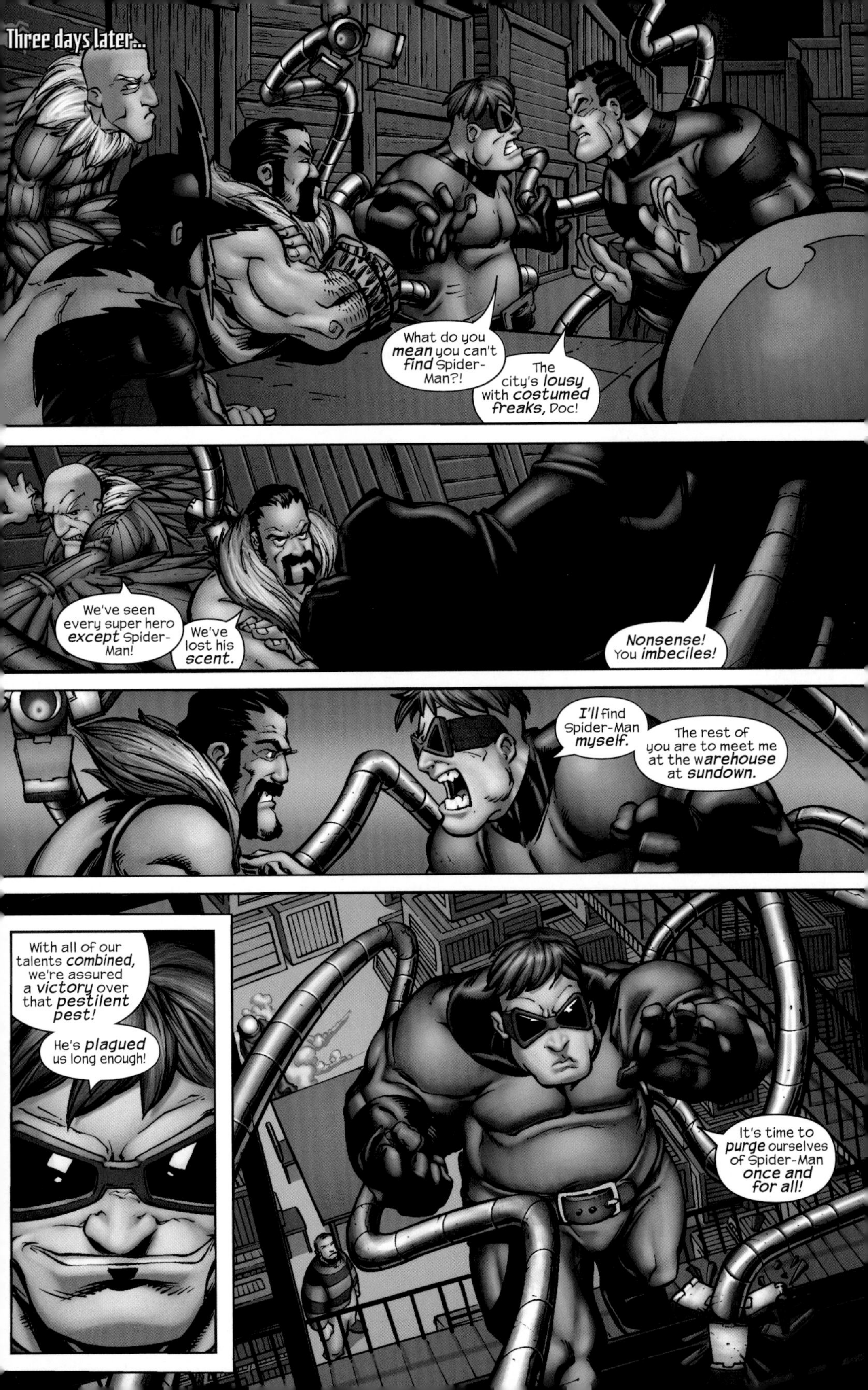

Three days later...
What do you *mean* you can't *find* Spider-Man?!
The city's *lousy* with *costumed freaks,* Doc!
We've seen every super hero *except* Spider-Man!
We've lost his *scent.*
Nonsense! You *imbeciles!*
I'll find Spider-Man *myself.*
The rest of you are to meet me at the w*arehouse* at *sundown.*
With all of our talents *combined,* we're assured a *victory* over that *pestilent pest!*
He's *plagued* us long enough!
It's time to *purge* ourselves of Spider-Man *once and for all!*

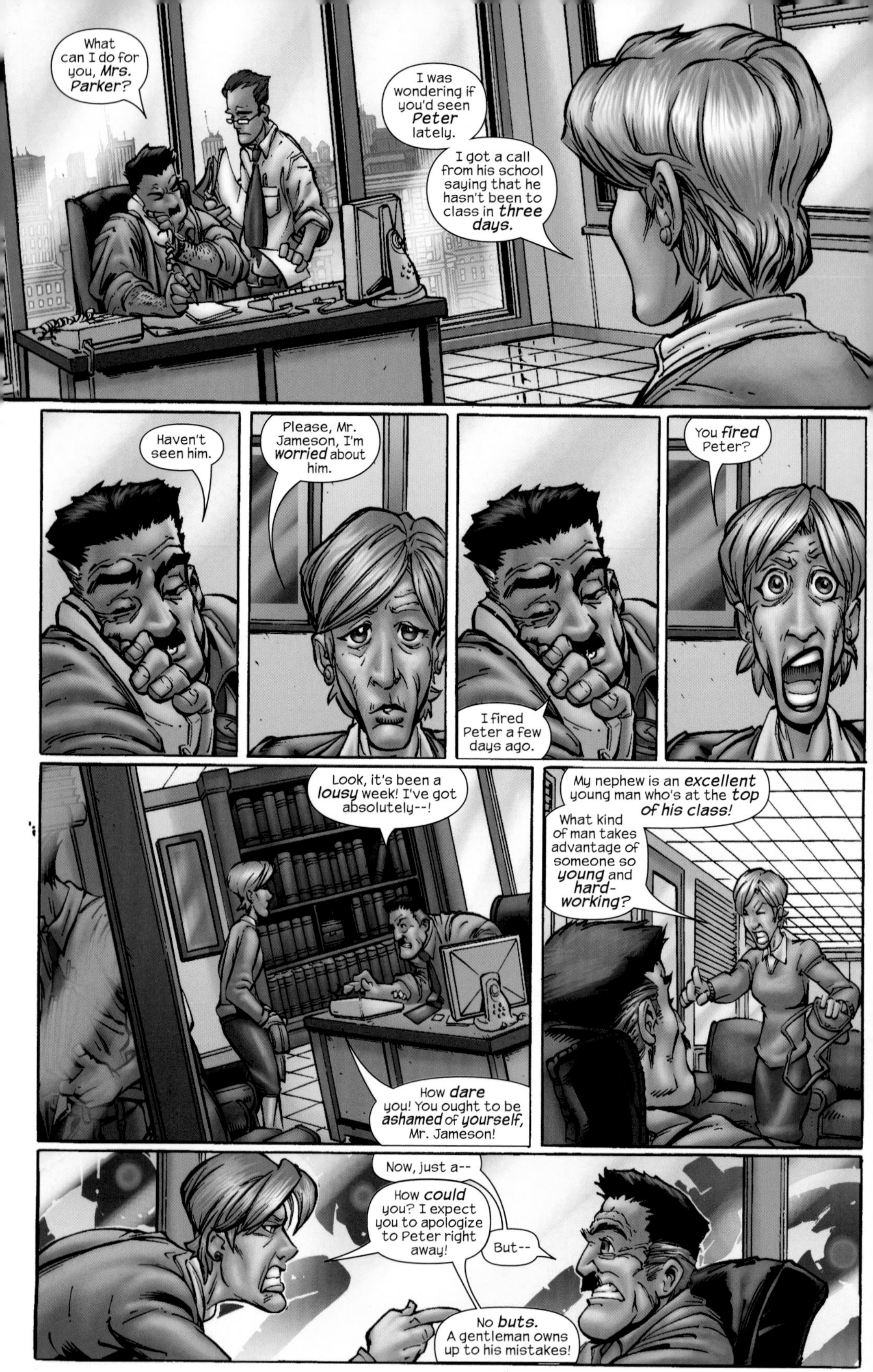
What can I do for you, Mrs. Parker?
I was wondering if you'd seen Peter lately.
I got a call from his school saying that he hasn't been to class in three days.
Haven't seen him.
Please, Mr. Jameson, I'm worried about him.
I fired Peter a few days ago.
You fired Peter?
Look, it's been a lousy week! I've got absolutely--!
How dare you! You ought to be ashamed of yourself, Mr. Jameson!
My nephew is an excellent young man who's at the top of his class!
What kind of man takes advantage of someone so young and hard-working?
Now, just a--
How could you? I expect you to apologize to Peter right away!
But--
No buts. A gentleman owns up to his mistakes!

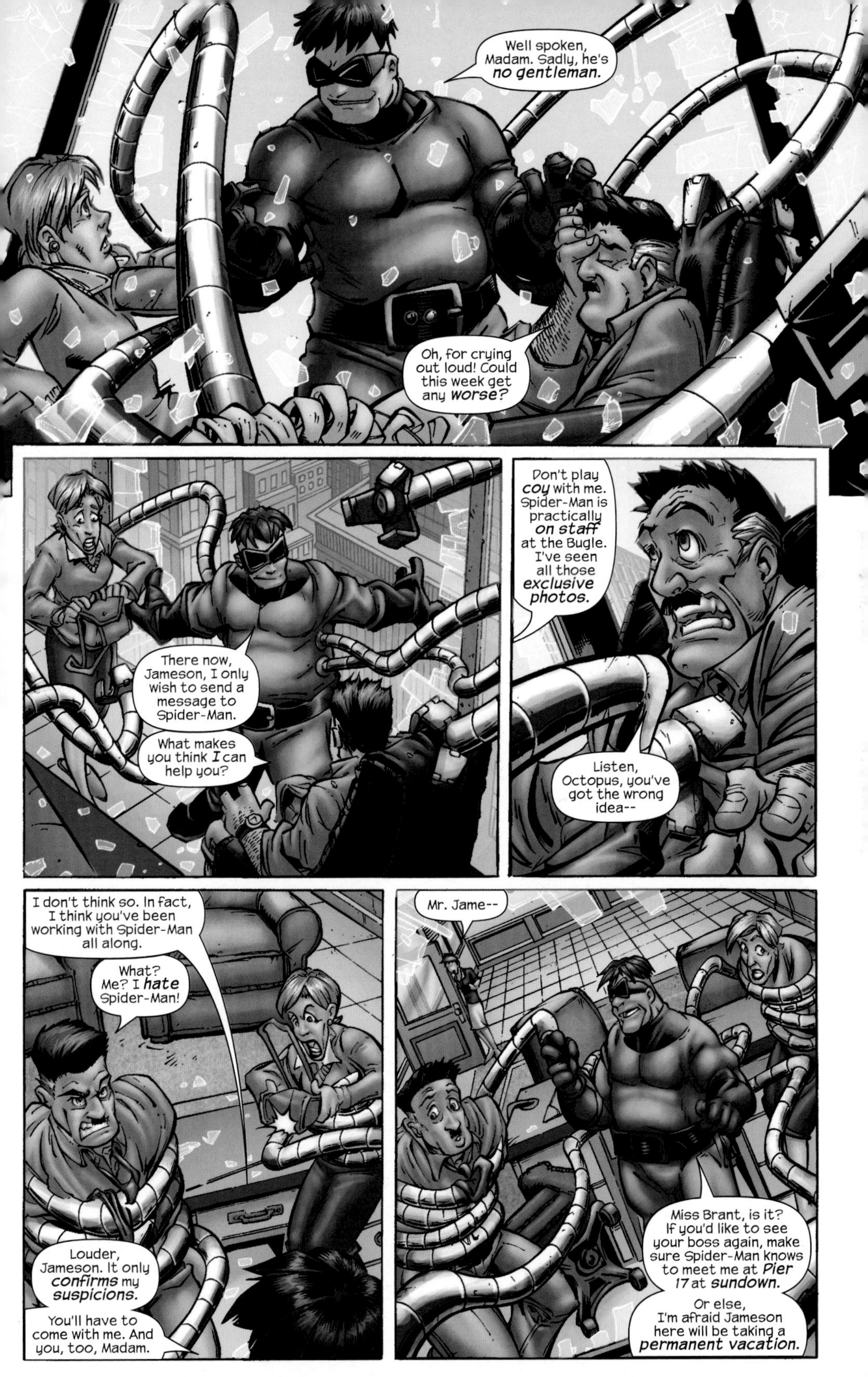
Well spoken, Madam. Sadly, he's *no gentleman.*
Oh, for crying out loud! Could this week get any *worse?*
There now, Jameson, I only wish to send a message to Spider-Man.
What makes you think *I* can help you?
Don't play *coy* with me. Spider-Man is practically *on staff* at the Bugle. I've seen all those *exclusive photos.*
Listen, Octopus, you've got the wrong idea--
I don't think so. In fact, I think you've been working with Spider-Man all along.
What? Me? I *hate* Spider-Man!
Louder, Jameson. It only *confirms* my *suspicions.*
You'll have to come with me. And you, too, Madam.
Mr. Jame--
Miss Brant, is it? If you'd like to see your boss again, make sure Spider-Man knows to meet me at *Pier 17* at *sundown.*
Or else, I'm afraid Jameson here will be taking a *permanent vacation.*

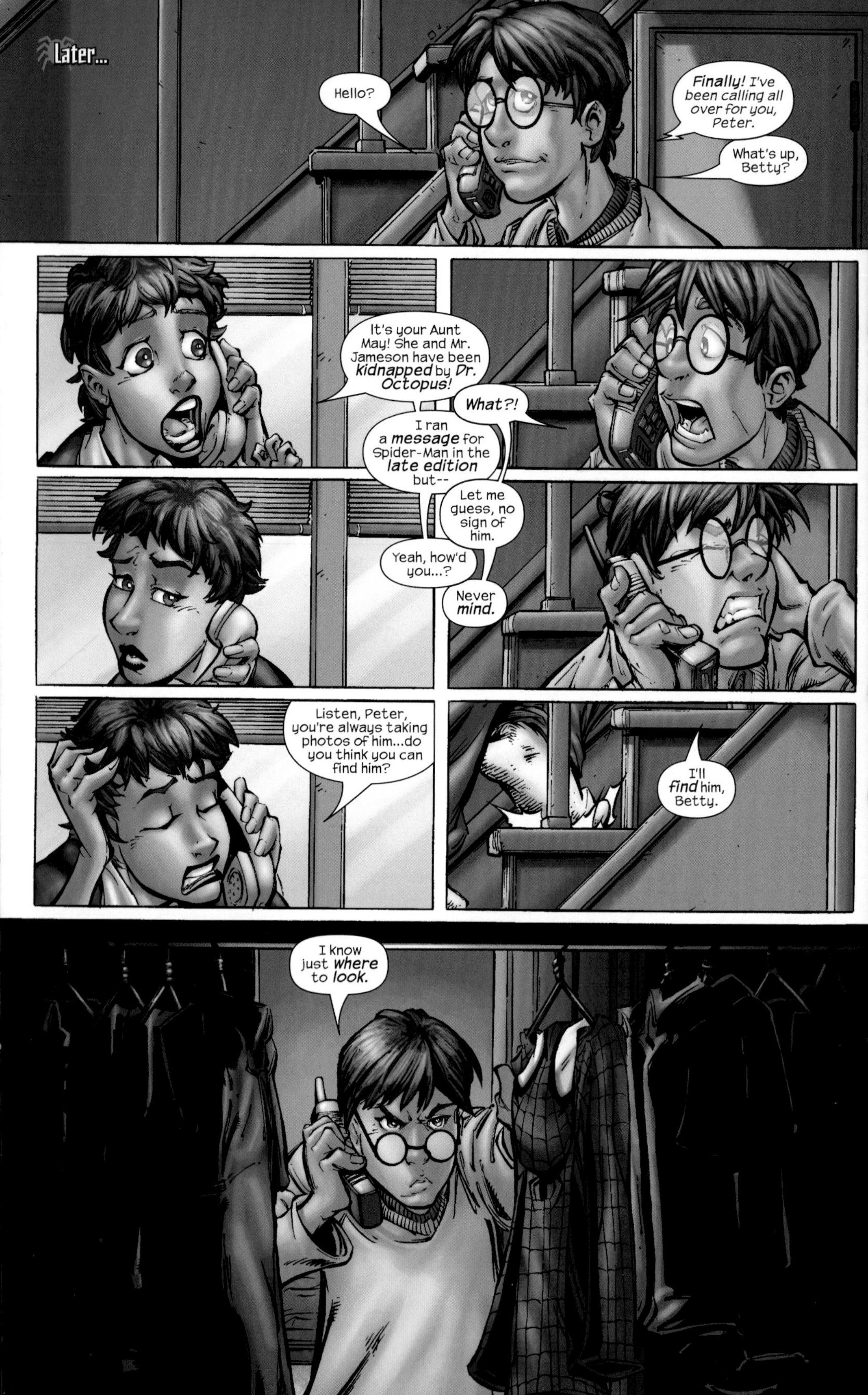
Later...
Hello?
Finally! I've been calling all over for you, Peter.
What's up, Betty?
It's your Aunt May! She and Mr. Jameson have been kidnapped by Dr. Octopus!
What?!
I ran a message for Spider-Man in the late edition but--
Let me guess, no sign of him.
Yeah, how'd you...?
Never mind.
Listen, Peter, you're always taking photos of him...do you think you can find him?
I'll find him, Betty.
I know just where to look.

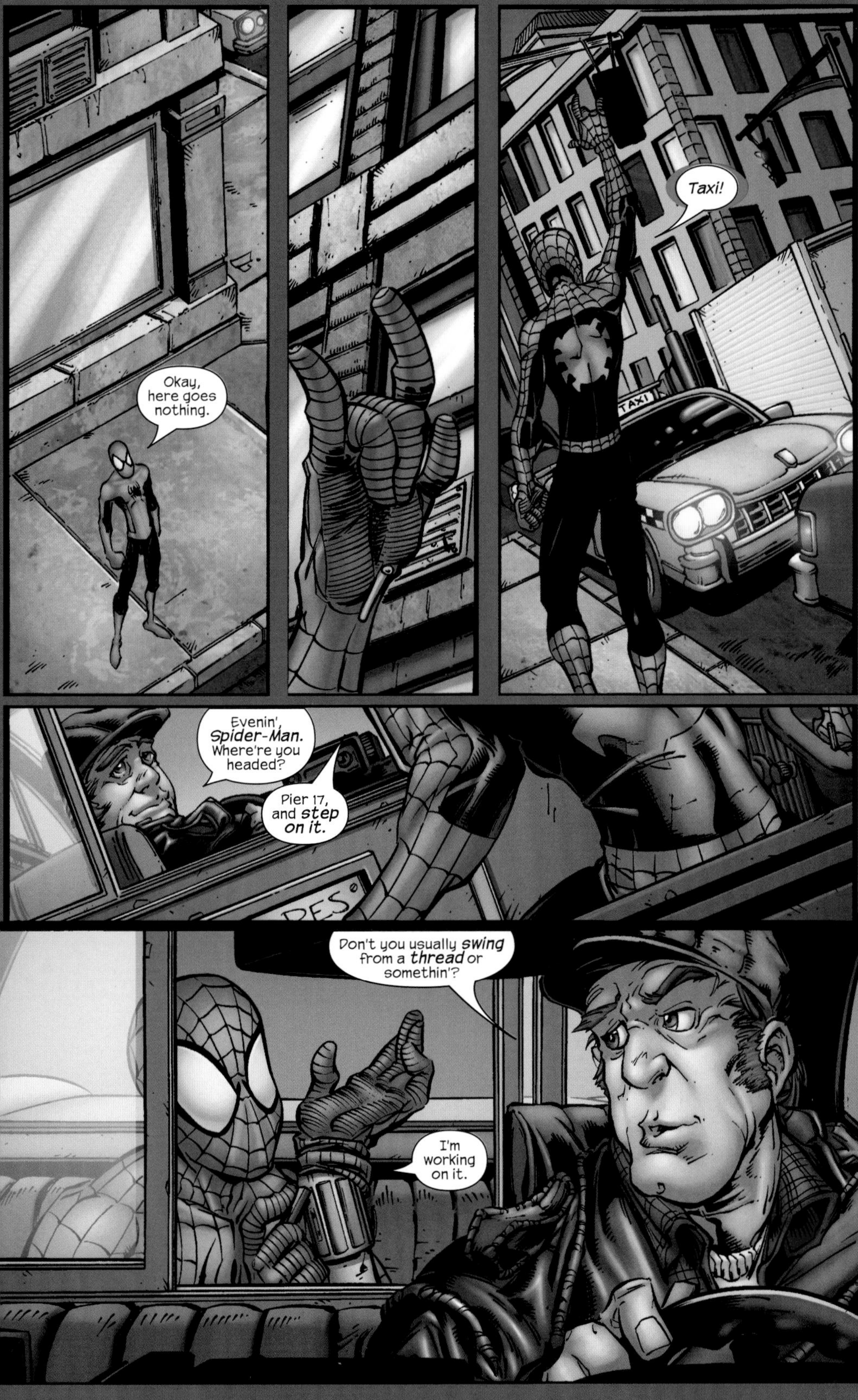
Okay, here goes nothing.
Taxi!
TAXI
Evenin', Spider-Man. Where're you headed?
Pier 17, and step on it.
Don't you usually swing from a thread or somethin'?
I'm working on it.

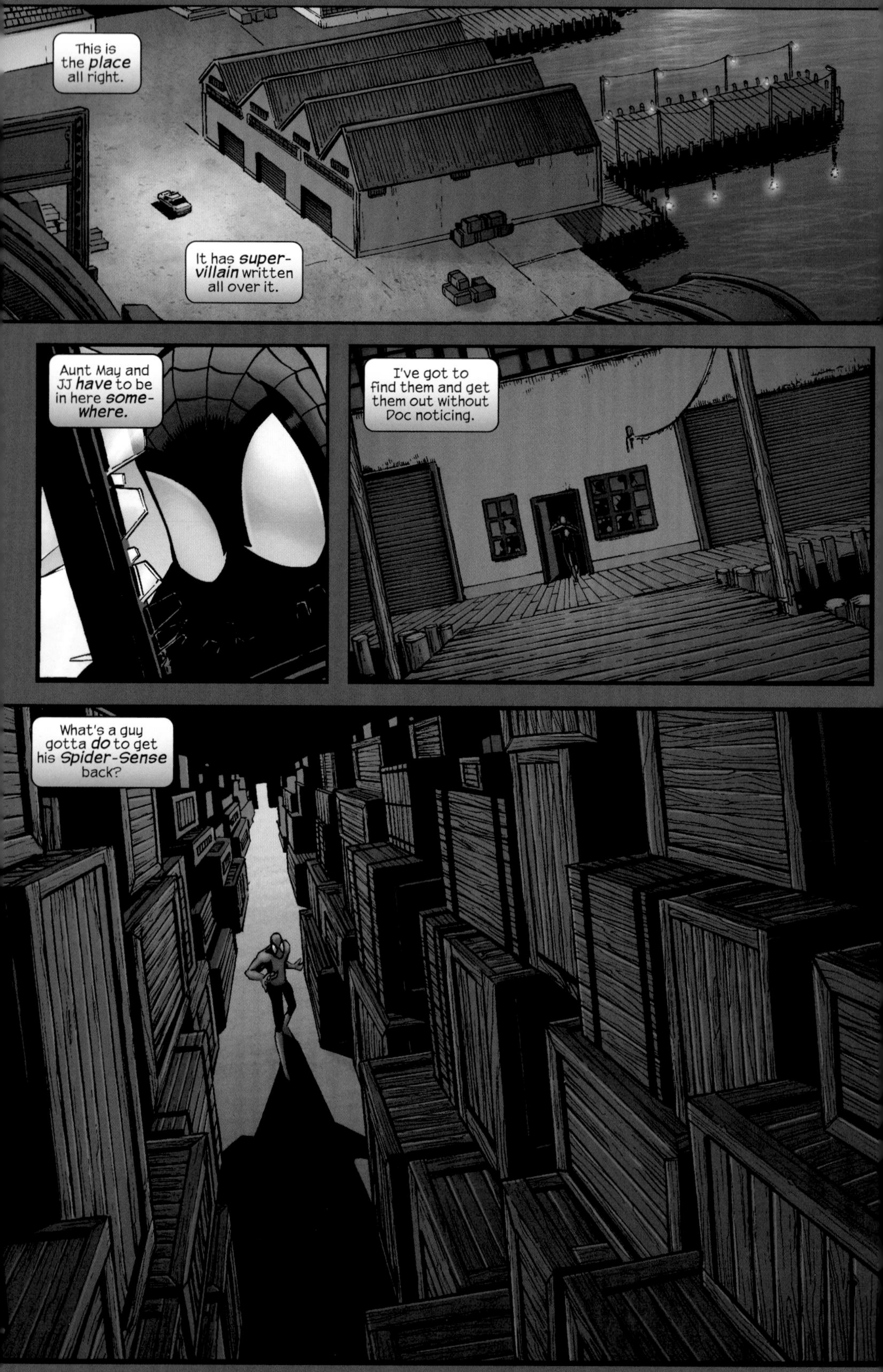

This is the *place* all right.
It has *super-villain* written all over it.
Aunt May and JJ *have* to be in here *some-where.*
I've got to find them and get them out without Doc noticing.
What's a guy gotta *do* to get his *Spider-Sense* back?

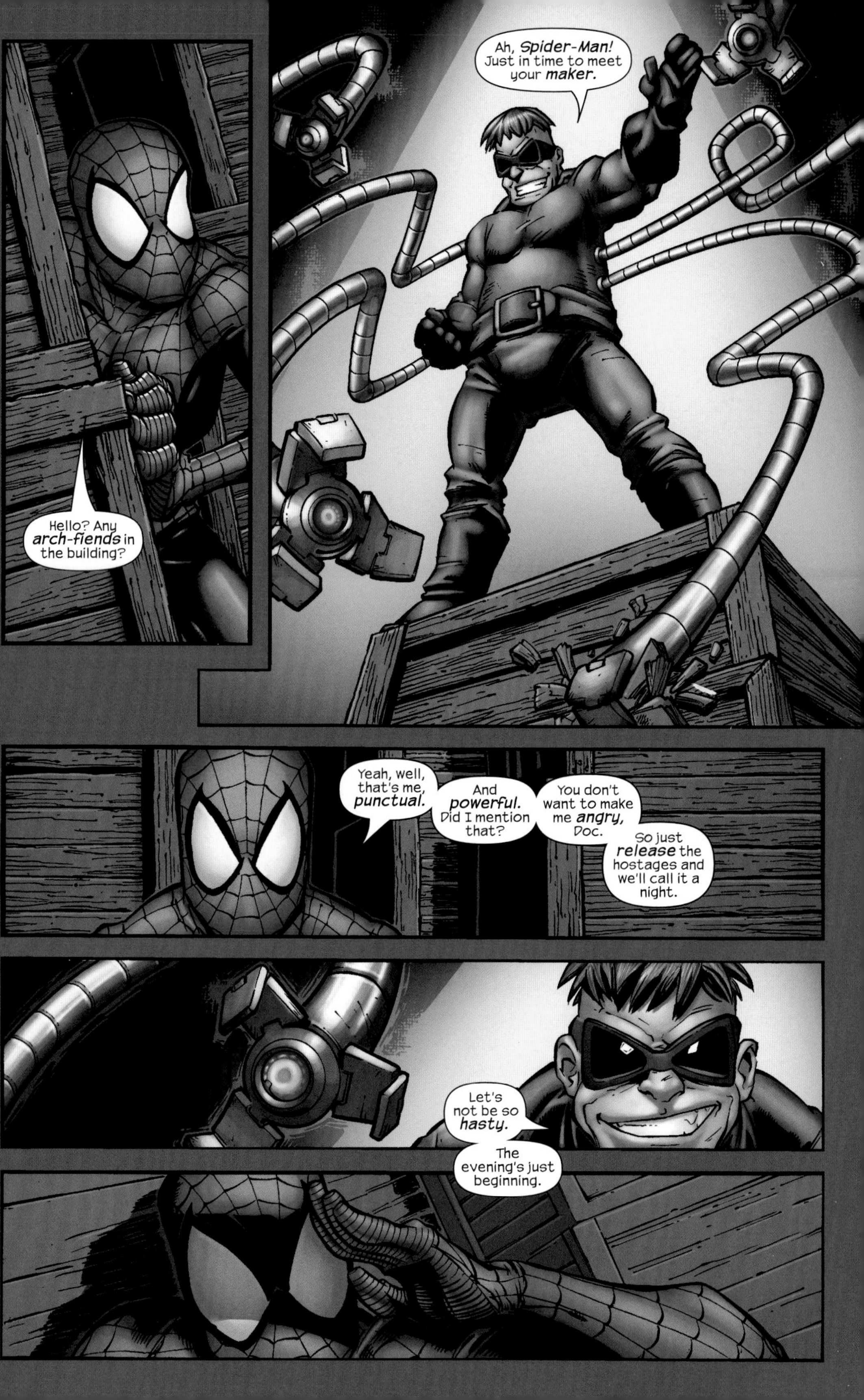
Hello? Any arch-fiends in the building?
Ah, Spider-Man! Just in time to meet your maker.
Yeah, well, that's me, punctual.
And powerful. Did I mention that?
You don't want to make me angry, Doc.
So just release the hostages and we'll call it a night.
Let's not be so hasty.
The evening's just beginning.

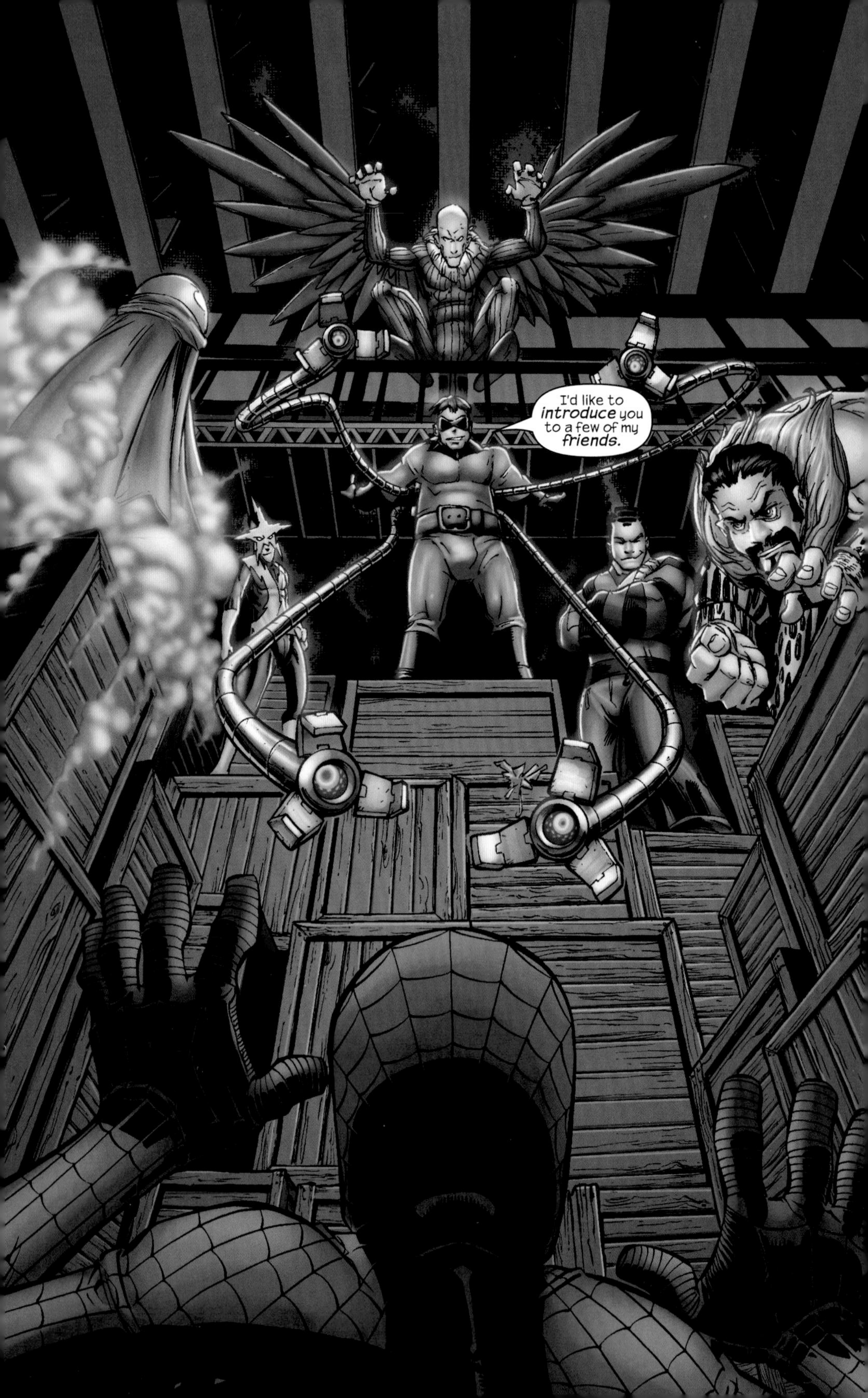
I'd like to *introduce* you to a few of my *friends.*

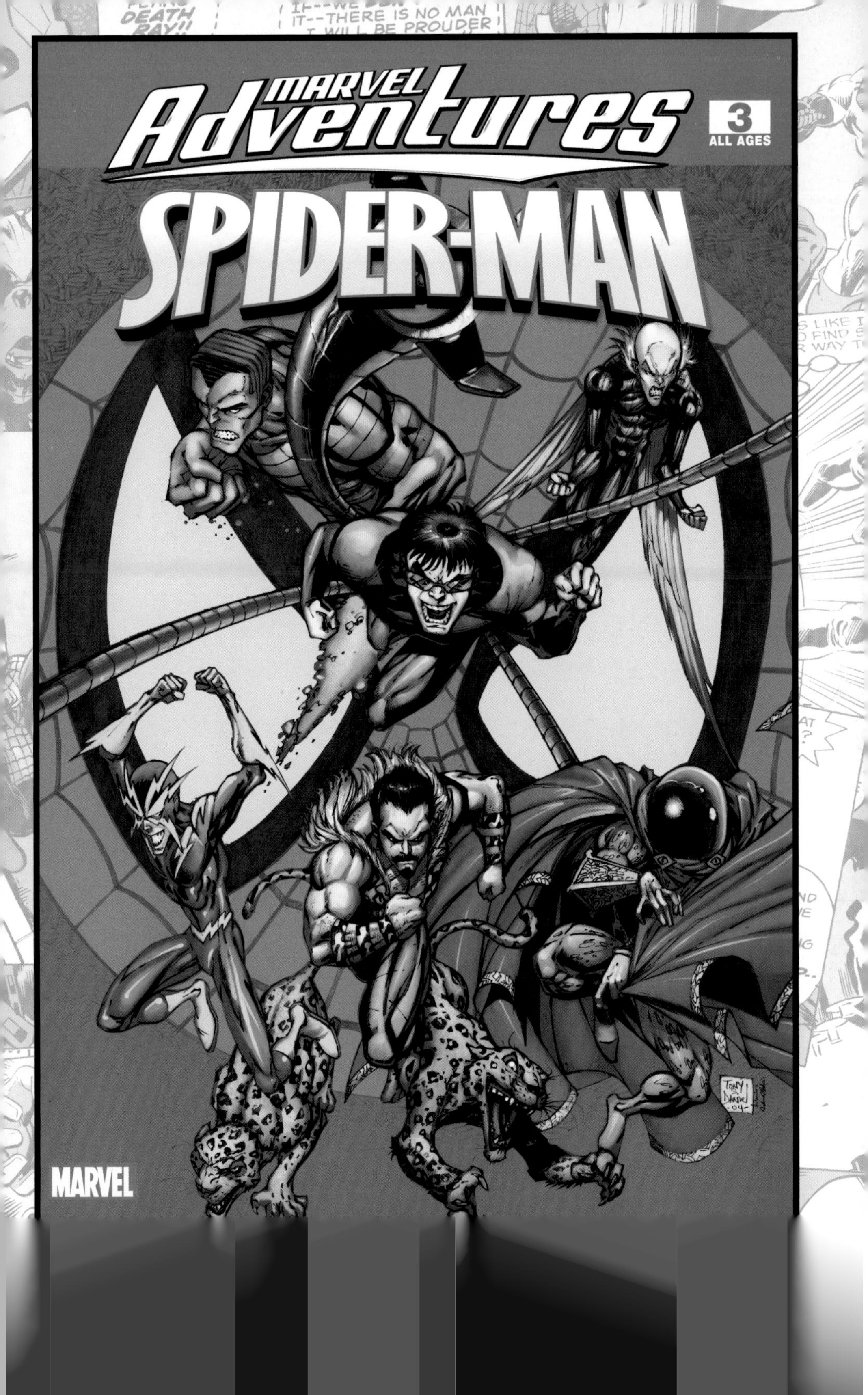
MARVEL
Adventures
3
ALL AGES
SPIDER-MAN
MARVEL

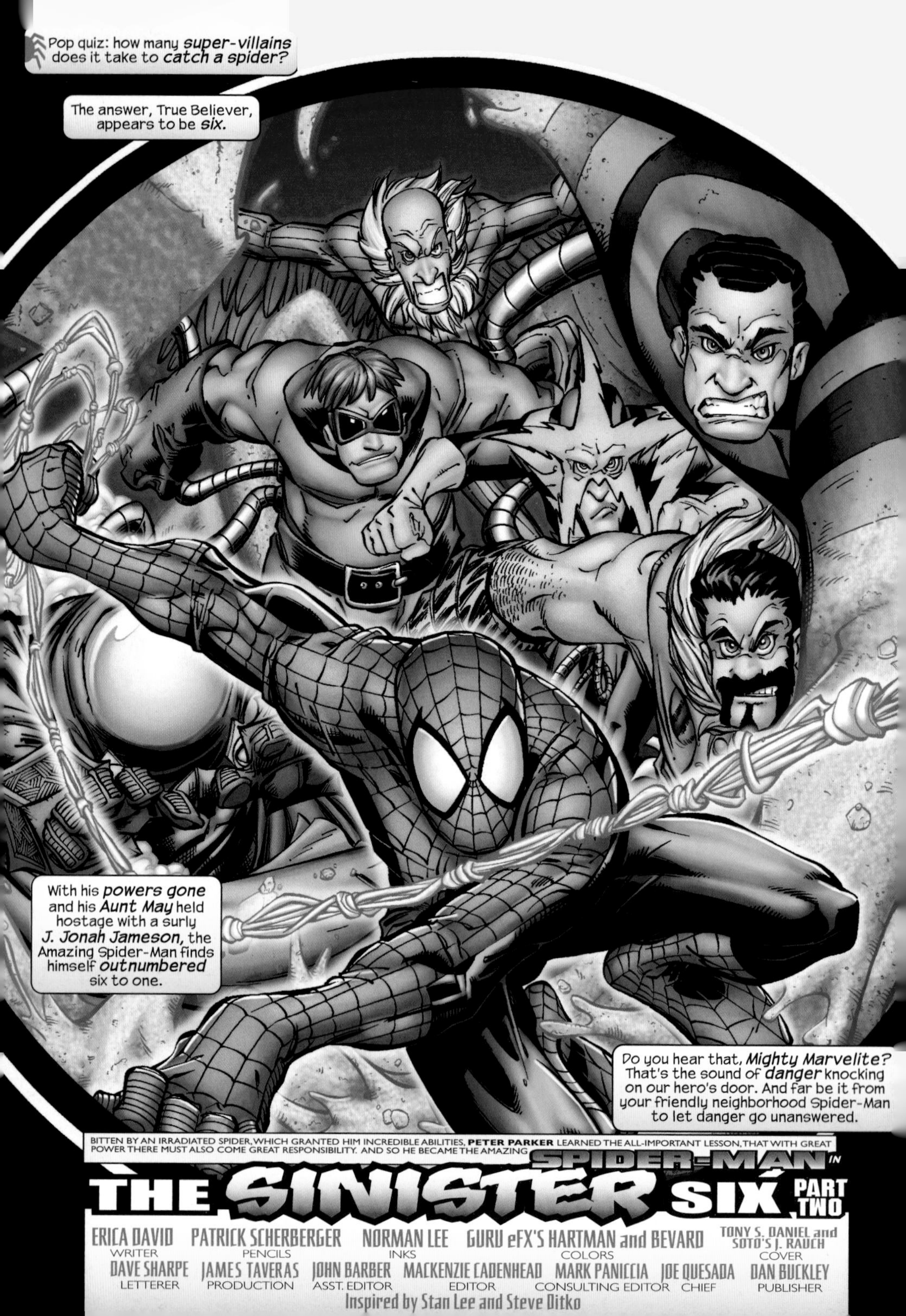

Pop quiz: how many super-villains does it take to catch a spider?
The answer, True Believer, appears to be six.
With his powers gone and his Aunt May held hostage with a surly J. Jonah Jameson, the Amazing Spider-Man finds himself outnumbered six to one.
Do you hear that, Mighty Marvelite? That's the sound of danger knocking on our hero's door. And far be it from your friendly neighborhood Spider-Man to let danger go unanswered.
BITTEN BY AN IRRADIATED SPIDER, WHICH GRANTED HIM INCREDIBLE ABILITIES, PETER PARKER LEARNED THE ALL-IMPORTANT LESSON, THAT WITH GREAT POWER THERE MUST ALSO COME GREAT RESPONSIBILITY. AND SO HE BECAME THE AMAZING
SPIDER-MAN IN
THE SINISTER SIX PART TWO
ERICA DAVID WRITER
PATRICK SCHERBERGER PENCILS
NORMAN LEE INKS
GURU eFX'S HARTMAN and BEVARD COLORS
TONY S. DANIEL and SOTO'S J. RAUCH COVER
DAVE SHARPE LETTERER
JAMES TAVERAS PRODUCTION
JOHN BARBER ASST. EDITOR
MACKENZIE CADENHEAD EDITOR
MARK PANICCIA CONSULTING EDITOR
JOE QUESADA CHIEF
DAN BUCKLEY PUBLISHER
Inspired by Stan Lee and Steve Ditko

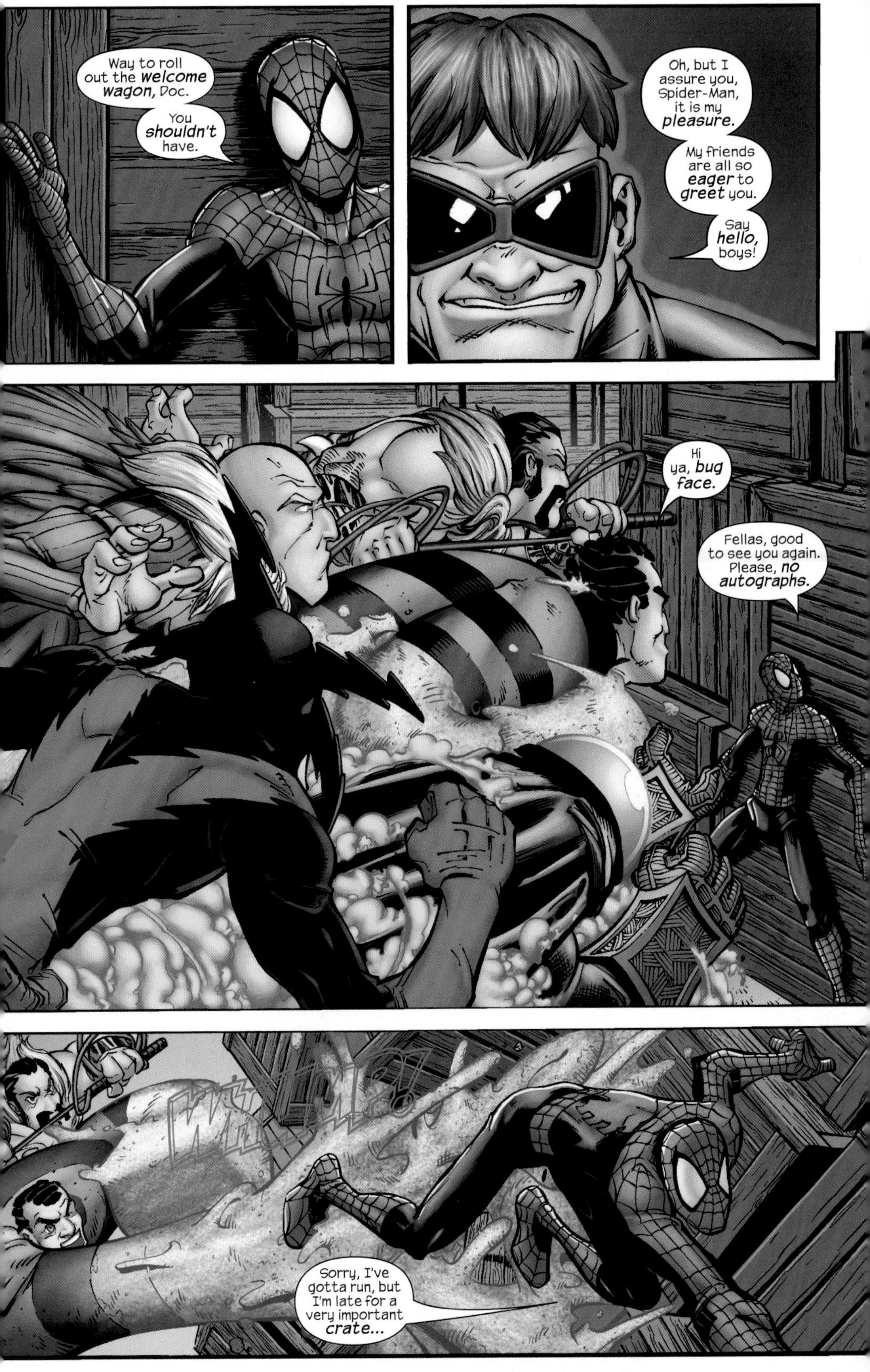
Way to roll out the welcome wagon, Doc.
You shouldn't have.
Oh, but I assure you, Spider-Man, it is my pleasure.
My friends are all so eager to greet you.
Say hello, boys!
Hi ya, bug face.
Fellas, good to see you again. Please, no autographs.
Sorry, I've gotta run, but I'm late for a very important crate...

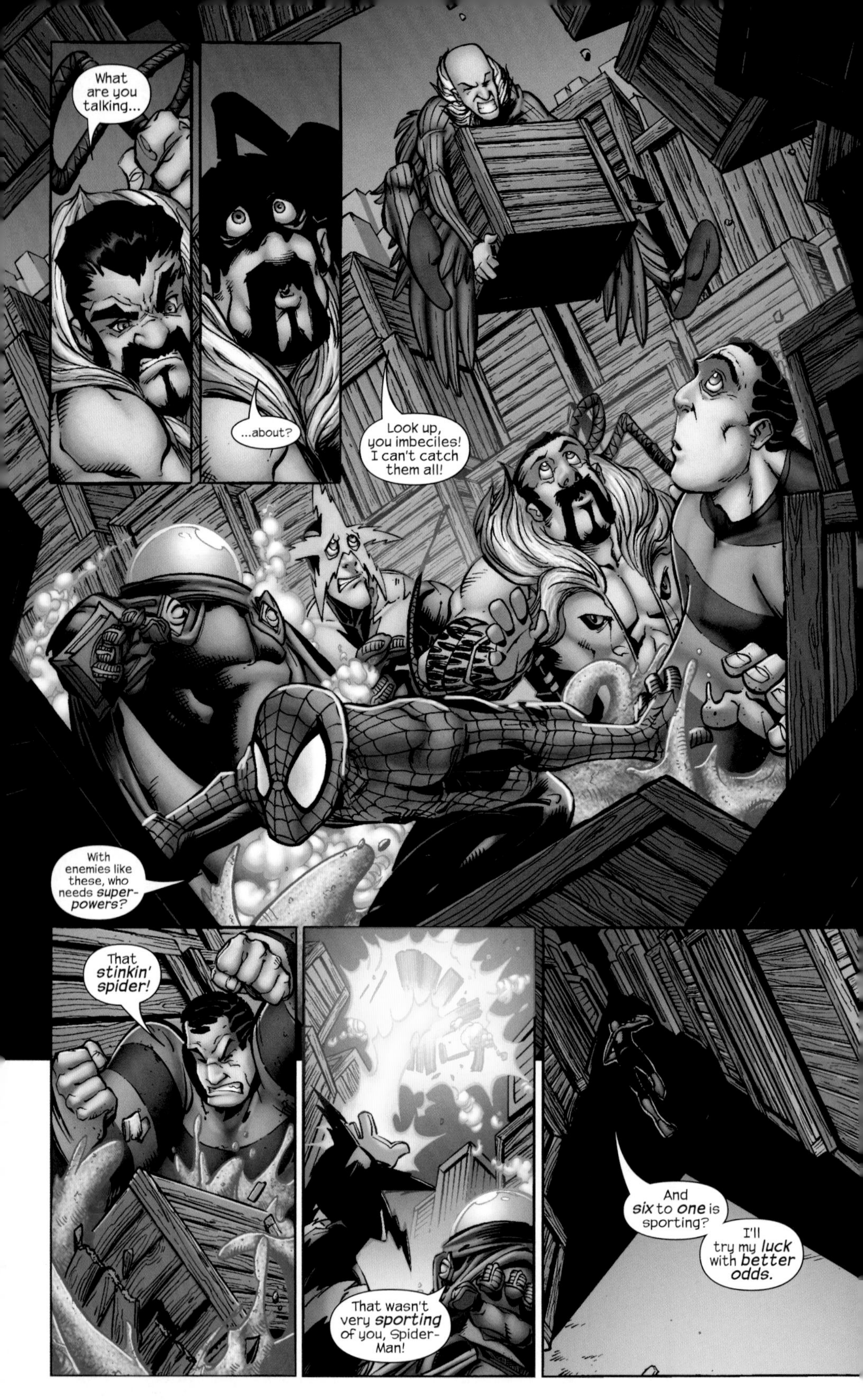
What are you talking...
...about?
Look up, you imbeciles! I can't catch them all!
With enemies like these, who needs super-powers?
That stinkin' spider!
That wasn't very sporting of you, Spider-Man!
And six to one is sporting?
I'll try my luck with better odds.

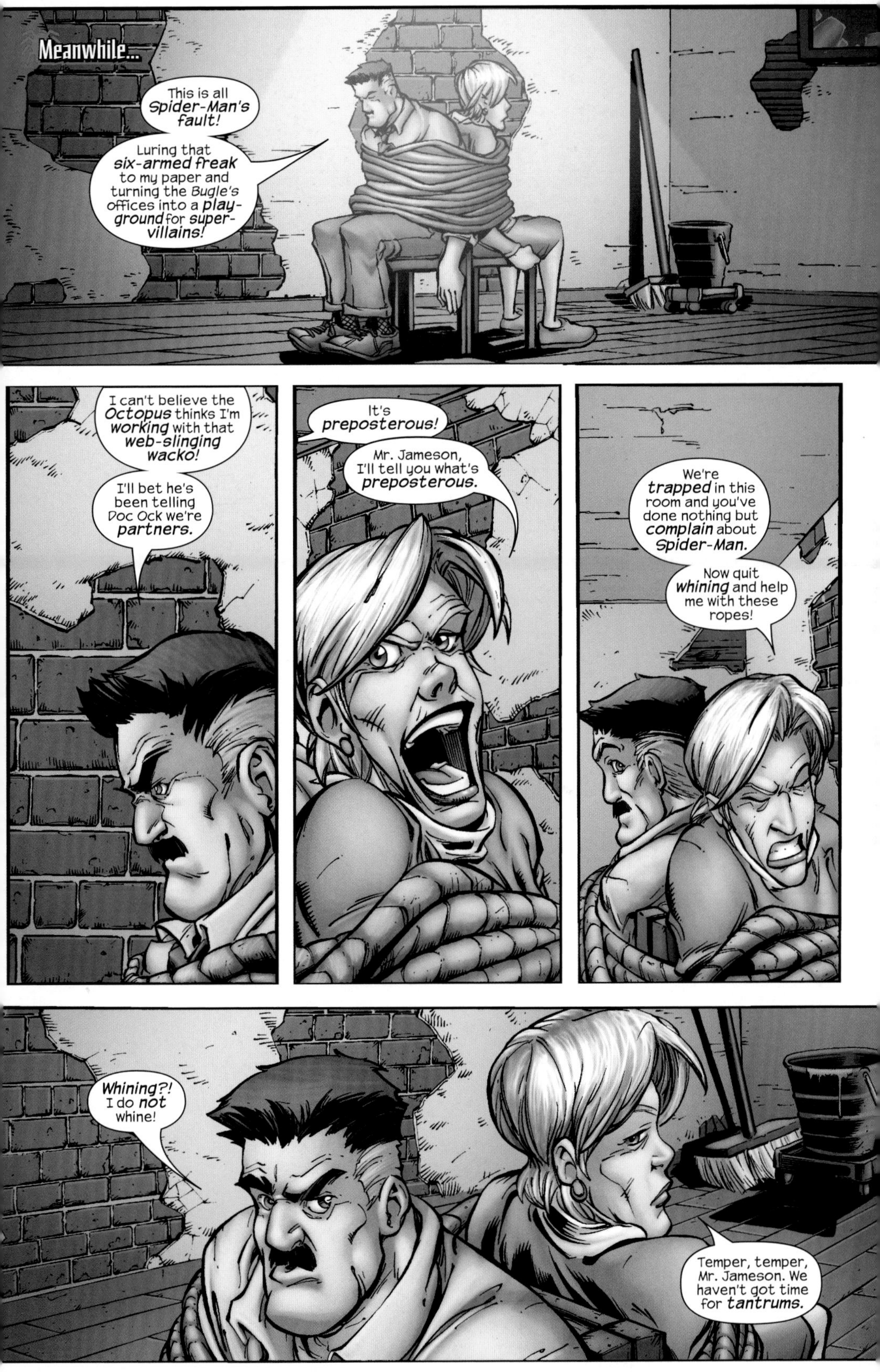
Meanwhile...
This is all Spider-Man's fault!
Luring that six-armed freak to my paper and turning the Bugle's offices into a play-ground for super-villains!
I can't believe the Octopus thinks I'm working with that web-slinging wacko!
I'll bet he's been telling Doc Ock we're partners.
It's preposterous!
Mr. Jameson, I'll tell you what's preposterous.
We're trapped in this room and you've done nothing but complain about Spider-Man.
Now quit whining and help me with these ropes!
Whining?! I do not whine!
Temper, temper, Mr. Jameson. We haven't got time for tantrums.

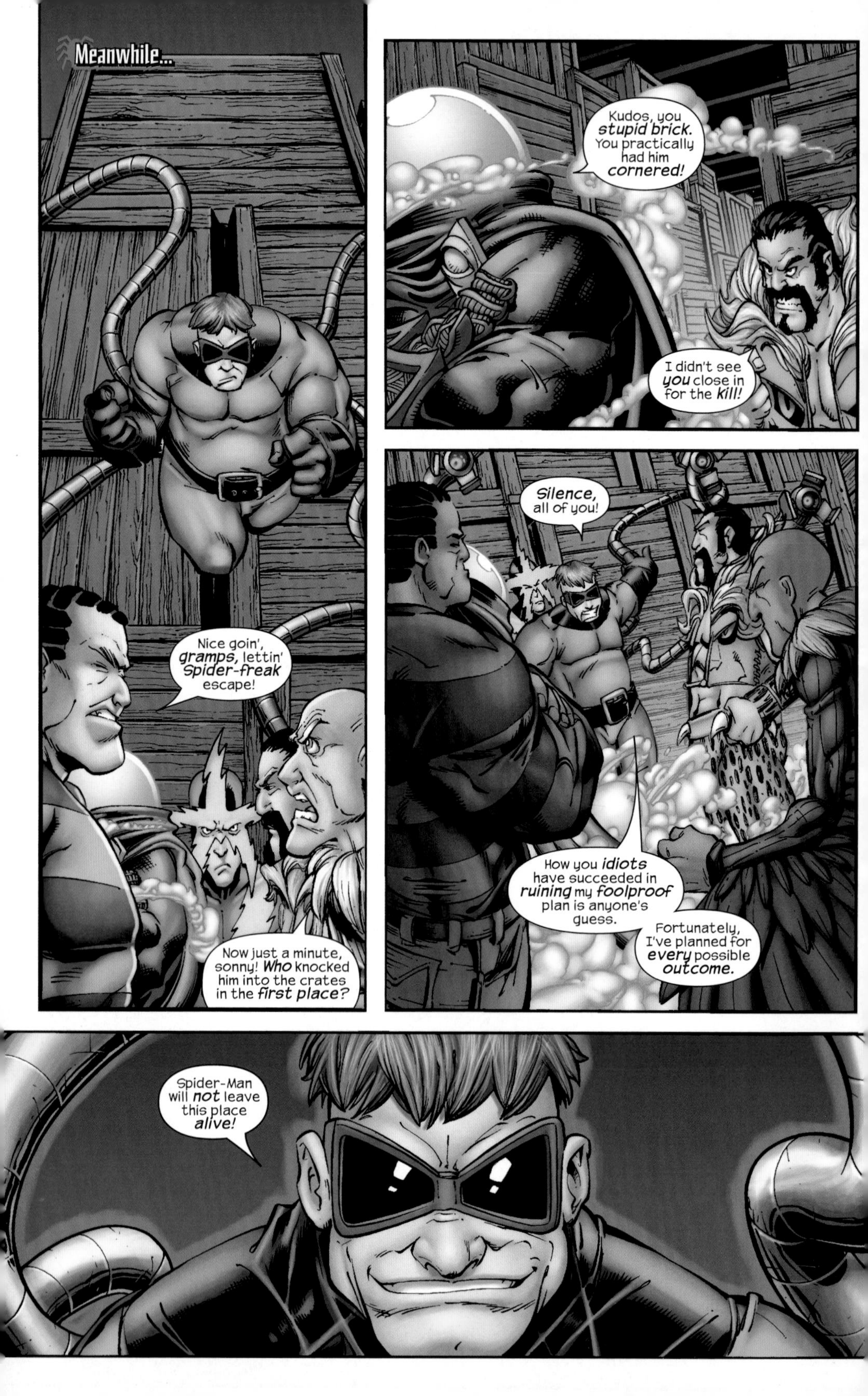
Meanwhile...
Nice goin', gramps, lettin' Spider-freak escape!
Now just a minute, sonny! Who knocked him into the crates in the first place?
Kudos, you stupid brick. You practically had him cornered!
I didn't see you close in for the kill!
Silence, all of you!
How you idiots have succeeded in ruining my foolproof plan is anyone's guess.
Fortunately, I've planned for every possible outcome.
Spider-Man will not leave this place alive!

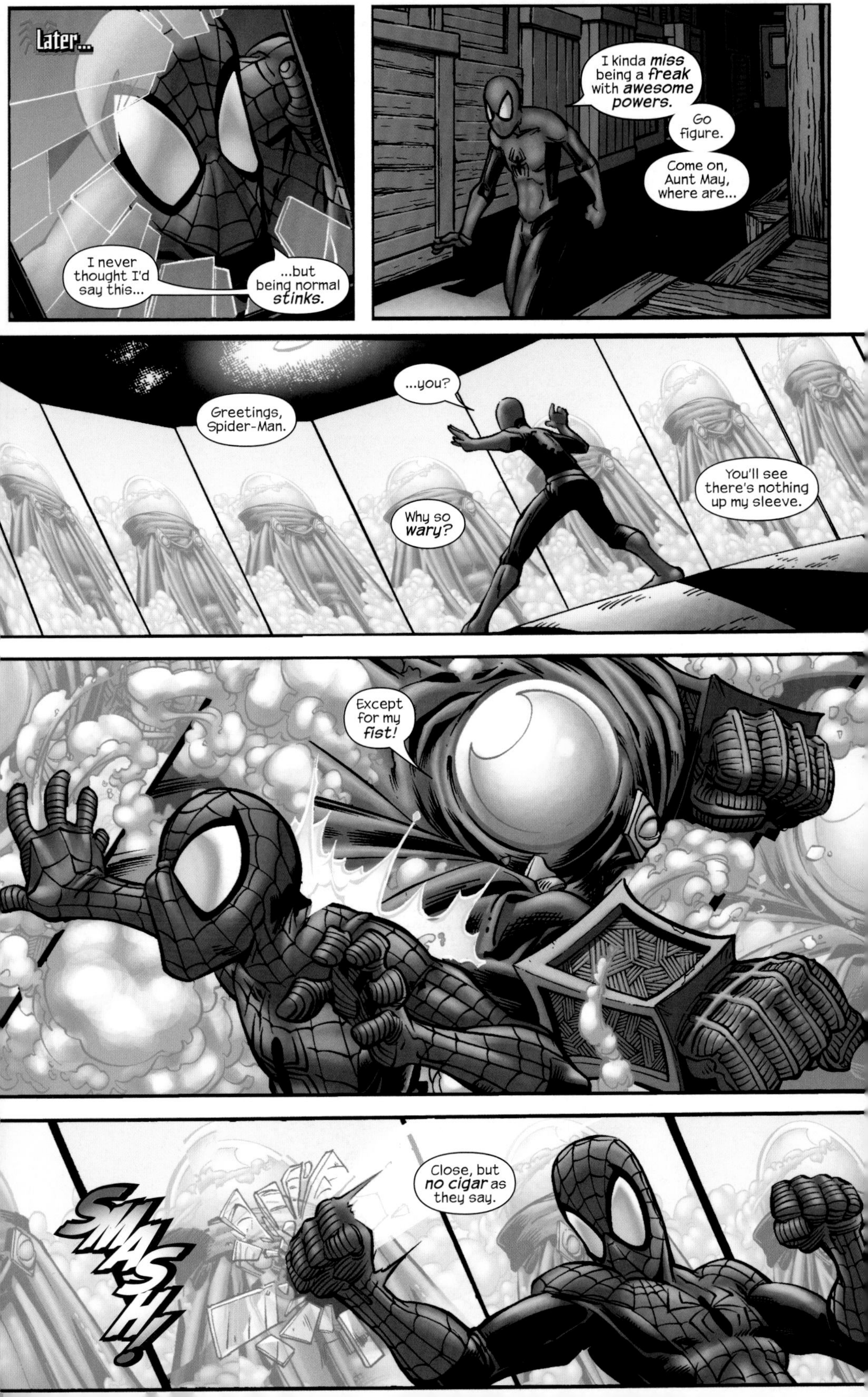
Later...
I never thought I'd say this...
...but being normal stinks.
I kinda miss being a freak with awesome powers.
Go figure.
Come on, Aunt May, where are...
...you?
Greetings, Spider-Man.
Why so wary?
You'll see there's nothing up my sleeve.
Except for my fist!
SMASH!
Close, but no cigar as they say.

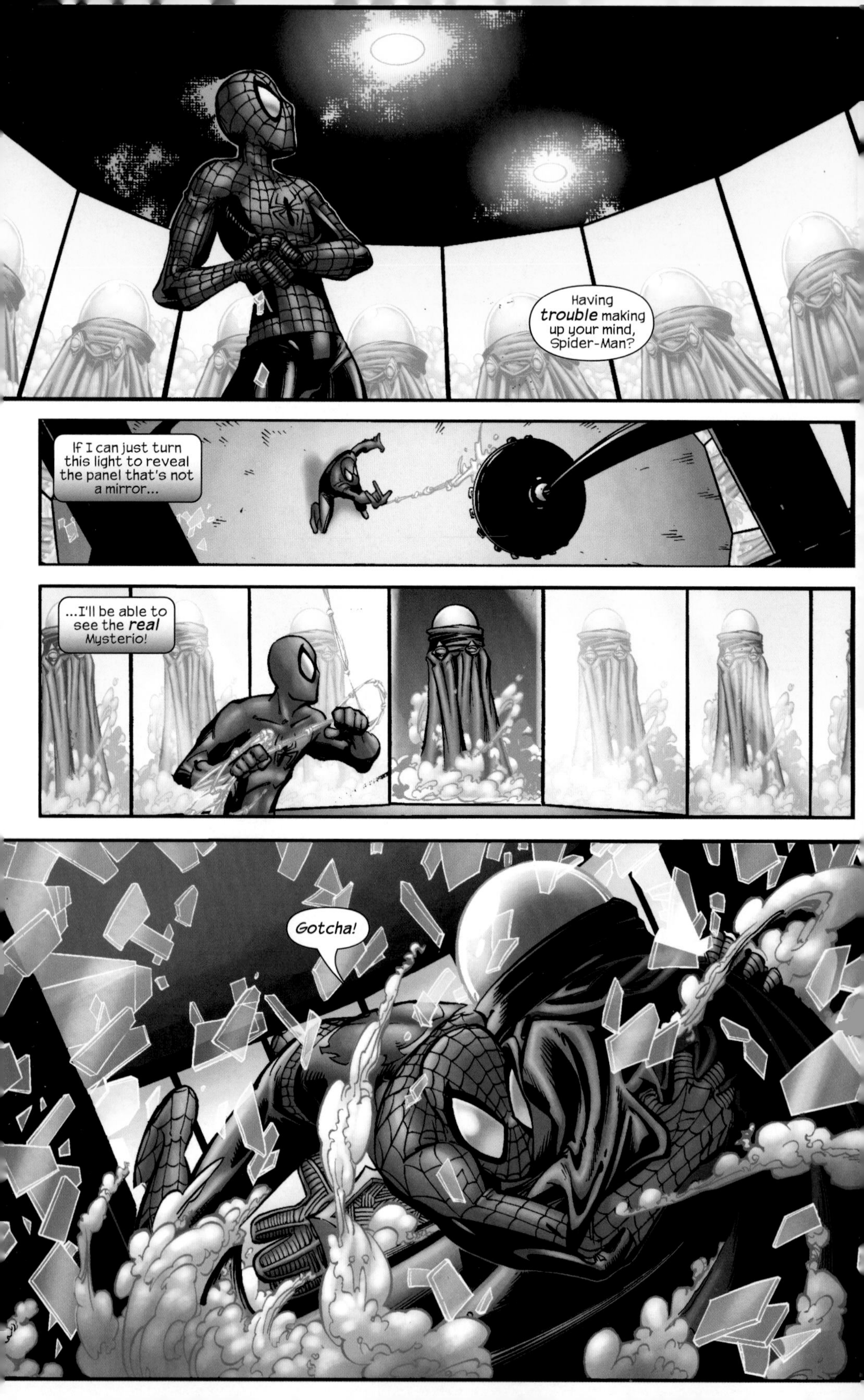
Having trouble making up your mind, Spider-Man?
If I can just turn this light to reveal the panel that's not a mirror...
...I'll be able to see the real Mysterio!
Gotcha!

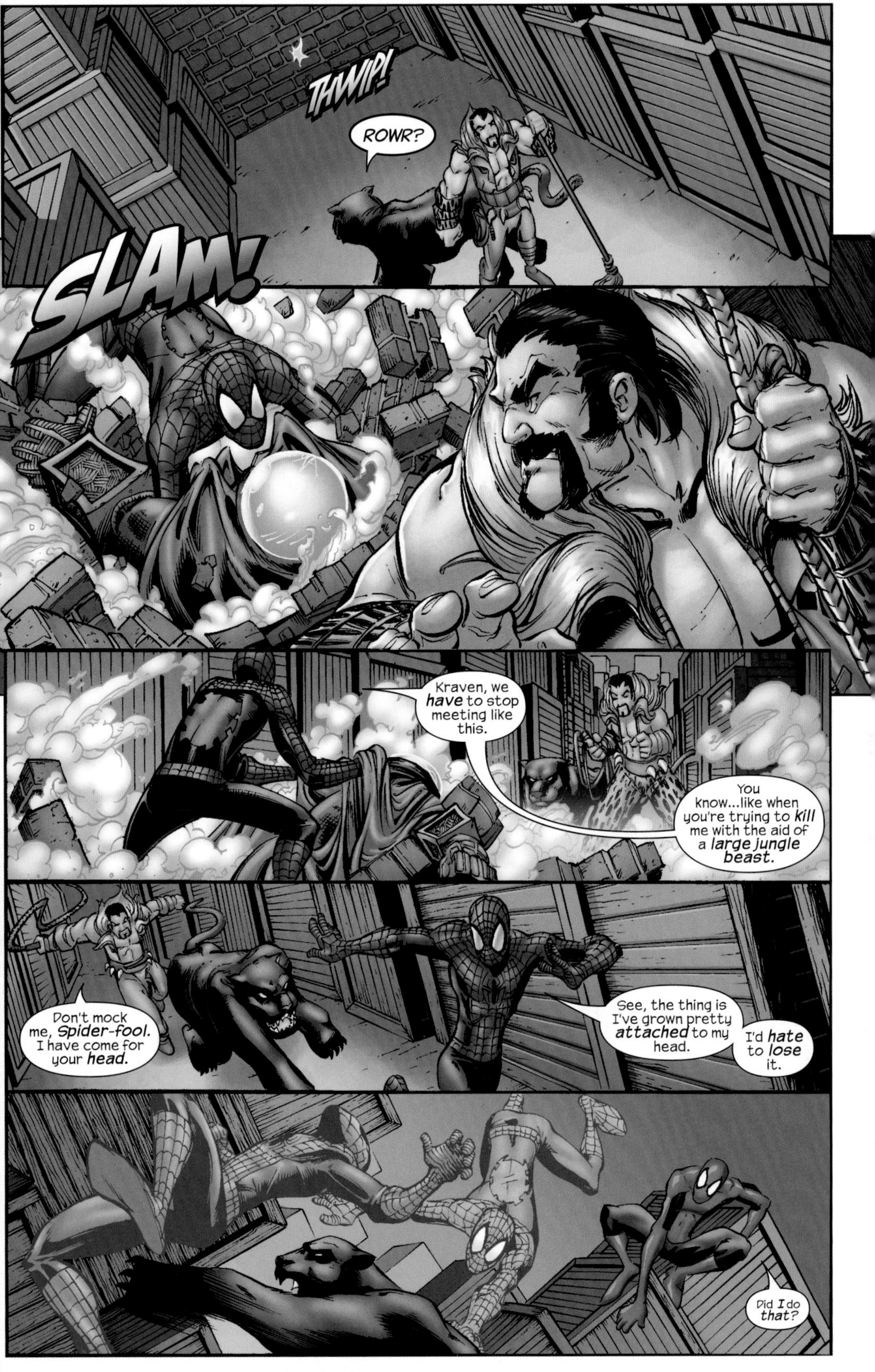
THWIP!
ROWR?
SLAM!
Kraven, we have to stop meeting like this.
You know...like when you're trying to kill me with the aid of a large jungle beast.
Don't mock me, Spider-fool. I have come for your head.
See, the thing is I've grown pretty attached to my head.
I'd hate to lose it.
Did I do that?

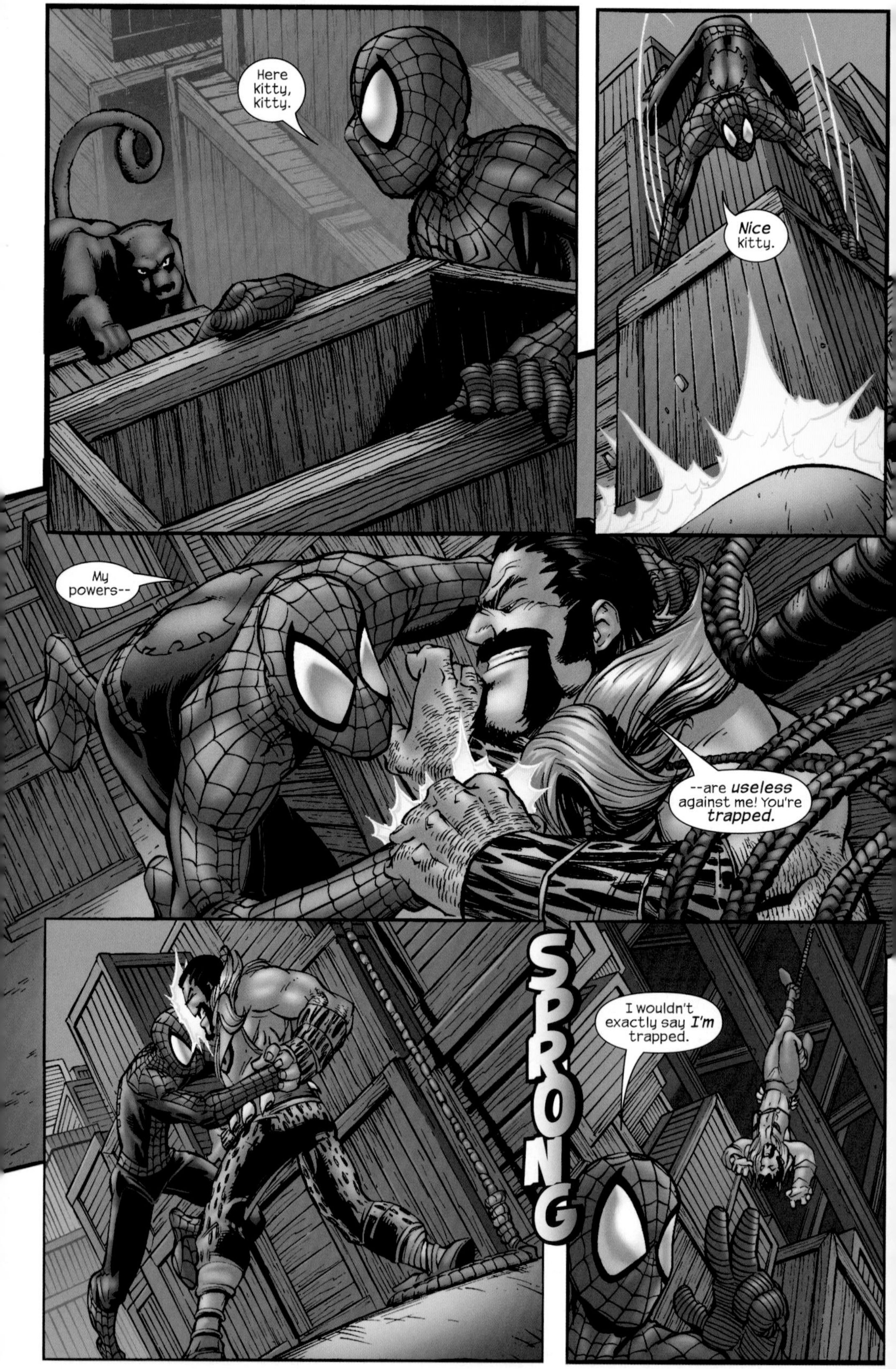

Here kitty, kitty.
Nice kitty.
My powers--
--are useless against me! You're trapped.
SPRONG
I wouldn't exactly say I'm trapped.

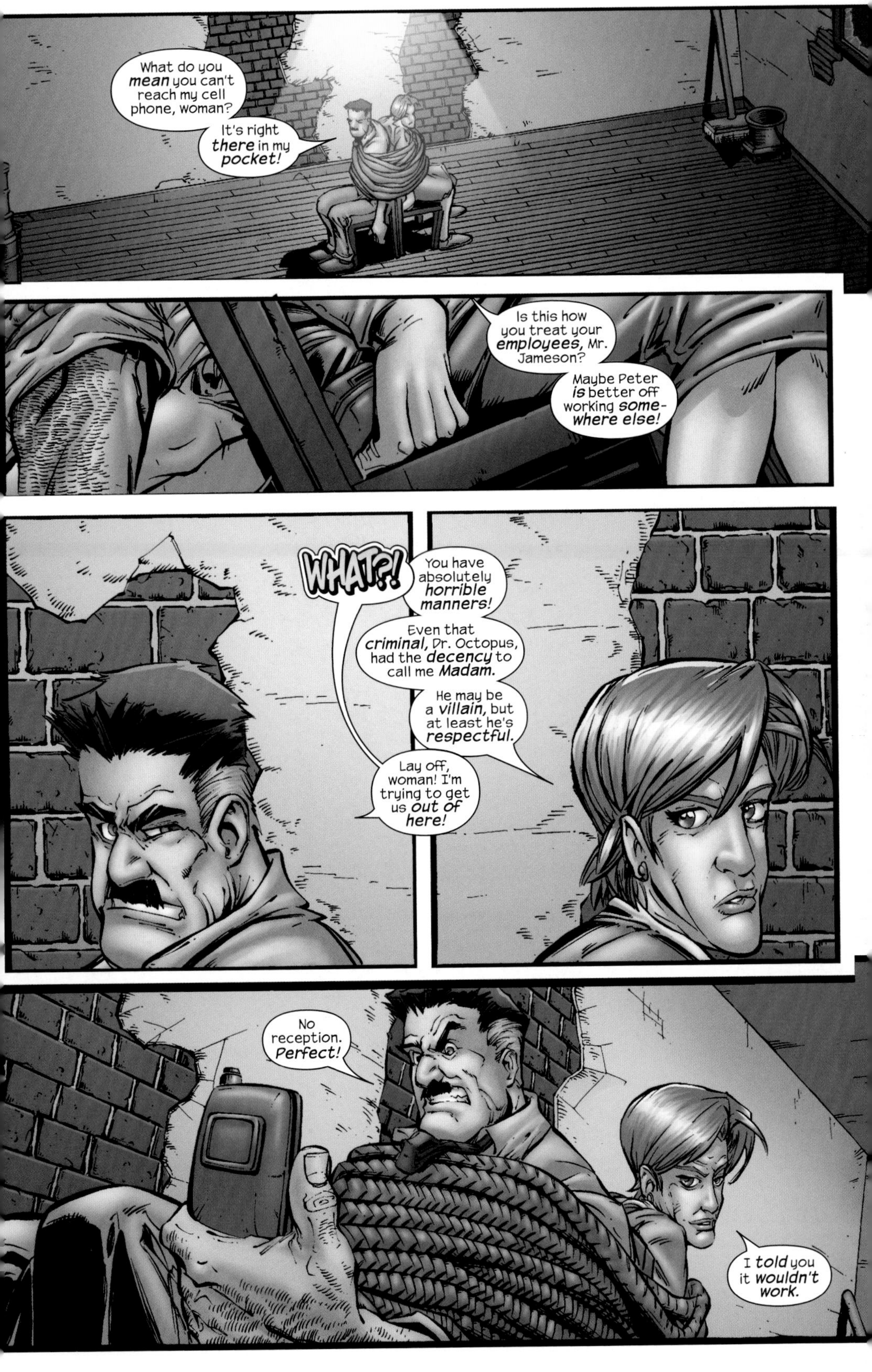

What do you *mean* you can't reach my cell phone, woman?
It's right *there* in my *pocket!*
Is this how you treat your *employees,* Mr. Jameson?
Maybe Peter *is* better off working *some-where else!*
WHAT?!
You have absolutely *horrible manners!*
Even that *criminal,* Dr. Octopus, had the *decency* to call me *Madam.*
He may be a *villain,* but at least he's *respectful.*
Lay off, woman! I'm trying to get us *out of here!*
No reception. *Perfect!*
I *told* you it *wouldn't work.*

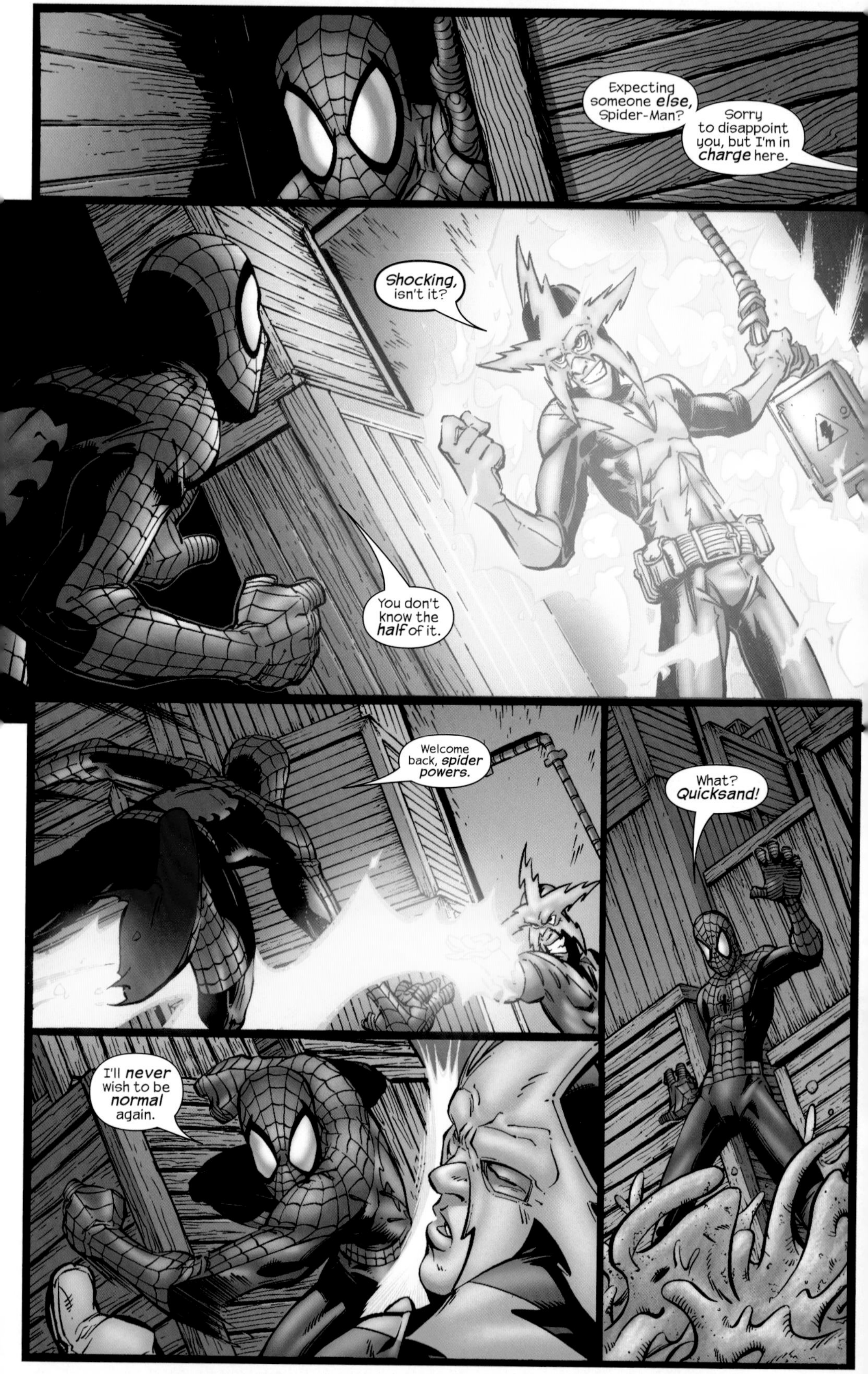
Expecting someone else, Spider-Man?
Sorry to disappoint you, but I'm in charge here.
Shocking, isn't it?
You don't know the half of it.
Welcome back, spider powers.
What? Quicksand!
I'll never wish to be normal again.

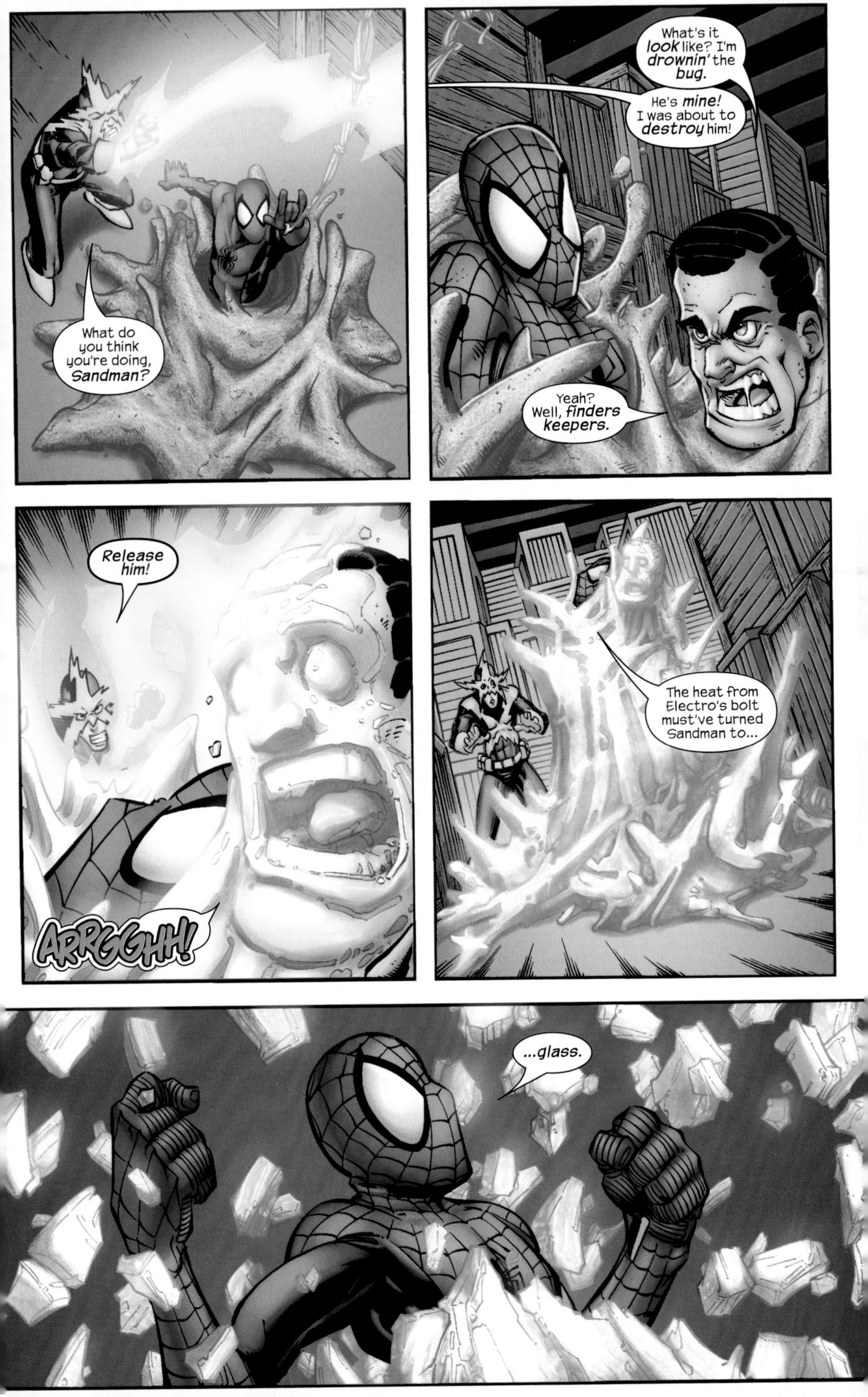
What do you think you're doing, Sandman?
What's it look like? I'm drownin' the bug.
He's mine! I was about to destroy him!
Yeah? Well, finders keepers.
Release him!
ARRGGHH!
The heat from Electro's bolt must've turned Sandman to...
...glass.

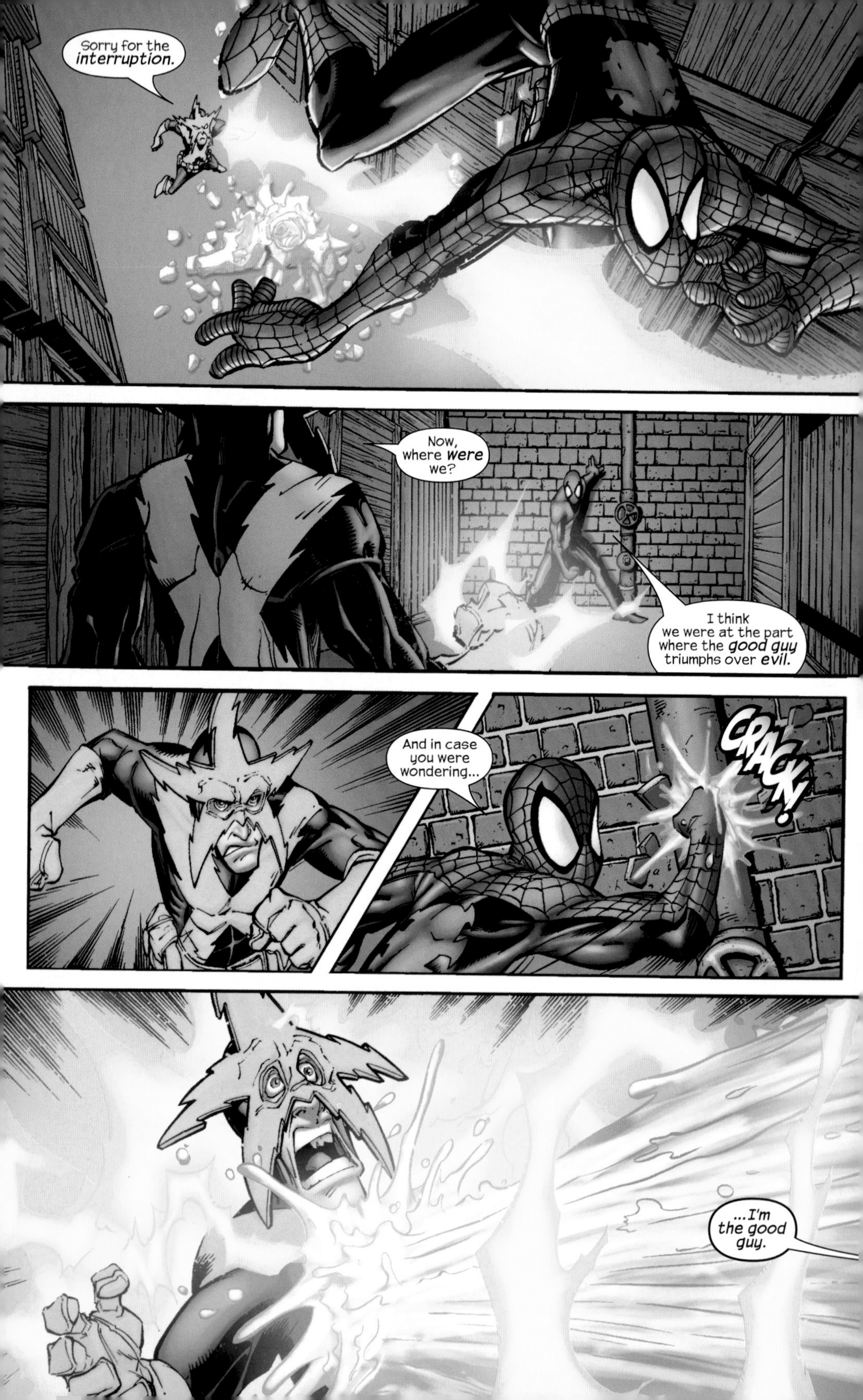
Sorry for the *interruption.*
Now, where *were* we?
I think we were at the part where the *good guy* triumphs over *evil.*
And in case you were wondering...
CRACK!
...I'm the good guy.

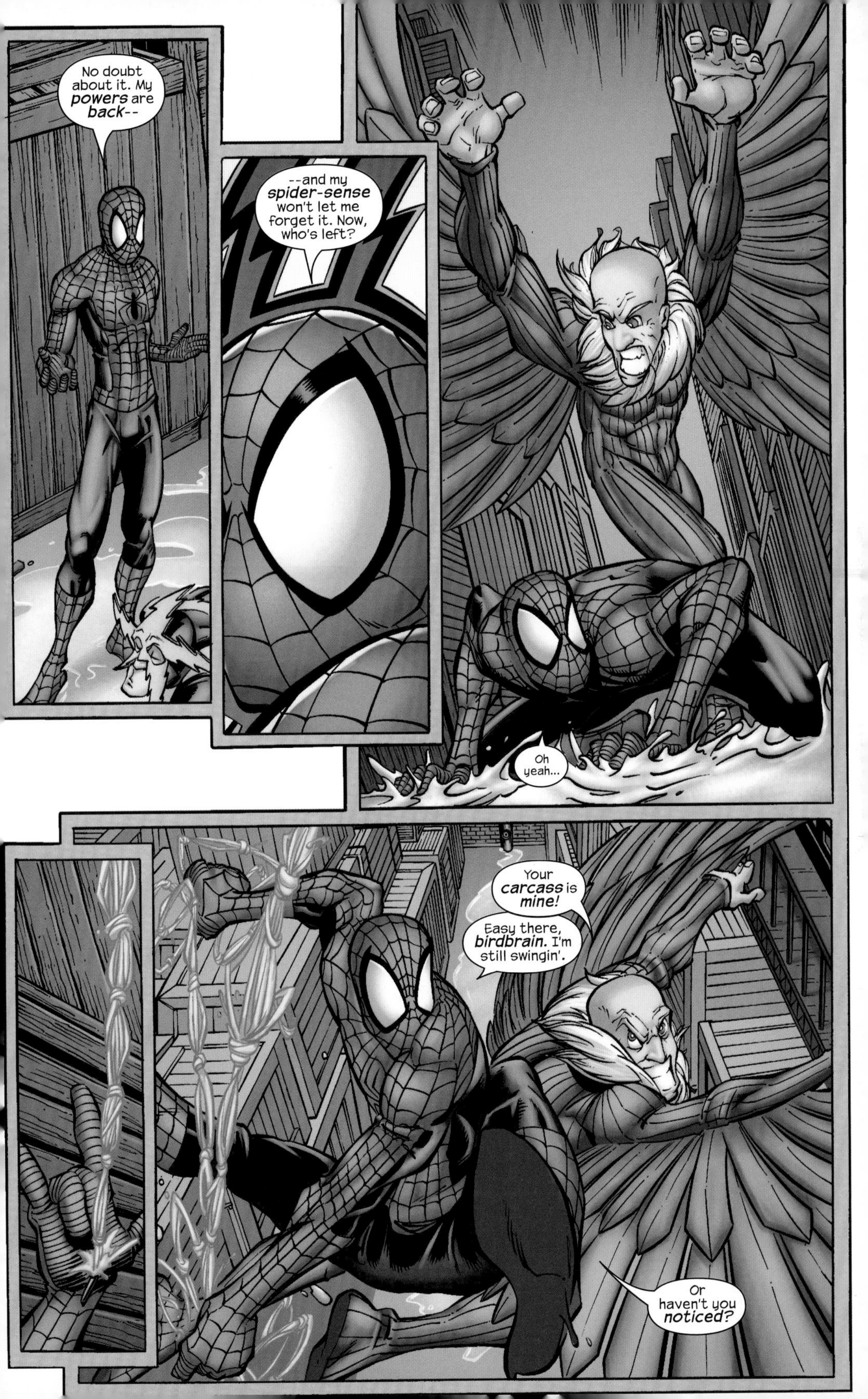

No doubt about it. My *powers* are *back*--
--and my *spider-sense* won't let me forget it. Now, who's left?
Oh yeah...
Your *carcass* is *mine!*
Easy there, *birdbrain*. I'm still swingin'.
Or haven't you *noticed?*

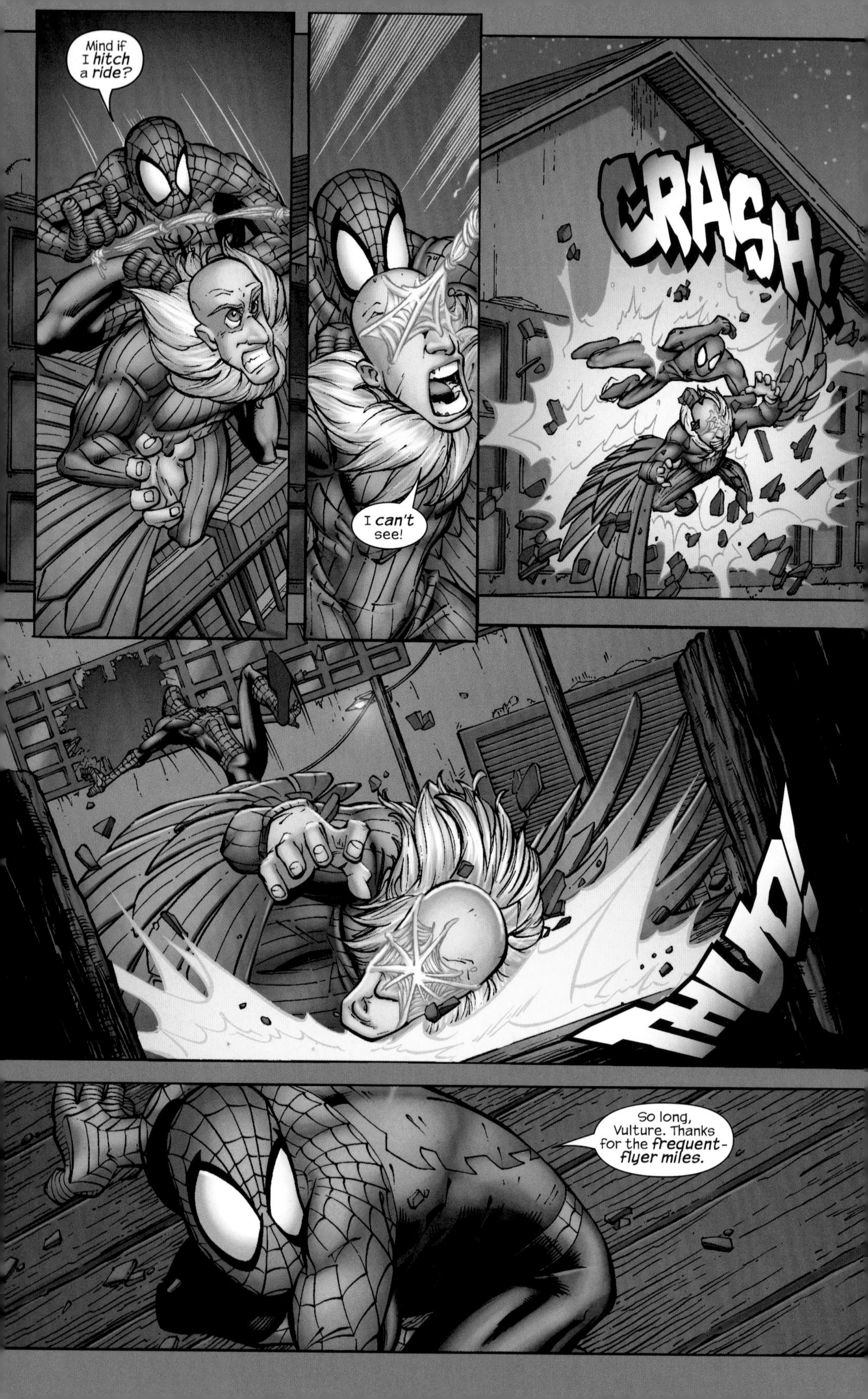
Mind if I hitch a ride?
I can't see!
CRASH!
THUD!
So long, Vulture. Thanks for the frequent-flyer miles.

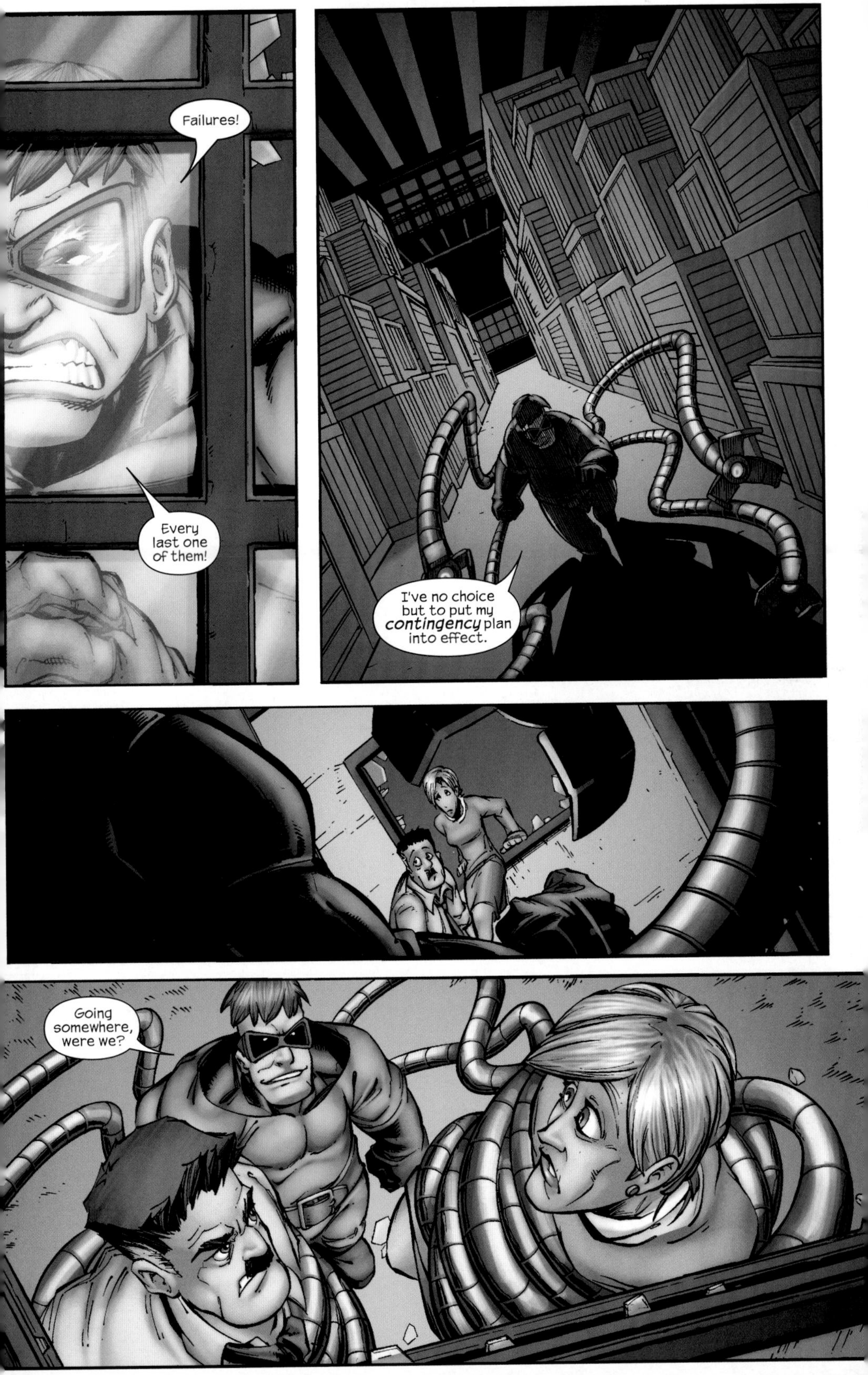
Failures!
Every last one of them!
I've no choice but to put my *contingency* plan into effect.
Going somewhere, were we?

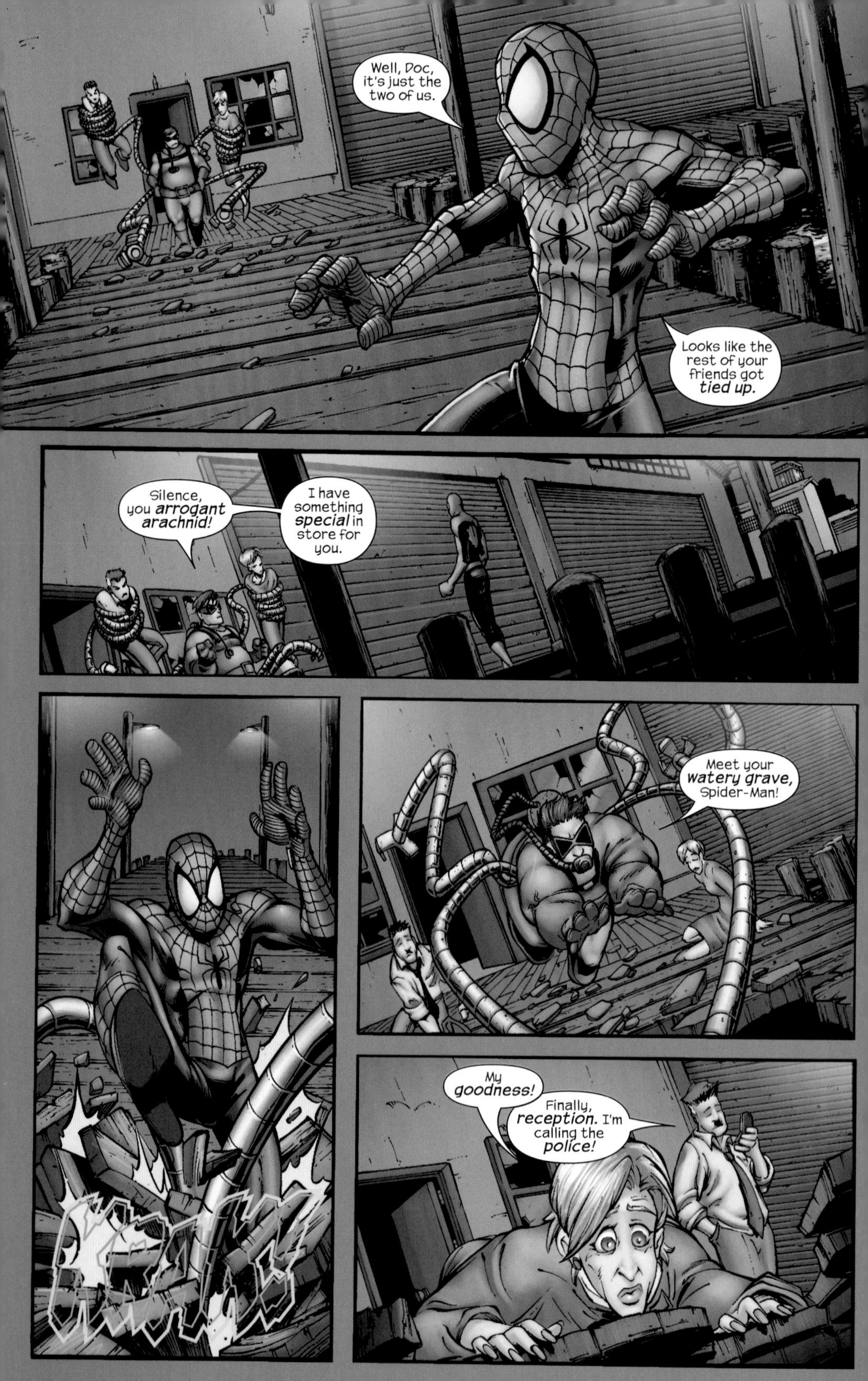
Well, Doc, it's just the two of us.
Looks like the rest of your friends got tied up.
Silence, you arrogant arachnid!
I have something special in store for you.
Meet your watery grave, Spider-Man!
My goodness!
Finally, reception. I'm calling the police!

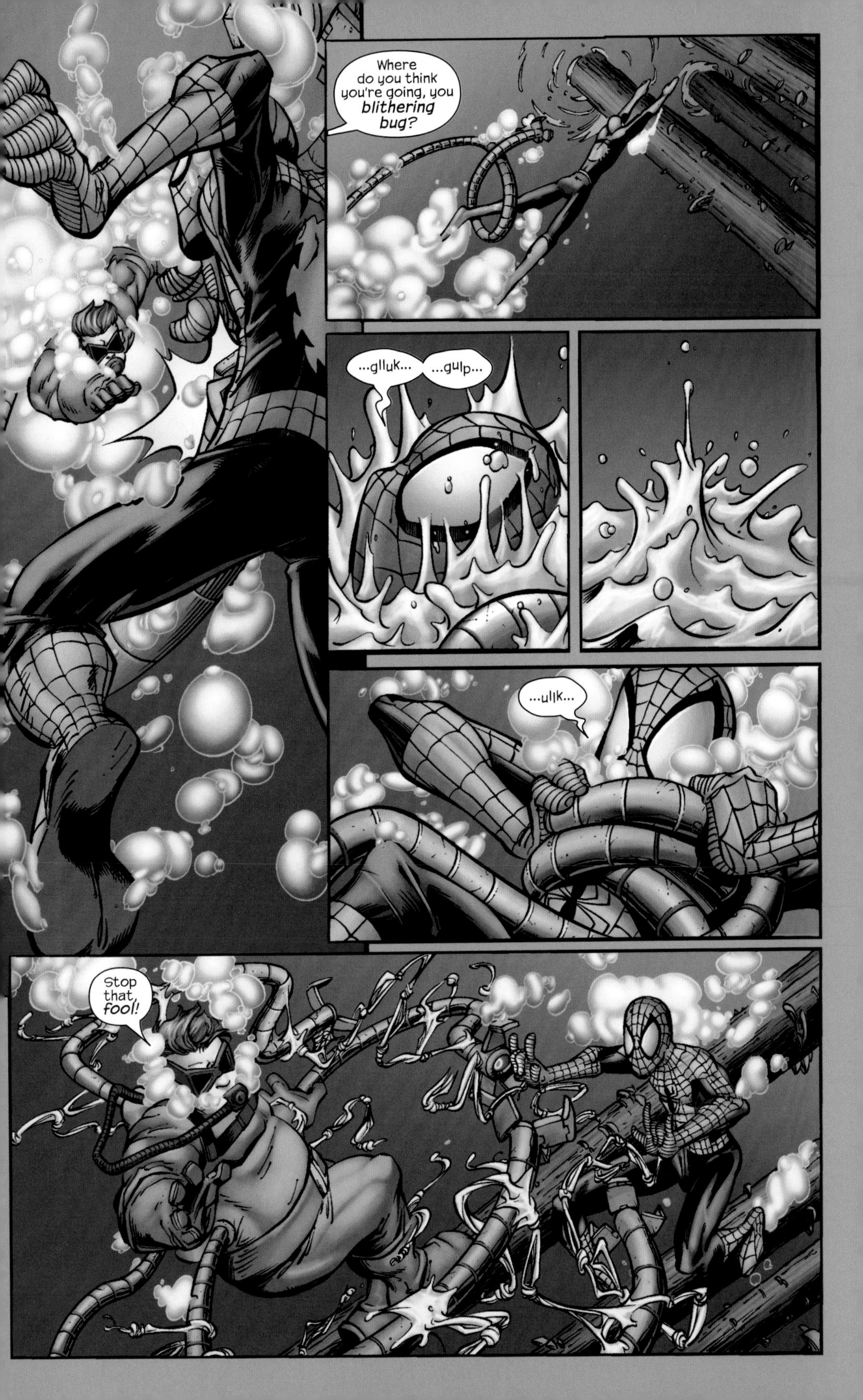
Where do you think you're going, you *blithering* bug?
...gllluk...
...gulp...
...ulk...
Stop that *fool!*

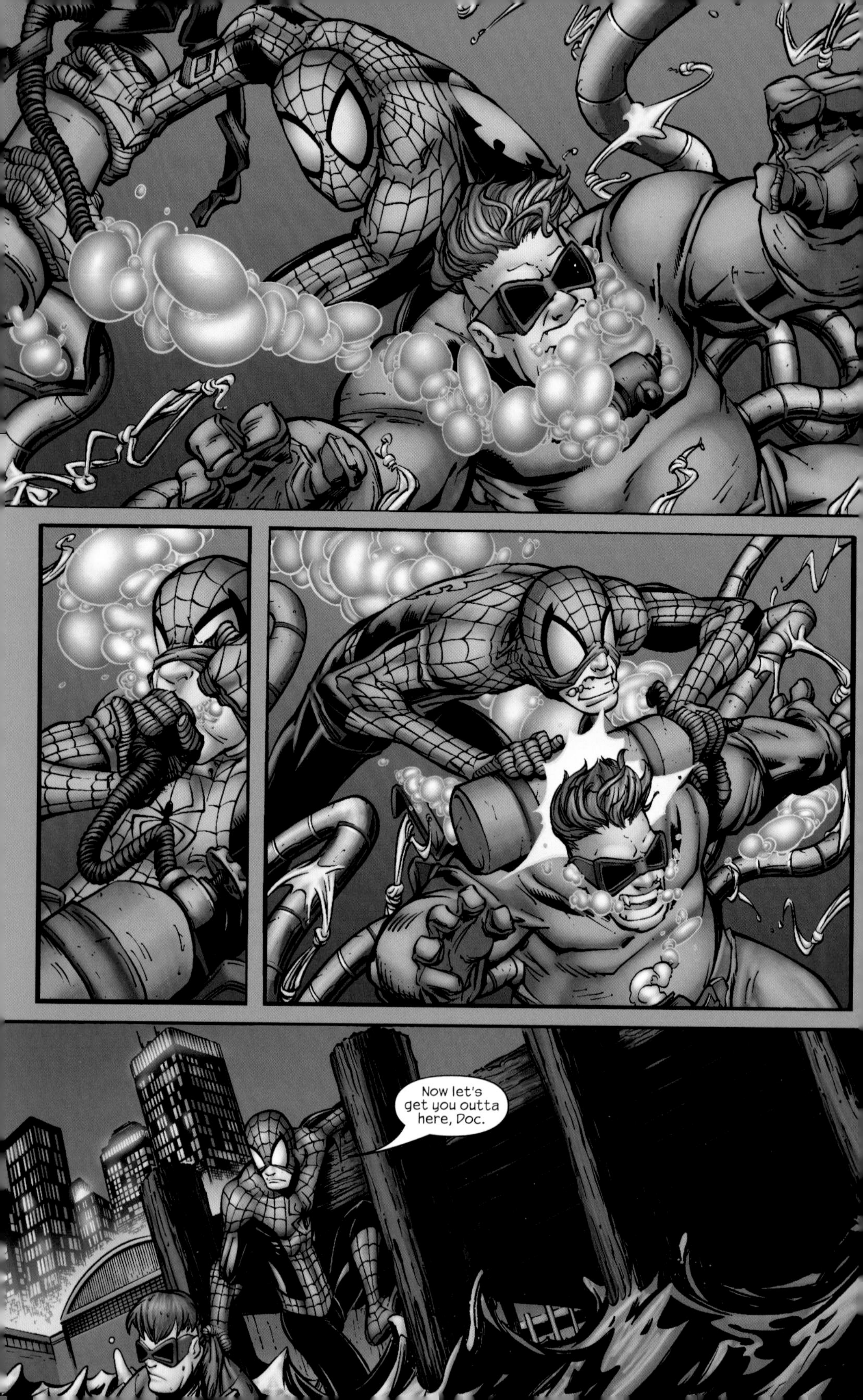
Now let's get you outta here, Doc.

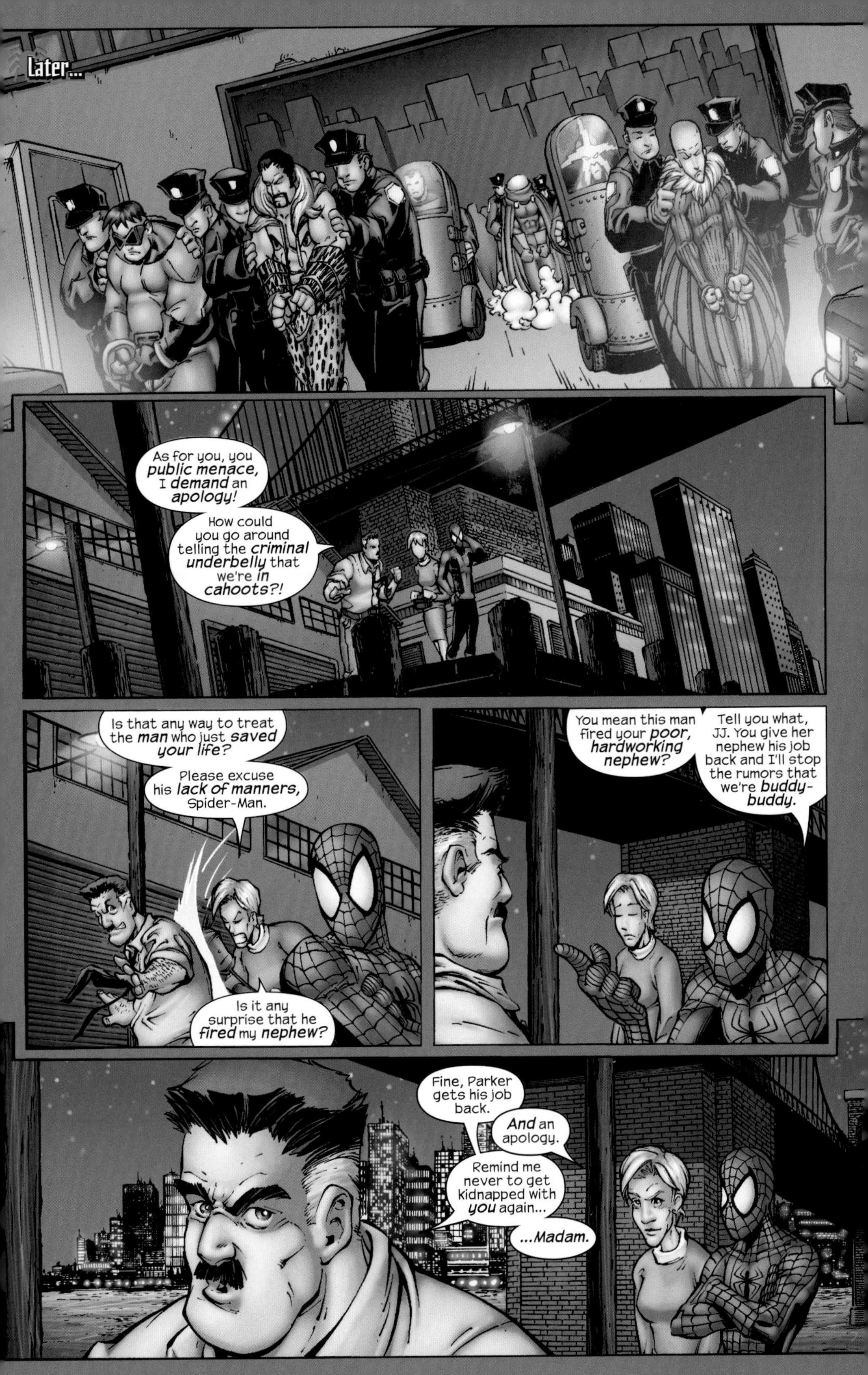
Later...
As for you, you public menace, I demand an apology!
How could you go around telling the criminal underbelly that we're in cahoots?!
Is that any way to treat the man who just saved your life?
Please excuse his lack of manners, Spider-Man.
Is it any surprise that he fired my nephew?
You mean this man fired your poor, hardworking nephew?
Tell you what, JJ. You give her nephew his job back and I'll stop the rumors that we're buddy-buddy.
Fine, Parker gets his job back.
And an apology.
Remind me never to get kidnapped with you again...
...Madam.

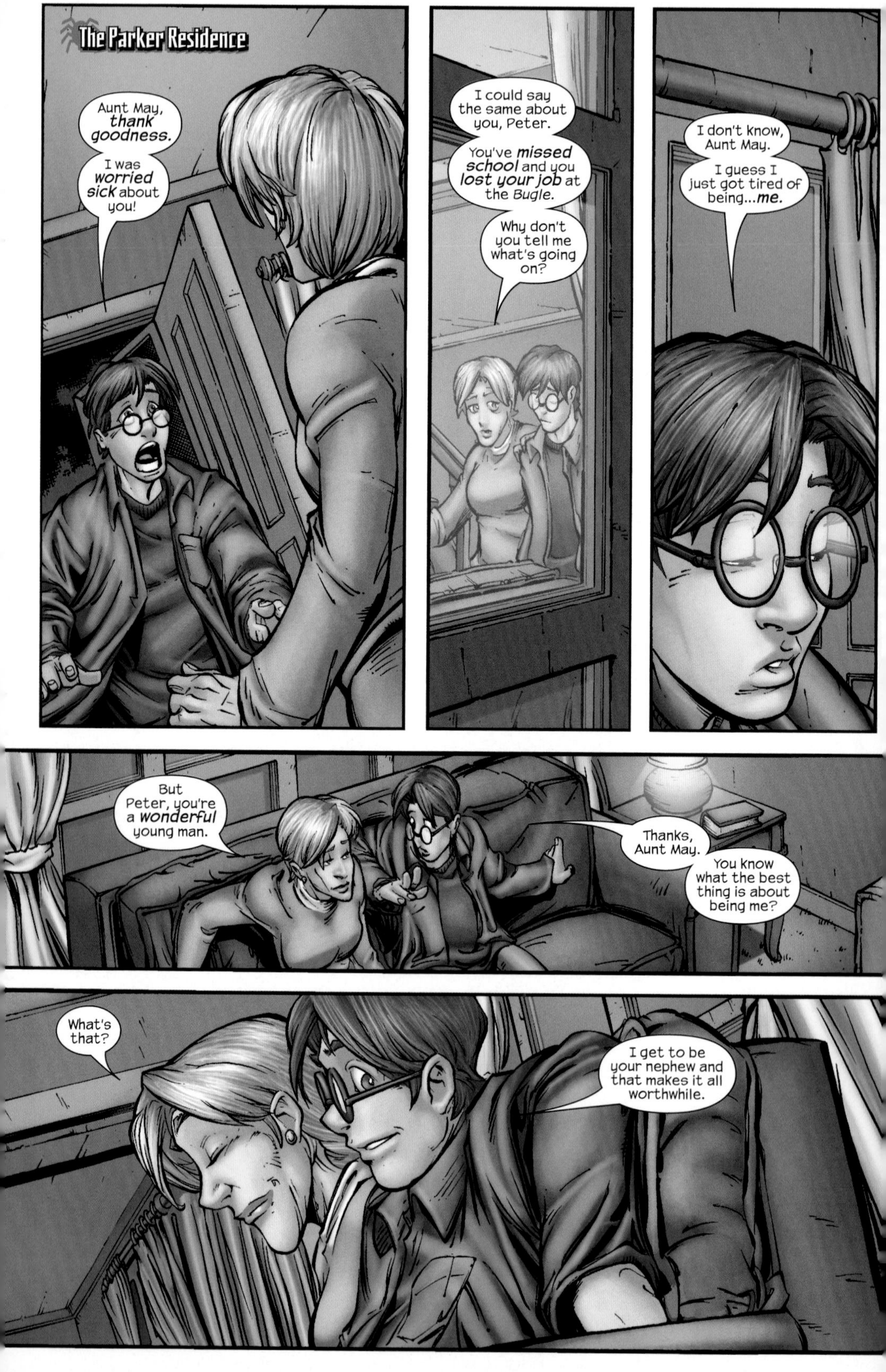
The Parker Residence
Aunt May, *thank goodness.*
I was *worried sick* about you!
I could say the same about you, Peter.
You've *missed school* and you *lost your job* at the *Bugle.*
Why don't you tell me what's going on?
I don't know, Aunt May.
I guess I just got tired of being...*me.*
But Peter, you're a *wonderful* young man.
Thanks, Aunt May.
You know what the best thing is about being me?
What's that?
I get to be your nephew and that makes it all worthwhile.

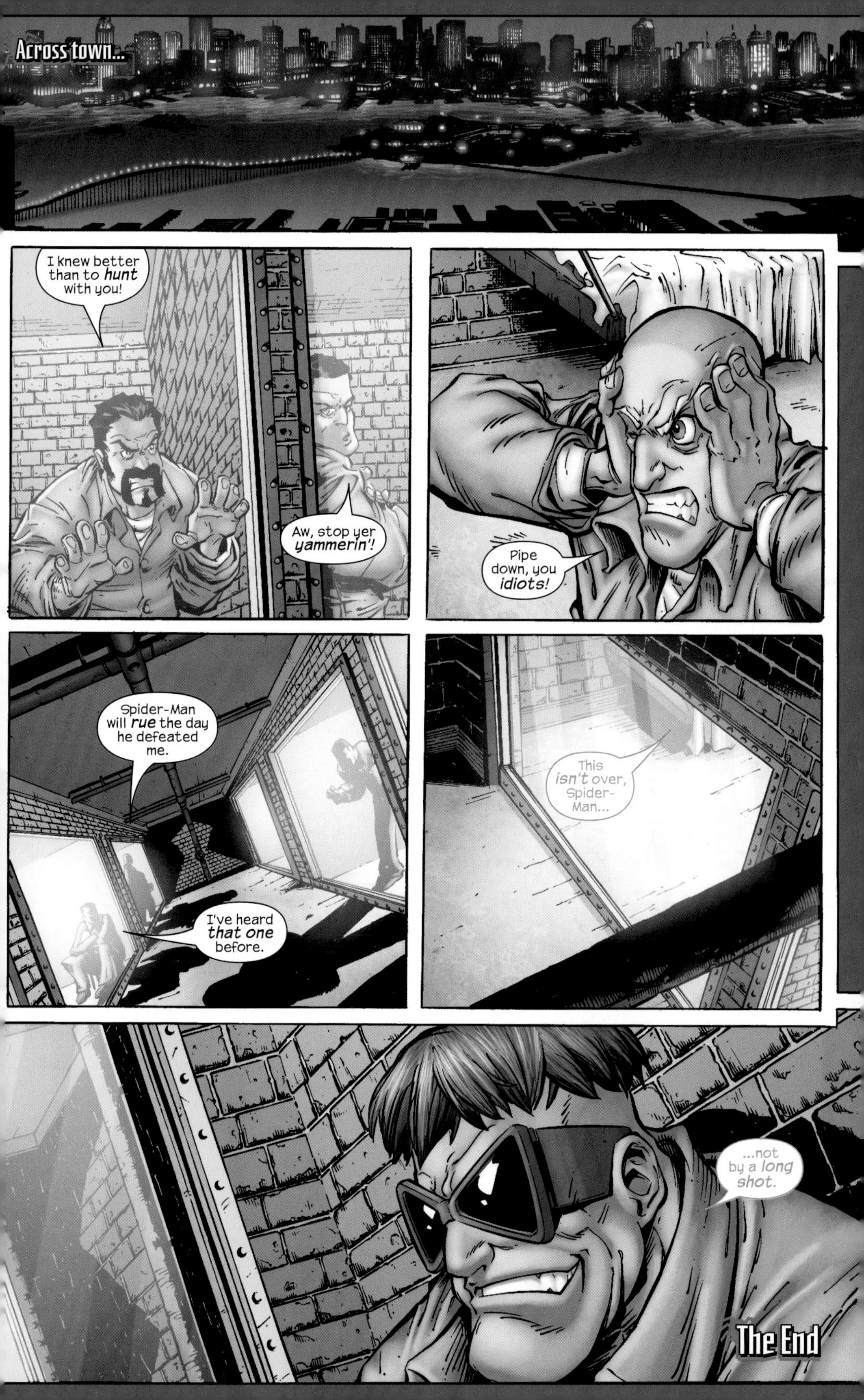

Across town...
I knew better than to *hunt* with you!
Aw, stop yer *yammerin'*!
Pipe down, you *idiots!*
Spider-Man will *rue* the day he defeated me.
I've heard *that one* before.
This *isn't* over, Spider-Man...
...not by a *long shot*.
The End

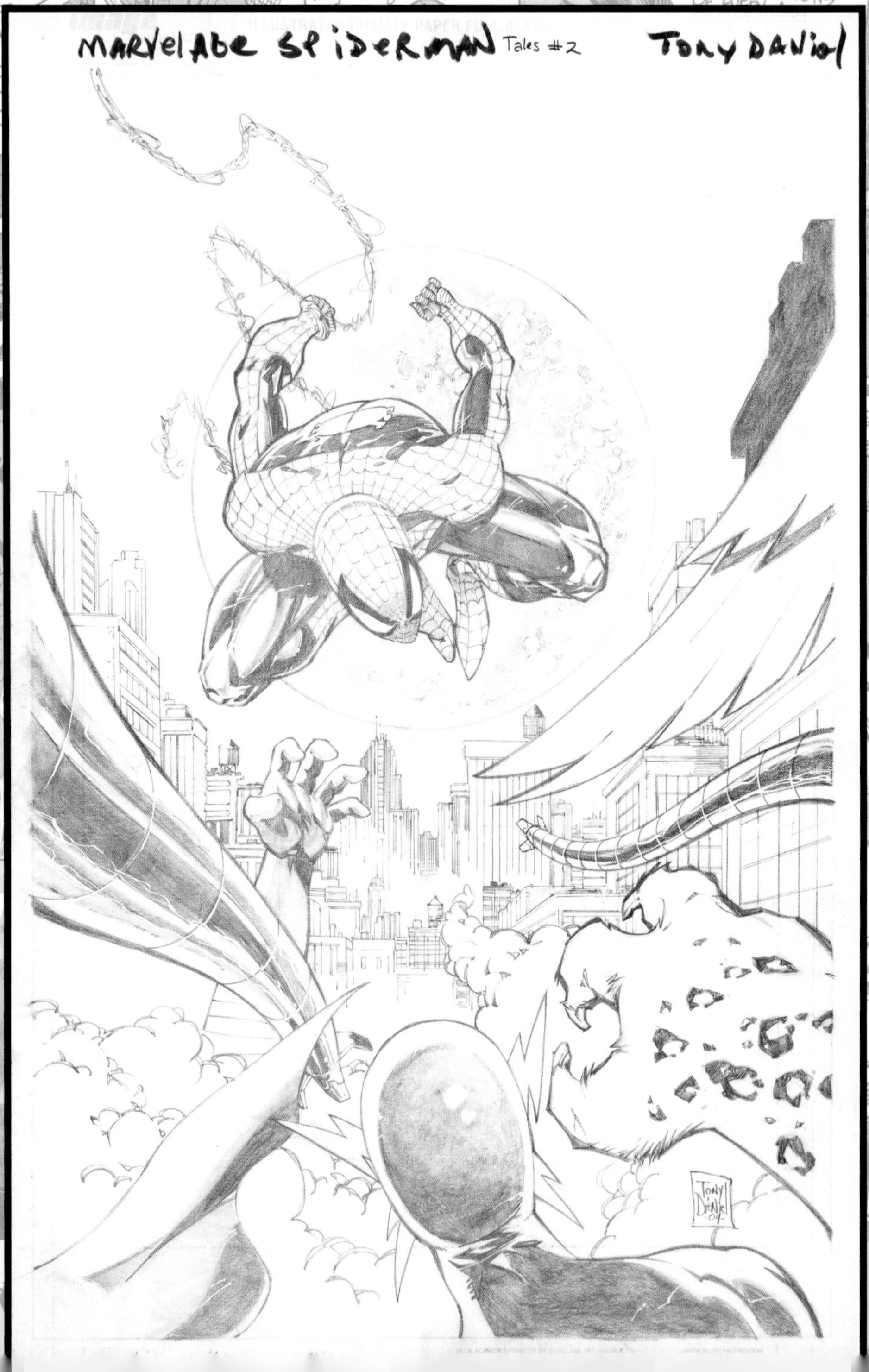
MARVELAGE SPIDERMAN Tales #2
TONY DANIEL
TONY DANIEL '04

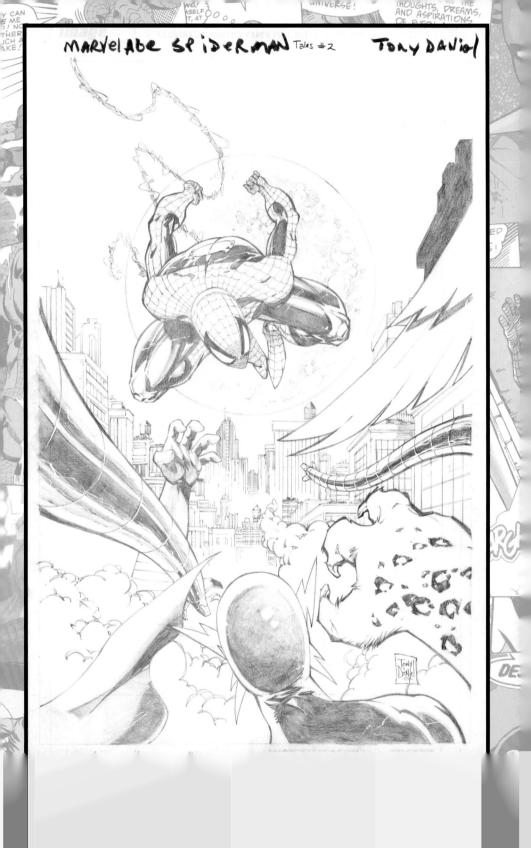

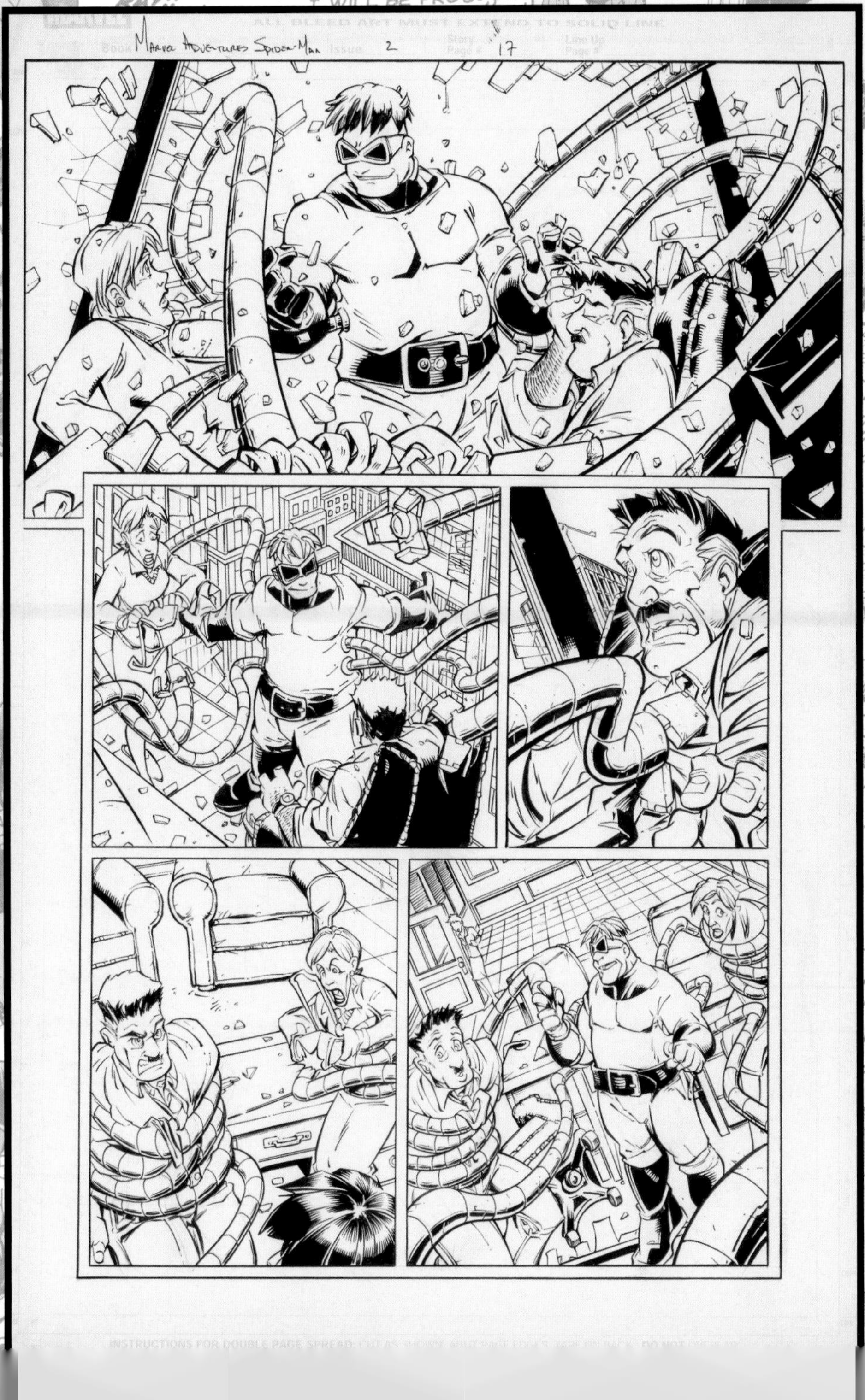
ALL BLEED ART MUST EXTEND TO SOLID LINE
Book Marvel Adventures Spider-Man Issue 2
Story Page # 17
Line Up Page #

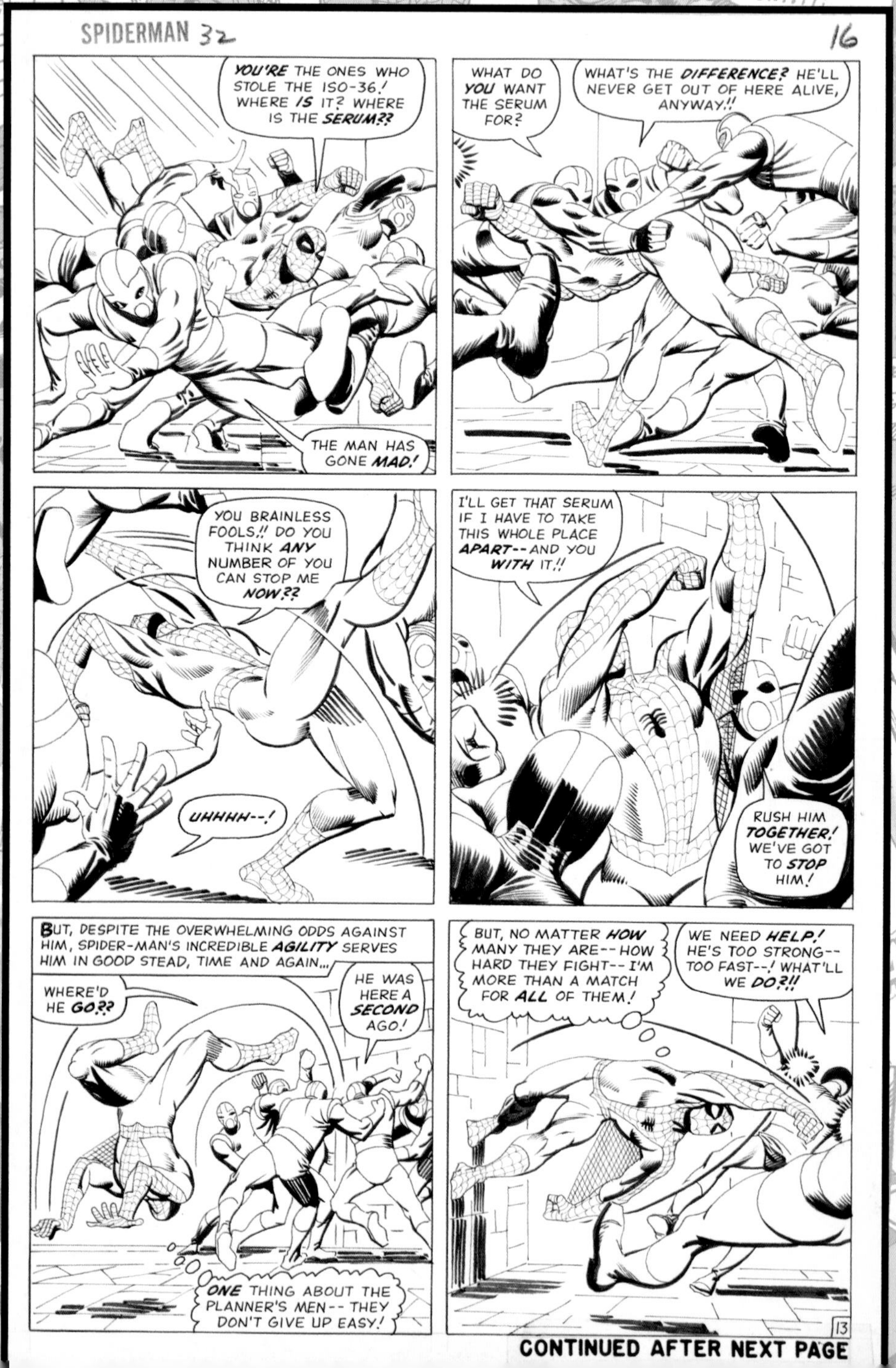

SPIDERMAN 32
16
YOU'RE THE ONES WHO STOLE THE ISO-36! WHERE IS IT? WHERE IS THE SERUM??
THE MAN HAS GONE MAD!
WHAT DO YOU WANT THE SERUM FOR?
WHAT'S THE DIFFERENCE? HE'LL NEVER GET OUT OF HERE ALIVE, ANYWAY!!
YOU BRAINLESS FOOLS!! DO YOU THINK ANY NUMBER OF YOU CAN STOP ME NOW??
UHHHH--!
I'LL GET THAT SERUM IF I HAVE TO TAKE THIS WHOLE PLACE APART--AND YOU WITH IT!!
RUSH HIM TOGETHER! WE'VE GOT TO STOP HIM!
BUT, DESPITE THE OVERWHELMING ODDS AGAINST HIM, SPIDER-MAN'S INCREDIBLE AGILITY SERVES HIM IN GOOD STEAD, TIME AND AGAIN...
WHERE'D HE GO??
HE WAS HERE A SECOND AGO!
ONE THING ABOUT THE PLANNER'S MEN-- THEY DON'T GIVE UP EASY!
BUT, NO MATTER HOW MANY THEY ARE-- HOW HARD THEY FIGHT-- I'M MORE THAN A MATCH FOR ALL OF THEM!
WE NEED HELP! HE'S TOO STRONG-- TOO FAST--! WHAT'LL WE DO?!!
13
CONTINUED AFTER NEXT PAGE

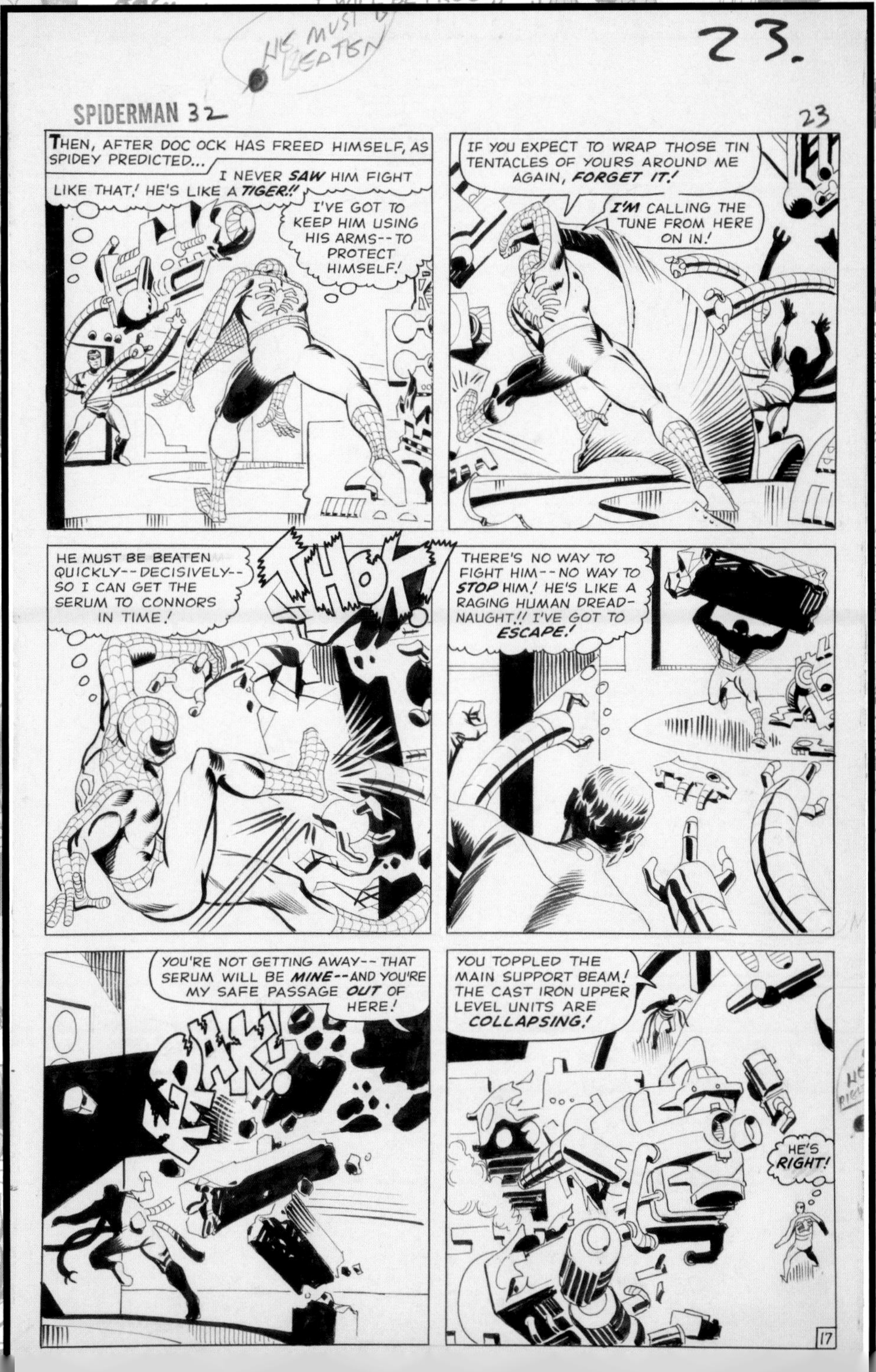
HE MUST BE BEATEN
23.
SPIDERMAN 32
23
THEN, AFTER DOC OCK HAS FREED HIMSELF, AS SPIDEY PREDICTED...
I NEVER SAW HIM FIGHT LIKE THAT! HE'S LIKE A TIGER!!
I'VE GOT TO KEEP HIM USING HIS ARMS--TO PROTECT HIMSELF!
IF YOU EXPECT TO WRAP THOSE TIN TENTACLES OF YOURS AROUND ME AGAIN, FORGET IT!
I'M CALLING THE TUNE FROM HERE ON IN!
HE MUST BE BEATEN QUICKLY--DECISIVELY--SO I CAN GET THE SERUM TO CONNORS IN TIME!
THOK!
THERE'S NO WAY TO FIGHT HIM--NO WAY TO STOP HIM! HE'S LIKE A RAGING HUMAN DREAD-NAUGHT!! I'VE GOT TO ESCAPE!
YOU'RE NOT GETTING AWAY--THAT SERUM WILL BE MINE--AND YOU'RE MY SAFE PASSAGE OUT OF HERE!
KRAKK!
YOU TOPPLED THE MAIN SUPPORT BEAM! THE CAST IRON UPPER LEVEL UNITS ARE COLLAPSING!
HE'S RIGHT!
17

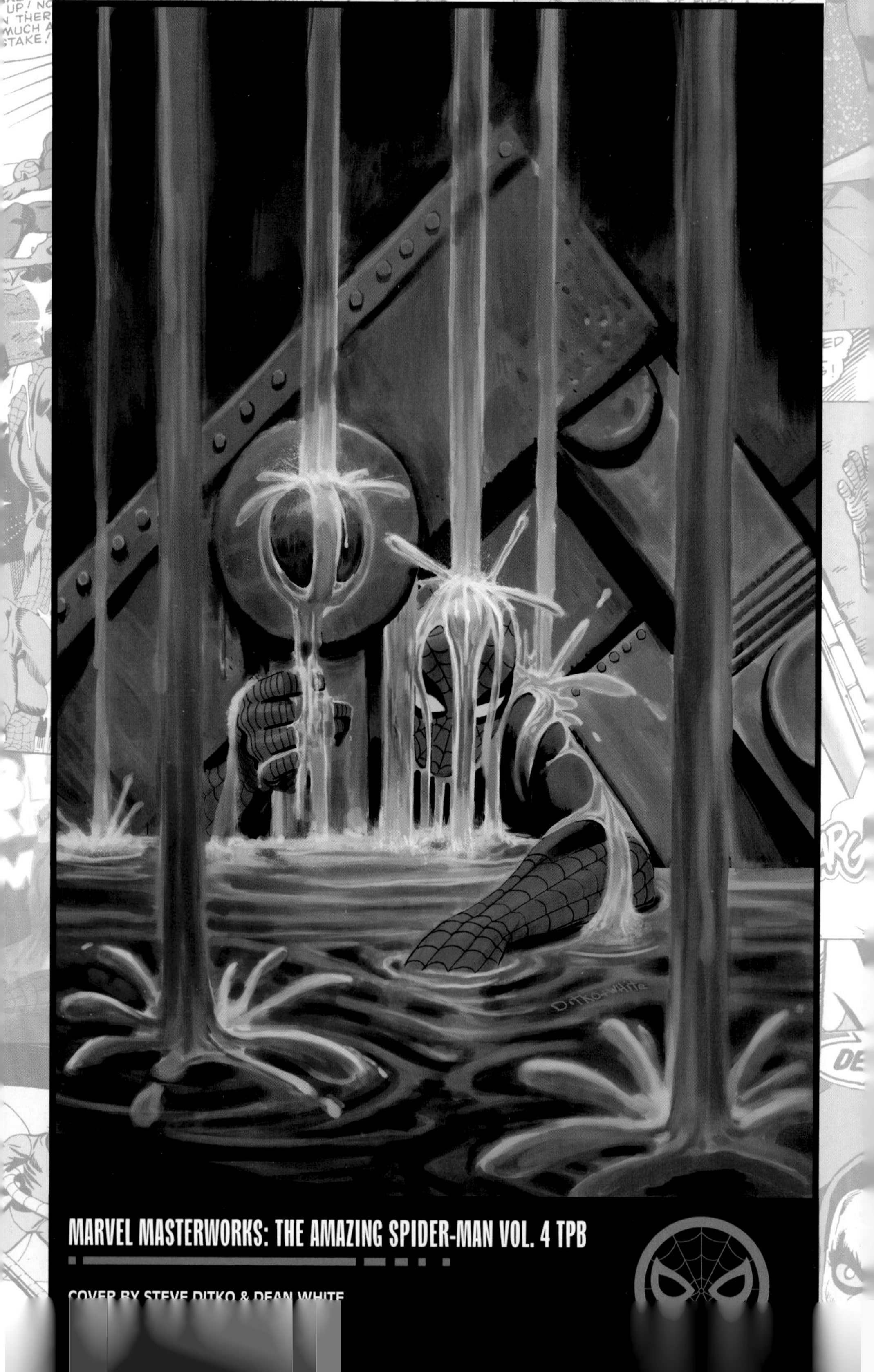

MARVEL MASTERWORKS: THE AMAZING SPIDER-MAN VOL. 4 TPB

COVER BY STEVE DITKO & DEAN WHITE